PAUL THEROUX'S MEMORABLE, AND MENACING FAMILY:

- MURF AND BRODIE, WHO "CAN POSSESS A CITY ONLY BY INCINERATING IT"

- THE MONSTROUS LADY ARROW

- ARABA NIGHTWING, A GUNRUNNING ACTRESS

- VALENTINE HOOD, THE "FATHER," WHOSE "COMPASSION IS AS FITFUL AND MURDEROUS AS A CYCLONE."

"Paul Theroux's most engrossing novel yet; tightly and suspensefully written."

—Joyce Carol Oates

"SPIKED WITH COLOR AND HUMOR AND NOISE AND CRUELTY . . . Theroux is always an original and gifted entrepreneur."

—*Kirkus Reviews*

"PAUL THEROUX IS A MAJOR LITERARY FIGURE OF FORMIDABLE PROPORTION."

—*Los Angeles Times*

Also by Paul Theroux
available now from Ballantine Books:

SAINT JACK

THE BLACK HOUSE

THE GREAT RAILWAY BAZAAR: BY TRAIN THROUGH ASIA

THE
FAMILY
ARSENAL

Paul Theroux

BALLANTINE BOOKS • NEW YORK

Library of Congress Catalog Card Number: 76-10212

ISBN 0-345-25751-0

This edition published by arrangement with
Houghton Mifflin Company

Manufactured in the United States of America

First Ballantine Books Edition: May 1977

For

ANNE, WITH LOVE

ALEXANDER, WITH ADMIRATION

JONATHAN, WITH THANKS

"I determined to see it"—she was speaking of English society—"to learn for myself what it really is before we blow it up. I've been here now a year and a half and, as I tell you, I feel I've seen. It's the old regime again, the rottenness and extravagance, bristling with every iniquity and every abuse, over which the French Revolution passed like a whirlwind; or perhaps even more a reproduction of the Roman world in its decadence, gouty, apoplectic, depraved, gorged and clogged with wealth and spoils, selfishness and scepticism, and waiting for the onset of the barbarians. You and I are the barbarians, you know."

—HENRY JAMES, The Princess Casamassima

THE
FAMILY
ARSENAL

Part One

1

SEATED ON A CUSHION at the upstairs window of the tall house, Hood raised the cigarette to the sun and saw that it was half full of the opium mixture. Filling it was pleasurable, like the willful care of delaying for love: to taste confidence. He winked and sighted with it, as if studying violence from afar, to take aim. He had a marksman's princely squint and the dark furious face of an Apache; but he was only finding his landmarks with the unfinished cigarette.

He moved it slightly to the left and covered a church steeple on the next road. In the slow fire of the late afternoon the tall granite spire had the look of an old dagger. Then to the right, past the far-off bulb of the Post Office Tower, a matchstick in metal; past a row of riverside warehouses the sun had gutted, and more burnt spires, and the dome of Saint Paul's —blue and simple as a bucket at this distance. Drawing the cigarette down he measured a narrow slice of the river between two brick buildings charred by shadow: part of a wharf, the gas works, the power station pouring a muscle of smoke into the sky, a crane poised dangerously like an ember about to snap, housetops shedding flames, then under his thumb the ditch at the end of the crescent where the trains ran.

The ditch wall was streaked with exulting football slogans: ARSENAL RULE and CHELSEA FOREVER and ALL WANKERS SUPPORT PALACE. That glint behind it was the river at Deptford, showing like a band of bright snake scales; but the snake lay hidden, and here when the wind was right on the creek it was a smell—a tidal odor of mudbanks and exposed pebbles, a blocked sink holding a dead serpent. Up close, in Albacore Crescent, the severe summer shadow gave the bending terraces of plumb-fronted houses the look of iron closets, clamped against thieves, and it was the emptiness of the street—indeed, the emptiness of this part of south London—that made Hood think that in each locked house there was at least one impatient man plotting a reply to his disappointment.

Spying with his cigarette in this way, Hood saw the father and son approach, sweeping the road. They made their way in a bumping procession, detouring around a blind abandoned Zodiac parked on flat tires, passing the widely spaced trees whose slender trunks were sleeved in wire mesh. The old man was on the broom, shoving at the gutter; behind him, the boy —no more than ten or eleven—fought with the handle of the cart, a dented yellow barrel on wheels. Even with the window closed Hood had heard the scrape of the broom and the bang of the old man's tin scoop as he emptied a load in the barrel. Hood had been waiting since dawn for Mayo to arrive, and the suspense had made his hearing keen: his frustration amplified the slightest sound.

He was in a room of snoring children. He thought of them as children: they were young and slept like cats in a basket. They were not conspirators—they didn't know the word. The girl, Brodie, was asleep across the room; Murf slept against the near wall, hugging a pillow. The crudely sketched tattoo on Brodie's arm (a small chevron of needlemarks: a bluebird), and Murf's earring and hunting knife, looked especially ridiculous on these contented sleepers. Sleep had removed anger from their faces and made their youth emphatic. Hood used his cigarette to study them. He thought: It is possible to believe in a sleeper's innocence.

Earlier—around two—Brodie had said, "Mayo got lost—or picked up. I'm crashing." And she had gone to the mantleshelf and pawed with her little hand in the drawers of the Burmese box and taken out a vial of powder. She faced him, hunching, ten inches from shoulder to shoulder, and shyly, because everything was Hood's in this house, she showed him the vial. She hesitated, looked to Murf for encouragement, then back at Hood, who had not moved or spoken.

"Please?"

"Don't say that."

Brodie nibbled her underlip. She said, "Then fuck you."

"Or that."

Hood frowned, and Murf laughed at the girl, showing the pegs of his teeth. And only then she seemed to realize her cleverness; she giggled and went round-shouldered. It was this that made them children: they could not be alone, but there was nothing they would refuse to do if they had company. Now they were happy, but even angry they were empty.

Quickly, Brodie had made two cigarettes and looked up for Hood's approval—he had taught her the trick of making a joint one-handed. She knew enough of her dependency on him to offer him the first one. He said no. Murf had rolled sideways and accepted it: "Fanks." Hood saw how their puffing weighted the air with warm opium fumes, and he had been tempted to abandon his vigil. But Mayo had promised to come—days ago. Hood knew she had what he wanted, the painting—the newspapers had reported her success before she sent him six inches of its fusty lining. He had sent an inch to *The Times,* but the story of her theft had slipped to the back pages: she was on her way. He had expected her at dawn today, and he would not have been surprised to see her steer her ice-cream van from the fog—the signs *Supertony* and *Mind That Child* bright with dampness on the van's side—and leap out with the painting under her arm. But she hadn't come then, nor at noon. Hood had forgotten to eat lunch, and sick of waiting and not realizing his impatience was aggravated by simple hunger, he resented his wasted day by the window; another day. He was quicker than any of them, so it was left to him to wait.

Waiting, a penalty, was his favor to them. He had not insisted on leading; he obliged himself to move at

their speed. He looked again at Brodie and Murf. They
slept smiling, Murf with his knees raised, Brodie on
the cushions where she had propped herself to smoke.
She had a smudge on her cheek that Hood found
viciously attractive, a blot that threw her pretty face
into relief and reminded him of the one fact he knew
about her: she had planted a bomb in a locker at
Euston. She slept in depths of silence that counter-
feited a happy death. Awake, Hood felt like a parent
in a room of napping children, and at five he had
crossed the room to the Burmese box that had lain
at the edge of his eye all day. He took it to the window and set to work. He crushed a cigarette and
pinched out the tobacco, and he began filling the empty
tube with alternate layers of tobacco and opium powder. He had delayed, tamping carefully, in the hope
that Mayo's arrival would interrupt him. It was the
reason he had used it to linger at the window for so
long; and when the cigarette was finished he had
avoided lighting the tightly twisted end and kissing
the purple smoke from it. Now he did not want to be
interrupted; the smoke was definite. It would warm
him and give him sleep, release him from waiting and
deliver him to a place of numb enchantment where all
promises were kept and what he attempted he mastered. And more: fountains of light, the caress of
moths' wings, syrup in his throat, sex like splitting a
peach with his teeth on the Perfume River, and all the
emerald heat of Guatemala.

Striking a match he heard the father and son again
and was distracted by their muffled voices. They were
in front of the house, the old man pushing into a pile
the litter of papers, the boy resting on the handle of
the cart, watching his father gasp. Hood shook out the
match and from his window looked down two stories,
annoyed by the interruption, but feeling an affection-
ate pity for them and a hatred for their grubby job.
The man was too old to be punching waste paper with
a broom and stooping with his pan; the boy too young
to be standing in the gutter with his clumsy barrel.
It seemed to Hood a shabby and undeserved penance,
which they performed sighing, with inappropriately

serious faces; and Hood felt mingled outrage and self-contempt, wanting to save them from a job he would not do himself.

He knew the third figure, a tall man in a plum-colored suit sauntering towards them on the opposite side of the street. And yet he was almost surprised to see him—he had once hammered that man so hard in a dream he was convinced the brute was dead. The man appeared cheerful, but that was deceptive. He crossed over, pitching forward into a tiger's slouch with each step, and Hood could see he was drunk. The man paused and jerked his face at the old sweeper, muttered something and passed by. He went five paces, drew a bag from the pocket of his jacket and removed a brown bottle from it. He crumpled the bag and lazily drop-kicked it into the gutter the man had cleared. He shouted and pointed to it, but the old man ignored the protesting squawk; he went on sweeping. The boy looked back anxiously, not at the shouting man but at the crumpled bag in the newly swept gutter.

Hood placed his cigarette on the Burmese box and slid the window open. The men faced each other: authority in a plum-colored suit; servitude with a push broom, the simplest example of unfairness; and the judging child.

"Pick it up!"

"—no attention to him," the old man was saying to the boy.

But the boy left the cart and started in the direction of the bag.

"Get back here," said the old man. "Don't listen to him."

The boy obeyed his father. This infuriated the drunk, and Hood heard again, "Pick it up!"

Now the old man turned and screamed, "Get off out of it! You stitched me up last week and you're not going to stitch me up again! Right, you made the mess and you can bloody well—"

The tall man staggered towards the father and son, howling with his whole face and swinging the bottle in his hand; his voice, his suit insisted. The old man

clutched his broom like a weapon and lowered his
puckered face behind it, crying, "Pack it in!" But it
was the boy's face that alarmed Hood: it had become
delicate with fear, as if it might shatter like white
china, and wincing it looked pathetically young. Not
daring to draw a breath, the boy wore the quick mask
of a nervous infant panicked by noise. The man was
threatening his father, now standing close, raising his
arms and working his mad face at him.

Hood had been with Mayo that other time. She
had said, "He's not political, it doesn't matter." "I'll
kill him," Hood had said; and she laughed and turned
away from the window: "You've got an Irish temper!
What would that effect?" Watching the man go then
he had said, "His ass, May. His ass."

He wanted to see the old man triumph and teach
the boy courage, and he looked for a flourish of the
broom handle, a whack or an insult to turn the drunk
away. Hood imagined himself leaping from the window, flying two stories to the bastard's back and dragging him to the street. In an uprush of anger he saw
himself with the man by the ears and tearing his head
off. But there was nothing. Hood seethed and stayed
where he was, the thick curtains in his hands, the val-
ance shaking above him. And the boy looked on, help-
lessly, at his helpless father, as the man struck, slapped
him (*"Dad!"*), nearly losing his balance, and spat out
something more. Hood saw the old man close his eyes
and tighten his grip on the broom; he saw the boy's
face break and the tears, and the drunk's expression—
that of a scavenger seizing a piece of meat in his teeth
and turning away to protect it. He saw all this with
terrible clarity, but he heard nothing more, for at that
moment a train passed in the ditch at the end of the
crescent. The train closed in on the quarrel, quickly,
without an announcing sound. Then there was for
fifteen seconds the drone of wheels on rails and the
rattle and screech of the carriages, sealing the humiliation by drowning it in a single wave of clatter; and
ending it, for when the train had gone by, leaving
the traces of a hum on the housefronts, the old man

had the broom on his shoulder and the boy was trundling up the road, following his father with the yellow barrel. The drunk slouched away, carrying himself crookedly to the hill.

2

ON THAT TRAIN, the 17:27 from Charing Cross, sat Ralph Gawber, an accountant. His thin face and his obvious fatigue gave him a look of kindliness, and he rode the train with tolerance, responding to the jump of the carriage with a gentle nod. In his heavy suit, in the harsh August heat, he had the undusted sanctity of a clergyman who has spent the day preaching without result in a stubborn slum. He held *The Times* in one hand, folded flat in a rectangle to make a surface for the crossword, and with the ballpoint pen in his other hand he might have been studying a clue. But the crossword was completely inked in. Mr. Gawber was asleep. He had the elderly commuter's habit of being able to sleep without shifting position; sleep took him and embalmed him lightly like a touch of sadness he would soon shake off. He was dreaming of having tea with the Queen in a sunny room of Buckingham Palace. Jammed in the corner, the standing passengers' coats brushing his head, the lunch pail of the shirtless man next to him nudging his thigh, he dreamed. Around him, travelers slapped and shook their evening papers, but Mr. Gawber slept on. The Queen suddenly smiled and leaned forward and plucked open the front of her dress. Her full breasts tumbled out and Mr. Gawber put his head between them and sobbed with shame and relief. They were so cool; and he felt her nipples against his ears.

He had caught the morning train dressed warmly
for the chilly summer fog which blanketed Catford
and gave him a secure feeling of privacy among the
bulky lighted cars half-lost in vapor. The fog cheered
him with forgetfulness, slowly and unaccountably, allowing him amnesia. But the sun had burst into his
compartment at London Bridge, dramatically lighting
the Peek Frean biscuit factory and releasing a powerful odor of shortbread. At once, he loathed his suit.
The boats on the river were indistinguishable in the
broad dazzle, and by the time Mr. Gawber had
walked the quarter mile to Kingsway he was perspir-
ing. It seemed to him, in traveling this short distance
to town from his home in south London, as if he had
left a far-off place, where the weather was different,
and had to cross a frontier to work.

All day at his desk at Rackstraw's he had been hot,
and twice he had gone to the tiled stairwell at the
center of the building, just to stand and be cool.
"Lovely day," Miss French had said. He had to agree.
Only the weather brought Mr. Gawber and his secretary together in conversation. He bore it and memorized the clouds for her. He would not tell her what
he secretly felt, that London looked deranged in
summer heat, collapsing and crowded, sunburnt necks
and ugly exposed navels, the paint blistering, the very
bricks sweating old poisons through their cracks. And
this summer something dreadful was happening: a
slump, or worse—an eruption. He'd seen the figures
and smelled smoke; the economy wanted a complete
rejig.

Before lunch he had asked, "What do we hear from
Miss Nightwing?"

"Nothing," said Miss French. "Monty's brought the
second post. I've been through it myself."

"She's very naughty," said Mr. Gawber.

"Oh, she looked lovely on telly the other night with
Russell Harty. She's going to play Peter Pan in the
Christmas panto. I'm sure she'll do it ever so much
better than that rabbity Susan Hampshire. But I said
to my mother, 'She may be a great actress, but her tax

is way overdue and she's making our Mister Gawber sweat tears.' "

"Miss French, I think I should remind you that Miss Nightwing's income tax is a confidential matter. She's simply forgotten to send us details of her expenditure. Rumors could damage her reputation." He gave her a grim smile of rebuke. "Do let me handle it, won't you?"

Miss French said, "They say she's a communist. She wants to outlaw Punch and Judy shows. Says they're cruel and decadent. Punch and Judy!"

He wanted to say how much they had frightened him as a child at the noisy fair in Ladywell Fields. He sighed, hearing Mister Punch's reedy threats. The heat was a cloak that weighted his back and made him slump. He squinted and tasted dust and wished it would rain. He said, "I shall ring her."

He dialed the number, but before it could ring the line seemed to burst and acquire an odd resonating clamor. In his ear, a male voice said, "That's marathon, I'm sure."

"Monetary," said a woman.

"Marathon."

"Monetary."

Mr. Gawber checked himself in an apology.

"Not monetary."

"It fits. With tapir at seven down."

"Tapir perhaps. But what about that ovoid at eight down? That would put paid to your monetary."

Mr. Gawber saw. They were doing *The Times* crossword. He had put his paper away; it was his practice to do half of it on his way into work and complete it on the way home in the evening. He had got tapir, but not marathon. He listened, fascinated, as if to friends, fellow puzzlers. But his embarrassment grew—and something else bothered him about the crossed line: the man and woman seemed shut in the same cellar room, and their voices murmured as if lost in utter darkness.

"All right, marathon," said the woman. "So with Elba at twenty-seven down and piano tuner at sixteen across we're left with that enormous blank at twelve across. Eight letters. Gosh."

" 'Bitten but—' "

"Please don't read the clue again, Charles."

"I'm stumped."

"It looks easy enough."

"Second letter 'a,' ending in 'n.' Could be another marathon."

Mr. Gawber held the receiver away from his face and reached for his newspaper. He carried out the activity as if learning a stratagem. He was not used to deceptions. He turned the paper over and put his finger on twelve across. Of course.

"You're always saying how awfully good you are."

"Rubbish."

"You're so full of corrections."

"I won't listen to much more of this."

"If you could only hear yourself."

The poor things, seeking the companionship of a puzzle in their darkness, had begun to row. Mr. Gawber became anxious. He had been holding his breath for so long his eyes stung. The woman turned abusive; Mr. Gawber blinked. He heard, "—bloody fed up," and took a deep breath.

"The answer to twelve across," he intoned in a voice he did not recognize as his own, "is macaroon. *Macaroon.*"

"Is that you, Charles?"

"No, my dear—why it *is* macaroon!"

"There's someone on this line. Who's there!"

The alert voice, a shaft from the darkness, spun a burr of panic at him.

"Who's there!"

Mr. Gawber clapped the receiver down and covered his face with his hands. He felt that voice had been heard throughout Rackstraw's. Shortly afterward Miss French said, "Mister Gawber, you're all flushed."

He said it was the heat. He had done no damage, but the episode was shaming—he should have put the phone down at the beginning. He respected privacy. If, on a train, the person beside him took out a letter and began reading it, Mr. Gawber doubled up to convey the impression that he knew it was a letter and was not reading it—he reminded others of their privacy. And he had frightened those people: what were they saying about him now?

He did not touch the telephone again until after four, regarding it as a dangerous and unreliable instrument. But his in-tray still held the unfilled tax form of Araba Nightwing, and pinned it to a curt letter from Inland Revenue. He overcame his shyness and dialed the number again. It buzzed and was answered. He gave his name, apologized for his intrusion, and stated his business briefly.

"I'm not paying," said the young woman in her famous voice.

"It's the law," said Mr. Gawber. "We'll have to get our skates on pretty smartly."

"Don't they know—don't *you*—there's a war on!"

"I couldn't agree more—"

But the line had gone dead, and he was now inquiring in darkness himself: "Miss Nightwing?"

It had been an upsetting day, and not helped by the heat. Mr. Gawber was glad to leave for home at five, to hurry away from the chattering that accused him of obscure errors. *Lovely day,* one woman says, smiling foolishly at the sun on the deranged street; *Who's there!* demands the one on the crossed line; *There's a war on!* the actress cries. These wrong voices moved through his mind, and he could not reply to any of them. For a moment in the cool stairwell at Rackstraw's he felt his strength return. He damned them softly and wanted the city to be destroyed to silence them. It was coming, in any case: the thunderclap. He had seen the figures. Then he would walk out of the building, put his umbrella up, and cross the smoking rubble of the Strand, now an empty beachhead of destruction: the ruin proving him right.

But it was an idle thought; the spite was unworthy of him. He boarded the train and resumed the crossword, and minutes later—while the train was stalled on its approach to Waterloo—completed it with unusual speed: Elba, piano tuner, marathon. Those strangers had made it easy for him. He drowsed in the crowded carriage and slept, while the evening papers crashed at his ears; he dreamed of the Queen, the sun, her body. New Cross, Lewisham, Ladywell: still he slept, and at Catford Bridge, his stop, the Queen leaned towards him and tugged at the front of her glittering dress. The train raced on to Lower Sydenham, where he woke. The carriage was nearly empty and nothing outside had the smallest wrinkle of familiarity.

He walked down the platform with such uncertainty his shoes seemed too large for him. He was walking with another man's feet. The name on the station signboard was recognizable, but this particle of the familiar in so strange a place confounded him. The platform had no roof, and when the train drew out it was empty —the other passengers had quickly deserted it. And yet he enjoyed it and was surprised to notice how he lingered to savor the feeling and acquaint himself with the station. He said to himself with wondering pleasure, "I've never been here before!"

Halfway down the platform a black man in a British Rail uniform was tipped against the door of a glassed-in waiting room. Mr. Gawber saw that he was talking to a fat black woman who was seated on a bench with a basket between her spread knees, two dimpled aubergines. The man was making her laugh in a way that gagged her and shook the brown pads of her cheeks. It was a race of willing comics: he had never believed in their anger. His neighbors—Mr. Wangoosa, the Aromas, the light brown Mr. Palmerston, the almost purple Mr. Churchill—positively skipped with good humor. The British Rail man yapped his lips, the woman's laughter kicked in her throat and she raised her feet and stamped them. The glass door was cracked, the walls were daubed with large red names: ARSENAL RULE, CHELSEA FOREVER, SPURS WANK. But the black people inhabiting it with their chatter lent it an air of ramshackle charm. In another mood Mr. Gawber would have seen it all as an example of decay pushing towards ruin. This summer evening it amused him and he felt able to share in their laughter.

"They all crazy like that up in Catford," said the black man. Then he straightened his cap and reached for Mr. Gawber's ticket. "Thank you."

Mr. Gawber showed his season pass in the plastic wallet. He said, "Caught napping!"

"Excess charge," said the black man. He plucked again at the fingerprints on his visor.

"Kah," said the woman. She looked away, pursed her lips, and blew.

"I've never been here before."

The black man took out a pad, inserted a carbon, and with a complicated care that interested Mr. Gawber, wrote figures on the thin top sheet. This paper-work seemed a suitable acknowledgment for the degree to which Mr. Gawber felt off-course, and he said again, "I've never been here before."

"Five pence additional," said the man. "Pay the cashier."

"Kah," said the woman.

"And that not all," said the man. "You know the George up Rushey Green?"

Mr. Gawber smiled: he knew the George. He wanted to enter the conversation, to give a conclusion to this oddly spent day, and hear the couple cluck: *You mean you never been here before?* He waited for the black man to see him waiting.

After a moment the black man turned to him and said, "But if you come here again, mister, get the right ticket."

Mr. Gawber said, "I'm looking for a call box."

"Don't have to take no train for that," said the man. He chopped the air with his hands. "Down the foot-path. Pass the shed. On you left. The Motive. Can't miss it."

Mr. Gawber paid his fare and found the path. The late-afternoon brightness cooked a smell of hot pollen from the cat mint, the cow parsley and the tall weighted weeds swayed in a thickness of foraging bees. The path narrowed, and soon Mr. Gawber was alone in the greenery, his suit flecked with seeds. He could smell the oily dirt and brake dust from the train tracks, but he could not see above the tops of the stalks and grasses. He almost laughed; he was de-lighted by this sense of being lost so near his home. *Norah, I'm somewhere in Lower Sydenham!* The sun heated the insects and made them crackle under the dusty oversized weeds which, left to grow here undisturbed, were exaggerations of the small pulpy ones in his garden. He saw tall saw-toothed things, spiky blossoms, dragon-tailed leaves, white-haired stalks, thistles and wild garlic. Assertive castaways. And he was gladdened by them. It was the perfect end to a day which had from the first seemed unusual: freedom!

He had been jostled out of his routine and he wanted to know every detail of its difference. He poked at this place with his umbrella's point. His life had been without surprises; he did not want surprises. But this was manageable and it cheered him. Past the shed and a terrace of eight houses with useless numbers and corrugated iron sheets nailed to their windows he saw the public house and its sign, *The Locomotive*. He entered, and, breathing wood planks and sawdust and beer, he went to the bar to celebrate his arrival instead of flying to the telephone to tell Norah he'd be late.

3

ALL THE WAY to the bus stop on the hill the pursuer was hidden from the man he chased by mothers smiling at the sun and turning their bodies gently as they walked. Pursuit was an easy secret in this crowd of casual shoppers, the women bringing a waist-high tide of children forward. Hood rolled steadily behind them as they paused and gathered like hookers—offering smiles, soliciting nods, not going anywhere—and he kept his eye on the plum-colored shoulder thirty feet ahead. He boarded the bus with him and followed him up the stairs to the top deck;

the man dropped into a front seat; Hood fell into the seat at his back. The conductor appeared, bowing as the bus lurched, clutching the knobs of his ticket machine: "Thank you." The man asked for a five pence ticket; Hood did the same. The bus swayed through the traffic, its roof occasionally striking branches— the leaves wiping streaks on the side windows. Hood stared forward at the man's head and found a dent in it, and just above the expensive collar saw the futile contour of cowardice in the furrow of the man's neck.

Hood shredded his bus ticket, impatience jerking his fingers. He had never been on this bus or gone in this direction, south in South London; so it seemed to him, on the move again, as if he was continuing the journey he had started abruptly in Vietnam. He forgot Mayo and her painting, Murf and his earring, tattooed Brodie. He longed to act. To abandon this chase would be an evasion of his strength. He craved the kind of blame that would release him honorably from the charge of inaction, a guilt like grace. He was in the mood for a scrap this hot afternoon, to frighten the bully and prove that weeping boy mattered. Just once, to take sides, and settle the sort of unfair fight a million men ignored every day.

An accident had brought him here. But there were no accidents; instinct was offered expression by a hollowing of chance, and impulse seized it. You didn't choose, you were chosen, claimed by a muscle that knew more than wisdom did of pain. That was justification enough: there was no law before passion's anger. Less than a year ago a man had said, *These people are not worth it,* and Hood had gone quite close to him and punched his face. Within an hour Hood had been suspended by the ambassador and ordered to Washington: he had punched a government minister. The act had freed him, but what looked in Hood to have been savagery, a casual reckoning of penalties, was extreme obedience. He had launched himself blindly and in doing so was granted the gift of sight.

He had always, even as a consul, acted with energy and then, examining his work, seen how the pattern had been fixed for him. Vietnam had been his first overseas post. It had been a short career, but having seen that muddy beleaguered town he felt as if he had seen the whole world's damaged soul. He considered himself one of Vietnam's last casualties, and yet the pattern was still fixed: Mayo's plan at Ward's Irish House, the house in Deptford, the snoring children; those sweepers, that drunk, this bus. He belonged here since he could not deny that boy the strength he had wasted at a desk in the State Department, a classroom at the language school or at the consulate on the Perfume River. He could have gone home, back to the States, but there was time, and he had five thousand dollars—his "hardship bonus." And London attracted him; he saw its convulsion at once, he spoke the language. It was too late to fight in Vietnam, but this was just beginning. He chose this struggle for its simplicity and spent several weeks prowling the streets to involve himself before meeting Mayo at Ward's. Then he had obeyed every impulse and was already half in love with her, and he tried to make her see that this was a battle in that same war.

There were skirmishes everywhere, in every back street of the world. Tonight, or soon, she would come back to Deptford with her captured painting, and he would say, "Remember that drunk, May? The one we saw that day? Well, I set him straight."

The bus continued to wheeze, leaning the upper deck at lamps and pub signs and parlor curtains as it rounded bends, and flinging a bridge's shadow down the aisle. All this was new—the long rows of terraces breaking into segments of eight and four, then farther down Brockley Rise clusters of two, pebble dash semis with brick and timber cowls, nameboards on the gate and roses set in rectangles of lawn. Down there on the pavement a running boy, and twenty yards later a solitary sprinter, the one the child chased. Hood glanced to the right as the bus stopped, and saw at the end of a rising road a wooded hill and a biscuit-brown church lying in a declivity of the slope, nearly hidden by the trees. The hill rose above the house-tops; Hood studied the foliage which, at this distance,

had the density of a box hedge. It was unexpected in
the closely mapped city to see a place that looked
nameless, but he knew from his own neighborhood,
near the tail of the Deptford Creek, how an ordinary
street would close in and stop and show a fence; and
beyond that was another district, all corners over-
grown and broken glass and discarded motor gaskets
and bushes spilling into the blocked street. The area,
no more than a white trapezoid on a map, a blankness
that might have been labeled *Unexplored* or *Here
Live Savages,* was sealed from view in the huge exposed city, as neatly hidden as if it were an island that
lay under the sea, the ultimate hiding place. He
marked the hill on his memory.

The terraces had begun again, tinier now, their
front doors directly on the street. They slid back and
gave onto a row of shops—fruiterer, chemist, news
agent, butcher, off-license, pub—then resumed, to
be interrupted farther on by a similar parade of shops.
They were far now from Deptford, and Hood wanted
the man to get off the bus. He thought: If you know
what's good for you, go. The time passed and Hood
felt the consequences worsen, for with each mile
the urgency he was rehearsing moved by degrees he
could compute, from simple assault, to grievous bodily
harm, to a maiming. The man was leading him to
that, delaying an incidental fight by an interval of waiting which made Hood only more angry.

A gasworks lying behind a brick building, enclosed
by a steel fence; a warehouse; a breaker's yard; a bath
house of brown tiles standing like a cottage at a junction; and the man in the plum-colored suit rose and
started down the aisle, balancing himself by gripping
the seats. He stared directly at Hood but did not see
him. When the man was on the stairs, in a corner of
the mirror's bulge, Hood jumped up.

The man walked unsteadily down Bell Green, as
if the sidewalk were in motion under him. He turned
into Southend Lane and stopped at a house front.
Hood memorized the number before he noticed that
the man was only tying his shoe. It struck him as
comic, the man attending to this detail, thinking it

mattered. That morning in Hué, Hood had set out his
suit for a ministerial reception, and the same evening
he was in Singapore; the minister—tearing off a band-
age to show the wound—was shouting to the press.
The suit remained on its hanger, the dress shoes beside the bed; and Hood was running.

On a corner, beneath a railway bridge, Hood saw
the sign, *The Locomotive,* and saw the tall man pause
and push at the door to the Saloon Bar. Hood followed
him in and stood beside him. On Hood's right a man
in a bowler hat and wearing a heavy suit leaned over
and smiled. Hood nodded, but said nothing.

Mr. Gawber said, "I've never been here before."

"Neither have I," said Hood.

"Ah, two lost souls! But first things first—what will
you have? I'd like to push the boat out."

"Large whisky for me," said the tall man in the
plum-colored suit on Hood's left. Then he laughed,
"Sorry, mate, I thought you was talking to me."

"Who the hell are you?" said Hood.

"I'll let you know, but it'll hurt."

"Try me."

"Step outside," said the man, passing his hand over
his face and distorting it with that gesture, seeming
to pull his mouth into an expression of rage. "They'll
have to carry you home."

Hood said, "They won't be carrying you home,
pal."

"You trying to slag me?"

"Just a minute, gentlemen," said Mr. Gawber, touching Hood's arm.

"The geezer's offering drinks and all," said the man
to Hood. "If he don't want to pay he don't have to,
but he's waving that fiver like he don't know what to
do with it. Now get off my tits."

"I think he's upset," said Hood to Mr. Gawber.

Mr. Gawber had listened to the exchange with a
kind of horror, and he considered leaving. But he
lifted the five-pound note again and said, "You don't
have change for this, do you?"

"No," said Hood.

"I'll mind it for you if you like," said the man,

grinning. "Stick him with his mates and all." He reached into his pocket, took out a wad of five-pound notes the thickness of a sandwich and riffled the edges with his thumb, flashing their blueness. Then he tucked them away and laughed, pushing out his jaw and snorting negligently.

Hood said, "I think I had you wrong."

"I seen you looking at me wad. Listen, I don't have to touch you. I could have you rompered for a fiver and get change."

"No harm done," said Hood.

"Very good then," said Mr. Gawber.

The man held his finger in Hood's face. "You better watch your gob."

Mr. Gawber ordered drinks: a whisky for the man, a half of bitter for Hood, a bottle of light ale for himself. The barmaid told him the price of each as she set the glasses down. "Forty-six pence," said Mr. Gawber, then he apologized for his speedy addition. "You must forgive me—I'm an accountant." He handed over his money and raised his glass. "It's a lovely summer evening. I've never been here before, and I doubt that I'll ever be this way again. A long life to you both."

"This is to the dogs," said the man. "First race in half an hour."

Hood said, "Don't lose your shirt."

"That's nothing." The man slapped his pocket. "I could lose all that and laugh. But I won't. Them dogs see me and start running. You don't know me."

"I saw you two come in together," said Mr. Gawber. "I thought you were chums."

"This is my dancing partner," said Hood.

"Never seen him before in my life."

"There you go, boasting again."

"Piss off." The man dipped his head and put his mouth to his glass.

"You forgot to say something, sweetheart," Hood said, tapping the man on the shoulder.

"Get your hands off me."

"Say thank you."

"Thanks Dad," said the man. He turned to Hood.

"You're pleading for it. Remember, I can pay someone to have your gob fixed. I could get Bill to do it. Or maybe I'll do it meself." He brushed his lapels.

"Sorry," said Hood. "I forgot who I was talking to."

"You're entirely welcome," said Mr. Gawber to the man. "To tell the truth, I came here quite by accident. Normally, I do the crossword on the train and that keeps me awake. But today a most unusual thing happened—"

He told the story of the crossed line, but he improved on it. The callers, whom he imagined in a dark cellar room muttering blind uncertainties, he made precise and dignified; and he made himself comic, a muddled old man, fussing with the phone, who didn't have the sense to slam down the receiver. Telling the story he saw how the whole day, from the morning amnesia of fog and the intrusions at Rackstraw's, to the arrival at the wrong station, had made this chance encounter at the pub possible: it was all preparation to bring his story here. He was pleased to have these listeners and he delivered his last line with solemn comedy: " 'Macaroon,' I said, *'macaroon.'* "

"I got a crossed line meself once. I'm always doing things like that. Some bird nattering to her old man. 'Never want to see you no more,' she says. 'Selfish bitch,' I says. 'Hello,' she says, 'did you say that, John?' 'You leave John out of this,' I says and hangs up the earphone. I'm laughing like a drain."

"Yes," said Mr. Gawber, who had winced at the word bitch. "One feels as if one has been admitted to a secret. But really the most worrying thing is that afterward, when you make another phone call, you sense that someone is listening. Most of my business is highly confidential, so you can imagine my state of mind." It had distressed him at the time to hear Araba say, *There's a war on!,* and he still wondered if anyone else had heard her.

"Don't worry about that, Dad. The coppers'll be on to you before long and have you in the nick. They hear everything. Just a matter of time."

"Oh, I know what they say about accountants. But don't you believe any of it. We're much maligned."

"Full of angles," said the man. "You get a good screw."

"Less than you might think," said Mr. Gawber. "Though it's interesting work. We've always had theater people on our books. Sid Hope, Derek James, Max Morris, Araba Nightwing." He saw he was making no impression; actors believed in their names, no one else did. He said, "Araba's going to be Peter Pan."

"I don't care how much cash you snatch," said the man. "I get mine."

Mr. Gawber was picking through the leather slots of his wallet. He found what he wanted, two old business cards, and handed one to Hood and one to the man. "Bit tatty, I'm afraid. I don't get much chance to use them. But there's my name at the bottom, R. C. Gawber. Do ring me if you've got a financial problem you'd like sorted out. Or just say hello!"

"I don't have cards anymore," said Hood. "But very nice to meet you. Valentine Hood."

"Not English, I think."

"American."

"Ron Weech," said the man. He finished his whisky. "I don't have any financial problems, thanks all the same."

"Then you're a very lucky man," said Mr. Gawber.

"Weech is loaded," said Hood.

"I get mine. See this watch? Fifty quid anywhere you name. Probably a hundred in the West End. I got it for ten in Deptford. Fell off the back of a lorry. See this shirt, see this suit? Lord John—I could show you the labels. I got more at home, all colors. You wouldn't believe what I paid for them. Fell off the back of a lorry. These shoes, this here belt, cuff links, the lot. I've got cases of fags at me house." He smirked. "And that ain't all. I know all the other fences. I'll see them tonight at the track. Mates, we are. 'Hi Ron'—that kind of thing. I get mine."

"You sound like a pretty clever operator," said Hood.

"I get mine—cash, birds. I wouldn't even tell you. What I want I get. Feller up in Millwall tries to sell me this Cortina. A hundred he wants for it, the geezer's a mate of mine. Fell off the back of a lorry. I got the hundred—you seen it, right? I could show you the motor. Tape deck, radio, the lot. All I have to do is paint it and get new plates. But I don't buy it. Why? I just don't want it."

"I wouldn't own a car," said Mr. Gawber.

"You would if you seen this one. Beautiful she is. All the accessories."

"Well, I mean it's silly to run one. My good lady doesn't drive, and I work in Kingsway. Where would I park the ruddy thing?"

"I know what you mean. What you're saying, Dad, it's a fucking nuisance, right?"

The obscenity stopped Mr. Gawber for a moment, like a spurt of flame in his face. He straightened his head and touched at his nose and mouth; the word had singed the hairs in his nostrils: he could smell it.

"I get it," said Hood to Weech. "You do what you like, go your own way."

"Straight."

"Quite right," said Mr. Gawber without conviction. "Good for you."

"I'm me own man," said Weech.

"He's got guts," said Hood.

"I should say so. Admirable." Mr. Gawber made a cautioning noise in his throat.

"I look after meself."

"I'll bet when you go up to the dog track they say, 'Look out, here comes Ron Weech.'"

"They respect me, why not? They know me there. This ain't my regular boozer—no one knows me here. I don't care." Weech glanced at an elderly man on his left who had been listening to the conversation and smiling with shy gratitude when Weech grunted his remarks. Weech snarled, "What are you grinning at?" The man swallowed and became sad.

"Look at that—Weech is a tough cookie," said Hood, as the old man carried his pint of beer and his cigarettes to the opposite end of the bar.

"It's a funny thing," said Weech. "Most people are suckers. I go by these building sites and I see the silly bastards breaking their backs. I just look at them and say, 'Suckers.' Sometimes they hear me—I don't care. It's incredible. Ever see them? These blokes, all about ninety years old, heartstruck and half caved in, and they're trying to get some dirty great fridge off the pavement and not moving it an inch. Suckers. Lorry drivers, postmen, shop girls, that hairy over there pulling pints—twenty quid a week, they think it's a bloody fortune. They're all suckers—"

As Weech ranted, Mr. Gawber crept back. He was disappointed, and a little fearful—he had expected something else. He saw clumsy violence in the way Weech swung his big hands and spoke, and a disregard on Weech's face, a sightless rudeness he did not want to call stupidity. He was angry with himself for having stayed and listened, and sorry his day had ended like this. He plucked his watch from the front of his waistcoat and said, "Has it really gone half-past? I must be off—my wife will think I've left the country."

"Don't be so bloody silly," said Weech. "Have another one on me."

"That's very generous of you, but perhaps some other time," said Mr. Gawber. "It's been awfully good talking to you. You want to be careful carrying all that money about."

"Don't worry about me," said Weech.

"He can take care of himself," said Hood.

Mr. Gawber gathered up his briefcase and umbrella and hurried out. He had always hated public houses; they were dirty and uncongenial, the haunts of resignation, attracting men whose loneliness was not improved by their meeting one another. They talked inaccurately about the world, swapping cheerless opinions. England itself was turning into an enormous Darby and Joan Club in which deaf, nearsighted wrecks played skittles, ignoring the thunder and the shadow of the approaching rain. The ranting man had alarmed him more than the voices on the crossed line. Sometimes he could believe such people did not exist; this evening, toiling in his heavy suit past insolent youths of dangerous size, he felt there were no others. A world of them. He was concerned for that well-spoken one, that American. Had breeding.

"There he goes," said Weech, seeing at the window
Mr. Gawber making his way down Southend Lane,
"the old brolly-man."

"He seems nice enough."

"A sucker," said Weech. "Thinks he's got cash. I
could buy and sell him."

"How about another drink?"

"Put your pennies away." Weech pulled out his
sandwich of notes again, worked one loose with his
thumb and slapped it on the bar. "Two large whiskies."

"You're going to miss the first race," said Hood.

"Don't rush me. I'll get a taxi." He looked at Hood
closely. "What's a Yank doing here, anyway? Tourist?"

Hood said, "I'm hiding."

Weech made a face, as if he didn't know the word.
He said, "Working?"

"Nope. I got fired."

"You look like a sucker."

"Listen, Weech," said Hood, lowering his voice.
"I'll tell you. I was an American consul in Vietnam—
a little town, you've never heard of it. I was there for
about eight months. Then one day the minister of
defense showed up for a reception. But before that—
in the morning—he gave me some shit. So I let him
have it. I don't know what got into me—I just poked
him in the snoot. The first time in the history of the
foreign service any officer of my grade did that." Hood
looked for a reaction. Weech stared. It meant nothing
to him. "They suspended me, but that was pretty feeble, because I knew a quick way out of the country. I
made myself a new passport—that's what consuls do,
you know—and I split. They're still looking for me,
but they're looking in the wrong place."

"You hit the bloke, eh? Colored bloke?"

"Vietnamese."

Weech grinned. "Me, I'm color prejudiced as well."

"I'm not," said Hood. "It was something he said.
He talked like you."

"I could turn you in, probably get a reward. What
did you say your name was?"

"Valentine Hood."

"I could go up to Grosvenor Square—it's there, ain't

it?—and cough it all. No problem. I go up there now and then and play the wheel at the Clermont. You're really thick—you shouldn't have told me that. I might do it."

"You won't," said Hood.

"Don't be so sure. I don't like geezers who slag me."

"Do you read the newspapers?"

"You think I'm a dummy, don't you?"

"I was just wondering if you knew about the painting that was stolen the other day."

"Yeah, the old-fashioned one." Weech sighed. "No fence would touch it. It's too big. It's worthless. There's a reward for it, ain't there?"

"Right, right," said Hood. "But the interesting thing is—I know who's got it. Yes, Weech, she's delivering it to me tonight. She might be there now. How about that?"

Weech peered at Hood, then picked up his whisky and drank it. He wiped his mouth with the back of his hand. He belched and said, "You're full of crap."

"You don't believe me?" Hood took the strip of wrinkled canvas from his wallet. It was brown, with a close weave on one side and on the other flakes of dark cracked paint, like old flattened nail parings. He showed it, holding it against the lamp on the bar. He said, "That's part of it. It's being sent to the papers, an inch at a time."

"That's a piece of rubbish," said Weech. "What is it, an old sticking plaster or what?"

"It's from the edge of the painting."

"I don't see no picture. I think you're slagging me again. Anyway, why tell me?"

"I want you to know everything, Weech," said Hood. "Oh, yes. Remember the Euston bomb? Well, the girl that did it lives at my house—she's hiding, too. Albacore Crescent, Deptford."

"Hey," said Weech, showing an interest in the address that he had not shown in anything else Hood had said, "I live just behind it!"

"What else do you want to know?" Hood searched his mind for more: he wanted to startle the man, to rouse him with a secret. "The girl's name is Brodie. She planted the bomb, but she didn't make it. That was another kid, Murf. He's supposed to be tough, like you. But he hasn't got your money, so he's more dangerous."

"You're making this up. I think you're a nutter."

"You leveled with me, Weech—about all those stolen goods—so I'm leveling with you."

"Stolen goods," Weech sneered. "I'm into the big stuff, Arab exports—get it? I wouldn't even tell you. But that picture—they say it's worth about a million quid."

"Not a million," said Hood. "But you could get ten grand as a reward."

"So I just say, look at Valentine's place on Albacore Crescent."

"Number twenty-two."

"Yeah, and it's all mine," said Weech. He gave a shallow laugh. "But if this was really true you wouldn't be telling me."

"It's true."

"Then I'll tell the coppers, I'll tell the American Embassy, I'll cough it to the *News of the World.*"

"No, you won't."

"I fucking will."

"You don't need the money. You're loaded."

"I'll do it for laughs. I'll do it because you slagged me. I'll get me picture in the papers."

"I almost forgot," said Hood. "I've got two kilos of opium at my house—that should interest the police. Here, it looks like this." Hood took out the cigarette he had made earlier in the evening and put it in Weech's hand.

"You're joking. It's just an ordinary cigarette. Look, it even says Silk Cut on the paper."

"Watch," said Hood. Taking it from Weech and holding it in his cupped hand he broke it open, spilling it into his palm. "That's tobacco," he said, prodding the brown strands, "but see that powder, those yellowy grains? Opium—all the way from the Golden Triangle."

Weech's face creased with interest. He said, "You're as bad as me."

"No."

"Maybe worse," said Weech. "But I could tell you stories. I deal on the continent. Arab hardware. Get it?" He grinned. "Bang-bang. You in the picture?"

Hood said, "You're a fucking punk."

"You're pleading for it," said Weech in a whisper, pushing at the bar with his large hands.

"You're a gutless son of a bitch."

"I'll nail you, straight I will."

"You couldn't nail a daisy."

Weech was trembling, working his fingers, nodding his head and gasping as if he had been deprived of air. He hissed, "You bastard."

Hood straightened up and smiled. "Well, I really must be going now. Nice talking to you, Weech. Keep your thumb on it."

And he was out of the door, stepping into the half-dark of the summer evening. The iron railway bridge and the derelict houses and the high weeds bled into a dim motionless shadow that, in this faltering sunset, was like a memory of light, incomplete and simplifying and without warmth. There was a moon, and traces of stars, but the day remained, proceeding slowly to the edge of night with the season's lengthened hesitation. Hood started towards the street, then turned back to the path that led through the tall cow parsley to the station. At the opening of this disheveled glade, where some of the pub's customers had parked their cars, he waited until the door banged and he saw Weech appear, swinging his arms.

"Over here," Hood called, keeping his voice low.

Weech blundered towards him, chewing on rage and paddling with his fists. Angry, he seemed too large for his plum-colored suit. When he was about ten feet away, Hood took a paper bag from his pocket and threw it to the path. It startled Weech: he jerked his face sideways, twisting his shoulders, as if he thought it might explode.

"Pick it up," said Hood softly.

"I'm going to nail you."

He came at Hood, lunging with his arms out, landing a glancing punch on his upper arm. But Hood batted him away, and Weech falling back kicked at him; he was tall and nearly toppled himself with the kick.

"Pick it up!"

Hood, breathless, had sobbed the command. He took Weech by the shoulders and pulled him forward and down as he raised his knee quickly, cracking it into Weech's face. Weech started to fall, but Hood kept him up, punching him erect with the force of his fists, catching the underside of Weech's jaw and lifting his head. Then he let Weech drop. He fell backward, against a car, and slipped down, leaning into each contour as flexibly as a descending snake. Weech's trouser cuffs were hitched to his knees and his sleeves to his elbows; his head was knocked over to one side, his ear against his shoulder. Hood knew he had broken the man's neck, for when he pulled him away from the car Weech's head flopped backward from the ledge of his shoulder and hung there staring blindly behind him, tugging his abnormally long neck. The failing light gave the horrible translucence of a membrane to his white throat.

Kicking at it with his heel, Hood opened the small side window of the car and unlocked the door. It was a Volkswagen, and though he had no trouble jumping the wires and starting it he could not get Weech into the back seat. He pushed on the man's legs, but the small space would not contain him. So Weech rode in front, propped by the seat and nodding each time Hood touched the brake. He drove fast up Bell Green and then along the bus route towards Brockley Rise.

They were such simple skills, like steadying a rifle to hit a target: following the bully and setting him up, hot-wiring a car, and finding a place to dispose of the body—that wooded mound he had seen was a park called One Tree Hill. It was all easy, and if there was blame it was in taking advantage of the simplicity of it. He had not known it would end like this, on a dimly lit path above Peckham. He had thought he would feel triumphant, but he was only angry and his

fingers stank of error. It was furiously petty; the man
was worth nothing; no one knew. But he was not
sorry. The memory of a thing not done was worse
than any deed. He had never wanted to go back, and
now he had proved he couldn't.

He dragged the body into the park and off the path
and sank it in grass. Laughter carried down the slope
from a thicket of bushes and low hiding trees: lovers.
Beneath him London lay on a plain, the humps and
spires showing in dim aqueous light, yellow distances
like a burnt-out sea drenched and smoldering under
a black sky.

4

VOLTA ROAD, CATFORD, was, in his eyes a corridor of cracked Edwardian aunts in old lace, shoulder
to shoulder, shawled with tiles and beaked with sloping roofs; the upper gables like odd bonnets with
peaks jutting over the oblongs of window lenses and
the dim eyes blinded by criss-crossings of mullioned
veils. With the long breasts of their bay-fronts forward
and their knees against bruised, clawed steps, they
knelt in perpetual genuflection, their flat gray faces
set at one another across the road, as if—gathering dust
—they were dying in their prayers. They were tall
enough to keep Volta Road in shadow for most of the
day. Among those four-story houses one's primness
stood out in the senility, paler than all the rest, with a
low hedge and clematis beside the door and a garden
gnome fishing in a dry birdbath, number twelve, Gawber's.

He walked towards it tonight in a mood of distress,
hurrying home to be calmed. Once, this road had the

preserved well-tended look of the nearby roads of
lesser houses, small-shouldered bungalows with freshly
painted trim, owned by families for their cozy size
and kept in repair. But the houses on Volta—with serv-
ants' bells in every room and names like *The Sycamores*
—had fallen into the hands of speculators and building
firms and enterprising landlords, who partitioned them
with thin walls, sealing off serving hatches and doors,
building kitchens in back bedrooms, installing toilets
in broom cupboards, bolting a sink or a cooker on a
landing so the stacked dishes were in full view of
the street. Many of the houses were hives or insects'
nests, every bedsitting room a tiny home in which
people were battened down like weevils, murmuring
to other families through the chipboard walls. The
density was obvious from the panels of buzzer bells on
the front doors or the clusters of unwashed milk bottles on the top steps.

Mr. Gawber had been born in number twelve and
he had grown up in it, moving into the front bedroom with Norah when, ten years after his father, his
mother died. He had attended the boys' school, Saint
Dunstan's, at the top of the road and the Anglican
church at the bottom. Now the church was Baptist
and mostly black; it had gone simple: he stayed away.
He had seen the street's residents grow old and die
or retire to the country, and after the war the houses
had moved into a phase of decline that was, even
now, unchecked. The occupants were numerous, they
were every human color, and the street was made
nearly impassable by their parked cars. The street had
been lined with elms; the trees had risen, almost to
the height of the housetops, and the boughs had met
over the street. After the war, they were cut down.
The killing had taken a week, and hearing the drone
of the saws Mr. Gawber felt they were cutting his
own arms off. The sticklike saplings planted in their
place had gone quickly, after one season of promising
leaves—that autumn, children had snapped their tender branches and used them for swords and spears.
The window boxes were empty, the hedges torn out,
the gardens paved for cars and motorbikes. In three

front gardens old wheelless cars rotted with their doors ajar. It was not a bad road—there were many worse—but it would never improve. Eventually it would be bought wholesale by the council and boarded up and rained on, then pulled down and tall apartment blocks built on it. That was the pattern. Out here there was nothing worth preserving, not even sentiment, for that had passed away with the older residents who had gone with the trees.

The native families were dispersed, and Mr. Gawber thought: I am a relic from that other age. Latterly, he had studied the new families. They were limpers and Negroes and Irishmen who wore bicycle clips; dog-faced boys in mangy fur coats and surly mothers with red babies and children with broken teeth and very old men who inched down the sidewalk tapping canes. All of them escapees who had arrived and would never go. There was a tall Chinese man and his wife in number eight and an Indian with a blue Land-Rover next door—he washed the huge thing on Sunday mornings with his radio going. Mr. Gawber had fit them into houses, matching their colors with names on the bell panels. He did not know them well; they did not seem to know each other, and oddest of all, none of the darker people wore socks. Tropical folk with tropical names: Wangoosa, Aroma, Palmerston, Churchill, Pang.

Estate agents and men with unreliable eyes and dandruff on their shoulders had tried, first with leaflets pushed through the letter-slot and finally by bumptious visits, to gain possession of Mr. Gawber's house. They sat on Mr. Gawber's sofa with their knees apart and spoke ominously of encroaching blacks, using these unlucky hostages, their own tenants, as an oblique threat; they told Mr. Gawber there was a nice class of owner-occupier and more fresh air in Orpington and often they alluded to the length of Volta Road that had already fallen to them, as if to show that it was only a matter of time before they would have it entirely. But Mr. Gawber held on. Orpington? He was a Londoner. And he would not surrender his father's house.

In winter it was tolerable; it had a bleakness Mr. Gawber liked. The cold rain composed it, blew the newspapers into corners, restored the black shine to the street and kept the limpers indoors. Rain tidied it and gave London back some of her glamour, even some of her youth: the city was designed for grim weather, not crowds. It was best in drizzle or gleaming darkly under a thin layer of ice. Then Mr. Gawber felt an affection for it and saw the pelted dripping lamps on the platform at New Cross as magical jelly molds mounted on Arabian posts; or he lingered on Catford Hill to watch the heaving rain-reddened buses.

But winter was distant tonight. Mr. Gawber walked down the sidewalk feeling spied upon. In the warm weather that started the poisons in bricks and woke the smell of decay, the life in those houses spilled into Volta Road—babies were wheeled out for approval, youths met and tinkered with motorbikes and taunted girls; arguments turned into fights, shameless courtships into loud weddings. There, on the steps of Palmerston's, he had seen one on a Saturday afternoon, a wedding party enlivened by music from steel dustbins, the guests' lavender buttocks on windowsills, all the people using the occasion to raise their voices. They hollered and laughed and late at night the party broke up, leaving pools of vomit all the way to the corner. This evening they were out: Wangoosa mending his bicycle, Churchill dandling his baby, the Indian tuning his Land-Rover, each one claiming his portion of the road. He wished these families away.

Mr. Gawber destroyed it with his eyes. He policed the ruins and found the idlers guilty of causing a nuisance and a breach of the peace, of unlawful assembly, uttering menaces, outraging the public modesty, and tax evasion. He blew a shrill whistle and had them carted off, then leveled the road, reducing the houses to a field of broken bricks and lumber; and he let the grass reassert itself and cover the rubble with its green hair. It would serve them right. The summer's disorder, those hot lazy mobs, made him wish for a cleansing holocaust—some visible crisis, black frost combined with an economic crash. It was certainly coming: a slump, a smothering heaviness, a power cut and a blinding storm stopping lifts between floors and silting up the Thames, and but for the tolling of funeral bells there would be silence. Hardship was a great sorter. He rather enjoyed the thought of deprivation, candlelight, shortages, paying with official vouchers and coupons, and cold baths with homemade soap. He included himself in the challenge. It would be a fair test to everyone, like the war, that last dose of salts. Let it all come down! The foolish would go to the wall, but those who endured, and jolly good luck to them, would be the better for it. It would not be easy for him at his age—even harder for poor Norah—but he'd survive the collapse. It was a matter of patience, belt-tightening and bookkeeping. In that sense he knew he was the older sort of Englishman: he valued decency above all things, and hardship, testing instinct, only made decency a greater prize.

Once, he had been calm, but this summer—was it those Irish bombs?—the city and its faces overwhelmed him with thoughts of ruin. He was not angry but apprehensive. His imagination exaggerated his simple feeling, and he never wished for the worst without an accompanying sense of shame and a frown of guilt he knew passers-by could read on his face.

The pain was not only his. Often he came home to Norah and knew from her eyes she had been blubbing.

He fitted his latchkey and peered through the red and green stained-glass window on the door for the shadow of Norah. Then he entered and met the familiar smell of dry carpets and dead relations. Home was that odor of furnishings and family, and an obscurer unfragrant one in the air of your own skin.

"Rafie?"

His mother had called him that. The name had stuck, though Norah only used it when she feared something was wrong, to get near to his worry.

"Sorry I'm late." He kissed her forehead. "You weren't worried, Noddy?"

"You've had a phone call," said Norah, insisting on

her alarm. "That Araba Nightwing. I didn't know what to tell her. Rafie, I had no idea where you were!"

"Shambles. Fell asleep on the train, pitched up in Lower Sydenham. Groping around the back end of the borough." He laughed, using his age to excuse his mistake: I'm getting feeble, don't mind me. Nothing about the crossed line; nothing about the men sparring dangerously in the public house; nothing about his destructive mood. "What did Miss Nightwing want?"

"She was upset. I couldn't understand a word she said. Poor girl."

"Not poor, Noddy. Her income last year ran to five figures. She's going to be Peter Pan."

"She sounded distraught."

"She's an excellent actress."

"She'll make a lovely Peter Pan."

"I'm sure." He mistrusted actors offstage: the most convincing were the most suspect. He could not deny their skill, but there was something about their swift ability to persuade that was itself unpersuasive. They did not have a voice of their own and when they attempted one it sounded vulgar and insincere. Their vanity was titanic, their capacity for bluff bottomless. Norah's respect for them amounted almost to veneration; he was suspicious in the same degree. He had had them as clients his whole life and still did not know them, which was why.

Norah said, "I'll get your tea."

The rest was ritual. He sheathed his umbrella in the tall blue jar, fastened his coat on a hook, laid his briefcase and bowler hat on the table by the stairs and washed his hands. That was London done with. Then he sat in his unlaced shoes and for minutes there was only the tick of the wooden clock in the hall and the sound of the tea going down his throat and Norah's finishing first and saying, "I needed that."

The room was dominated by a painting, blue stripes, an orange sun, a conflagration of red in one corner. He had accepted it in lieu of a small fee, but now the artist was famous and the painting was very valuable. Visitors remarked on it—because of its size and its fiery color—and Mr. Gawber told its story. He was glad to have the story; he had never found the painting much good. And next to the bookshelf, photographs of actors he'd represented, one now in the House of Lords, another the wife of a shipping tycoon, a suicide, a murder victim, several outright failures, a singer who made her name during the war and who in peacetime sank into obscurity: all smiling into their signatures. A fan of theater programs twenty years old lay on a small table as casually as if they had been used the previous night—Norah's doing, and it was she who had framed the program of the Royal Command Performance.

Norah said, "The butcher saved me some nice chops."

They ate together in the back dining room, facing each other across a table whose grain he had memorized as a child on winter nights between algebra problems: there were yellow lyres and unstrung harps in the beautiful wood. But tonight he stared, seeing faces in the table, and he replayed the day's conversations, all those extraordinary voices: *Who's there? Don't be so bloody silly. There's a war on!* If he didn't understand, was he dead?

Norah said, "You've gone all quiet, Rafie. Is there anything wrong?"

Everything. The overheated world had split its shell like a cooking egg. Deranged, deranged. The news was written in blood, and smudges of blistered paint said ARSENAL RULE! Let it all come down; now he only bought the paper for its puzzle. Norah leaned to inquire, but he said nothing.

Norah said, "We'll have a good holiday. You'll see."

He hated the word. He didn't want a holiday's brief deception of well-being. He had no intention of repeating last year's disappointment, when he had sat in a shirt and tie, but with his trousers rolled to his knees, behind a canvas windbreak on a crowded Cornish beach. He had seen gluttonous Yorkshiremen turn into lobsters and tug at children with their claws. Sand blew between the pages of his book, which the sun prevented him from reading. The high-spirited par-

ents, to amuse their children, disfigured the beach
with deep trenches too far from the tidemark to be
altered by the sea, and so the scars on the sand remained as an appropriate parody of invasion on this
littered beachhead. Holidays required skills he did
not possess: pounding posts into the sand; humping
and unflexing beachchairs; acting as a waiter—with a
clumsy tea tray—for Norah. He endured it, praying for
it to end, wishing the skies to darken and those families to be rained on. It was the sun—the sun maddened
the English and turned them into farting Spaniards.
The holiday, that rest at Polzeath, had exhausted him,
and though Norah still spoke of it with pleasure it had
taken two weeks at Rackstraw's for him to regain his
former grip on things.

Norah said, "If we'd had children we'd have our
own grandchildren by now. They love the beach."

A sadness. It was a son they'd had. He had lived for
twelve hours and they hadn't had the heart to name
him. *Baby Gawber,* the death certificate read. Mr.
Gawber had seen him only once, and that was thirty
years ago, but not a day went by that did not throw
up that memory of the infant. He seemed to grow into
manhood in his mind, and Mr. Gawber always recalled
with solemn clarity the chipped paint in the room
where he had been told the news. For the second
time that day, he remembered his boy.

Norah said, "You'll want to listen to the wireless."

It was late. The proms concert was half over. He
wouldn't listen. The second half was always modern,
thin and incomprehensible, unexpected pluckings and
bongs and vagrantly sorrowing note shifts. It was soul-
less stuff. He preferred the coughing between movements to the music itself.

Norah said, "You've left half your meal. I did those
runner beans especially for you."

They tasted of dust. There was dust in the air, and
outside in the street he could hear—even from this
back room—the shouts of his neighbors, frighteningly
loud, the honk of common speech. It could have been
a riot, the voices looters', the slapping feet fleeing fel-

ons'. But no, it was always that in summer, the ordinary tyranny of noise.

Norah said, "They're at it again."

Mr. Gawber finished his meal. He ate the beans for Norah's sake and knew as he did so they would rouse him in the night and make froth in his stomach. He went into the parlor and listened to Norah busy at the kitchen sink. At nine o'clock he heard the television, the yak of typewriters that preceded the news, and the factual voice of the newscaster, Robert Dougal: Ireland, bombs, the Prime Minister warned today, record crowds. Phrases reached him; he did not want to hear more. The newscaster said good night, and he heard Norah's "Good night, Robert!" She usually replied to salutations on the damned thing.

At nine-thirty—the bell shook him badly—the telephone rang. It was Araba Nightwing, breathless, drawling with apology in her deep attractive voice.

"I'm at the theater, Mr. Gawber," she said. "It's the interval, so this will have to be short, I'm afraid. I'm so glad I finally reached you. I've been thinking about you the whole day—well, ever since you rang—"

"I understand," he said. "It's quite all right." In the background he heard the thump of chair seats, the babble of the audience, shouts.

"No, it's not—"

He winced and held the receiver away from his ear.

"—it's unforgivable. I don't know what got into me. It's just this frightful business—all these rehearsals—and I've got so much on my mind these days. I've just been to the continent—Rotterdam, nothing special. But I was rude to you."

"No harm done."

"I'm an absolute bloody bitch."

He winced again: who was listening? "Miss Nightwing—"

"You're too kind to say it, but it's true. I wouldn't hurt you for the world. How can you be so kind to a bitch like me?"

"I find it very easy."

"Because you're so good! I don't deserve it. But this

play is such rubbish I can't help myself. People say it's destroying me. I can't help that, and I was a bitch before it opened, as you know. Last year it was the same thing, that business with the fascist bank."

"Swiss bank, but that's best forgotten."

"I tried to ring you before the show. Your wife said you weren't there."

"No—I—" Was she asking for an explanation? "I was held up. Rather a long story."

"It's the story of my life. Mr. Gawber, I want you to know that I'm very sorry. I don't want you to get involved in this in any way."

Involved in what? He said, "It's just the small matter of your tax return. You've had a good year. An excellent year. Unfortunately."

"Oh, *God!*"

"We'll have a chat. It'll sort itself out. You'll see."

"But I don't have the slightest intention—there goes the first bell. I must fly. My face—"

"Don't make yourself late, my dear."

"The reason I rang is that I have some tickets for you and your wife. They're good seats, but the play's pretty dreadful, utter crap really, a McGravy sit-com, *Tea for Three*. Naturally it's a smash-hit, it's always full—Americans and the coach crowd. But it's a night out and you could come backstage and meet Blanche and Dick. They're awfully sweet."

"Are you sure it's no trouble?"

"I think that was another bell. No, no trouble at all. The tickets are for next month, the nineteenth—I hope that's all right. I'd love to meet your wife. I just wish this play was better."

"We'll be delighted—"

"Tickets at the box office. Don't pay attention to what I say. I don't care if they expel me—I hate myself. You're the kindest man I've ever met. Another bell! Bye!"

Norah watched him put the receiver into its cradle. He sighed and reported what the actress had said.

"But that's splendid!" Norah said. *"Tea for Three*'s had wonderful notices."

Glamour: he was glad. The day had been saved for

her. He so seldom knew how to please her. She would have her hair done and meet him in town. An early dinner at Wheeler's; Norah would have the prawn cocktail and he would have whitebait, and somehow Norah would find an occasion to say, "The lemon sole looks good." At the play she would eat half a pound of chocolates. She would remark on the scenery—she loved plays for that. Stage sets dazzled her, and though she could never recall the title of a play, much less a line, she could describe in tedious detail the sets she'd seen before the war at the Lewisham Hippodrome in Catford, now torn down. There was nothing she liked more than to see the curtains go up and reveal on the stage a great frigate's butt, fully rigged, with sails. Shakespeare was not always a good bet, but she remembered the fantastic trapezes in one play and the cushions when Araba had played Cleopatra; and she still mentioned the pyramids and the golden disc of sun in that play about the Incas. *Tea for Three* did not sound promising—perhaps a parlor—but Mr. Gawber was hopeful. In any case, Norah would come away praising the bookshelves, the crockery, the wallpaper.

He would hate the play for its fakery, unless a door stuck, or some sudden accident intervened to give the play a brief jolt of reality. He always enjoyed seeing heavy men in blue boiler suits striding on stage between scenes to rearrange the furniture; those thumps and grunts; or simply an unexplained crash behind a closed curtain. Otherwise he would find it a mediocre puppet show—why didn't they use puppets?—and he would sleep without changing position, the way he did on the train. Play dialogue and the presence of actors and even the heat and light of a theater—the great mob ignoring itself—embarrassed him. It was like filing into church, but the wrong one.

That night in bed, he still heard voices in the road and the feet of people passing below. He wanted the limpers on their beam ends. He had started the day happy, in that fog, and then the day had heated and turned strange for him, disturbing him to his very bones. He had tried to give it order, but failed; there were too many contending voices. So it closed in a babble, the people darting at his eyes—no wonder they called them gorillas. That was the whole of his life, a kind of concealment, guarding against alarm. And it was odd because it was all caution, so secretive, just the two of them hiding in their enormous shadowy house: it was the way he imagined conspirators to live.

5

"THE KIDS WERE asleep," Mayo hissed. "I had to climb the back fence and break the door to get in."

Hood laughed, but darkly: she had given him a fright. He had entered by the back and seen the great crack in the door and the smashed tongue of the lock. Then in the kitchen he, had seen a small man in an old pinstriped jacket, a tweed cap, and gloves. He was on the point of kicking him in the ankles when the man turned: Mayo in her burglar's get-up, and she had said, "Where the hell have you been?"

Now she said, "Murf can fix it. I'll buy a new door."

They were still in the kitchen; her gloves and jacket were on the chair. She slipped her cap off and shook out her hair. Hood pulled the broken door shut and said, "I thought you were supposed to be good at that sort of thing."

"I got in, didn't I?"

"Don't take housebreaking literally, sweetheart. You nearly tore it off its hinges! What a burglar. It's lucky you don't depend on it for your living. You'd starve."

"You still haven't said where you've been."

"Don't race your motor." He stared almost bewildered at the painting that had lain stiffly rolled on the kitchen table when he came in. It was Flemish, and though it had been pictured in most of the newspapers in the past week, the real thing had none of the clarity of the little black and white reproductions. It was smaller than he had expected; it had a coarseness of texture; it yielded no pattern. The reflection of the over-bright kitchen light crazed its roughened surface with glare, giving it the opacity and flaky shine of a piece of old leather. It was creased and scratched; it wouldn't lie flat. Hood looked for a long time at the dark varnish before he recognized under the layers of that leathery yellow the face, the hat, the arms, the long boots. It was not large, and yet he had to study it in parts, losing the order of its composition as his eye moved in ellipses from section to section. At first he saw only rough shapes, like separated jigsaw pieces, and it was not until he set it at an angle to the light—spread it on the floor and stood on a chair above it—that he grasped the whole of it: the figure in the chalk-white collar and somber hat posed peevishly by the window; the summer landscape outside that was dead still, and the carved posts of the interior furniture. It was dark, nearly all shadow, almost crudely done in melting solids, and it had the rank smell of a dusty attic. Artists painted not moods but conditions in their self-portraits, and this one by Rogier van der Weyden showed the sullen impatience of an unwilling exile.

"So this is what all the fuss is about," said Hood, hopping from the chair. "It's not as good as *The Just Judges.*"

Mayo said, "It's a good painting, Val."

"Quit leering at it." He looked at it again, but now it had once more become a dense curtain of cracks. He saw a curious unlit antique, smeared with yellow glaze. He said, "It's as ugly as money."

"It got them screaming."

"Screaming for money—the ones who have it. Collectors and art dealers. The rest don't give a damn, and they're the ones who matter. I think we should burn this turkey right now."

"You wouldn't dare." Mayo was controlling her voice but could not conceal the tremble of anger in it.

Hood knelt and clicked his lighter. It spurted: a jet of flame shot to one corner, sparking at the fibres on the edge.

"Stop that!" Mayo stepped on his hand. She was still wearing her men's shoes. She pressed the thick sole down, tangling the lighter in his fingers, then freeing it. But there was no mark on the painting, just the greasy smell of singed cloth in a thread of smoke. "You're a barbarian."

"That's what they say about you."

"Let them."

"But they're wrong, because if you were you wouldn't think it was such a big deal to score an old master. You would have set that stately home on fire. Anyway, why didn't you leave a bomb behind?"

"I think I know how to deal with them."

"I think I know why," he said. "You're a barbarian with taste."

"Stop getting at me," said Mayo. Angry, she lost her slight Irish accent; her voice rose to a higher register of annoyance, gained precision and assumed a smart pitch of indignation that was haughty. "Besides, you're missing the point."

"Lay it on me."

"It's a symbol, you idiot."

"Now there's a word that's really hot shit. Where'd you pick that up?"

"Stop playing dumb. You know what I mean."

"Sure. But symbols are a bad substitute for reality —they're always the wrong size. Go the whole way or don't go at all. Set the bastards on fire, don't pick their pockets." Hood spat with force into the sink. "Jesus, I'd like to meet the guy that sent Brodie to Euston. A railway station? You must be joking. Who was it?"

"You'll find out," she said, growing calm at his sudden anger. "All in good time."

"I'd like to have a word with him. I'm not getting anywhere with Brodie. She sits around staring at her cartoon posters and watching television. She worries about her complexion. And what did she do? Blew a hole in a locker. Now they've roped off the lockers and closed the Left Luggage window. You give them a symbol and they give one back to you."

"All you can do is mock," she said. "Well, go ahead —no one's hunting you."

"Not yet, but listen, honey, I think you underestimate yourself. You've got your painting and you're tickled to death. So we'll hang it up. Very expensive, right? The art world is horrified. But I've got news for you—we're not declaring war on the art dealers and you won't get anywhere with symbols."

"That's what you say."

"It won't work. You don't want to win, you just want a few famous enemies."

"And what do you want?"

"I want scalps," he said. "I'll get them. You can't lose if you make all the rules."

Mayo swore and stooped to roll up the painting. Hood looked at her back and for a moment felt sorry for her. It was a small job but she had done it well; she had taken it seriously. But she hadn't seen beyond the theft, to the time when that pretty painting would be only a burden.

"Be serious, May," he said. "Would you get into the sack with a phallic symbol?"

"I go to bed with you, don't I?" she said lightly, regaining her Irishness and tucking the last few inches of the painting into the roll.

He had met Mayo at Ward's in Piccadilly in the late spring soon after he arrived. She was drunk; she told him, a perfect stranger, of her plan to steal the painting; and that carelessness worried him: who else would she tell? He had spent the night with her and at last moved in and tutored her in caution. They agreed to work together and afterward—long after he made love to her, since they isolated themselves and hid from each other in sex—he came to know her. She was a short brisk woman in her mid-thirties, habituated to gestures of tidying, as if attempting to sort the clutter in the house and match the order in her mind. But she was the only neat one in the place, and it made her preoccupation hopeless. She was slim, but the men's work clothes she wore, the blue bib-overalls, the

loose denim shirt with baggy sleeves, made her seem
stocky, and she tramped clumsily in her heavy shoes.
Her hands were small and beautiful, her face plain
but unmarked. The clothes made her seem convinc-
ingly a man until she turned and showed her face.
Then she seemed wrong for the clothes, and the
posture—the upturned collar, the masculine stress in
her voice—only exaggerated the prettiness of her
mouth. There was something else: the work clothes
were clean and the shirt still bore the vertical creases
from the box. And yet, in her mask and gloves she had
succeeded; her description had been repeated in all
the papers with the photograph of the Rogier self-
portrait—they were looking for a member of the Provisional wing of the I.R.A., probably armed, with a
slight build, a black jacket, and the trace of an Irish
accent: a man.

Mayo put the painting on the table. She said, "Are
they still asleep?"

"Apparently."

"How do they do it?"

"They don't do anything else," said Hood. "They
fight, make love, then fall asleep. When they wake up
they start fighting." It was true: the quarreling of
Brodie and Murf invariably turned into lovemaking.
He had seen it enough times to know when to avoid
them. They didn't take off their clothes; they wrestled
themselves into an embrace and fumbled until their
threats became sighs. It was sexual struggle made out
of the most childish assault, and in the same fighting
postures they slept, with their faces close.

"Are you giving them coke?"

"It's not coke—it's low-grade opium. And I'm not
giving it to them, they're taking it."

"I wish they'd take a little interest in the Movement. And I can tell you one thing—the Provos don't
allow their people to take drugs. It's an offense."

"I should have known. All that clean living," said
Hood. "It shows."

Mayo waited, then said impatiently, "Sometimes I
can't stand you. You wonder why I don't tell you anything. Listen to yourself. You're always asking about

the Provos, but if I told you about it you'd only laugh."

Hood said, "Just tell me what you do in Kilburn."

"That's my business," she said. "I'm going to make myself some scrambled eggs. I'm hungry." She slid the frying pan onto the stove and started the burner. She said, "Hard drugs. You'll turn her into an addict. And she's—what? Sixteen? Jesus."

"She's already been in the slammer—you said so yourself."

"So what? She's a child."

"Tell that to the Provos."

Mayo went into the larder saying, "Has she told you about her family?" There was a clatter, a thud; Mayo came out cursing, carrying a box of eggs.

"I've heard all about it."

"Terrifying," said Mayo.

"It didn't sound so bad to me," said Hood. "I must have disappointed her."

"I suppose you laughed."

"Not very loud."

"You should spend more time with her."

"The anxious parent," said Hood. "She's a screamer and he's a latent tip-toe. I try to treat them as equals— it's quite a challenge."

At Ward's in June, where Mayo had introduced Brodie to Hood, the young girl was refused a drink. But she had taken it as a great joke and in the Ulster and Munster Room, while Mayo and Hood were drinking, had said, "I'm underage!" She had started to roll a joint and Hood showed her how to do it with one hand. Mayo said, "She's on the run," and Brodie, with the tobacco in her hand, had watched Mayo say this; she smiled as if she had been complimented on her clothes. They treated her with excessive kindliness, as if they had just adopted her. Hood remembered how they had driven back to Deptford in the ice-cream van, how he had said, "So you're the Euston bomber." She had looked at Mayo and giggled. Then she had asked Hood to stop at a corner shop. She had gone in and bought a bag of toffees, which she poked into her mouth for the rest of the drive. Hood said, "She looks scared to death." Murf had come later, with his satchel of blasting powder and his case of clocks. The dark curtains went up on the front windows in the house on Albacore Crescent. Hood had trusted Mayo, but from the moment he set eyes on Brodie and Murf he had felt insecure with this fragile family. He knew he could not rely on them: they were too reckless to be trusted, they took no precautions. They had no experience, so they had no belief; but still he felt protective towards them.

He had asked Brodie what it had been like to plant the bomb. She said, "It was in this carrier bag. I shoved it in one of them lockers. Is that what you mean?" He pressed her for a motive. She was imprecise, uncomprehending. Yet she could be specific when she talked about herself. "Mayo saved me," she said. "I was a mess." He inquired further. She said, "Anorexia." Her smile appalled him more than the word.

The frying pan smoked with overheated fat. Mayo seemed not to notice it. She cracked the eggs on the side of the bowl, but they broke and dripped in her hand. Hood said, "Let me do that. You're making a hash of it."

"Get away," said Mayo. She moved aside, spinning the bowl to the floor. "Now look what you made me do."

She knelt quickly to pick up the fragments of yolk-smeared glass, and Hood helped, tossing them into the wastebasket. Then he saw Brodie's bare feet, her thin ankles. She was at the door to the hall, squinting in the light, yawning lazily.

"What's all the noise?" She saw Mayo. "Oh, you're back."

"Hello, love," said Mayo. "You all right?"

Brodie nodded and broke into another yawn, her mouth wide open; her teeth were small and unstained. "Okay," she said, pushing her hair back. "I just heard the racket and I was wondering."

"Get a load of her," said Hood. Brodie wore her purple T-shirt. There was a wrinkle of sleep—a pink welt—on her cheek, and another across the tattoo on her arm.

"I was getting the most fantastic flashes," she said. She moved towards the painting. "Hey." She unrolled it on the table, still yawning, keeping the canvas spread with her hands and touching it, seeming to study it with her slow fingers, like a learner at Braille, tracing the collar, the contours of the man's dark clothes. At this angle, Hood saw a gleam in it he had not noticed before, a softer light falling across the figure's hand, relaxing it and answering the light on the face, dignifying the skin with a gentle sallowness. And he saw a tension of concern that was almost a smile on the mouth and the beginnings of motion in the legs —one knee canted left as if starting a dance step. The clothes were not the stiff material he had seen earlier, but the level pelt of blue velvet with bluer folds crushed into it. Around his neck was a silver chain with square links and depending from it the medallion of a dead animal: a fox. Brodie smoothed the paint with her fingers, helping Hood see, and still touching it, still identifying its deft features, she said, "Anything on telly?"

He wanted to reply—to mock—but he was gagged. He was angry with himself, for the girl's dismissal, that pale child's blindness, parodied his own reaction. *Anything on telly!* She had bettered him and with this new glimpse of the painting he felt reproached.

"Have you had anything to eat?" asked Mayo.

Brodie said no and let the painting roll itself on its own stiffness. She yawned again. "I'll have a cup of tea."

"You'll have to do better than that, my girl. Look at yourself—you're getting skinny. Have some scrambled eggs at least."

"I'm not hungry—"

"You'll do as I say—"

Hood listened: mother and daughter, scolding and whining. Watching them bark and circle each other nagged all his desire away; their careless noise drove off his lust and killed his affection and left him with annoyance. Brodie brushed an eggshell to the floor;

Mayo picked it up; and that simple action—the girl blundering, the woman righting it—caused in Hood an unreasonable anger. He wanted to shout. Instead he moved Mayo aside and finished making the meal himself, saying, "Tell her to set the table."

Brodie insisted on eating with the television on. Hood said, "One of these days I'm going to put an axe through that thing."

Brodie pointed. "He's on 'Dad's Army.'"

"Eat," said Mayo.

"Aw." Brodie picked up her fork and went on smiling at the television program. It was a comedy, a pair of mimics quacking.

—*Do you play an instrument?*

—*I pick my nose.*

—*That's a start. Speaking of noses, what would you do if your nose went on strike?*

—*Picket!*

"Murf's missing it," said Brodie.

"Who taught you to cook?" said Mayo.

"If you don't like it don't eat it," said Hood.

"Stop fighting," said Brodie. She put down her fork and picked up a banana from the basket of fruit. She peeled it, took it in her mouth, and champed at the television.

"See her eat that banana, honey? A symbol that she hates her father. Remember that." Hood rose, went into the kitchen, and came back with the painting. He held it against the wall, where Brodie's "Magic Roundabout" poster was tacked. He said, "How about putting it here?"

Mayo was clearing away the plates, Brodie still watching television; neither one made a comment, but when Hood began prizing the tacks from the "Magic Roundabout" poster, Brodie said, "Don't do that."

"I need the tacks."

"Don't take it down. It's mine. There's more drawing pins upstairs."

"Then pick your ass up and get them."

"No." Brodie glowered at the television.

"Stop it, you two," Mayo called from the kitchen. Hood threw the poster aside and put up the self-portrait, securing its top edge with a row of tacks. Its lower edge lifted and curled like a scroll. Hood stepped back. The man seemed to have moved slightly from the window and his gaze was no longer tense but mildly relieved, starting to smile. Hood had the impression that the wide-brimmed hat the man held in his hand had, earlier in the evening, been covering that fine hair. The peevishness, the anxiety, was gone from his face: Hood saw contentment in the dark eyes and light starting at the edges of the room where there had been shadow and old varnish.

He said, "What do you think?"

"It's poxy," said Brodie. "I like mine better"—the poster was on her lap—"but I'll put it in my own room where you can't touch it."

"I'll do the same with this," he said.

Mayo drifted in saying, "I've done the dishes— thanks for the help." She looked at the self-portrait. "Incredible," she said. "It works beautifully in this room. Too bad we have to keep it upstairs."

"Look at her leer," said Hood. "She wants to eat it."

Images jumped on the screen, a newsroom, an aged face: the late news. Brodie said, "Rubbish." There were shots of the seaside: *"Record crowds—"* Hood sat between Brodie and Mayo on the sofa, his long legs extended, his hands clasped across his stomach. The drone of news made them remember—the unpaid electric bill, the broken door—and Hood listened, fascinated by how trivial their murmurs were, those low neutral voices on the old companionable sofa, in front of the crackling television. They stared at the television to ignore it, and it struck him as comic, their arrival at such simple topics, trading the bland family assumptions about the light bill, the missing bath plug, the burnt pan, the smashed bowl. "We'll have to do some shopping." It related them; domesticity obliged them more than crime, and Hood almost laughed. The bomber went on murmuring to the thief: family matters—and he, the murderer, agreed to make cocoa.

"Nothing about the picture," said Hood when the

news ended. "Looks like you're out of the running, Mother."

"We'll send them another inch," said Mayo. She stretched, flattening her small breasts against her shirt. "I'm going to bed."

Hood followed her to the top of the house, three flights. She paused on the last landing to kick off her shoes, and when she did Hood lifted her and kissed her. She stared at him with a wife's detachment, considered his eyes, and moved past him. In bed Hood threw his arm around her and said, "Honey?"

"I'm whacked," she said. "Not tonight."

He spoke to the ceiling: "I had a fight today."

Mayo turned to him. "Who was it?"

"I don't know," he said.

"You fool." She settled against her pillow, and he waited for her to say more. But she only sighed.

"I snuffed him," he said. She said nothing: her sigh was sleep.

The house was purring an hour later when, wakeful, restless, Hood descended the stairs. He had not slept, but he knew how. He tore a pinch from his plug of opium and rolled a pill in his fingers: that was all the weight he needed to take him fathoms down through the world to Guatemala, to the Perfume River and beyond to the slowest rehearsal of damp sexual knots, the watery orbit of triumphant love. He swallowed the pill with a glass of water and the buzz in his ears changed to a new frequency, a low drawl that tugged and burred at the back of his eyes. The room was dark, but the painting had a light of its own, the white narrow face of that laughing man who stood, Hood saw for the first time, with one hand on the silver knob of a sheathed dagger. And the window he had seen as motionless with summer was alive with excited shapes, fat baffled men with buckets, bawling children a rearing horse, a flock of fleeing chickens, riot. Rogier heard, but his back was to confusion, and on that face Hood saw his own alert eyes.

Part Two

Part Two

6

OFTEN, SEEING A workman propped by a smoking ditch in the road, Hood dressed the man in ermine, envisioned a pronged crown where his tattered cap was and made that shovel a scepter to lean his chin on. He gave them the benefit of his belief: the rag-and-bone man a stallion, the postman impressive robes. The regal face was puffed and florid; the laborer's lank hair and heavy jaw only made the imagining more vivid. They might look broken, but they never lost that look of watchful cunning he had seen in powerful men—the potbellied general in his birdbill cap supervising the shelling of empty hills. Hood convinced himself that the shouting hag in Deptford with her handcart of whelks and cockles and her sign *Live Eels* could be transformed into a braying baroness. It was a swift flight of the mind, and he rarely saw a pack of slender children that could not be possible inheritors: the urchins changed by the eye into princelings.

The slim woman he saw in velvet, a high-collared cape and buckled shoes, with pearls at her throat and a jeweled pistol crammed into her sash. She was agile, with blue eyes and a sly suggestion of toughness on her mouth. She had a boy's bounce and black hair that was straight and bright and caught the sun like metal. She glided in the heat, always away from him. But that, like the oaf in ermine, was mostly fanciful: he did not know her, he had only timed her movements, as she left the house in striped slacks and a yellow blouse and sandals. She rarely smiled, but that was half her beauty; the rest was motion, the silver bracelets that rode on her arm and visibly jangled, and the sideways swish of her trouser cuffs and when she shook her hair the sight of her earrings, large hoops that jumped against her cheek, and all the light she brought forward on her skin made him think she could not cast a shadow. She aroused him the moment he saw her, the housewife in Deptford with the large child, and he wondered if perhaps she was ordinarily pretty and he committed to enhancing her. He did pity her, and he felt saddest on Tuesday when her mood was bright and she chased the boy and made him laugh, because she was alone and did not yet know she was a widow.

She went out in the mornings with the boy, whose round head was screwed tight to his shoulders; he looked unrelated to her, his size was wrong, no feature matched. She shopped, carrying a string bag. If it was sunny after lunch she spent the afternoon in a corner of the park on Brookmill Road—the child flopped in the sandpit and she regarded him vaguely, keeping her distance, plucking at the pages of a book. Then, on the Thursday—a week after Hood had begun to watch her—the police arrived at her house, braking hard, and took her and the child away. An hour later she returned and her posture was so changed they might have taken her away to beat her. She seemed to crouch with grief, her black hair over her eyes, and she held tightly to the child as if, surprised by danger, she were performing a hopeless rescue and moving towards more danger. Her spirit had been arrested; she was weakened; and when she turned to speak to the policeman at the wheel her gaze saw nothing. She entered her house stooping.

Hood watched from a bench on the corner. He chucked the paper away. She knew.

On the following days, apart from one morning—the funeral, he guessed—she continued her routine, the morning shopping, the afternoon at the park, varying it once with a trip to the laundry. Her slimness had become angular, she had grown thin in a matter of days, with a stiff sorrow in her shoulders and a frailty that took the ease out of her walk. Once she looked directly at him with hollow deep-set eyes, and Hood knew she was not sleeping. There was something stunned about her, not saddened but shocked. It was different from grief now; it was as if she had awakened in a foreign country and was listening for a familiar voice. He understood her displacement. Then she wore sunglasses, which emphasized the smallness of her head and gave her the hunched foreshortened look of an insect. She stayed closer to the child, holding his hand, though he pulled hard on her arm. She was subdued, but the child was livelier than ever and bigger with infantile glee.

*

In the house on Albacore Crescent Hood was awakened by the sound of typing, Mayo—always purposeful when she got up—pecking away in the next room. This went on for several minutes. Then she came into the bedroom and said, "I have to go to Kilburn. Tell Brodie there's another envelope inside this one. She's to take it to the West End and open it and post the one inside—without leaving prints on it."

"Why don't you tell her yourself?"

"She's asleep—I looked. Explain it when she's wide awake or she'll forget. And you might remind her that her prints are on file at Scotland Yard, so she'd better be careful. Got it?"

Hood took the envelope and rolled over to hide his face from the London sunlight which in midsummer dawned as early as it had in Vietnam, dazzling the curtains and heating the dust in the room before he got out of bed. That same heat was mingled with the smells of carpets and varnish, the sound of flies. He said, "Got it," into the pillow and heard her go.

It was simple enough, but everything was simple as long as you stayed anonymous: the man who had been told everything was safe because he was dead. The charade with the notes meant nothing; the painting had nothing to do with him. He was glad to have it in the house—it was graceful and indefinite; it warmed him like the sun's curious hum and startled him each

new time he saw it; but he did not feel responsible for
it, only lucky that it was on the wall, a patch of order
where he could rest his eye. It was a window, nothing
more, accessible and well placed, but not his. Mayo
always called it "My Rogier"; he called it "Death
Eating a Cracker."

The ransom notes: in them he saw all of Mayo's
futile diligence. He had sent an inch of the canvas
himself and laughed when it was pounced upon by an
art critic who saw in the theft and this ripping a terrible crime, as if he had posted the man a bloody
finger or a victim's nose. Then he had watched Mayo
follow that up with her ransom notes and a list of her
demands. He was interested but detached, as the canvas strip, now verified as authentic, was sent an inch
at a time. To *The Times:* Mayo said they had a
knowledgeable art critic on the staff—even on the run,
in hiding, she did not forget her snobbery. In the
week Hood had followed the widow's movements,
three notes had been sent, with a crusted fragment
and a code word in a plain buff envelope. They were
mailed in different parts of the city, at Clerkenwell,
Earl's Court, Shepherd's Bush, anonymous places,
densely populated. But though the demands had
grown insistent—she was threatening to destroy the
self-portrait—the response had become muted, and
indeed there had been no response at all until a cash
reward was offered for its recovery. "What if they ignore it?" Hood had asked, and Mayo replied, "They
wouldn't dare." But it was a hollow certainty, since
Hood guessed that she had placed a higher value on
the painting than anyone else—higher perhaps than
the person she'd stolen it from. And so the spate of
notes: this was the fifth.

She had, almost from the moment they had met
at Ward's, kept Hood at the edge. They were lovers
before they were conspirators, but she had another
life, other friends, and though her casual allusions to
them gave them an obscure importance, this prevented
him from knowing her well. Her secrecy made their
friendship incomplete. She was over-anxious to reassure him, and so he imagined that her urgencies—

sexual, political: she turned one into the other—
could not but be adulterous. She used his affection like
a pledge of purpose, and making love to her was
only another aspect of this commitment: comrades
became lovers, lovers conspirators, and promises
whispered to her in bed she repeated later as evidence
of political involvement. "You told me," she once
said to Hood, "that you'd never met anyone like me."
He said, "Yes, in the sack." Their very intimacy excluded him; he was so close to her she could say,
"All in good time," and keep him in the dark. Patience
was the lover's obligation. It would have been easier,
he would have known more, if he had never been
her lover, and while he mocked her secrecy she replied
by criticizing his impatience. He sometimes wondered, like the cuckold, if he was being humored, all
the gentle foolery of occasional sex a cover for her
betrayal.

He had been given one specific task. He saw it as
trifling, she said it was important. "The Provos don't
change people," she said. "We have chemists, teachers,
drivers—they're all good at their jobs. The only difference is now they work for us. If a carpenter
joins and says he wants to be a hit-man, we tell him to
get lost. We've got enough of those. We want skills."
So Hood, the consul, was ordered to prepare an American passport for the Provos. He had the necessary
equipment, a stock of passport blanks he had stolen
when he ran from Hué, with unrecorded and so un-
traceable numbers; the stamp, the official seal. He had
been given a small photograph of the person—the
prospective traveler—a bespectacled man with an
old-fashioned hairstyle, almost certainly a disguise.
He had glued in the picture, forged the passport,
stamped and sealed it and given it to Mayo to deliver. "They like it," she said. And later: "They
might have some more for you to do." But he wasn't
contacted again. He had brought the passport blanks
to London almost as an afterthought; he had only
believed in his anger. He was told he could be valuable,
he did not know if he was trusted; and though Mayo
said, "They're going to contact you," she said it in

that remote wifely way and it did nothing to lessen his impatience. The passport business was the work of a morning, but he knew he had done nothing until he had killed Weech, and he wanted to do more.

"Deal the cards," he heard Murf saying.

"What else?" said Brodie. "Was that all?"

"Naw, the silly bitch put treacle on it and let everyone lick it off. She was stoned. Anyway, what about you? What's the sexiest thing you ever done?"

Hood listened. He heard a giggle.

"I wore five belts."

"Leave off!"

"Straight. Tight as anything."

"Five flaming belts."

"And nothing else. But there was another one—she was a groupie, too—she had this plastic mac, the transparent kind. She'd put it on and they'd tie her up like a parcel. And then, you know, they'd do stuff to her."

From the doorway Hood could see Murf's head, inclined forward, listening to Brodie. He looked like a bat; he had the ears and the snout and the gray pinched mouse-face, the hunched bony shoulders that were like folded wings. There was a solemnity in the smallness of his head, and the gold ring and cross in his ear lobe only called attention to the size of his ears, which stuck out enough for the sun to light them pink from behind and show the tracery of their veins.

Murf said, "Deal the cards."

Hood entered the room, rapping on the door as he did so and noticing, above the two children sitting naked and cross-legged on their mattress—their sheets twisted around them—the "Magic Roundabout" poster tacked to the wall with felt pennants nearby (*Souvenir of Brighton, Chelsea*). On the dresser there was a clothed doll—a stiff-armed Spanish dancer in a mantilla—some cigarette papers, a toy mouse, Murf's hunting knife, a Chianti bottle with a red candle in the top, a record player, and on the turntable a bag of toffees.

"Rise and shine."

Brodie turned, smacked a toffee in her mouth and said, "What do you want?"

"I've got a surprise for you. Today, you're going to leg a bomb in Trafalgar Square. This is the big stuff, right? Get Lord Nelson flat on his back and fry those lions. All you do is stick some jelly on the column and you're laughing. What do you say?"

Murf said, *"Boom widdy-widdy."*

"Shut up, bat-face, and get your clocks out."

"Leave him alone," said Brodie, glowering at Hood.

"It's your big day, sweetheart. Better than Euston—and this is only the beginning."

"Don't pay no attention to him," said Brodie. She shuffled the cards, hit the pack on her knee, and flapping her elbows, let the sheet fall from her breasts. They were small and very white behind the russet discs of her childish nipples. She scratched lazily at one with her thumb and said, "He's crazy."

Hood stayed in the doorway, watching Brodie cut the cards again. "If you think blowing up Nelson's column is crazy, why did you put the bomb in Euston?"

"Maybe they wanted me to. Ever think of that?"

"Deal them bitches," said Murf impatiently.

"But you had a reason, right?"

"Yeah. These rich people—they're messing the other ones about, and like the other ones don't have anything. I don't know. It's all politics and shit."

"It's aggro," said Murf. "The rich ones don't want to know."

"What if you were rich?"

Brodie laughed and cupped her breasts and squeezed them. "Heavy!"

But Murf lowered his head and spoke seriously, muffling his words by jerking his mouth to the side. "Well, I wouldn't be rich like that, for one thing," he said. "They didn't earn the money, did they? I mean, someone give it to them. Their fathers or uncles like." *Fing, favvers, unkoos;* the boy nodded, putting his ears in shadow.

Hood said, "But what if someone gave it to you?"

"I never thought of it. Maybe buy meself a boat—

one of these cabin cruisers. Or a car. Maybe a stereo. Shit like that." He grinned. "Maybe start meself an army."

"Stop hassling him," said Brodie, who was both severe and defensive. She was quicker than Murf and seemed to sense he was being mocked. "What do you want him to say?"

"Keep your shirt on, sister," said Hood. "I was just wondering what I'm doing here, so I thought I'd ask you two."

"I like it here," said Murf.

"We don't get hassled, except by you," said Brodie, still sucking the toffee.

"Okay, let's be friends," said Hood, touching her shoulder.

"I think he wants to raise you," said Murf.

"Watch it, sonny, or I'll kick you through that window, ears and all."

In a low voice, Murf said, "Deal them cards."

"This is for you." Hood handed Brodie the envelope and told her what Mayo had said, making her repeat the instructions. Murf took the cards from Brodie's lap and dealt them. Once, Hood had seen the boy play solitaire, shuffling and cutting the pack carefully, and arranging the cards on the table; and he had noticed how, muttering his tuneless chant, *boom widdy-widdy*, he had paused, wet his thumb and cheated.

"We'll need fares," said Brodie.

"You've got money."

"Spent it." She sucked the toffee, held it in her teeth and opened her mouth for Hood to see, making a face.

"Here." Hood gave her a pound.

"It ain't enough."

"It's plenty."

"A quid and all," said Murf, still dealing the cards. "Maybe buy meself a boat with that."

*

Before they went out they dressed themselves in Indian shirts, long muslin smocks with flowers embroidered on them—Brodie's was sleeveless and showed her tattoo. They wore wristlets, strings of amber blobs and dungarees that had been patched and sewn with badges and army insignia; they carried shoulder bags they had bought at a jumble sale in Deptford. These flapping costumes made Hood think not of gypsies but of children dressed up as gypsies, amateur players slouching down Albacore Crescent and past the pillar box to some trivial farce. Their costumes revealed more of what was childish in them than their nakedness had. Play-actors—but they could not be blamed: they did what they were told. They disappeared at the end of the road, near the melancholy sight of a man in blue overalls brushing up a circus poster.

Hood had known what to do—the thought had been with him all week—but his certainty had made him delay. Certitude unmarked by doubt was suspect, a trap, and he had been proved wrong too recently not to pause. He had been so sure of the dark flaws in the Rogier self-portrait, and then beneath the caked varnish and all the dusty black he had seen the pinpricks of swallowing light, the change in the man's expression, the riot at the window. And Weech: he had obeyed that impulse without a single doubt. Now he wondered if he had made a mistake. He hadn't counted on the wife and child: he owed that family something.

Mayo was certain, but Mayo's movements were brisk with evasion. Hood had always visualized the business of plotting as something which went on all day and late into the night—the poring over plans, the scenarios of assault and seige, the meetings, gaining a controlling advantage by stealth. The exercise of secret crafts. But where was the craft? Mayo watched television when she was in the house, and though she spent some afternoons away from Deptford, when Hood asked her where she had been, she'd say, "Shopping," and prove it with a bag of groceries. She never had visitors; he had seen no one at the house but her and the two children, marriage's parody enacted in a Deptford hide-out that had become a family home. So he was kept at the edge of action, captive in the kind of solitude that can madden. He had not come so far for that, and the inaction worked on him, it roused him, lit his imagination—he was made furious by the continual stalling.

He put Weech's wallet, the money and the bunch of keys in the pocket of his black raincoat. He had given the widow time to leave, but he would be quick —get inside and leave the stuff, then split; he wouldn't snoop. Already what he knew of the woman depressed him: he didn't want to know any more. He went to the house, found the right key for the lock and eased the door open.

The house was unusually cold, holding a chill on its walls that muted the sounds of his entering. His face tightened in the morguelike air, as if the whole place were made of stone slabs that were masked by the arsenic-colored wallpaper. He waited in the damp passage and listened before proceeding farther into the closed clammy rooms, noticing the toys, the telephone directories heaped by the phone. The rooms were neat, bare, anonymous: a sitting room, a dining room—a few pieces of new furniture, a table, a television, a shelf of china figures. A plastic clock filled the tiny kitchen with its ticking. He would leave the money there, weight it with the wallet and keys, and go; but he paused and looked again in the sitting room and began to prowl.

On the upstairs landing there was a twisted slipper, and farther on a throttled cloth animal. He tried the doors: a toilet, a bedroom with a white wardrobe and a mirror reflecting a counter of jars and bottles; then a child's room with an unmade cot and a clutter of toys and torn comics. The frail claim of habitation in the layer of cheap objects. But there were two more rooms. They were locked, and Hood fished out Weech's bunch of keys and opened the first room. It was filled. Light filtering through the drawn net curtains fell on a great heap of merchandise, a solid wall of brown cartons, a row of new televisions—some still padded in bars of plastic foam; and among these were smaller objects, radios, record players, hair dryers shaped like pistols, and hubcaps, automobile chrome, sink fittings, cameras. He read the cartons: they were cases of cigarettes, tobacco, whisky, perfume, and the boxes lent to the stale air of the room a cardboard aroma of newness. The floor was so littered with goods there was no room for Hood to walk.

In the last room, also locked, there were old newspapers tied into bales, and a broken bed, a lampshade, a sofa with a burst seat and two large tin trunks, padlocked. There were markings on the trunks, numerals, the word *Maatschappij* and a Dutch name. Hood found the right keys and released the hasps, opened the padlock on the biggest one and lifted the lid. And he whistled. Inside, piled to the top, were Sten guns which had been broken down, barrels lying beside stocks; digging down he found boxes and clips of ammunition. The second trunk held more ammunition, low-caliber pistols and fist-sized hand grenades, and what he recognized as Armalite rifles. The sight of this small arsenal made him self-conscious. Without examining it further, he shut the trunks and, securing that room, went back to the first room to make sure it was locked.

He was trying the door when he heard a bang and the rattle of a glass pane downstairs; then a thud, a child hitting the floor. Finally, a woman's voice: "—because I said so, that's why!" He heard footsteps downstairs, the woman crossing the house, the sound of the radio being switched on, the child yelling. He locked the door and pocketed the keys.

He did not sneak. He coughed and came down the stairs hard to alert the woman, and before he had gone ten steps he heard the radio switched off and the sound of her running to the foot of the staircase. She drew back when she saw him and tried to speak, but before she could utter a word Hood said with easy familiarity, "Can't seem to find your gas meter anywhere, lady. Where do you hide it?"

"Who are you?" The woman was breathless with fear, and she did not seem to notice the child kneeling behind her, holding her legs. "What do you want?"

"Nothing much," said Hood, continuing down the stairs. "Say, he's a big fella. Hello, tiger."

"How did you get in?"

"The door was open a mile," said Hood, still grinning. "I was upstairs waiting for you to come back."

"You're from Rutter," said the woman.

"Sort of."

"Bastard. Well, you can tell him it's all locked—you've seen for yourself. I don't have the key."

"I'll tell him that."

"Sent you around, did he?"

"Nope. I don't work for him," said Hood. "He works for me."

"I've seen you somewhere," said the woman. "But you ain't English."

"Maybe you haven't heard about the American branch."

"Ron never mentioned it. But he never told me anything. Look," she said impatiently, "I want that stuff out of here and fast. The coppers'll be asking— Oh, Christ!" She pushed the child aside.

Hood said, "I'll see what I can do."

"So you just walk into people's houses? You've got some nerve!" The woman had become calmer, and calm she regained her indignation. She glared at Hood. "Okay, you've had your look, now get out."

"Who's that man, Mummy?" The boy whined, thumping her leg.

"Big kid," said Hood. "What's his name?"

"Jason. He's a villain. Just like his dad."

Hood said nothing. He looked at the boy's large head and saw the man's malice.

"Were you a mate of Ron's?"

Hood hesitated, then said, "I knew him."

"Some layabout done him."

"So I heard." He stared, trying to perceive a reaction on the woman's face.

She shrugged. "He was asking for it. He thought he was so flash, with all his big talk about his connections, Rutter and all. And look what he leaves me with—two rooms full of stolen junk."

"Do you know what's in there?"

"I don't want to know, but if the coppers get wind of it they'll break the bloody door down."

"You'll be all right," said Hood.

"That's what Ron used to say. You're just like him —all talk, and underneath you're nothing."

"Maybe I'd better go," he said. He wanted to be away; he wished he hadn't seen the arsenal, the strewn toys, the woman in the cold house. For the first time he felt his anger turning against him, souring into guilt, endlessly repeating. It was physical self-loathing, as if his skin had become an evil sack for the sour feeling. "I'll see you later."

"What are you afraid of?" said the woman. "Me?"

Jason began to slam a toy car on the floor and make the grunting sounds of a motor.

"I'll be all right," said the woman, mocking. "Eighteen quid a week, widow's pension. And all his big talk about Rutter." She walked down the passage to the kitchen, and Hood followed, stepping over the child. The kitchen was a narrow cubicle: a tiny table, a shelf of cups, a worn biscuit tin, the plastic clock, and a sink with a scrubbed wooden drainboard. He saw that he could not leave her. She put a kettle on the stove and when she turned to him again her face was creased.

"It must be tough," he said.

"It's not what you think. Not Ron. He was a real bastard—he nearly killed me once. Used to throw things. Always walking out on me and then coming back. He had to come back—for the kid, for the stuff upstairs." She sighed, and now Hood saw a slight scar, a half-inch of whiteness on one of her eyebrows. "It's locked. I'll bet there's tons of it. I can't sleep thinking about it—it's stolen, you know, every bit of it."

"I can help you get rid of it."

"It's all locked."

"I'll pick the lock."

"I still won't get to sleep."

"Maybe I can take care of that, too."

"I've tried sleeping pills. They don't work."

"Not sleeping pills."

"Bit of the other, eh?" The woman set out two cups. "Just like Ron."

"No, no," said Hood. "I've got what you need."

The woman eyed him suspiciously. "You weren't waiting. You sneaked in here. What do you want from me?"

"I was waiting for you," Hood said, and he sat down.

7

IN THE TRAIN, Brodie licked the cigarette, set its twisted end on fire, puffed it hard and passed it to Murf, who crooked his skinny fingers like tongs on a coal and sucked a lungful of smoke from it. He gave it back, wheezing a gust of air the color of steam: "Fanks."

They rode with their feet braced on cushions, in an empty eight-seat compartment, rocking away from Deptford. The great brown warehouses flew at them, knocking the train's own clatter through the window with an odor of rope and fried bricks. Smoking pot usually flung them hilarity: they tasted marvels. The sun glanced on the river between buildings and shone in the mirror on the wall opposite, spangling the ceiling with swimming reflections like discs of light from water. The mirror flashed a window of blue sky at them, caught more of the river's dazzle, a boat dissolving into a prism, a jumping council estate. Murf crept over to it and drew out a broken crayon. He wrinkled his nose, set his bat's face against it, and scrawled on the glass ARSENAL RULE.

"Freaks me out, that does," said Brodie.

"You got a buzz on," said Murf.

"No," she said, pointing to what Murf had written on the mirror. "That. They'll think it's football villains."

"Forget it." He took the cigarette, puffed it and passed it back. "Football villains don't do that."

"They do and all," said Brodie. "Write stuff all over the shop."

"Get off. I'll show you." He took his hunting knife from its sheath and kneeling on the seat swung at the mirror, landing the knob of the handle on its center. There was a crunch; the mirror at once deepened and glittered and a web of hairline cracks shot from the beveled edge and met at a crusty dent. But the spikes of glass, held together by a tight chrome frame, did not fall. Seeing that the train was drawing into London Bridge station Murf scrambled to a sitting position and grinned at the shattered mirror. "That's what them football villains do. Make holes."

"The viwuns mike owls," mocked Brodie, screwing up her face. "Here, hold this roach. Give me your blade."

She looked to the side. The train had drawn out of the station. Now the shimmering river was close and she could see across the water to the Monument, its bright gold head ablaze on the tall column and behind it the lid and spires of Saint Paul's on a hill of low silver-blue towers. She stood unsteadily, hesitating at every intrusion of the city passing beside the train. She raised the knife to strike the cushion. They pulled into Waterloo.

"I hate these stopping trains," she said, and put the knife down.

The compartment door opened, and a woman with a shopping basket got in. Murf snatched the knife and slipped it beneath his shirt.

"It's the last hit." Brodie gave him the cigarette.

"This is a non-smoker," said the woman. She sniffed, muttered, and threw down the window.

"Hoo!" Murf leaped to the door, laughing crazily. He unlocked it and kicked it open. They were crossing Hungerford Bridge—the trestles banged, making the iron spans ring; below, the river was molten with sunlight.

The woman seized her shopping basket.

"Piss off!" said Murf and pointed to the open door.

The woman screamed and rocked back in the seat, and she stayed in this position, almost on her back—her feet raised—until they drew into Charing Cross.

"I'm going to report you," the woman said on the platform.

Murf lifted two fingers at her, and they hurried past her, laughing.

In the Strand, Brodie said, "How much money have we got?"

"Sixty pee."

"I know where we can double it. Come on."

They crossed the Strand and scuffed into the Crystal Room, an amusement arcade, making for the one-armed bandits. Side by side, they fed pennies into the machines, yanking the handles, watching the fruit spin. Near them, pin tables coughed and came alight.

Murf said, "Cherries!"

There was a clatter, three pence rattled into the metal dish; Murf clawed it out and moved to a new machine, while Brodie continued to tug on hers. At the end of several minutes they counted their coins.

"Rubbish," said Brodie. "Twenty-eight pee."

They went over to a machine with shifting trays and slides that nudged clusters of pennies into a chute. They fed nine in and won two very black ones. They lost a shilling trying to raise a cigarette lighter with a metal claw. Then they went back to the one-armed bandits and lost all but seven pence.

"Not a sausage," said Murf.

"It's fixed."

"I know where we can double it, she says. Bugger it," said Murf. He went to a tall machine with a rifle on a revolving stand. He put in his coin and began firing—*tunk, tunk*: bells rang, the scoring wheel spun, the lights flashed, and boys playing machines nearby wandered over to see what the commotion was.

Murf was triumphant. Hunched on the platform, his ears sticking out, his teeth clamping his tongue in concentration, his bat's face contorted against the rifle stock, he fired on. He cleared two rows of ducks, knocked down the deer, the rabbits. *Tunk, tunk;* and he made the bells ring.

"Look at the cowboy," said an old man, holding a ragged parcel in his arms.

"Dead easy," said Murf, and picked off the last object, a wheeling tin bird with a light bulb on its wing.

The old man said, "You got a free game coming to you."

"It's all yours, Dad," said Murf.

"Rather have the shilling."

"Take the game!"

They weighed themselves with the last two pence —"We're skint," said Murf, posting the coin—and set off, along the Strand to Trafalgar Square.

At the base of Nelson's column Murf craned his neck for a look at the standing figure on top. He squinted as if solving a problem, then said, "I reckon you could do it. You could blow up this bitch beautyful if you legged it right."

They wandered around the square, tiny in the basin of dark stone, the looming masonry. The buses circled, and on one of them, Mr. Gawber looked down. He saw flocks of filthy pigeons, and people who looked like pigeons; he liked the size, the proportions of the square, and saw the people penned, sunning themselves, scaring the pigeons. It was the people who needed a scare: their idleness made this noble place a dago plaza. Two grubby ones were palavering under Napier. The panic would make them see, the crash would teach them. His bus turned into Saint Martin's Place; he whispered his memo: "Lunch. Picture insurance. Arrow."

Murf and Brodie speculated on the square. Murf said he could bring down the Admiralty Arch by blasting away the central supports with plastic explosive—"then nip on a Number One bus." Two well-placed charges were all that were needed to launch the colonnaded porch of the National Gallery across the square. Brodie, still giddy from the cigarette, saw the steeple of Saint Martin's church toppling as Murf described how he'd bomb the pillars. Or an underground charge, a parcel of nitro in the tube station might do the trick, cause an earthquake in the Bakerloo cellar that would send the whole of South Africa House sprawling: they saw it leap in all directions, airborne columns, chunks of marble, glass splinters, all this hugeness in whirling motion. They saw it rising, in smithereens, but nothing more—not the leveling, the smoke: they could not peer beyond the explosion to the flat acres of still rubble and all the dead.

Up Cockspur Street to Pall Mall they swung along, elated, envisioning bursting buildings. They stopped before the Athenaeum, where dark-suited men were going into lunch. Murf said, "Wouldn't that go beautyful, all them posts crashing—"

Brodie's eyes drummed the wobbling pillars outward, drew the flaming rooms into the sky with cartwheeling men and spinning hats, and the great gold statue pitching forward, dissolving to a sprinkle of dust, and all the paving stones in Waterloo Place flying.

"London's great."

"Fantastic."

It was the only way they could possess the city, by reducing it to shattered pieces. Exploded, in motion, it was theirs. The grandest buildings held them, because in that grandeur, in all the complication ornateness required, were secret corners for bombs. Nothing that could not be razed with a tremendous noise had any interest for them: they celebrated this part of London. They walked up to Piccadilly Circus, sharing another cigarette; then over to the Eros statue where they squatted among the youths with rucksacks and street guides who were roosting and stretching their necks like heavy birds.

"I got it," said Murf. "There must be fifty or a hundred heads here. Let's sell some of that pot. We could get a fiver at least."

"No." Brodie watched the Circus spin, a cascade of lanterns and lighted tubes: the Magic Roundabout —it was here, among the freaks, the center of London, her life, the world. She felt a kinship with everyone who chose to sit here by the statue.

"Look, we don't have any money."

"I don't want any. I hate the shit." Brodie turned

her pale querying face on the others who sat on the steps. They were perfect to her. She saw a girl with a tattoo: a sister.

"You can walk back to Deptford," said Murf. Brodie yawned. He said, "Come on, let's hustle some cash."

"I'd rather hang out."

"So hang out," said Murf. *"Boom widdy-widdy."*

They sat, not speaking, for ten minutes.

Murf said, "I'm sick of hanging out."

"You're a real pain."

"Me arse hurts. And what about the letter?"

"I've got the stupid thing."

"I wish we had some money."

"Money, money," said Brodie. "I can get money —anytime I want."

Murf grunted.

"You don't believe me?"

"Yeah, every day." He grunted again. "I hate this poxy place."

"Follow me."

They walked to Berkeley Square where, at the corner of Conduit Street, they paused to gape at the Rolls Royce showroom. A man was driving a Rolls into the square, a salesman in the street mimicking a traffic policeman, stopping the flow of cars so that the driver could negotiate his way off the sidewalk. Murf had been fretful since leaving Piccadilly, sucking his teeth at the expensive shops and complaining about Hood for only giving them a pound, cursing the machines at the Crystal Room for swallowing the last of their money. When he saw the cobalt blue Rolls and the plump face at the wheel he began to pant. The salesman stuck out his hand, demanding room for the bulky boatlike car.

"Bastard!" screamed Murf, holding his fists up to his ears. He was twitching with rage, and hopping, as if he were a small instrument of nerve strung on bone. He wanted to slash the tires, burn the car, rip the man. He saw money lumbering slowly past his mouth, taunting him. "I'd like to brick that fucker," he said,

but only Brodie heard him. He screamed again at a
higher pitch, "Bastard!"

"You crack me up," said Brodie. Murf was still
trembling as they walked to the lower end of the
square. Brodie tore the letter open and dropped the
smaller envelope into the pillar box in front of
the bank, then led Murf across the square.

A young man in a fawn-colored suit and two pretty
girls reclined on the grass sharing a bottle of champagne and food from a small basket.

Murf approached the picnicking group. He stiffened:
"Bastards!"

The man got to his feet and turned his champagne
glass slowly by its stem, eyeing Murf. The girls
stopped eating. Murf stared at them, then pushed at
his ears.

Brodie took his hand. "What are you doing?"

"I'm going to flash it." He fumbled with his buckle.

Brodie giggled. "Let's go," she said, and pulled him
away.

They walked up the west side of the square and
along Hill Street. Murf said, "If I ever see that fucker
in Deptford I'll brick him."

"It's around here somewhere," said Brodie. She repeated the house numbers, then stopped. "There."

"What's this supposed to be?"

"Money. I know the old girl who lives here."

"You been here before?"

"Lots of times," said Brodie. "Come on."

"I ain't going in," said Murf quickly. He looked
anxious and there was a note of appeal in his voice.

"Why not?" Brodie went up the steps and pointed
her finger at the bell.

"No," said Murf. "Don't."

"Look at him!"

Murf's face registered surprise and fear as Brodie
darted her finger against the bell; and he quailed as
he heard its distant purr in the enormous house.

8

"FUCK IT," SAID Lady Arrow, hearing the bell
go and banging her fist so hard on the desk top a
silver snuffbox the shape of a beetle jumped open and
spilled some of its fine dark powder over her papers,
the pages of a financial statement. She pushed her
work aside and stood up, still cursing. But her diction
shaved obscenity from the words; she enunciated
them overprecisely and with the wrong stress, as if
speaking a foreign language from a phrase book.

She was a gray large-boned woman and had a long
lined face, a look of coarsened hauteur with highlights
of fatigue. Her hair was drawn back tightly across
her skull and fixed behind with a ribbon of ragged
velvet. She was not pretty, she made no attempt to
appear so, she had a disregard even for neatness, she
was not clean; she was very tall. The height that in
another woman would be an embarrassment, causing
an awkward stoop, Lady Arrow gave its full length,
which was well over six feet; and she could accentuate
it by holding her head up and slightly back, giving
herself another inch. She could appear clumsy, but
her clumsiness intimidated: she was an insulting size.

She wore a roughly woven smock, open at the
throat and bound at the waist by an expensive piece
of silk rope; a pair of crushed slippers, a man's watch.
Although her hands were large, her fingernails, which
were bitten to the quick, gave her fingers the blunt
stubby look of garden tools; those of her right hand
were smudged with ink stains, those of her left with
traces of snuff, the same shade that darkened her
nostrils and now her financial statement. These hands

were active, limbering and foraging, making repeated
clutchings. She allowed them this movement and she
seemed at times, as she watched them closing on her
lap, like a strangler practicing alone in a room.

Lady Arrow was a collector. It was from her mother,
an early campaigner for women's rights—there was
a statue of her, flourishing a bronze banner, in a
London park—that she got her height and her interest,
as a girl, in social justice. Her father, a Labour
Member of Parliament, had been an amateur art
historian—some of his collection was still in the house,
as he had left it, now dusty and much neglected; the
rest was in museums on permanent loan. She had in-
herited his taste for acquisition but not his eye. Though
she dramatized it by exaggerating her early unhappi-
ness, it had been a close family, a secure and humane
upbringing; and yet the family traits, combined in
Lady Arrow, formed something new. The result was
a greed for possession, not of objects but of people.
She had always believed that she was carrying on a
family tradition; she was a proprietress of fame. Her
money mattered: the assurance of her wealth blinded
her to difference and allowed her a vulgarity that
was beyond affectation. It also made her unassailable.
She said the opposite. She spoke of the difficulty of
being rich, the impossibility of anyone understanding
her except the very poor, with whom she felt a special
kinship.

It was a unique arrogance of emotion, the senti-
mental belief that both great wealth and the distress
of poverty granted a simplicity of feeling. To be rich
or poor from birth was to know a kind of bravery,
and Lady Arrow insisted that rich and poor alike
enjoyed a common skepticism; neither experienced
true shock or the deception of awe; they were hidden,
immovable, and did most to turn the world. Lady Arrow's belief was a wish mingled with envy: in a
restaurant she would see waiters hurrying to the kitchen
laughing, whispering, perhaps mocking, and she would
want to leave her table of chinless companions and
join those waiters. She envied them their confident
humor, and she could share it—she frequently did at

her own lunch parties on Hill Street—because they
shared an enemy. The middle class threatened both—
selfish, predatory, unprincipled, artless, exposed and
lacking any warmth; drooling and cowardly in the
most wolfish way. They were the mob—the accountants in Lewisham, the parvenus in Barnes, the trend-
spotters in Islington, the predictable *Guardian* readers
in their Basingstoke bungalows; she feared the children
most—their enameled souls, all their hunger and outrage.

The poor could not be outraged, nor could the rich
be moved. Her mother had described to her the
first night of *Pygmalion* (Shaw had been to Hill Street,
the play was a great favorite in the family), when,
at Liza's sharp reply, "Not bloody likely," the whole
theater had suddenly broken into applause—it was
joy, relief, a cheer for vitality. Lady Arrow herself,
on the radio program "Any Questions?," had used the
word "fuck," pronouncing it in her usual way, as if
she were conjugating a German verb. She was the first
to do so, and there was a hush, but there was no
applause. She was not asked back to the show, and
later some man, a mediocre drama critic, claimed
credit for first saying the word. The BBC, dominated
by the wolfish middle classes, had demanded an
apology. Lady Arrow refused and only hoped that
she had wounded them or terrorized them in some
practical way.

She would not be ordered by them, or anyone. The
privilege of ownership was hers, by right, amounting
itself almost to a duty: she was the collector. But
her proprietorial instinct extended beyond mere objects, the assembling of pictures or jars in a room to
be catalogued and gaped at. She had known from an
early age that she could do anything she wished: the
vision excluded nothing. It encompassed the country
that, when she first knew this, was nearly the world.
So she took up—not causes, but those who promoted
them, not ideas but those who held the ideas, not
action but those who acted. She chose the people
with swift skill, like fruit tested for ripeness with a
pinch. It was a deliberate campaign of recruitment

and she carried it out with persuasive gusto. She offered what she believed to be the considerable protection of her friendship, and sometimes temporary shelter, to the mother and child fleeing a mistake, the working-class poet putting a book together, the rising painter, or simply the man who had come to mend the pipes and agreed to stay the night. She made no distinction between friends and lovers, men and women: she slept with both and found a wicked delight in teaching an anxious girl the narrow pleasure of her own sexuality, introducing her to the taste with her foraging fingers and watching her surprise—the small, astonished, moonlit, frightened face.

She recruited them, broke them in with sexual tutoring, then paraded them at her lunch parties—the handyman, the African refugee, the poet, the Welsh Buddhist, the ex-convict, the terrorist, the actress, the shy girl she had loved the night before. And she invited her own contemporaries for witnesses—the successful, the powerful, the very rich: golden pigs, balding mice. There in her drawing room the Minister of Home Affairs might meet a sullen young man and never guess that the boy had, a few weeks before, been his prisoner in a London jail. To the eminent lady biographer of a dead queen she would say, "Jim and I have been reading your book with enormous pleasure, haven't we, Jim?" and the taxi driver Lady Arrow had manfully seduced would nod, avoiding the biographer's eyes. Later, Jim might gain courage and say to a guest, "I once had a fare from Lord Snowdon—seemed a nice bloke." Thieves and the people they burgled, bombers and their intended victims, agitators and their effigies in flesh and blood, the morally sententious and their mockers—how were they to know?—mingled freely, met and chatted in the Hill Street house, like parents and children. She tolerated one and encouraged the other, for she saw her role as essentially maternal: they were hers.

On the piano there were three framed photographs—her husbands in a curious sequence of age. The first, a painter, had been quite old—she married him when she was nineteen—the next a middle-aged banker, and the last, whom she had married in her own middle age, fairly young, a television director. The photographs might have shown her father, her brother, her son—they didn't match her. But the three marriages had given her an even greater profusion of relatives, an extended family that verged on the tribal. This, taken with her aristocratic habit of referring to famous people with great casualness as her relations—"He's supposed to be some cousin of mine," she would say of a man in the news—made it seem as if there was no one on whom she did not have some claim. Those whom she could not prove a relation either by marriage or blood, she collected in other ways, either confronting them with memorable directness ("I want to get something straight between you and me, my darling") or striking up occasional liaisons which she alluded to by saying—and it might be an African prime minister—"He's an old boyfriend of mine!" in that loud silencing voice.

There were always tragedies, disappearances, desperate phone calls at odd hours. She understood: the poor were seized by the same tide as the rich, and jailed, or their friends were. She knew: she was a regular visitor to prisons. Yet that had started in the most conventional way, out of nervous concern, as a duty, her reply to the cautious gentility that led others to visit the sick in hospital wards, the lame and the blind, Chelsea pensioners and the like. Lady Arrow set off in a different direction, to Wormwood Scrubs and Holloway. She brought gifts of cigarettes and fruit and spent afternoons helping the convicts with lessons from correspondence courses. She organized drama groups: lifers at the Scrubs put on Conrad's stage version of *The Secret Agent* (Lady Arrow played Winnie), Holloway did Beckett and Brecht, Brixton a Christmas pantomime. She had plans—for a murderer to play a murderer, a thief a thief; to do *The Importance of Being Earnest* with the girls at Holloway, herself as Lady Bracknell; and lately she had thought of O'Casey's *Shadow of a Gunman* done by I.R.A. prisoners in Wandsworth. The convicts were released and she saw them at her house, those lunch parties. She was uncritical, helpful, attentive, welcoming; she performed, seeing herself as a character in an unwritten novel by someone like Iris Murdoch, and while she remembered any slight with unexampled malice, she invited dependency for the way it obliged the dependent and so she could say without risking contradiction, "You can't refuse me—you're one of the family!"

She brought her pondering hands to the level of the doorknob, pulled it and crossed the landing. At the foot of the stairs, Mrs. Pount, her cleaning woman, held the front door open a crack. Mrs. Pount was plump, clean, correct, and wore a floppy white cap which she tugged, peering through the crack, as if the cap were a badge of authority empowering her to turn away callers.

"Two youngsters to see you, ma'am."

"Is it urgent?"

Mrs. Pount muttered to them, then turned her face to Lady Arrow, towering at the top of the stairs: "They say no."

"Then send them up," shouted Lady Arrow.

Brodie and Murf crept past Mrs. Pount into the house, and as if sensing the vastness of the place and startled by their movements repeated in the several mirrors—corridors of themselves prowling towards gilt frames—they bent slightly and hurried forward. Murf held his head down and seemed to paddle sideways to the stairs. Brodie pawed a greeting to the tall woman standing by a potted palm who, with the sun behind her and her face in shadow, was unreadable.

"Dear Brodie!" said Lady Arrow, watching the two ascend, pulling themselves up on the bannister and kicking the carpet. It had always interested Lady Arrow to see how slowly strangers moved in her house, how uncertainly in all that space, as if they had plunged from the entryway into a wide hole and had to fight their way up a vertical wall. She had met Brodie at Holloway, and had found her careless, intelligent, and pretty; she had listened with horror to Brodie's story of her parents, her ordeal—dreadful, and yet like her own, disturbing. She too had suffered. In the prison the girl had shown little interest, but her visits since to Hill Street had given Lady Arrow encouragement, and she longed for her in a way that made her feel old and foolish and vulnerable.

She wrapped a long arm around Brodie and hugged her warmly. "So sweet of you to come—and who is your charming friend?"

"Murf," said Brodie. "He's scared."

Hearing his name, Murf drew back. He felt the woman's gaze bump the top of his head and he stepped back to take her in. But after a single glance he looked down again at his feet.

"Come in and sit down," said Lady Arrow. "You both look exhausted."

She threw open the doors, making more light and space, another vastness from the vastness of the landing. She sat and put her legs out and said, "Now I want you to tell me what you've been doing. I haven't seen you for ages."

Brodie took a seat near her, holding a cushion for balance. Murf looked lost. He fled to a chair some distance away and sat on the edge gingerly, as if he feared it might collapse; his knees were together, there was a look of worry on his face, and his hands made the feeding gestures of smoking, his fingers straying to his mouth.

Lady Arrow said, "Walking the streets! I suppose that's what you've been doing—walking the streets!"

"Here and there," said Murf. But he choked on it. He cleared his throat and repeated it softly.

"We had to come up this way," said Brodie. "I reckoned we should pop in and say hello."

"I'm so glad you did. But you caught me on one of my busy days." She waved her hand at the desk. "Look at all those letters. And every one of them wants a reply. It's all rubbish. What do you do on your busy days, Murf?"

"Me?" He swallowed. "Sit around."

"Usually we just hang out," said Brodie.

"Yeah, listen to the radio," said Murf.

Lady Arrow said, "I thought only blind people listened to the radio."

Murf looked away wildly, as if searching for a reply, and finally fixed his anxious eyes on the row of photographs propped on the piano.

"Them are all her husbands," said Brodie.

Murf gave a grunt of surprise. He said, "Free?"

"Free, free!" said Lady Arrow, raking her thighs with her fingers. "You're priceless, Murf. How many times have you been married?"

Murf shook his head. "But I lived with a bird once, in Penge it was. Couple of years ago. She was under-age, and then I was had up—threatenin' behavior, utterin' menaces and—" He stopped abruptly, pushed at his ears and said nothing more.

"Young people are so sensible. How I envy you!" She stared at Murf, then at Brodie. "Do you know how lucky you are?"

Brodie hunched and locked her hands around the cushion.

"Do you?"

Murf wagged his head, neither yes nor no.

"You are," said Lady Arrow. "Extremely lucky."

Brodie said, "I won five pee at one of them amusement arcades. Fruit machine."

"Good for you," said Lady Arrow. "I do envy you. I'm always going by those places—they look so cheerful and scruffy. I went in once, but it wasn't much fun. The machines are way down here"—she measured with her hand—"they're not made for freaks like me. I had to hunch so."

"Murf won a free game on the rifle range."

"*Did* you?" said Lady Arrow loudly.

Murf sniffed and cleared his throat again, but he did not speak. He saw the woman's long face smiling at him and he looked away.

Brodie said, "Been over to Block B?"

"Holloway?" said Lady Arrow. "Let me see. This is August—June, I went in June. That was for the Brecht—it went down wonderfully. Can't you just see me as Mother Courage? All the girls were asking about you—you were so popular. You really must go back."

"No fear," said Brodie. "I hate that place."

"But you have ever so many friends there."

Brodie was laughing, a little girl's mirth, chirp and hiccup: "Back to the nick!"

"Don't think of it like that. I'm doing Beckett with the girls now—it's super fun. Believe me, England's prisons are full of splendid people."

Murf said, "And bent ones."

"That's just a word they use," said Lady Arrow.

"Straight up," said Murf. "Mate of mine came out of the slammer with a crimp." He looked at Brodie. "Arfa—he's crimped."

Brodie shuddered and made her goofy face. "Back to the nick! No thanks, I'll stay where I am."

"Where are you living at the moment?"

"Deptford way," said Brodie.

"Deptford!" said Lady Arrow, tasting the word, as if Brodie had said Samarkand. "Deptford!"

"It's not too bad," said Brodie.

"Yeah," said Murf. "It's okay."

"Deptford! Marlowe was stabbed there—in a pub."

Murf said, "Well, it's a rough area."

"Christopher Marlowe," said Lady Arrow.

"I got no time for them pubs," said Brodie.

"Worse than Penge," said Murf.

Lady Arrow smiled and flexed her hands. She was delighted, but only her fingers showed it. She said, "Deptford is near Blackheath, is it not?"

"No," said Brodie.

"I'm sure it is."

Murf said, "Black'eaf's in Kent, something like that."

"Shooters Hill way," said Brodie.

"I'm going out there sometime soon," said Lady Arrow. "A friend has just taken Mortimer Lodge. Perhaps you know her. Araba Nightwing, the actress? Perhaps not."

"Is she on telly?" asked Murf.

"She does quite a lot of television, but she's in a West End play at the moment. Charming girl, very

committed, very involved. You must have read about
her campaign for banning Punch and Judy shows. She's
going to play Peter Pan this Christmas—it's quite a
feather in her cap. Which, I should say, is a good
cloth cap and bright red. She's a Trot." Lady Arrow
waited for a reaction, but Brodie and Murf only
fidgeted. "So many of the actors are, you know—
Trotskyites. I say, what do you think of this bomb
business?"

Brodie gnawed at her lips, bringing a pinkness to
them. She said, "Interesting."

"Isn't it?"

Murf glanced at Brodie with a dumb furtiveness
and saw her swallowing a smile, pursing her pink lips.
He said, "Not half."

Lady Arrow said, "The Old Bailey, and another
in Oxford Street, and the Stock Exchange. All the
right targets. And Victoria Station, too."

Murf looked again at Brodie, then lowered his
eyes.

"And Euston," said Brodie.

"No," said Lady Arrow. "I'm sure you're mistaken."

"Straight up," said Murf.

"*Was* there one in Euston? I had no idea."

"Blew up some lockers," said Brodie. "Where you
put your cases."

"But I have no cases," said Lady Arrow. "I travel
with a carrier bag. I throw in my plastic mac and a
bottle of Cyprus sherry and I'm off."

"Did a lot of damage," said Brodie, persisting.

"A ten-pounder," said Murf. "Legged to a clock."

"I don't remember that one," said Lady Arrow.

"June fourteenth," said Brodie. "Well, around then."

"We were doing the Brecht. I didn't notice—we
were working flat-out. I can hardly keep up with all
these explosions," said Lady Arrow, sitting up and
drawing in her long legs. "But do you know what I
say when I hear about them?"

Murf stared.

"Do you?"

Murf cleared his throat and again wagged his head noncommittally.

Lady Arrow said in her harsh trumpeting voice, "I say, 'Jolly good luck to them!' That's just what I say." She was silent a moment. "What do *you* say?"

"Something like that," said Murf.

"Murf's got a mate in the Provos," said Brodie.

"Not exactly a mate. More a friend, like."

"That's just what this country needs," said Lady Arrow, continuing. "A good shaking up, root and branch, the whole business. Oh, I know there are some people who don't approve of the means. Stockbrokers, people in the City, all the money men." She shook her head. "No, I'm sorry, but they're sadly mistaken. There's only one way to change this old country."

While she spoke, Murf's head sank to the level of his shoulders, his earring brushed his collarbone, and he eyed Lady Arrow with keen apprehension. Brodie, too, crouched with an expressive alertness, as if she had had a whiff of danger. Lady Arrow was talking fast and as she continued she sat straighter in her chair, gaining height; Brodie and Murf drew away, as if the tall ranting woman was ganging up on them.

"—They call them murderers, barbarians, assassins, terrorists!" Lady Arrow threw out her chest and the bracelets shot down her gesturing arm when, conspiratorially, she hissed, "Don't you see? We are the terrorists!"

That "we," so easily given, did not appear to include Brodie and Murf. They watched the woman, waiting for her to erupt again.

But Lady Arrow, beaming with triumph, did not see how she had silenced them. She took the beetle-shaped box and tapped it lightly on the back of her hand, then said, "Snuff?"

Brodie said no. Murf still stared.

Lady Arrow lifted her hand and drew the snuff into her nostrils with an energetic snort, working the back of her hand and her fingers against her nose. She gave a slight sob but did not sneeze. She saw how the two were watching her; she said, "When are you going to invite me to Deptford?"

"You wouldn't want to go there," said Brodie.

"But I would!"

"Maybe when it's fixed up," said Murf.

"Don't do that. Don't do a thing to it. You'll just fuck it up—"

Murf's eyes widened, his mouth fell open. His face then tightened into seriousness. He heard but he did not understand.

"—I want to see it the way it is."

"It wants to be toshed up," said Murf. "But the trouble is with toshers—they're all villains."

"Viwuns," said Brodie, and made a face. "Yeah, he's right. There's nothing in it. In the house."

"But there's nothing here either," said Lady Arrow. Brodie frowned. Murf said, "This is quite a nice setup."

"Everything—it's nothing! They're the same. This room is desperately commonplace. It might be absolutely bare." She dismissed it all with a sweep of her arm: the marble fireplace, the bust wearing a crushed felt hat, the paintings stacked against the wall, the piano, the glass case of Chinese jars, the desk with its clutter of papers, the tall drapes, the shelves and shelves of books, and the room itself with its high delicate coping of plaster, the molding of roses and trailing leaves. "Nothing," she said. "I know because I have everything. It doesn't amount to a row of pins —all this is nothing. Take it, take anything you like."

"That's what I was wondering," said Brodie.

But Lady Arrow was on her feet. "Can I interest you in a genuine Jacobean inkstand—notice the engraving?" She flourished it. "Or this splendid bust— he's supposed to be an uncle of mine. Take it if you can carry it. And the paintings—there's a Turner watercolor somewhere in the middle of that stack. Come now, Murf, haven't you always wanted a piece of Wedgwood?" She handed a blue pillbox to Murf and looked at Brodie for approval.

Murf held the pillbox up to the light, studied it, and then carried it to Brodie. She took it and touched it with disappointment.

"In that amusement arcade, um, I won five pee."

Brodie juggled the pillbox nervously. "But then I lost the lot."

"Not a sausage," said Murf.

"Do you think we could have a few quid?"

"A loan, sort of," said Murf.

Lady Arrow put her hands on her hips and said, "Would you believe it? I haven't got a penny. I never have cash. It's so awkward to carry around."

Murf said, "What we do is we usually spend it."

"Maybe just the train fare," said Brodie. "That's forty pee for both of us."

Lady Arrow went to the desk and slapped the papers. "Not a penny."

"That really freaks me out," said Brodie.

"Funny," said Murf showing the stained pegs of his teeth.

"I know what we can do," said Lady Arrow. "Let's ask Mrs. Pount. She's always got money. She won't mind."

Mrs. Pount was buzzed. She entered the room timidly, in her white cap, twisting the buttons on her cardigan in expectation.

"I say, Mrs. Pount, do you have a quid or two you could give my friends here? Of course, I'll pay you back."

Mrs. Pount took a purse from the stretched pocket of her cardigan and opened it slowly. She poked in it with her fingers, saying nothing.

Lady Arrow said, "And I can give you back that other loan at the same time. We'll settle up. Now don't leave yourself short."

"Here," said the old woman. She unfolded a pound note and gave it to Lady Arrow. As she did so the front doorbell rang. She said, "I'll get that," and left the room, snapping her purse shut.

Lady Arrow held the pound in Brodie's face. "When are you going to invite me down?"

Brodie said, "You'll hate it. It's not like this."

"If it's not then I'll adore it."

Brodie reached for the pound, but Lady Arrow moved it away, and waving it and smiling wickedly, she said, "When?"

"Anytime you want," said Brodie. She pinched the pound.

"You didn't have to say that," said Lady Arrow, letting go.

At the door Mrs. Pount said, "It's for you, ma'am. Mister Gawber."

"That means you must go, my dears," said Lady Arrow. "But please leave your telephone number."

Brodie scrawled the number on a pad and left, giggling to Murf.

Mr. Gawber paused on the staircase to let them pass. He said cheerfully, "Good afternoon!"

The door slammed on their laughter, ending it with a thud.

"You got my message," said Lady Arrow. "I was up to my neck in financial statements."

Mr. Gawber took a chair and when Lady Arrow seated herself behind the desk he said, "I chased up those claims forms. It seems they'll have to conduct an investigation of their own as well as get a police report."

"Let them," said Lady Arrow crisply. "But frankly I am in no mood to put in a claim."

Opening his briefcase, Mr. Gawber said, "Here they are. You sign at the bottom. I'll do the rest." But he did not hand them over. He held the papers away from her and said, "It would be ill-advised for you not to put in a claim. It was a valuable item, and I'm worried about your cash flow."

"Mister Gawber," said Lady Arrow flinging out her long arm and seizing the papers, "I have told you before, I have no wish to die solvent."

"I'm so glad you said that," said Mr. Gawber.

9

"WHY DO YOU take this stuff?" she had asked
the first time, watching Hood roll a pill of sticky opium
in his fingers.

"Because I don't dream." But here in this brown
bead he held the colors of love, a prism of bravery,
a bath of warm feathers, an erotic beak, long cinnamon-
scented wings, and a flight under diamonds to Guatemala.

"Ron never did either." She pouted sadly and a
frightened tearful look came into her eyes. He
thought she was going to say more—she opened her
mouth but expelled only a sigh. Now she was cautious
when she mentioned her murdered husband.

Hood understood that she had disliked and feared
Weech and had wanted him dead. But now that he
was dead she felt obligated—accused—by that dislike, as if she were responsible for his death. There
was no grief in her, only a tremble of resentment,
half sadness, half anger, because she had her wish. She
was left alone with the guilt, as empty and resource-
less as if she had been cursed. She had no friends;
she had a house furnished with stolen objects and two
rooms of loot she had never seen; a child with blotchy
legs whom she seemed at times to look upon as an enemy; and a dread that made her wakeful—that she
was being punished for the way she had felt about her
husband.

She trusted Hood in a hopeless way, asking nothing,
offering nothing, resigned to his attentions, like an
orphan taken up by a strange parent. Hood had
waited for her to reveal some aspect of support—a

mother somewhere she might return to, an old boyfriend she could live with. But she was alone, her
family was dead, she had no plans. Having come to
her with promises he could not leave her, for though
she did not react to him—"You again," she said flatly,
when he dropped in—he knew that to stop seeing
her would be to deprive her of opium, withdraw her
sleep. That desertion would ruin her.

He had succeeded with her so far because he had
shown her how to sleep: a pellet of opium while the
child napped upstairs. She was no smoker—she
couldn't handle a cigarette lightly enough; she fel-
lated it and missed the smoke. But the brown beads
brought dreams to her trance of exhaustion. Hood sat
and saw the liveliness on her mouth, the relaxation
of the drug, a chromatic slumber that induced in her
a sense of well-being, even cheerfulness, as if in her
sleep she had been caressed. That was opium, the
imagination flattered. The drug was all praise. Hood
said, "It's the only way to fly."

"You could do me while I'm asleep," she said
the third time, lying on the sofa and tugging down the
hem of her skirt and smoothing her knees with a kind
of absent-minded innocence.

"I'd rather look at you."

"I'm not much to look at. My tits don't stick out.
That's what Ron used to say."

"They're not supposed to stick out." Hood licked
the pellet and put it in her mouth. He lingered at it,
making it a sexual suggestion, this transfer from his
mouth to hers.

She held the pellet against her cheek like a gum
ball. "Hey, when I'm asleep, don't touch me, okay?
Just don't touch me."

"All right, Mrs. Weech," he said.

"And don't call me that." Her name was Lorna,
but Hood never said it. It sounded too much like
forlorn, alone.

She slept, and he was aroused. He lay his head on
her stomach and waited until she woke.

The drug restored her, gave her rest, removed suspicion from her mind, and yet she said she still never

slept at night. She told Hood how she lay awake on her bed, sometimes going downstairs in the dark and washing all the floors in the hope of tiring herself so she could sleep: and he imagined her pounding her mop in the hall or standing alone in her small kitchen before the black window. He wondered if by killing her husband he had inflicted a fatal wound on her memory. But it was not that at all, not the guilty feeling of bewildered resentment that kept her awake. The two locked rooms worried her. She speculated on what they contained—burglars' loot, forbidden things, a whole cupboard of snatched purses, parcels she'd seen her husband sneak in with, boxes he'd dragged upstairs, danger. Weech had been secretive: his thievery was a mystery to her, but all the more sinister for that. She was afraid it would be discovered by the police and she would be thrown into prison and the child taken away from her. She knew nothing of trials; arrest meant years of solitary confinement in a cage, helping police with their inquiries. She pleaded with Hood to help her.

He told her not to worry. He said, "I know where we can stash it."

"But the rooms are locked."

"So we'll unlock them."

"There's no keys. Ron was robbed!"

"We'll unlock them with a crowbar."

He did not dare use the keys he'd taken from Weech's pocket. The wallet, the money: he had been too ashamed to think of a lie, a pretext for giving them back to her. He unscrewed the plates from the locks and burst the mechanisms with a hammer. The bolts flew. He kicked open the door to the first room.

"Oh, God, what do we do with all this clobber?" The sight of the stack of new televisions, the radios, the crates of cigarettes and whisky alarmed her. She saw a reason for her worry. She stamped the floor and swore and belched with fear. She was less frightened by the two steel trunks in the second room; Hood didn't open them. She said, "It's probably clothes."

"This is going to take some doing," said Hood. "It's a lot to shift. But where did it all come from?"

"You know—you're one of them."

"I almost forgot," he said. "I'll have to get a truck. I'll need help."

"Please do it now. Tonight."

The ice-cream van with its faded signs *Supertony* and *Mind That Child* had been parked in Albacore Crescent since the night Mayo had come back with the painting. Every day—it was one of his family chores—Murf started it up to charge the battery, because it was so seldom driven. Hood went to the house.

He found Murf with a small nervous man he had never seen before. Seeing Hood the man shuffled his feet and coughed. He wore buckled sandals and torn socks and a greasy necktie; his breast pocket bulged with pens. He had been smoking with Murf, and Hood saw the man drop a marijuana roach behind him, find it with his heel, and crush it into the floor.

"Who's your friend?"

"This here's Arfa," said Murf. "Arfa Muncie."

"Start talking, Muncie."

"Go ahead." Murf sniggered. "The great Arfa."

Muncie started, then coughed and cleared his throat. He looked terrified. "Me? I run the secondhand shop down the road. Victoriana. You must have seen the sign."

"The only sign I see is 'Palace Are Wankers,' " said Hood.

"I'm a Chelsea supporter," said Muncie. "Him, he's for Arsenal. Football, see."

"Arsenal rule," said Murf, and winked at Hood.

"Cut the shit," said Hood. "What do you want?"

"Arfa wants to buy that picture," said Murf.

"What picture?"

"The, um, poxy one upstairs."

"I'll give you a tenner for it," said Muncie eagerly. "Too bad it don't have a frame. Ones with them gold frames fetch up to twenty-five. More sometimes. Depends if they're chipped."

"It's not for sale," said Hood.

"Give you another ten bob," said Muncie. "Okay, fifteen."

"You're going to give me the clap if you keep that up."

"He was just asking," said Murf, seeing Hood's face darken.

"Get out," said Hood to Muncie. Muncie backed to the door and left. Hood turned to Murf. "You really have your head up your ass."

"Leave me alone."

"Sorry, I've got a job for you, sport."

Hood explained what he wanted Murf to do. Murf refused. But Hood had a threat: he would tell Mayo that Murf was planning to sell her painting to his friend Muncie for ten pounds. Murf agreed and sulked until nightfall. In darkness they went to Lorna's house and loaded the ice-cream van. Five trips were necessary, but Murf was interested, panting, the weight of the cases making him bowlegged as he tramped back and forth. "There's more and all," he kept saying. "It's fucking diabolical." *Diabowicoo*: he meant it; it was the first hint he'd had that Hood was mixed up in something unlawful. Until then, he had been antagonized by Hood's mocking abuse; he suspected him of being an intruder. Hood jeered at him and he never had a reply. But he was impressed by the amount of loot and looked upon Hood with a new respect, an admiration for what this secret transfer of goods meant. Hood had talked tough, and now Murf believed he was tough. He grinned at all the television sets and strained and swore as he helped heave the metal trunks. "Diabolical. I wish Arfa could see this stuff. He'd shit."

They carried it to the top of the house on Albacore Crescent and filled one of the unused middle rooms. The harvest of another impulse; Hood thought: I'm in it up to my neck.

"I know where it come from," said Murf. "Fell off the back of a lorry, right?"

Weech's phrase. Hood said, "Never mind."

"Who's the bird?"

"Which one?"

"At the house, where we got all this stuff. I seen her mooching around upstairs." Murf licked his lips. "She got your nose open?"

Hood grabbed the front of Murf's shirt and marched him backward against the wall. "There's no bird," he said. "You didn't see one, did you?"

"Yes, no," said Murf. He gagged. "Hey, leave off!"

"You didn't see a house." He twisted Murf's collar, choking him.

"I can't breeve!" Murf's eyes bugged out, his earring danced.

"Did you?" said Hood softly.

"Okay, okay," said Murf, and Hood let go.

"You're murder," said Hood. Murf rubbed his throat and looked uneasily at Hood, who said, "You've got a lot to learn."

"I won't say nothin'."

"Keep your friend Muncie out of here and your trap shut. You'll be all right, but if I see you"—he snatched at Murf's ear, but the boy ducked—"if I see you messing around again and shooting your mouth off, I'll go ape-shit. And if I go ape-shit, pal, you're in trouble."

"I'm knackered," said Murf. "Hey, want to turn on with me? Here, I'll make you one." He fumbled with his cigarette papers and took out his stash.

"Produce it."

They squatted in the dimly lit hallway. Murf nudged him and said, "Muncie's a fence, but nothing like this. 'Ncredible. Hey, I meet all these geezers and I think they're posh, and they're really villains. This old girl the other day and now you." He laughed at the thought of it and showed Hood the cigarette; he smiled in friendship, moving his lips apart to reveal his stained tooth-pegs. "This all right?"

Hood said, "Make it a fat one, squire."

*

The next day, Mayo said, "You *found* it?"

"Right," said Hood. "Ask Murf."

THE FAMILY ARSENAL

"I don't know nothing," said Murf.

"But you know we found it, don't you, squire?"

"Oh, yeah, I know that," said Murf. "But I don't know nothing else."

"So that's why you wanted the van. I leave the house for six hours and I come back to a muddle. Give me the keys."

Hood handed her the keys and said, "There's no muddle, sweetheart. Everything's fine. We found the stuff, now stop shouting."

"Are you lying?" asked Mayo.

"Do snakes have elbows?"

"Where did it come from?"

Hood said, "When I get a few answers from you, sweetie, you'll get some from me."

"I've been straight with you."

"Sure you have. You haven't told me a thing."

"It's too soon. But I'll tell you this. There's something big, a Provo offensive in England. We don't want to blow it."

"Hear that, Murf?" said Hood.

"Yeah."

"Something big. An offensive."

"Yeah."

"But she doesn't want to blow it."

Murf sniggered.

"He thinks you're full of crap," said Hood to Mayo. "He's a bright boy."

"Hop it, Murf," said Mayo. "I want to talk to Hood alone."

"See you later, squire," said Hood. Murf winked and hunched out of the room.

"I'm glad you two are finally getting on."

"We're pals, Murf and me. He doesn't know whether to scratch his watch or wind his ass, but we're pals."

"Those televisions upstairs, all those boxes," said Mayo. "I don't like secrets."

"You're not telling me anything, so I'm not telling you anything. I thought I could help. I can shoot and I can move faster than those drunks in Kilburn. But who do they trust? Teenagers—these tenth-rate screamers and tip-toes. It's a joke, and so far I haven't done a goddamned thing."

"You did that passport."

"It takes ten minutes to make a passport. They don't even realize that it's harder to forge a visa than a passport—ask any consul. Look, I didn't join up to make passports—I joined to take scalps." Hood glared at Mayo. "Well, I get the message. I'm on my own."

"That's not true," said Mayo. "We need you."

"Prove it," said Hood. "Tell me something I don't know. Tell me why they're stalling."

"They're not stalling," said Mayo, but she turned away as she said it and Hood read evasion on her back.

"Yes, they are," he said. "You're trying to protect them. They're supposed to be so efficient, but as soon as I saw Brodie I knew they were a bunch of amateurs. Professionals don't risk a whole campaign by sending a kid like that to do the dirty work—and Murf has the political judgment of a tuna fish. No, they're beginners—like you with your painting. Sure, it's a nice painting, but you're the only one who thinks so. You're wasting your time. All these secrets, all this waiting—tomorrow, next week, next year. It means one thing: they don't know what they're doing. They've got no skill, so they've got no nerve. And you want me to believe there's some big secret! Honey, I know their secret—they're incompetent. They're stupid. They're stalling. Admit it."

"They *have* got a plan, Val," said Mayo. "There's going to be an English offensive. In terms of head-lines, one bomb in Oxford Street is worth ten in Belfast."

"They've got a plan," he said. Their opiates were plans, plots, counterplots, circular stratagems, this drugged sentry duty to which they attached importance. Threat and plot replaced action, the motions of militant bureaucracy blinded them to the fact that they had no power. But they were satisfied with the self-flattery of their secrets, like addicts sucking a pipe of smoking promises. "Well, they haven't got me."

"Don't say that. If you leave I'll be blamed. I told them we could trust you."

"Did they need you to say that?"

"You're an American. You were in the State Department. How were they supposed to know you weren't a spy or—"

"They thought I was a spook?" he said sharply. "At first."

"Why didn't you tell me that before?"

"Because I knew you weren't."

"How do they know I'm not one now?"

"The passport you made. It worked. He wasn't picked up, whoever used it."

"I still think it's a pretty sloppy outfit. You can tell them I said so."

"Maybe I will."

"And another thing," said Hood. "Tell them I know they're stalling. They've got a plan. Big deal—a plan is just a piece of paper, or in their case one Guinness too many. Any drunk can have a plan. There's only one thing to do and that's act. What are they waiting for?"

"All right," said Mayo, wearied by the argument. "Something's gone wrong. There, are you happy now?"

"What is it?"

"I can't tell you. I don't know."

"They're drunk."

"It's serious. Something to do with supplies. All the contacts were made—that's why they needed the passport. They think they've been burned."

"Supplies," said Hood. "You're talking about hardware. What about their supply lines? What kind of mob is this?"

"This isn't America, Val. We don't buy machine guns at the local ironmonger's. We have to get them on the continent—from Arabs, thugs, anyone. Then they have to get them into the country. It's bloody hard."

"You're wrong, sister. It's easy," said Hood. "Just send one of those creeps around here and I'll tell him how."

"You're so belligerent all of a sudden," said Mayo.

"You've got all the answers, haven't you? Well, I saw that room full of stuff upstairs. What do you propose to do with your twenty television sets?"

Hood said, "Get twenty people and watch them."

Mayo shrugged, but the talk had rattled her; she started out of the room.

Hood said, "And what do you propose to do with your painting?"

"I don't want to think about it," she said.

"I'll be sorry if they pay your ransom," he said. "I'm beginning to like it."

The painting's secret had been revealed slowly. It had changed from day to day, from week to week, and now nearly a month since he first saw it the image had set. It was definite. He had seen Rogier as confused, furious, hesitant, holy, insane; one day the thin smile was mocking, the next day it was benign, then it was not a smile at all but a mouth mastering pain. It was the portrait of a fabulous villain in black. It was a patrician gentleman gleaming with wealth. It was an anxious bridegroom pausing at the window of experience. It was an icon with saintly hands and small feet, a man suffering an obscure martyrdom, his soul shining in his face. Hood gave it titles: "The Expelled Consul," "The Jailer Lord," "The Hangman," "Death Eating a Cracker." One time it was not a man at all; he'd had an opium dream in which it was revealed as a woman, slender, like a heron in black, with small breasts, hungering in a high attic—the onset of loneliness, the moment of widowhood. All these, then none of these. The legs were apart, the boots planted almost athletically on the square of carpet; the arms were rising on the handle of a silver dagger, the eyes were awakened with fury and pricked by the red light of imagination. The neck was tensed to turn, the hands to fight. It was the instant between decision and movement, a split second of calm. It was, passionately, a man of action.

"You're bourgeois to like it," said Mayo.

"You were bourgeois to take it," he said. "A real revolutionary would have burned it weeks ago."

For Mayo it was proof of her commitment, and

when Hood challenged her with doing nothing she said, "At least I've got the picture," using the theft to seek exemption. Hood said, "Right. You're stuck with it." She did not see that it was purely theatrical, the dramatic flourish of a well-publicized burglary. But incomplete, a hollow gesture, since there had been no word from the owners, no further response from the newspapers. The sanctimonious warnings had ceased, the aggrieved art critic who had called it "a national treasure" was silent. The loss was accepted; its last mentions had the serene factuality of obituaries. And none of Mayo's demands had been met. The reward offered was laughable and would barely have covered the cost of reframing it. There was not much more that could be done with it. The frayed bottom edge had been sent to *The Times;* to send any more would mean cutting into the painting itself, slashing the finished work. Mayo appeared unwilling to do this, and Hood knew that he would prevent her from damaging it. She had threatened in one of her letters to burn it. He reminded her of that threat, but hoped she wouldn't do it. It seemed more valuable to him now than anything he had ever known; it calmed him to have that masterpiece of action in the house, the reassurance of a perfect man; and it filled him with resolve, like a summoning trumpet.

She kept it tacked to the wall of the bedroom cupboard, her trophy, regarding it with embarrassed pride. Hood noticed her standing before it, inhaling it, growing hostile in a glum way, as if she saw nothing in it but a man. The image did not move her; the painting itself mattered. It was hers. Her attitude, then, was one of simple ownership: possessing it somehow bore witness to her dedication, enhanced her little role. That idea drugged her, helping her to ignore whatever remained of the plot. To steal money was a crime; to steal a million pounds' worth of art was a political act. She was no ordinary thief. Once she had looked at the self-portrait and said, "It's butch."

Butch! Hood came to despise that in her; how casually she acknowledged the painting, with what pompous certainty she spoke of the future. The painting taught him all he knew about her.

She said nothing about her family, who, Hood guessed, must be wealthy—they had left that mark on her, or rather no mark at all, but an absence of blemish which was itself vivid as a scar. The impression she gave was one of aggressive independence, as if she had simply arrived. She gave no hint of preparation; no doubt, hardly a motive, only the smug certitude that anything was possible. It was a snobbery of assurance Hood had seen in the rich, an awareness of power: what could not be changed could be bought wholesale and owned, or stolen without blame, or killed. Privilege: only the powerful knew the enemy; but they had no true enemies, they could not be touched. The poor might suspect a threat but their world was outside Rogier's window, a confusion of the unseen.

Mayo, Lorna: he compared them and made his choice. The house on Albacore Crescent was a family, parents and children; the television, the kitchen, the bedroom. Hood had, in a modest way, supervised Brodie and Murf; and he had gone to bed when Mayo had, obeying a kind of marital signal, looking to her for sexual encouragement, the unspoken suggestion that meant they would make love. "I'm tired" or "I'm not tired." He had lingered, and finally he sat up reading and let her go to bed alone, penalizing her by pretending not to understand the hints that familiarity made obscure. She hadn't insisted on sex. By mutual agreement he slept with her, watching how she stiffened on penetration and clung to him, relaxing as if unlocked with his blunt key. Then his feeling lapsed. He said nothing. These days, Mayo went to bed alone.

Murder had brought him to the widow. He now visited her out of a cautious curiosity; and, afraid of giving her false hope, he kept his distance. The guilt he saw in her intensified his own. He regretted that. He did not want to think that in killing Weech he had done anything but rescue his victims—and Lorna was one of them. The murder was an act of preservation. But with Mayo's refusal to bring him into the plot, and

with her objections to the cache of loot in the room—
fear again: he did not want her to know of the arsenal
—he turned more and more to Lorna.

He had been treating her for her unspecific grief, a
drug for her guilty anger. He liked her company, then
he preferred it to Mayo's; and finally he needed it,
found in this widow's trust the solace of the drug itself, and dreaded wounding her with his love.

"Put the kid to bed," he said one afternoon.

"He won't go," said Lorna. "He wants to go out."

"Can't you do something with him?"

"In the way, is he? Look, if he gets on your
nerves you don't have to come round here."

"My nerves? What about yours?"

"I'm stuck with him," she said, and Hood could see
that everything she had feared in her husband she
hated in the child, who was the brute, blameless in
miniature.

"He should be in school. I see kids his size going to
school. It's September—they've started already."

"Playgroup," said Lorna. "He'd like it."

Hood said, "Then send him."

"Just like a Yank," she said. "You never think of
the money side. I'm on a widow's pension. I can't
afford things like playgroups."

"They'd let him in free if they knew that."

"I'm not a beggar."

Hood took out his wallet. He said, "How much?"

"I don't want your money."

"Please take it," said Hood. "You can pay me back."

"Stuff it."

"Don't talk to me like that," he said angrily. "Understand? Don't say that to me."

It was the first time Hood had ever raised his voice
with her. He was sorry; she looked scared: she had
known other threats.

"I'm not giving you the money. I'm giving it to
him." Jason lay on the floor, playing happily. An un-
common sight; usually he screamed for his mother's
attention when Hood was around. Hood saw him as
he saw the mother, through the narrow aperture of

pity. He called the child and said, "Want to go to a playgroup, sonny?"

"No," said Jason, wrinkling his nose. "I want to do a shit on your head." He laughed a crass adult laugh.

"Ron was sarky like that," said Lorna.

"Look," said Hood to the boy, "you want to go to a playgroup. I know you do, so take this"—he gave the boy a five-pound note—"give it to the lady and you can go."

"Keep digging," said Lorna. "It costs twelve quid."

It rained the next day, a heavy downpour ending a week of sun and dropping autumn on to that part of London, chilling the trees and darkening the brickwork of the angular terraces and washing all the traces of summer away. Where there was green, as in the park on Brookmill Road, it was sodden and depleted; and the city looked smaller and fragmented in the mist —it was a sea of sinking islands. Hood put on his black raincoat, turned up the collar and trudged around the corner to Lorna's.

She said, "I knew you'd be over today."

Hood entered and, opening his coat, took out a paper bag that was flecked with rain.

"What's that?"

"I'm going to do some cooking."

The house was cold and unusually quiet; the toys were put away; he could hear the clock ticking in the kitchen. He looked across the parlor and said, "It's a good place for him. He'll like it."

"So will you."

"What makes you say that?"

She looked at him; resignation tugged at her smile. "I know what you want."

Hood ignored her and opened the paper bag. He took out a thick blackened pipe, some tweezers, a candle, and a cigarette lighter. He pulled the cushions from the sofa and spread them on the floor; and he squatted, setting out the simple apparatus. She watched him and shook her head.

Her voice was flat: "You're going to do me."

Hood lit the candle and broke off a piece of opium. He took it with his tweezers and heated it in the flame.

It sparked, then grew black, but it did not light. It thickened to a rounded blob and became glossy and then was encircled by fire. He said, "Lie down."

Lorna came near and sniffed. "What is it?" She lay beside him, propping herself on a cushion. Hood took the pipe, poked the softened plug of opium inside and clicked the lighter over the hole.

"Put it in your mouth," he said, handing her the pipe. He told her how to puff it, and they passed it back and forth until the fragment was reduced to a coal. Then he scraped the bowl and started again. The candle lit her face, the flame giving her cat's eyes: she was lovely, feline in this small light. The rain pattered against the window, while they lay on the floor smoking. She did it with her lips, holding the pipe stem tentatively, using her tongue, kissing the smoke, and he was half in love with her as the room filled with the aroma of sweltering poppies. They lay side by side, barely touching, breathing slowly; they puffed the pipe and did not speak. He felt an urgent shudder, a dumb hilarity in his groin. Then it weakened and passed through him, warming him. There was thunder from the river, but the warehouses hid the lightning flashes. In the rain and opium smoke he smelled Hué, the fleeting gulp of a bobbing sampan. She was the first to sleep. He watched her as he prepared a fourth pipe, then he moved very close to her and kissed her still lips: they were cool with sleep. He puffed and closed his eyes and he was traveling to the drum and whine of a *raga,* an eastern lament, sorrowing for a love that was distant and danced like a flame in water. He opened his eyes: already the dream had begun to roll.

10

PITCHFORKED AWAKE BY a sharp pain in her back, Norah sat up in bed quickly, pushing at the mattress with her hands, making Mr. Gawber's whole body leap. She switched on the bright bedside lamp, blinding her feebly inquiring husband, who turned and groaned. He lifted his pocket watch from the side table and swung it to his eye. It was just past eleven-thirty—he'd had one hour's sleep. Norah, motioning to stifle a sigh, managed to amplify it. She jerked on the bed, testing her back, drummed her legs and sighed again, drawing the noise slowly through a grievous scale, high to low, the sound of a person spinning down a deep shaft and never striking bottom, only whimpering at the end and growing into silence. They were both fully awake now, and in pajamas and nightdress, their hair fluffed into tangled white wigs, they looked blanched and ancient, whitened by frailty, two hundred years old. Mr. Gawber quaked. The light jarred him like noise. Norah said, "I can't sleep."

He pretended not to hear; but how typical of her to wake him to tell him that! She was no solitary sufferer. She demanded a witness, involved him in her discomfort, made him endure it. Invariably she touched him with her pain, and there was not an upset she'd had that he had not somehow shared. She sighed, he groaned. It was in part the penalty of the double bed, marriage's narrow raft.

"Wake up, Rafie, I can't sleep."

"What is it?" He exaggerated his drowsiness.

"I feel ghastly. Yes, I think I'm coming down with

something." She tried her fingers, tasted her tongue, blinked—to locate symptoms.

"Probably"—he yawned: a stage yawn, almost a pronouncement—"probably just wind."

"No," she insisted. "I've got pins and needles. A splitting headache. I've gone all hot." She got a grip on her head and out of the corner of his eye Mr. Gawber saw her swivel it. She looked as if she might be trying to unscrew it.

"Leave your head alone. You'll just make it worse."

"I'm feverish."

"Poor thing." Without wishing to he yawned again, an authentic rebuke.

"You don't care." She started to cry softly. "Oh, my head. It won't stop."

He said, "I believe you're coming down with something."

"It's flu," she said and was calm. She listed her symptoms once more.

"I'm not surprised. There's a lot of it around. Thornquist was out all last week."

He wanted to be sympathetic, but Norah's illnesses were always so laborious that it annoyed him to hear her complain of their annoyance. He resisted consoling her. Then her aches and pains gave him some satisfaction—she deserved them for the pain she caused him. By a queer process of reversal, charity made antagonistic, he came to enjoy hearing her say how it hurt.

The bright lamp knocked against his eyes. He said, "Do turn the light off."

"How can I find my medicine in the dark?"

She thumped the mattress again, bouncing him, and went to the bathroom, switching on lights. She returned with a bottle of Doctor Collis Browne's Mixture. It was an old bottle, containing a fluid now unlawfully potent, the active ingredient being opium. She was a regular user of patent medicines and pills: green lung tonic, fruit drops, stinging ointments, syrup of figs, dragées that stained her tongue purple. She was troubled by wind; she took iron for her blood.

Old ailments, old cures. She measured the Collis Browne into a soup spoon and sucked it noisily.

"Do you a world of good," Mr. Gawber muttered.

Norah lay panting. Mr. Gawber reached across and turned the light off. She snored.

But he stayed awake, alert, panic preventing sleep. Perhaps it would happen like this, a fiscal cramp that couldn't be unknotted with a dose of the old mixture; a sickening for which there was no name or cure; a fever that couldn't be shaken off. The workers all down with something, brokers with their fingers badly burned, industry halted at a stage of senility, a hardening in the usually swift canals, blockage, and the old country supine, helpless on her back like he himself in a ridiculous parody of repose.

He found his small radio and put in his earplug. He moved the dial. Radio Three had gone off the air. He spun the wheel to the World Service. He heard,

> . . . let no star
> Delude us—dawn is very far.
> This is the tempest long foretold—
> Slow to make head but sure to hold.
>
> Stand by! The lull 'twixt blast and blast
> Signals the storm is near, not past;
> And worse than present jeopardy
> May our forlorn tomorrow be.

Kipling, the old mixture, favorite of puzzle-setters. Mr. Gawber passed the night like this, worrying about England as if she were a dear old aunt in failing health, and not whether or how soon the death would come, but how she would look, laid out among her indifferent mourners. The medical analogy he knew to be fanciful, and Kipling's "Storm Cone" was romance. Whenever he thought of the catastrophe ahead one image remained in his mind: the war. He hadn't fought, yet he had felt it keenly. It was a dark brown newsreel in his memory he could run at any time, and that flicker from the past was a flicker of the future. Powdered eggs, rationed sweets, sugar coupons, bread queues, the occasional bombed building in the middle of a terrace, like a missing tooth in a wonky denture; books printed illegibly on villainous paper, the brave voice of Churchill on the steam radio and the officious Mr. Mullard from number twenty-nine over the road—and now in Bognor—in his warden's helmet. Coley for tea, the sizzle of snoek, the sound of buzz bombs. War! It had shaped him. He remembered it on this long night with a certain cheer, because the war had helped him to find in himself an access of strength. He was not afraid.

Still Norah snored, and dayspring—who said that? —dayspring was mishandled. The traffic began on Catford Hill, and on Volta Road the clank of the bottles in the milk float, the grinding front gates, the plunk of the letter slot. And the September sun —for once he was glad dawn came early. He went down, made tea, and brought Norah a cup. She slept as if she had been coshed, bludgeoned there on her half of the raft: her mouth was open and she sprawled face up, ventilating her sinuses with rattling snores. He woke her gently. She blinked and smacked her lips and said, "I had a dreadful night."

He was silent at breakfast, though he allowed himself a glance at the crossword, the letters, the obituaries. An item on the front page shocked him.

"You know what that means, don't you?" Norah said.

. . . *unclothed and partly decomposed body,* he'd seen. Why did they print such things, and which ghouls read them? He folded the paper and said, "What's that, my dear?"

"I won't be able to go to the play."

Indecent—worse: hideous. He saw the body and tasted it on his toast. "What play is that?"

"Tea for Three," said Norah. "I was so looking forward to it."

That too? How trivial and sour the title seemed over breakfast. He said, "I'd completely forgotten about it. You might be feeling better tonight. I must say, I'm feeling a bit off. That's enough breakfast for me."

"I won't enjoy it. It won't be the same."

"Then I shall cancel the tickets."

"You can't do that. It's a gift—Miss Nightwing will be terribly upset. She was counting on us to go."

"But what will I do with the extra ticket?"

"You can take someone from the office. Miss French."

"The inevitable Miss French."

"One of the clerks. Mr. Thornquist. They'd be glad of a chance. And you can tell me all about it."

"Are you sure you can't go?"

"Rafie, I feel ghastly. I have this rotten feeling in my stomach—"

She described it with disgusting care, checking Mr. Gawber's reverie. Sick people knew their ailments so thoroughly. He clucked and tilted his head in concern; he listened and felt a vengeful glee rising to his ears. He was ashamed, but even that did not diminish the pleasure of hearing her drone on about her stomach. She had deprived him of a night's sleep.

He promised to get tickets for another play: they'd see *Peter Pan* at Christmas. A penance—he would have to sit through two plays for her gastric flu. And she said she couldn't face making his lunch. So the crush of a noontime pub as well, elbows and soapy beer and the prattling of loud clerks in the smoke. The catastrophe would finish them, but he wanted it soon. Sometimes he wished there were a chain he could pull to start the landslip quickly.

"Why are you smiling?"

"I'm not smiling." Was he? What did that mean? "I've got something stuck in my tooth."

"Is there anything in the paper?"

"No."

He left for work, glad to be free of the house, the stale air of the sickroom. He crossed the frontier of the Thames and was restored by the rain-freshened air in the solider part of the city. He chose the Embankment route to the Aldwych, walking behind the Savoy, pausing at the statue of Arthur Sullivan where the heart-breaking nude sorrowed on the plinth; then along the neat paths to the stairwell below Waterloo Bridge. The graffiti howled from the walls, unpronounceable madness and the threat that had become so frequent: ARSENAL RULE. Two homeless old men bumped their belongings down the stairs in prams, like demon nannies with infants smothered under teapots and ragged clothes. The men and their prams were secured with lengths of string. It was an omen: soon the whole population would be shuffling behind laden prams, crying woe.

His reflection was interrupted by the tickets he had been lumbered with. Who to take?

In the course of the morning he worked through a short list. The receptionist yawned at him. Not her, in any case: people would talk. The messenger, Old Monty? He had a room in a men's hostel in Kennington. A clean man, he smelled of carbolic soap and was always speaking to Mr. Gawber of weevils and black beetles and how the other men never changed their shirts, and how they left the bathroom in a mess. He had been in an army band: Aldershot, Indian camps, Rangoon. "I should have stuck with the clarinet," Monty said. He'd enjoy a play. Mr. Gawber risked the question, but Monty said, "I always do my washing on Thursdays." Rodney, the stockroom boy? Rodney brought fresh pencils at eleven o'clock, but Mr. Gawber didn't like the way he dropped them on his desk, with a clatter that hurt his teeth. In such a careless gesture he saw the boy would resign one day soon. It was the pattern: they became clumsy, then they quit. Not Rodney.

"Ask Ralph—can't you see I'm busy?" said Thornquist irritably waving a secretary away.

And not Thonky.

Sadly, the inevitable Miss French. But she said, when he approached her, "I hope you're not going to ask me if those letters are typed. They're all here, just as you gave them to me. I couldn't read your writing."

He was proud of his handwriting. It was a good uniform hand, sacrificing loops for a workmanlike clarity. The woman was lying. Not her.

He picked up the phone and dialed. There was a buzz, a jumble of clicks, then, "—but if I sell now at thirty-three I'll be out of pocket to the tune of four thousand."

"By tomorrow morning it will be five thousand," said another voice.

"Sell now," said Mr. Gawber, and hung up.

*

Hood took out the business card and confirmed the Kingsway address, found the entrance and just inside on the wall the name *Rackstraw's* on a column of varnished boards. He ran up the steps three at a time and met the receptionist who, with headphones at rest on her neck, was reading a magazine.

"Mister Gawber, please."

The girl looked up from her magazine. "Do you have an appointment?"

"No."

"You'll have to take a seat."

"I'll stand." He saw the girl return to her magazine. Then he said, "You can tell him I'm here."

"There's someone ahead of you."

"I don't see anyone, sweetheart."

"He's got an appointment. He's not here yet." Now the girl was not reading, but simply holding her elbows out and flipping pages to avoid facing another question.

"I wish you'd do something. I'm in a hurry."

"I'm doing everything I can." She didn't look up. "This is a busy office. Appointments only. That's the rule." She turned pages quickly and shook her head. "I don't make the rules."

An elderly man in a dark blue messenger's uniform came through the outer door. He stopped at the desk and made a swift reflex with his heels.

"That packet's from Mister Thornquist," said the girl crossly. "It was supposed to be delivered an hour ago to the City. By hand."

"Sorry," said the man. "I was doing the post."

"The post doesn't take two hours, Monty."

"Parcels," said the man. "They wanted weighing."

"Listen, Monty, that packet's been sitting there—"

"Back up," said Hood striding over to the girl. She was startled. He said, "Why are you talking to him that way?"

"I'm sorry but—"

"Cut it out. Don't use that tone with him."

The man stared.

Hood said, "Don't let her talk to you that way."

"Thank you, sir," said the man. "I was just going to say that myself."

Hood turned again to the girl. "If I catch you giving him any lip I'll come back here and slap your ass."

He walked past her to the office door.

The girl stood up. "You don't have an appointment."

"Move over, sister," said Hood with such fury the girl sat down and twisted her magazine in both hands.

Hood marched through the office of typists quickly, saw a glassed-in cubicle in which Mr. Gawber was working at a desk, and headed for it. He knocked and went in.

"Yes, yes," said Mr. Gawber rising, trying to remember the name.

"Valentine Hood."

"Exactly," said Mr. Gawber. "I never forget a face. I should be royalty or a tax inspector or a politician. Cursed with total recall! Lower Sydenham—about six weeks ago—and your friend." He tapped his forehead. "It's gone—what was his name? But his face is there, oh his face is there!"

"He wasn't a friend of mine," said Hood.

"Of course not. Nasty piece of work, wasn't he?" Mr. Gawber made passes with his hands. "Now do have a seat—what can I do for you?"

Hood said, "You told me that if I ever had a financial problem I should come to you—"

Mr. Gawber listened with apprehension. He took a pencil and holding it like a cricket bat said, "I'd like to interrupt you before you go any further. I might have given you the wrong impression. We're mainly a firm of accountants, which means we don't handle loans or mortgages. Some people think—and I don't blame them one bit—that we're bankers." He batted with the pencil. "Chap was in here last week, sitting where you are now. Tradesman, I imagine. Awfully nice chap. Wanted some cash. Had to tell him he'd got the wrong end of the stick. Bowled!" Mr. Gawber studied the pencil he had been batting with. "He was terribly creased. There are so many misconceptions about this business."

"I didn't come here for a loan," said Hood.

"I'm so glad you said that."

"Mine's more a question of procedure, about directing funds. I'm sure an accountant should have the answer."

"I couldn't agree more."

"I'd like your advice on transferring money to another person's account without that person knowing where it came from."

Mr. Gawber leaned forward, as if he hadn't quite heard the proposal. He had heard, but a detail bothered him: when a man said "person" he always meant a woman.

"I owe this person some money," Hood went on, "and the person will be offended if I just hand it over—pride, I suppose. The only solution is to transfer it. From an unknown source, as they say."

"How much is outstanding?"

"A lot, I'm afraid. But I'd like to transfer it in installments, a certain amount every week."

"Does this, um, person have a bank account?"

"Yes," said Hood.

"Then it's really quite simple," said Mr. Gawber. "I don't know how they handle these things in your country, but here—apart from Coutts, lovely old firm —banks don't specify the source of funds on the statements anymore. The money comes in, it's credited, and that's the end of it. There might be a deposit notice, though—a chit through the post. Your name might appear on that."

"Or yours."

"If we acted for you."

"It would simplify things," said Hood.

"I couldn't agree more," said Mr. Gawber. "Now if you give me the name of the young lady's bank and the account number—"

"I didn't say it was a young lady."

"Of course you didn't!" Mr. Gawber blushed and he rubbed his eyes in embarrassment. "Why did I think that? I'm terribly sorry—you must forgive me."

Hood smiled. "No problem. It's a young lady, all right. Here's her check. The account number's on the bottom." He unfolded the check he had torn from a book in Lorna's handbag.

"Weech," said Mr. Gawber, examining the check. "That rings a bell. I'm good on faces, but so bad on names. Should I know her?"

"No," said Hood, and attempted to distract Mr. Gawber with the details of his own account.

Mr. Gawber wrote on a pad. He said, "Very odd. I hope you don't think I always go canvassing for new accounts in the public houses of Lower Sydenham. That was my first time in the area. A little mix-up. But I told you, didn't I? It started with a crossed line on that telephone. Had another one this morning. But what an extraordinary day that was. I suppose you've forgotten all about it."

Hood said, "I'd better be going."

But Mr. Gawber didn't want him to go. Hood was more than a witness to that day; and now he recalled the other fellow, a tough rowdy man whose every word had alarmed him. Hood had not been afraid —he had stood between them and given Mr. Gawber a kind of protection. He was tired now. That night's sleep lost. Norah was paying for her disruption, but he needed someone, a little company. Alone, depressed, he would think only of the catastrophe. He said, to stall Hood, "No, you're absolutely right."

"I'm off," said Hood.

"No, I couldn't agree more," said Mr. Gawber. He doodled on his pad. "We'll have to tighten our belts, like everyone else."

Hood rose and backed to the door of the cubicle. He said, "I'll write you a letter to make it official."

"You're not going so soon?"

"I'm wasting your time."

"Not at all—I'm enjoying our little talk," said Mr. Gawber. "Have a cup of tea. I'm sorry I can't offer you anything stronger." *Tea:* he remembered. "I say, Mr. Hood, do you have any plans for this evening?"

11

LIKE FILING INTO church, but the wrong one. Mr. Gawber felt very tired and wayward, and he paused with Hood in front of the theater deliberately to anger himself. The critics' praise was displayed like gospel verses on a Baptist motto-board, calling doubtful people in: I LAUGHED TILL I CRIED—THAT RARITY, A SHEER DELIGHT—RELIEF FROM THESE DARK TIMES—I BEG YOU TO SEE IT!—THE SADDER MOMENTS ALSO RING TRUE—IT DESERVES TO RUN AND RUN—A SHATTERING ACHIEVEMENT—I DIDN'T WANT IT TO END! He knew there was even an organ inside, flanked by boxes that might have held choristers. The lobby had all the carpets and brass of a presbytery, and there glassy-eyed people smoked, chattering excitedly, searching faces for friends, a commotion of tentative greeting. Clerical-looking ushers in dark uniforms stood at attention, tearing tickets near the doors to the stalls. The people passed by them, entered the theater—a stupendous hollow temple trimmed with pagan gilt—and dropped their voices to whispers. They shuffled down the aisles pinching their stubs: an attitude of somberness that was almost stately. Church-going for them, too, but they were reverential.

Mr. Gawber bought a pound of chocolates. It was habit. He excused himself and fell into that queue as soon as he arrived. He tucked them under his arm, and picking up the tickets at the box office—a slight thrill seeing his name importantly lettered on the envelope—led Hood to the seats. They were down front, so near to the footlights they could hear the mutters of stagehands behind the curtain pushing furniture into position. Then Mr. Gawber sat with the box of Black Magic on his lap, wearing an expression of extreme anxiety, as if he expected the place to catch fire at any moment; or a bombing? Public places had become terrorists' targets. He hugged the box and stared at the curtain. It was more than discomfort—it was a rapture of fear on his face so keen it could have been mistaken for joy.

"Looks like a full house," said Hood, and saw Mr. Gawber's grasp tighten on the chocolates. Allowing the old man to escort him, Hood had experienced a son's cozy serenity. Mr. Gawber had acted with polite conviction, almost gallantry, steering Hood down the Aldwych, occasionally warning him about pickpockets, and apologizing in advance for the play he promised would be appalling. But Mr. Gawber had said little else. His guidance was unobtrusive—paternal nods that were helpful and mild and with a hint of pride. He was like the father who remains silent because so much is understood; and Hood was relieved that no brightness was demanded of him. He had been unwilling to go to the play, but he had nothing better to do, and Mr. Gawber had shyly insisted: "I'd consider it a great favor." Now, seated in the theater under a sky of lights and paint, he felt he had stumbled into an anonymous pause, outside time, like a formal reverie which would leave him empty. He expected nothing of the play but for it to end.

The mutterings from behind the curtain grew louder, the bump of furniture quickened, and the curtain itself bulged on the backs of the stagehands. There was a crash and a muffled cry: *"Balls!"*

"This is the part I like," said Mr. Gawber.

Hood glanced at him, puzzled. He wondered if the old man was cracked. The curtain had not risen. Mr. Gawber relaxed and clasped his freckled hands.

It happened again, porkers' grunts preceding a wooden thud that made the hem of the curtain dance.

"Forgive me," said Mr. Gawber, shaking with laughter. He snorted into his handkerchief. He was enjoying himself now, his look of fear replaced by a cheery appreciation of the random bangings. This, for him, was the only comedy: harmless error, unplanned and unexplained.

The houselights dimmed, silencing the murmurs in the audience and bringing a hush like piety.

The curtain went up on a modern kitchen the width of the stage, as efficient-looking as an operating room, with chrome and bright fittings and a muted yellow decor. Sunbeams leaned against the windows. A large stove, a refrigerator the size of a wardrobe and a series of oblong cupboards at eye level, one with its door open revealing shelves crammed with cans of food: there was a gasp of approval from the audience. On counters that ran between the appliances and on a table at the center, the cooking paraphernalia had been set out—spice jars, bowls, a pitcher of milk, an electric blender, copper pots and whisks, ingredients in cartons, and a varnished firkin labeled *Flour*.

"That's the kind I want," said a woman behind Mr. Gawber, biting on a chocolate wafer.

"Looks awfully expensive," said the man next to her.

"But there's masses of working surfaces. Nice units. Fitted cupboards. Vinyl."

"Is that a gas cooker?"

"Electric," said Mr. Gawber softly to himself.

A red light flashed on the back panel of the stove and a loud buzzer rang. It rang continuously in the empty kitchen and after a minute of this piercing sound a ripple of mirth—embarrassed, expectant, then confident—ran through the audience, responding to the buzz. This unattended signal, mimicking rage, went on for another few minutes, causing hoots and finally shouts of laughter.

At the side of the stage a door opened and a woman in an apron rushed across the kitchen. She was recognized by the audience and applauded. She acknowledged this with a small girl's pout. She was a plump slouching woman with heavy arms, brittle make-up, stiff blue hair and a drooping mouth. She wore bracelets that flopped and tinkled above the sound of the buzzer. She glared at the noise, making impatient passes with her hands.

"Blanche Very," said Mr. Gawber. "She's an old-timer. Norah loves her. We saw her as Ophelia at the Hippodrome in Catford. That's going back a few years."

The buzz droned on. Blanche Very took a wooden spoon from a counter and whacked the control panel, magically stopping it. This sent the audience into peals of laughter. The hilarity depressed Hood; and Mr. Gawber sat with his mouth fixed in a grim bite.

Blanche Very drew on a pair of thick red mittens, then peeked through the window of the stove and groaned—more laughter: it was abrasive and forced—and pulled the oven door open, releasing a tremendous cloud of black smoke.

"*Knickers!*" she cried, bringing out a tray of burned scones.

The audience was now hysterical and a woman sitting near Hood was stamping her feet and wiping her eyes and nearly gagging with croaks of merriment.

"It's her timing," said Mr. Gawber. "Can't see it myself, but there it is."

For the next several minutes Blanche Very measured and sifted flour, broke eggs, poured milk, and banged about the kitchen, making each busy gesture into casual blundering and repeating it when she raised a laugh. At one point she opened a cupboard, revealing another assortment of food, impressive for the size of the packages and the way it was stacked, from top to bottom. There was a significant hush in the audience at the sight of it that did not quite conceal an envious hunger.

—*Now let's see here. 'Baby's Bottom Muffins.' That's it.*

She worked from a hefty cookbook, which she

held up in one hand and read slowly, satirizing the recipe by giving it a Shakespearean stress and intonation. As she spoke the side door opened and a man came in. He wore slippers, clenched a newspaper in his shaking hands, and puffed a pipe. He was recognized and applauded.

"Dick Penrose," said Mr. Gawber. "They're married. I mean, in real life. Though Norah says it's touch and go."

Penrose winked at the audience and Hood saw that all the movement of the head and hands was not for comic effect but rather an elderly twitching that was uncontrollable. It was as if he were being pelted with rain. He shook and walked arthritically, fooling with his paper, blowing on his pipe. Like the woman, he was dressed and made up to look more youthful than he was. The program notes described them as "a childless couple in early middle age, perhaps forty," but their pinkness was powder. Hood saw two old people in clown's masks.

—Did you call me, love?

—No, I said 'knickers.' I've burned the scones. They looked like pieces of coal.

—Save them. Might come in handy this winter when the miners are on strike and the Arabs are squeezing our assets.

There were bawls of appreciation, and even scattered clapping, for this.

"Right," said Hood. "I've seen enough. I'm leaving." He hitched forward and started to rise.

But Mr. Gawber was asleep. He slept upright, facing the stage, holding the pound of chocolates on his lap, like a train passenger in a tunnel. His posture was attentive; only his eyes, tightly shut, indicated his slumber.

—Speaking of Arabs. Hear about the one that was trying to get back? Goes into an airline booking office and hands over a hundred quid for his ticket. Feller at the desk says 'You're ten pee short.' So this Arab walks outside and stops a City gent. 'May I have ten pee, sir? I want to go back to Arabia.' 'Here's a *pound,' says the gent, 'take nine more of the buggers with you.'*

Hood folded his arms angrily.

There was some business with the electric blender. The woman left the top off and switching it on sent the mixture flying in blobs that plastered the kitchen and shot into their faces. The jokes were about food— the shortage of sugar, the cost of flour, the hoarding of butter; and the audience reacted as if their own grievances were being accurately represented.

—*Three weeks on the Costa Packet. Isn't it smashing to be back? Imagine, a cup of tea without grease in it!*

—*And no enterovioform for dessert anymore.*

—*Blimey, they even put garlic in the corn flakes.*

—*Wasn't it shocking? Why did we do it?*

—*Perversion, that's Europe. But I've been looking forward to this. High tea. Good English food after all that Spanish muck.*

Mr. Gawber swayed in sleep. Hood was restive; the stupid happy faces of the audience, the idiocy onstage, the gaping at food, the ineffectual humor put him in a mood of the sharpest rage. He could destroy them for this fooling. They were acting out their strength, celebrating their petty hatred. But the worst of this malice was the acceptance of things as they were, the assumption of oily foreigners, the assumption of greed, the assumption of funny little England. That and the moronic display of food— stacked, burned, thrown about—which titillated the audience like naked flesh. Hood saw it as the coarsest pornography—hunger's greedy ridicule.

He wanted to wake up Mr. Gawber and tell him he was going; he could wait in the lobby until it was over. And he had half-risen to leave when the boy made his appearance onstage—a handsome boy in an old army shirt and woolen cap and boots.

—*You mean, while we were in Majorca you were sleeping in the garage?*

—*Yeah. I'm a squatter.*

—*Spanish style? Well, there's a time and place for that.*

—He means he's moved in.

—He can bloody well move out. He'll rust me mower.

—You can't throw me out like that. Anyway, maybe I can help.

Hood sat down. The boy, unseen by the man, winked at the woman, who was obviously attracted to him. The man gave in and allowed the boy to help with the dishes. This was the beginning of a prolonged and punning flirtation, with winks for emphasis, that lasted throughout the first act. The audience screamed at the farce the woman made of the cooking and barked at the sexual innuendo. But Hood was looking closely at the boy, studying the face, the ears, the set of the mouth.

The woman tossed a bowl into the sink, splashing and soaking the boy's shirt.

—Oh, I'm terribly sorry. You're drenched.

—That's okay. It'll dry.

—Here, take that off. Can't have you catching cold.

—I'll get you one of my shirts. Won't be any worse than the one you're wearing.

The man plucked at the boy's shirt, but the boy objected and covered himself. The man snatched and with fumbling fingers worked at the buttons. He opened the wet shirt and shook loose two well-developed breasts, nodding softly in his astonished face.

That was the end of the first act.

Mr. Gawber woke and smiled. He said, "Disappointing."

"Who did you say the girl was?"

"Araba Nightwing. Client of mine. Awfully nice girl. She's going to play Peter Pan in the Christmas pantomime."

"I'd like to meet her."

"Would you?" Mr. Gawber seemed surprised. "I can arrange that. It's the least I can do after putting you through this. We'll go backstage afterward. But I think it's only fair to say that her company can be rather, um, frenzied. How about a tub of ice cream?"

He hailed a woman passing with a tray and bought

two ice creams. He gave one to Hood and said, "Or more than frenzied, if there's a word for it. It's the profession, you know. All that publicity. Money. Then unemployment. It does things to them. They never stop acting—it's very trying. They cry and it's not sad. They laugh and you wonder why. I'd applaud if only they'd stop, but they take it as encouragement. Norah loves them, poor old thing. I always think they could have puppets instead of actors. Big puppets, of course."

"The Japanese have them," said Hood, digging at the ice cream.

"You don't say," said Mr. Gawber. "I thought it was my own invention. Big puppets, absolutely lifelike. I'd feel better about it. It wouldn't be so embarrassing somehow."

"It's a good idea."

There was a thump behind the curtains. Mr. Gawber laughed. "Oh, I say!"

Hood said, "I hate this play."

"Then we shall go," said Mr. Gawber, crushing his empty ice cream cup and shifting in his seat.

"No," said Hood, "I want to meet that actress."

"She's got quite a reputation."

The warning bells rang at intervals of a minute and then the lights dimmed, the chatter ceased, and the curtain rose. Mr. Gawber went to sleep at once. The second act was a reversal of the first: now the boy was exposed as a girl in a tight-fitting dress. The woman was angry. The man flirted. There were whispers.

—She'll have to go.

—But you wanted her to stay!

—That was when she was a boy.

—But you've got to admit she knows how to cook.

The cooking, the preparations for tea, had gone on. The woman made mistakes; it was the girl who made the cakes, the scones, the kippers and poached eggs. This amazed and delighted the audience: cakes baked before their eyes, an egg poached on stage, the scones brought steaming from the oven. The food was theater. A little cheer went up each time a new item

appeared and was set out on the table. And it was the
cooking that won the woman over. At the end of the
play they sat around the table, the woman champing
on a cake, the man leering, the girl looking at once
seductive and demure.

—*We dreamed about this in Spain.*

—*A real English tea!*

—*Kippers, cakes, and scones.*

—*Toast.*

—*No garlic.*

—*And a bit of crumpet.*

"Awfully disappointing," said Mr. Gawber, blinking as the curtain came down.

There were five curtain calls, and then the audience
was depleted, but smiling in the glare of lights. They
filed out with mincing stateliness, as they had entered.
Hood noticed how fat and satisfied they looked, repeating the lines of the play with sleek self-assurance,
laughing through downturned mouths in hearty agreement.

At the stage door Mr. Gawber said, "I feel such a
jackass doing this."

Hood said, "I'll ask for her."

A porter in a peaked cap said, "Help you?"

"We're looking for Miss Nightwing."

"Come in. I think she's still inside," said the porter.
He spoke to another man. "Has she turned in her
key?"

The other man, at the window of a booth just inside
the door, glanced up at a board on which were a
number of keys with tags. He said, "It's not here.
She must be changing."

An old man walked towards them, carrying a
leather satchel. He moved slightly stooped and his
head shook. He wore a thin brown overcoat and a
small trilby hat. His face was deeply wrinkled and
pale and he looked very tired as he passed and
handed a key to the man in the narrow booth. "Night,
George."

"Night, Mister Penrose. Mind how you go."

Mr. Gawber whispered, "Dick Penrose." He saw
the old actor struggle with the door and pull his

satchel through, and he thought: Poor old fellow, he must be seventy. He felt a tug of pity seeing the actor alone, so exhausted, stepping into a damp wind gusting from Drury Lane. He had never seen an actor after a performance, and he could not separate the two men in his mind. He watched the battered door, sorrowing for the man, then turned to face Araba Nightwing, who tripped into him and burst into tears.

"Mister Gawber!" She held him tightly and sobbed.

"This is my friend. Mister Hood, I'd like you to meet Miss Nightwing."

Araba's crying ceased. She smiled at Hood. Suddenly she said, "Your wife—what's happened to her!"

"Under the weather, I'm afraid. A bout of flu. Nothing serious."

"I was going to suggest a drink," said Hood.

"God, I need one," said Araba. She wiped at her tears and wiped away that mood. She gave her key to the man in the booth and they started through the door. There was a shout from the hallway.

"Has my old man ditched me again?" The speaker was a short fat woman with a face the color of plaster. The voice was Blanche Very's and she was still shouting as the stage door banged shut.

They went up Catherine Street to the Opera Tavern, Araba wrapped in a black cape, speaking slowly in her deep attractive voice, repeating how kind it was of Mr. Gawber to have come to the play. She did not speak to Hood directly, and it was not until they were in the pub and seated under the old theater posters and signed photographs that he was able to get a good look at her face. The shine, the pinkness she'd had in the play, was gone—that mask was off—but there remained traces of the make-up flecking her long cheeks. She was tall, with large perfect features forming true angles and sloping planes which, because they fit so exactly, did not give the impression of largeness. She had the sort of beauty that is at once familiar and strange, a remembered face, full of clues. Her lips were full and she spoke emphatically without noticeable effort, but

with an anger she hadn't used in the play. The scarf
she'd wrapped tightly on her head in imitation of the
great Twenties actress she was often compared to, hid
her hair, and, tailing to drape her shoulder, gave her
the look of a desert princess. But it was her eyes that
struck Hood—they were green, and she seemed to be
able to intensify their light to give a point to her
words. She still spoke to Mr. Gawber—he was
jammed against the wall—but she watched Hood with
those green eyes, studying him closely, almost suspiciously.

"Sometimes I don't think I can bear it a minute
more. It's such a fag, and there's a matinee on
Wednesdays. I don't know how I do it—I have to
suck sweets to keep awake. It's dreadful."

"You seemed to be enjoying yourself," said Hood.

"I am an actress," said Araba.

"Yes, the play was very interesting," said Mr.
Gawber.

"Interesting?" she said, using her voice to doubt it.
"No one's ever said it was that." She addressed Hood.
"What did you think of it?"

"I'm not a very good judge of plays," said Hood.
"The audience seemed to like it, though."

"I don't want to talk about them," said Araba.

"We've heard your good news," said Mr. Gawber.
"About *Peter Pan*."

"It was the boy-girl part in this thing that did it. It's
just a gimmick. *Peter Pan* is a big play—I wonder if
you know how big? I hate some of the audiences, so
many queers think of it as their own vehicle. I'm only
doing it for the kids. They understand it—they go out
hating their parents. That's how it should be. God, I
love acting for kids! They really appreciate what you
do for them. They don't have any hangups. They're
terrible critics—if they think it's a lot of old rope they
say so; if they feel like screaming, they scream. I love
that."

They were seated near the door, drinking half-pints
of beer, and from time to time young men with blow-
waves and back-combed hair, and girls peeking from
beneath wide-brimmed hats, had called out "Araba"

and "Darling." Araba had smiled and gone on talking about acting for children ("There's no ego-trip involved—they're not interested in stars and personalities"). Now they were approached by a short woman pushing through the crowd, holding a small dog Hood had first taken for a handbag—it was square and still, with tight curls. The woman had freckles on her thin face and chewed an empty cigarette holder. Under this veil of freckles the woman—who was no larger than a child—had the sly mocking face of an old elf. But there was about her size and the way she was dressed a neatness that was sharp and unconcealing: the small body showed through the green coat as the slyness had through the freckles. She said in a high voice, "Poldy wants to say hello." She spoke to the dog: "Say hello to Araba, my dear. Get on with it— don't just sit there."

"McGravy, I'd like you to meet one of my dearest friends, Ralph Gawber."

Mr. Gawber said, "Very pleased to meet you. This is Mister Hood."

"Mister Hood is not a very good judge of plays," said Araba.

McGravy said, "Send him to *Tea for Three.*"

"I just saw it," said Hood.

"What's the verdict?" said McGravy.

Hood considered for a moment, then said, "It's got a lot of food in it, hasn't it?"

"It's all about food," said McGravy.

"And that was one damned hungry audience. I could see them licking their chops."

"Everyone's starving nowadays," said McGravy, looking uncertainly at Hood, who was smirking. "It'll get worse."

"I sometimes think that," said Mr. Gawber.

"It's the system," said Araba, and her eyes flashed. "All this deception. All these hangmen. And these leeches—bleeding people to death. It makes me want to throw up."

"Parasites," said McGravy, cuddling her dog until he growled his affection. "Well, they'll get what they deserve."

"I think that needs saying," said Mr. Gawber.

"Bloodsuckers," said Araba. "It's a Punch and Judy show, but it can't go on like this."

"I couldn't agree with you more," said Mr. Gawber.

"It really is rotten," said McGravy. "It's like a boil that needs lancing—then it'll all come gushing out, all the corruption and lies."

"I'm so glad you said that," said Mr. Gawber. He leaned forward, encouraged. Two hours of sleep in the theater had rested him. He said spiritedly, "No, the workers have had it all their own way since the war, but now they're simply malingering, holding industry to ransom. A period of recession wouldn't be a bad thing. A crash might even be better—dose of salts. I agree, unemployment's a bitter pill, but the workers have to realize—"

"Who's talking about workers?" said McGravy sharply in her high child's voice.

"Let him finish, sister," said Hood.

"Whose side are you on?" McGravy demanded.

Mr. Gawber said, "Aren't you talking about workers?"

"No," said Araba, patting Mr. Gawber's hand. "We're talking about the power structure, my darling."

"But the unions," said Mr. Gawber. "With all respect, there's your power structure, surely?"

"The union leaders are in league with the government," said McGravy. "It's a plot—"

"Dry up," said Hood.

"I had no idea," said Mr. Gawber.

"Let's talk about the play," said Hood.

"I'd rather not," said Araba.

"Wait, Araba. Perhaps he has some insight he wants to share with us."

"My insight," said Hood, "is I think it's the biggest waste of time since Parcheesi." He smiled. "A load of crap."

"Come now," said Mr. Gawber. He thought it tactless of Hood to say it, but all the same agreed and felt a greater fondness for him.

"It made him mad," said Araba.

"It's supposed to make him mad," said McGravy.

"But it is a wank," said Araba.

"If only it was," said Hood. "I was sitting there and saying to myself, 'What's the point?' "

"If only he knew," said McGravy, grinning at Araba.

"What don't I know?"

"Several things," said Araba. "But the first one is that McGravy wrote it."

"Oh, my," said Mr. Gawber. "You've put your foot in it."

McGravy stroked her dog and let him nuzzle her. She turned to Hood. "You were saying?"

"Nothing," said Hood.

"Go on, I'm rather enjoying your embarrassment."

"It's not embarrassment, sister, and if you think I'm worried about hurting your feelings, forget it. If you wrote that play you must be so insensitive you're bulletproof."

"I wish *I* were," said Araba.

"Who are you anyway?" said McGravy.

"Just part of the audience," said Hood.

"Drink up, please," said a man in a splashed smock, collecting empty glasses from the table.

"I have a train to catch," said Mr. Gawber.

"Let's get a coffee at Covent Garden," said Araba to Mr. Gawber. "Then we'll let you go home."

They trooped up to Covent Garden, turning left at the top of Catherine Street, where long-bodied trucks were backing into fruit stalls at the market. There were men signaling directions with gloved hands, and behind them stacks of crates and displays of vegetables. In spite of the trucks it had for Hood the air of a bazaar—the dark shine of the cobblestones, the littered gutters and piles of decaying fruit; the men jogging with boxes on their heads and others bent almost double under the weight of sacks. Mr. Gawber thought he saw the two men with the laden prams he'd seen earlier that day in the stairwell below Waterloo Bridge; he remembered the warning, ARSENAL RULE, and then actually saw it, splashed on the arches of Covent Garden Market. Over by the tea stall gaunt men stood inhaling the steam from cups of tea.

"I love it here," said Araba, whirling her cape open, performing.

The men saw her and grinned. McGravy's dog, lively for the first time, yapped at the tea drinkers. Mr. Gawber was uneasy: the men were wretched and looked dangerous; he wanted to go home. But Araba had bought four cups of coffee from the man in the stall—he had tattoos, and a torn singlet, and a hat folded from a sheet of newspaper—and she was handing them out. Mr. Gawber kicked the squashed fruit from his shoes.

"They don't treat you special here," Araba said. "They're real people."

But the men were gathering and muttering a little distance from her. In the half-light of the high lamps Mr. Gawber saw their faces as shadowy and criminal, and their eyes as thumb-prints of soot over whiskery cheeks. McGravy's dog continued to howl at them.

Hood said, "Your play. Both of you must be making a lot of money."

"It's for a good cause," said McGravy. Again she said to Araba, as she had in the Opera Tavern, "If only he knew."

"Let me guess your sign," said Araba. "Aries. The Ram. Am I right?"

"Pisces," said Hood. "Sorry, sweetheart."

"My actor clients are frightfully keen on horoscopes," said Mr. Gawber. "They read their stars in the newspaper and get ever so excited."

Hood had not taken his eyes from Araba's. He said, "Let me guess your passport number."

"How extraordinary," said Mr. Gawber.

"It begins with a 'Y.' Seven digits. And it's light blue—"

"Ah, you're mistaken," said Mr. Gawber. "Bad luck. British passports are navy blue."

"This is an American passport," said Hood.

"That's enough!" cried Araba, and seeing her fury in the lamplight the men at the tea stall laughed. She gathered her cape, said good night to Mr. Gawber and walked away, making her exit between the great stacks of crated fruit.

Part Three

12

SHE GOT OUT of the taxi in Deptford High Street, looked around, and felt cheated. Then she walked to assess it, to give it a name. No name occurred to her; she wondered if she had come to the right place. But she had: there were the signs. Deeply cheated, tricked by the map and her imagination. She had wanted to like it and had prepared herself for a complicated riverfront slum with the kind of massive mirrored pubs she'd passed on the Old Kent Road; damp side lanes and blackened churches and brick-peaked Victorian schools contained by iron fences and locked gates; with a quaint decrepitude, credibly vicious and with visible remnants of danger, a place where you could believe a poet might have been stabbed.

She had expected something different, not this. It was ugly, it was shabby—but not in any interesting sense. It was, sadly, indescribable. She had wanted to be startled by its grime, and the taxi ride across the vast gray sink of London had been long enough to suggest a real journey to a strange distant place. Deptford was only distant: characterless, without any color, a dismal intermediate district, neither city nor suburb, boxed in by little shops and little brown terraces— many defaced with slanted obscure slogans—and very dusty. You could become asthmatic here: the air stank of dust and chemicals and the unhelpful sun was the size of an apricot. She looked for the river (she could hear boats farting in water) and saw a green gasworks. Closer, a power station poured out heavy clouds of tumbling smoke that gave the sky an ashy hue. The smoky sky seemed no higher than those square chimneys. If anyone asked she would say Deptford was like the scar tissue of a badly healed wound. She was oppressed by the council estates, cheap towers of public housing draped in washing lines. All those people waiting; she could see many of them balancing on flimsy balconies, staring gravely down at her.

She might have gone back to Hill Street—her disappointment was great enough—but it had been so hard for her to get here! Not only the taxi (the driver first refused to take her that distance—she had had to agree to pay an extortionate fare), but the invitation, too. She had telephoned the house five times and either no one answered or else a strange male voice demanded to know who she was. "Who are *you?*" she'd asked in return, and hung up. When, finally, Brodie picked up the phone the girl was evasive, and it was only by Lady Arrow blurting out that she wasn't in the least interested in getting her pound back—indeed, she'd gladly give her another one if it was needed—that Brodie said to come over and told her the address.

"Albacore Crescent! I can just imagine it."

"It's on the map. Just get off the train at Deptford."

"We'll have tea somewhere," Lady Arrow had said, and now she laughed at the thought of it, seeing nothing in ten minutes of walking but two fish-and-chip shops with steamy windows, and a take-away Chinese restaurant. She was angry for noticing they were filthy; she didn't like to think of herself as a fastidious person. Here, everywhere she looked, she had to face the limits of her tolerance. And she thought: This is what it means. When people say they're living in Deptford they mean this, the gasworks, the nasty little shops, these poky houses, the smoke. Really, a pitiful confession.

Across Deptford Broadway to the hill and then into Ship Street, where she saw the entry to Albacore Crescent. She had not wanted to arrive by taxi, she deliberately avoided taking it to the door: she was ashamed. But it would not have mattered—the house was larger than she expected, and all the blinds were drawn. See-ing it, she remembered why she had come. It was more than a glimpse of Brodie at home, how she lived, what she did, who she saw, a piecing-together of the girl's other life to make a story for herself she hoped she figured in—a way of ordering it, like an artist, so that it could be set aside. She wanted that, but she wanted more: Brodie. At Hill Street she had resented Murf's hold over her, the companionable glances, the laugh-ter, the assumption that she was his. She wanted to separate her from Murf, break his hold over her and have the girl to herself.

Lady Arrow was not discontented with her life, but she knew it lacked any edge, and it was enclosed—too secure. Other people, living close to the ground, spent more congenial days, like the waiters she envied, whispering intimately to each other in restaurants where she was dining. And sometimes she thought that even the girls she visited in prison had more to challenge and amuse them than she did. The plays she brought them gave her a chance to act with them. She would not be shut out from anyone's life, and she was surprised that Brodie's seemed so inaccessible: five phone calls and what amounted to a bribe to gain entry!

She rang the bell, heard footsteps on the stairs, and listened to the snapping of locks, bolts at the top and bottom of the door being shot. Brodie's pale eager face appeared at a crack.

"You're barricaded in!" said Lady Arrow as she stepped through the door, seeing the locks and bolts and heavy chains.

"We don't usually come in this way," said Brodie. "We're supposed to use the back door."

"I hope I'm not infringing the rules—but who makes these rules? I say, is that your ice-cream van?"

Brodie was shrugging at the questions. "Sort of. It belongs to someone, but they're not here, see." She was vague. In a thin sleeveless shirt, Brodie's breasts budded at the pockets, and Lady Arrow saw the tattoo, the bluebird chevron on her white upper arm. Brodie's trousers were much too large for her; she held them by the waist to prevent them falling down.

"Hey, Murf—she's here!"

Murf put his head through the parlor door and nodded. His head was small and the sun behind his ears lighted them to look like the membranes of kites, one with a gold tail, the swinging earring. He wore a jersey with a chewed collar, a pair of girl's tight pink slacks, and in his bare feet he clawed at the rug with his toes. He plucked at the slacks that sheathed his legs and pushed at his thighs. Lady Arrow thought of a pet beast, ridiculously costumed.

"They're mine," said Brodie. "Them slacks. I've got his on. We decided to wear each other's clothes today."

"What a splendid idea." Lady Arrow moved down the hall and she smelled—what?—something she couldn't name, a hairiness of sour perfume.

"Murf said it turns him on."

"Except it don't," said Murf. "It was just an experiment, like."

"A pity it's not working," said Lady Arrow. "But then how awkward for me if I'd come and found you fucking. I'd hardly know where to look!"

"Yeah, well," said Murf, averting his eyes, pushing at his ears. "That's how it goes. Have a seat."

"Is this all yours?" Lady Arrow entered the parlor and paced. "It's quite huge. I think it's a success, I really do. And I imagine there are lots more rooms in the back and upstairs. It reminds me of a dovecote, all these little rooms rising to the roof. Whatever do you do with them all?"

"There's some other people," said Brodie.

"Yes, the owner of the ice-cream van."

Murf glanced uneasily at Brodie, then said with mild aggression, "We don't know nothing about that there van. Maybe someone nicked it and left it there."

"I understand," said Lady Arrow. "You can trust me with your secrets."

"We don't have no secrets," growled Murf, still facing Brodie, who got up and left the room.

"Of course not," said Lady Arrow. "Why should you?"

"Have a seat," said Murf again, pulling a stuffed chair away from the wall and awkwardly presenting it.

Lady Arrow ignored him. She leaned into the hall and said, "Does it extend very far? It seems to go on forever, more rooms in the back—and a garden as well."

"Here," said Brodie, entering the room. In an attempt at etiquette she had placed an unopened bottle of pale ale on a green saucer with a souvenir opener. "Oh, I forgot the glass."

"Don't bother," said Lady Arrow. "I never drink beer. I'll have some of this." She tapped some snuff onto the back of her hand, lifted it to her nostrils and tipping her head back inhaled it. She snorted and blinked, then she said, "Aren't you going to take me on a tour?"

"Sure, there's some pretty groovy places around here. We could go down to the power station. Murf's got a mate who works there. Or we could take a bus to the *Cutty Sark*. It's up Greenwich."

"I meant a tour of your house."

"There's nothing to see," said Brodie. "Just more rooms."

"But how many?"

"Six or seven."

"Why it *is* huge!"

"You can't go up," said Murf. "I'm redecorating the bathroom."

"Do let me have a peep."

"Have a seat," said Murf, and now he looked as if he might spring up and throw her into the chair.

"Oh, all right," said Lady Arrow. "But I'd much rather have a tour of this lovely house. By the way, who owns it?"

Murf said, "Some people."

"You are a mysterious fellow, aren't you? But you'll see—Brodie will vouch for me—I don't pry. I'm just interested. I was hoping we could be friends. Don't you want to be my friend, Murf?"

"Sort of," said Murf and picked self-consciously at Brodie's pink slacks sitting so uncomfortably on him and clinging to his skinny thighs.

"I'd like that," she said. But she thought: No, what's the point, what am I doing here? She had tried to flatter them by taking an interest in the house; but flattery didn't work—there was narcissism even flattery couldn't penetrate, and her compliments, so close to satire, only made them suspicious. She had guessed, alighting from the taxi at Deptford, that it would be a failure and now that was confirmed. She had expected too much, and she could see she was unwelcome. It occurred to her that she might take a hundred pounds from her purse and say, "Here—it's yours." It was a hopeless thought: they were children. You could give them anything, and they wouldn't notice; but you couldn't take a thing from them. They made themselves inaccessible. She had been foolish to think that she could take Brodie away and keep her. The young were not free enough to know affection, and why, she wondered, did they always insist by their lazy silence on being kidnaped?

Then she saw the Chinese carvings, the jade eggs on wooden tripods and the ivory figures on the fireplace. On the far wall was a painted scroll. Until then they seemed like the cheap plastic chinoiserie she'd seen in other working-class houses. But these were delicate; they were small beautiful things, finely done. Even across the room they glittered.

"Who do these belong to?" She walked over and lifted the carving of a camel. It was ivory, heavy and cool, resting perfectly in her hand. It had a red saddle and tiny gold tassels. You had to hold a carving in your fingers to know its value, because a craftsman had held it. And now she could see the brushstrokes on the scroll, a column of anxious swallows in a pale landscape.

"They belong to some people," said Murf.

"There's a few over here." Brodie brought her a carved red-lacquer box, and Lady Arrow was reminded of an idle child on a beach noticing an adult's interest in shells, offering to sustain that interest—

tempting the stranger's desire and yet knowing nothing even of friendship—by searching for more and trailing along until they were both alone in a far-off cove. There was such casual cruelty in innocence.

"It's quite beautiful," said Lady Arrow, opening the lid. There was a mirror on the underside, and Brodie's face reflected in it, framed by the lining of yellow silk. She wanted her, and again she was mocked by her reason for coming. The face slipped from the mirror. "Chinese."

"And this," said Brodie, finding a silver frog with filigree on its back. She handed it over. Lady Arrow felt the heat of the girl's hand on the silver.

"Very, very nice," said Lady Arrow. "Don't you think so, Murf?"

"I don't know," he said. "It don't belong to me."

"This is my favorite," said Brodie. She held out a tarnished brass ashtray with a crude pagoda and a Thai dancing girl etched on it.

"I like that one," said Murf. "When you give it a polish it comes up nice and shiny."

Lady Arrow studied it. It was a cheap bazaar trinket, ugly and roughly done, the native's revenge on tourists. You could cut your hand on it. She smiled at Brodie, agreeing, but she looked at the other objects and thought: She doesn't know the difference; as long as she values this ashtray she will never know me.

Murf said, "I'm going upstairs to take Brodie's gear off. I'll be right down." He left the room walking in a self-conscious way in the tight slacks.

"Anything I can get you?" asked Brodie.

"Call me Susannah," said Lady Arrow. "I'd love a cup of tea."

"Right." Brodie ran.

Lady Arrow could hear her shifting the kettle in the kitchen. She went to the door and listened: Brodie was still occupied. She climbed the stairs, distributing her weight, testing each step, taking care not to make them creak. She passed a bathroom, then saw the room in which Murf was changing—he was stamping out of the slacks—and another room, open and simply empty. She went up another flight, to the top of

the house. It was darker here—the doors were shut.
She tried one: locked. The second was open but held
only a stack of newspapers and an old sofa. Then she
was at the front of the house, in the large room with
the low double bed—whose?—and the Indian cushions:
almost a salon. The sour perfume she'd smelled earlier
was strongest here—and she noticed the Burmese box
on the mantelpiece, the silk robe, the view from the
window. It was her first sight of the Thames: the
power station, the old church, the Isle of Dogs, and
at a great distance, Saint Paul's. She wanted more.
She went to a long cupboard and threw the door
open, and gasped. Seconds later she was laughing very
loudly.

"Hey!"

Murf was on the stairs. She hurried into the hall,
but he was fast, moving nimbly on all fours up the
last flight. He bounded to the landing and ran to
the door of the back room, then crouched in an
attitude of truculence, like a startled sentry, protecting the room as Hood had ordered.

"I told you not to come up here! You're not supposed to—this here room's private."

He had surprised Lady Arrow with his speed and
noise, interrupted her laughter. But now she saw the
absurd boy with the reddened ears, puffing and holding himself so importantly in front of the door—the
wrong door!—and she laughed all the harder.

"Sneak!" he said. "I'll fump you!"

13

SHE WAS DELIGHTED, she was justified, she
knew why she had come: it was an inspired visit. And
she had a claim on them. She would stake it emphatically. Now she could reach the girl, separate her from

Murf; and though she felt like an intruder and vulnerable to humiliation (it had happened before: that hysterical procuress at Holloway had screamed from her cell, "Here she is again to look at the monkeys!") —her voice alone sometimes made her an enemy— she knew Brodie was hers. And the others, whoever they were: all hers. The knowledge of strength, her certitude, was comedy. She had cracked a great joke.

Downstairs she was still laughing at the thought of it, and again she saw the brass ashtray, the piece of junk they'd singled out and preferred to the small Chinese treasures, and she knew how they could make such a silly mistake. But what worthless thing were they protecting in that other room?

"Your friend was upstairs," said Murf. "Nosing around."

"It probably don't matter," said Brodie.

"It's private," said Murf. He spoke to Lady Arrow. "I told you it's private, didn't I?"

"You're being awfully boring, Murf," said Lady Arrow. "What is it you don't want me to see?"

"Nothing. It's just private."

Lady Arrow had become calmer, acquired the serene smugness of ownership, though for moments she fell silent, remembered, and laughed. The situation was under control. She sat down, jamming her hips into the chair, and she had the immovable solidity of a householder in her own parlor, as if her bottom were cemented to a plinth.

Murf said, "You better go now."

"But I haven't had my tea," she said and motioned for Brodie to bring it. She took the cup and smiled at Brodie over the rim. "You didn't tell me you lived in such a fascinating house."

"It's okay," said Brodie.

Lady Arrow drank her tea, smiling between sips.

"When she finishes," said Murf, "she's pushing off. I'm not taking the blame for this."

"Dry up, Murf, it don't matter."

"Blame? For what?" said Lady Arrow.

"Sneaking around upstairs. Sticking your nose where it don't belong."

"Did I see your precious room?"

"You wanted to."

"What a lot of balls you talk, Murf," said Lady Arrow. "Brodie, isn't there anything you can do with him?"

"Brodie knows the rules," said Murf. "No visitors. She didn't want to tell you, so I'm telling you straight."

Wules, strite: she almost laughed. She said, "You came to my house, didn't you? Did I make a fuss? I'm simply returning the visit, doing the civilized thing."

Murf had no reply. He glared at Brodie and repeated, "She knows the rules."

"It's not even five o'clock. You can't chase me away so soon."

"Maybe when you finish your tea," said Brodie. "Murf's right. We've got this stupid rule."

"That rule cannot possibly apply to me," said Lady Arrow. She raised her cup and drained it.

"Right," said Murf, "that's it. You're finished—out you go." He stood up and advanced on her; he was more belligerent in his own clothes—faded jeans, a black jersey, an old waistcoat—than he had been in Brodie's. He tottered near her, but even standing he was not much taller than Lady Arrow, who was seated.

"I adore bad manners," said Lady Arrow, smiling at him with her long sallow face. "Yours are quite terrible, Murf, but I assure you mine are much worse." She turned to Brodie. "I think I'll have more tea."

"No more bloody char," said Murf.

"Brodie," said Lady Arrow, holding out her empty cup. Murf put his hands on his hips and glowered at her. She said, "Oh, do sit down and stop being such a ham."

"They're coming back," said Murf to Brodie. "They're not going to like this—"

Lady Arrow looked abstracted for a moment, then burst out laughing. Wonderful!

"—and I ain't sticking up for you this time. It's your lookout."

"It's this bloke that lives here," Brodie said, turning from Murf to Lady Arrow, who was beaming at the blank wall. "He won't like it if he sees you here."

"I'd very much like to meet him," said Lady Arrow. Another competitor—who? And what hold did he have? But she was unconcerned. Brodie was slim, with a fawn's small coy face, and short hair—so awkward and small-breasted she could have been a boy. It was a type Lady Arrow especially desired, the light uncertain body, the clear skin. She wanted Brodie in a boy's beautiful suit and velvet tie, and to make love to her before an enormous mirror, undressing her slowly and hearing her clamor for breath as she slipped the clothes from her skin.

"He's got this bad temper," Brodie explained in a monotone, tucking her white arms against her side and hunching her shoulders. "Like he breaks things."

Murf was close to Lady Arrow. He showed her the pegs of his teeth and said, "He'll break your neck, lady."

"I've got a very strong neck, my boy," said Lady Arrow, and she thought: *Brike your neck*—they can't hurt me, I own them. She was buoyant. Upstairs she had proven herself unassailable. The boy with dowels for teeth stood near her mouthing threats, but there was nothing more he could do, and she pitied his helplessness. "I would love another cup, Brodie."

"There's no more tea," said Brodie.

"Don't deny me."

"Take a walk!" cried Murf, working his shoulders menacingly.

"Dear girl," said Lady Arrow, "I do believe he's frightened you. But you have nothing to fear—you'll see."

Brodie was being obstinate, and Lady Arrow saw she would have to fight to have her—she would win, but she didn't want to destroy Murf. She hated the way Murf nagged—he looked so silly trying to threaten her with that face and those ears, the scrawny shoulders, the grubby waistcoat. She believed she could have knocked him over quite easily, but she only laughed.

There were bangings at the back entrance, the slam of a door, the thud and pause of boots.

"It's him!" said Murf, and now he looked desperate. "Get out, get out!"

"Take your filthy hands off me," said Lady Arrow. To free herself from Murf's pushing she simply stood up. Then she was out of reach, and again she felt sorry for him. His anger was so futile. Perhaps it was futility, nothing more, that made him angry.

Brodie said, "Please go."

"I don't think I shall," said Lady Arrow, but she had barely finished the sentence when she saw the parlor door open and the hawk-faced man enter. He was tall, with stiff black hair and he almost frightened Lady Arrow with his squinting eyes. He wore a black raincoat and black boots, but what disturbed her most was that he said absolutely nothing. Through his posture and his fixed expression of sullen inquiry he communicated threat like a crow. She saw him as her equal, and in Brodie and Murf's cringing she saw his hold over them. But she would not be sent away. This was her competitor for Brodie. She was glad he looked strong, and yet to win was no victory—the advantage was hers. He shut the door and stared at her.

"I told her to get out," said Murf, his voice becoming a quack. "She wouldn't go. Brodie let her in. But don't worry—she don't know anything—"

"Shut up," said Hood, without turning to look at Murf's little gestures, his accusatory leaps at Lady Arrow. Hood bore down on her with his narrowed eyes.

"This here's Lady Arrow," said Brodie. "She's a friend of mine."

"A very old friend," said Lady Arrow.

"You said it." Hood smiled.

It took a moment for this to register. Then Lady Arrow straightened: she would make him regret saying that.

He said, "Anything I can do for you?"

"Yes, you can tell Murf to stop accusing me of spying. He won't listen to me."

"He's just doing his duty," said Hood. "We don't want strangers here."

"I'm hardly a stranger to Brodie," said Lady Arrow, slurring her words to load them with sexual intimacy. "But if you insist, I'll go."

"I insist."

"It wasn't Brodie's fault at all. I invited myself. I didn't realize you had such strict rules. But I quite understand. Under the circumstances, it would be rather awkward if you had people dropping in."

"Under the circumstances, I think you'd better get your ass out of here," said Hood evenly.

Lady Arrow smiled. "They warned me you were naughty."

"Piss off," said Murf, standing just behind Hood, seeming to shelter from the gaze of the tall woman.

"Don't get excited, squire," said Hood. "She's going."

"What a pair of monkeys you look," said Lady Arrow. "But I know you're perfectly harmless. You wouldn't touch me."

"Wouldn't I?" Murf stepped forward and crouched as if preparing to pounce on her.

"Easy, squire." Then he spoke to Lady Arrow. "What are you waiting for?"

"I'd like a word with you before I go. I'm sorry, I don't think we've been introduced."

He told her his name, then he said, "I don't have anything to say to you."

"Perhaps not, but that's beside the point. I have something to say to you. Do you think we could be alone?"

"No," said Murf. "Tell her to get out."

"Run along!" said Lady Arrow impatiently. "Brodie, be an angel—do take him away."

Brodie said, "Come on, Murf. Let's go."

Murf appealed to Hood: "Don't listen to her. I caught her snooping, but she didn't see nothing. She's Brodie's mate—I didn't want her here, but Brodie said—"

"Upstairs, squire," Hood said softly. He had not moved. He had entered the room and folded his arms;

his posture was unchanged, nor had his eyes shifted from the tall woman's face.

Murf muttered a complaint, and he kicked at the floor, but he did not reply directly to Hood. He screwed up his face at Lady Arrow, then turned and swaggered out of the room, still muttering. Brodie shrugged and without a word followed him. Her abruptness hurt Lady Arrow, who until that moment had expected the girl to return with her to Hill Street. She wanted her and she resented whatever hold this dark man had over her.

But she said, "How very Victorian you are—what a stern parent. You remind me of my father. You walk in and they flutter like doves. I suppose they accept it because they know so little, but when they know that you have no right to order them about they'll hate you. I'm sure you don't understand Brodie at all."

"If that's all you have to say, you can go."

"Mister Hood, I believe in freedom."

"That's fine with me, Mrs. Arrow."

"Never call me that—Susannah, if you like," she said, and went on in a different tone. "Freedom must be taken, snatched if necessary, whatever the cost. Do you think a woman like me has no interest in such things?"

"A woman like you is probably interested in a lot of things," said Hood. "But take my advice—don't get interested in us. You might be disappointed."

"I find all of you fascinating," said Lady Arrow. "Do you mind if I sit down?"

"Don't bother. You're not going to be here very long."

"Now you're being stern with me, and I'm twice your age. Do I know your father?" She smiled. "Really, you shouldn't take that tone. I'd like you to visit me some time. I think you'd enjoy meeting my friends, exchanging ideas with them. They have more in common with you than you might think."

"No thanks."

"I think you'll change your mind," she said with playful malice.

"Look, sister," he said, "I don't think you're my type. If you're through you can hit the road."

"Oh, God," said Lady Arrow in admiration, "I wish I could say that like you."

Hood moved, and Lady Arrow reacted, startled by this slight gesture, Hood unfolding his arms. He took off his raincoat and threw it over the back of a chair.

Lady Arrow strolled to the small fireplace and said, "Yes, I think you will change your mind and visit me." She selected one of the carvings, an insect worked in ivory, and weighed it in her hand. She said, "I've been admiring your art collection. It's really rather beautiful."

"Presents from people I happen to like. Put that down before you break it."

"They're hard to get in England—very scarce nowadays. I imagine you were in Asia—they're the sort of pieces one finds there, aren't they?"

"If you say so." Hood took the carving from her hand and put it back on the mantelpiece.

"Brodie and Murf haven't the vaguest idea. Oh, I'm sure they find them pretty, but they don't know their true value. Brodie is so sweet. She thinks that brass ashtray is some sort of treasure. That scroll. It's silk. Ch'ing Dynasty, is it not? It's late, but it's lovely. No, they don't know how valuable things can be. Children are unmoved by sham and humbug. But they are unmoved by sincerity and beauty, too. Such simple creatures—not blind, but so shortsighted."

Hood was going to speak, to prevent her from saying anything more he agreed with. She had come close to echoing his own feeling in calling them children and defining their simple slowness. But Lady Arrow interrupted him. She said, "May I say you are a most fortunate man, Mister Hood?"

"Your time's up," he said.

"But I'm not finished!"

"Now," said Hood, raising his voice to insist.

"Yes, I've been admiring your art collection. In these rooms—"

"Listen," said Hood.

"—and upstairs," Lady Arrow went on. "That

painting. Your little man was awfully cross, but in the event he didn't seem to know I'd seen it."

"You've got a nerve."

"Not me, Mister Hood," said Lady Arrow. "It's you who have the nerve. But I admire you for it. You see, I own that painting. Yes!" She laughed in long mocking shouts, trumpeting in his face. "It's mine! It belongs to me!"

Hood relaxed; he stepped away and smiled. "Which painting are you talking about?"

"You know! The one in your cupboard."

"I painted that myself. It's called 'Death Eating a Cracker.'"

"It was my father's. You can call it anything you like."

"'The Widow,' 'The Jailer,' 'The Saint,'" he said. "It's just a copy."

"The Rogier self-portrait," she said. "And you needn't try to deceive me. I can assure you it's the original."

"You're lying, sweetheart."

"No, I'm not. I was ashamed to admit it—it was so valuable. How can you own a thing like that? It was on loan—that got me a tax deduction, for charity, believe it or not. It was so embarrassing I loaned it anonymously. I've had so many calls from the curator—he wanted me to make a statement. Weren't you surprised by the silence? The lack of response? And do you know, I was glad it was stolen! Relieved —I can't tell you how relieved I was. Now this! It exceeds my wildest dream. It is magnificent!"

"What are you going to do about it?"

"Absolutely nothing. One can't be burgled by people one admires. You can trust me, Mister Hood, I won't tell a soul. I might even collect on the insurance —my accountant's been insisting on it. You're welcome to that, as well. I do feel it's a bit much for you to want to chase me away. You see, when I saw that picture in your cupboard I suddenly realized what a family affair this has all become. I wish I had planned it this way—arranged for someone to steal my own painting. But that sort of thing takes genius. However."

Hood said, "I'm going to check on everything you say."

"Do that, Mister Hood. You'll see I'm telling the truth."

"Okay, now beat it."

"Not so fast, my man," she said. "You can't order me now. You see, your project very much concerns me. I support you! I believe we can be friends at last, and I consider this house as much mine as yours. Frankly, I was rather hoping Brodie would come back with me. She's not yours, you know."

"She's staying here."

"She'll come to me eventually," said Lady Arrow. "And you'll visit me now, won't you?"

Hood pursed his lips, but said nothing.

"I'm sure of it," said Lady Arrow, and she picked up her handbag. At the door she said, "I can't tell you how pleased I am that things have turned out this way."

"Keep going," said Hood in a flat threatening voice.

He banged the door and locked it, but when he went back to the parlor he clapped his hands and laughed—a yell of gladness, and still chuckling he sat down and waited for Mayo. The picture stirred him from its hiding place at the top of the house.

14

AT MIDNIGHT THERE was still no sign of Mayo. He wondered if she could be teasing him with her more frequent absences; she knew he was waiting and was deliberately hiding herself. She made her inaction secret to give it drama. She was whining in Kilburn

over a pint of beer or in bed with an Irishman—for
her a political act. She had deceived him over the
passport, tricked him into forging one for the well-
known actress, whose single attribute, so far as he
could guess, was her theatrical ability to alter her
face. You had access to a wig, so you were a conspirator. Araba had struck him as hysterical and
insincere, a fraud, persuasive only to those who didn't
know the real thing. The trick had made him doubt
his own judgment—the victim losing respect for himself when he knows how easily he has been
victimized. But he had said nothing to Mayo: he
would have his own secrets.

He had drawn the cushions to the center of the
upstairs room and he lay on them in his bathrobe,
with the cupboard door open wide and the lamp tilted
to face the painting. He pondered it and smoked a
pipe of navy-cut sprinkled with hashish grains. He
had a feeling of wealth, the comfortable security of
resting in undisturbed solitude. For the moment he
wanted no more than this, and the self-portrait only
added to his pleasure: now it could not be snatched
away; he didn't need to hide it; the owner didn't care.
It shone on him. Its greatness lay in the way the cubes
of color gathered to match his own mood. It was consoling: it did not reproach him—perhaps the greatest
art never did—it exalted the eye. It shimmered with
certainty, it was the surest vision, an astonishing light.
What Mayo and the others did to enrage him the
painting corrected: it was the only solace he had re-
ceived, this illumination. And like a light it printed a
small white star on his retina that stayed to remind
and console him long after he turned away.

There was a knock at the door. Mayo never
knocked. It was Murf.

"You busy?"

Hood pulled the pipe out of his mouth and blew a
gray white cone of smoke at the lamp, watching it
untangle in the light. "Come in, squire. Where's
Brodie?"

"Watching telly. She thinks you're narked. She
said she's sorry." Murf bobbed nervously and pushed

at his ears. "I don't know what that old girl told you, but she's lying. She didn't see nothing."

"It's okay. But you can tell Brodie she's got some pretty hot-shit friends." Hood puffed the pipe. He felt high, happy, a buzz inching down his ears like a centipede with sparking feet. "Don't let me catch you bringing any lords and ladies down here, squire, or I'll have to change my socks."

"I hated her," said Murf, who had started to sweat. "I wanted to brick her."

"No kidding. What for?"

"She was laughing at me." He pushed at his ears again, a combing motion with his palms. Hood had noticed how he did this when he was upset, made self-conscious by a stranger. But the ears, as if exercised with brushes, sprang out wider. "Just standing there, laughing like a fucking drain. I could have smashed her face."

"I know the feeling," said Hood. "Don't let it get you down."

"Hood?" Murf sighed, whacked at his ears, and shook his head. "There was something else. I said she didn't see nothing. Well, maybe she did. But it wasn't my fault. She come up here while I was changing. I caught her on the stairs. Laughing, she was. I don't know for sure, but maybe she come in here."

"Maybe," said Hood. "You couldn't help it."

"Honest, I couldn't. Brodie was supposed to be watching her. Maybe she seen your picture. Anyway, she didn't nick it, did she?"

"It's still here," said Hood. Murf leaned and looked at it, cocking his head to the side as if to understand it better. "What do you think of it?"

Murf said, "It's a bloke, ain't it? Old-fashioned bloke—them boots, them clothes. Yeah, I like it. First time I seen it I thought it was poxy. Who's this flaming great tit, I says. Then Arfa sees it and he says it's a antique, it's worth something, they're paying for them up the West End. He's got ready money, he says. I thought maybe I could do you some kind of favor, flog it to Arfa. Sorry about that. Anyway, I had a crafty look at it. Later, this was. I'm staggered!

It's all shiny, sort of moving and blowing up in me mush. Bloke's looking at me, yeah, like he's going to jump out and kick me in the goolies."

Hood loved him for that. He had despaired of ever changing Murf. The boy was unaffected by the afternoon concerts on the radio Hood had listened to before he began spending his afternoons with Lorna. No symphony, not the finest phrase had altered those blaring ears, and nothing Hood had ever shown him —the Chinese scroll, the carvings from Hué—had worked his eyes wider than a squint. He had given Murf a Chinese treasure and Murf, making a claw of his fingers, had handled it like a turd. The silk shirt from Vientiane, his present to Murf for helping shift the arsenal and the loot, had become a rag on his skinny shoulders; the pocket bulged and drooped where he kept his stash of tobacco. He carried himself like an ape, with his arms hanging loose. He had one skill: the clock-legged bomb. But a sense of loyalty had brought him to the room tonight; he had told the truth; his response to Lady Arrow was crudely accurate—Hood himself had wanted to smash her in the face. And his description of the painting—how civilizing a thing it was!—had insight. In that small crooked boy Hood saw a shy friend.

Hood poked his pipe stem at the painting. He said, "I've been trying to figure out who it is."

"Funny bloke." Murf scratched his head. "Sort of smiling and sad at the same time."

"And look at his eyes."

"You think he's going to say something," said Murf. "Yeah, I like it." He caught his lips with his fingers in embarrassment and pinched them. He said, "Reminds me of you, he does."

"No." But Hood peered at the painting.

"Maybe not," said Murf. "He's posh like you, but not only that. Yeah, I think he does. Straight."

Hood said suddenly, "What do you want, Murf?"

"Nothing."

Nuffink. "I want to give you something, squire. Anything."

"I don't know," said Murf carefully. "But there's one thing."

"Name it."

"Just don't," Murf began and caught his lips again with his fingers. "Just don't laugh at me."

Hood waited for more. Was this a warning, a condition to prepare him for the wish—or the wish itself? Murf fidgeted and said no more, and Hood saw that it was all he wanted, to be free of ridicule. The woman's laughter had wounded him and made her his enemy. Hood said, "Okay."

"Me mates don't laugh at me."

"Then we'll be mates."

Murf grinned, filling his cheeks, as if he had food in his mouth; and he put out his hand, offering it as an equal. He said, "Shake."

Hood reached up and wrung his hand—Murf's palm was damp with nervousness—and he said, "Now I'm going to hit the sack."

Murf hesitated. "Mayo didn't show."

"No," said Hood. "Maybe it's something big."

"Yeah." Murf sniggered. *Something big:* now it was a private joke they could both share. "Are you going to tell her about the old girl?"

"Do you want me to?"

"She'll laugh at me."

"I can say I was here the whole time."

"Right." Murf brought up another gobbling grin. "And she's bending your ear, this old girl. Then you're out of the room, you're having a wash. You don't know nothing. Then she goes sneaking upstairs. You hear this fucking laugh of hers."

"And I caught the bitch in this room."

"Beautyful."

"That's what I'll tell her then."

Murf said, "Good night, mate."

*

Mayo did not arrive until the next morning, and showing her face at that early hour, with an over-brisk apology but no explanation for her lateness, and yet

with a guilty pallor made of smugness and fatigue—
the satisfied smile and yawn—she had the cagey
adulterous look of a woman returning to her husband
and children after spending the night with her lover.
Romance: if not actual, then a metaphor, since she
had always treated her political involvement like an
affair, her energy hinting at brief infatuation.

Brodie stirred her bowl of cornflakes with a spoon
and said, "There's no more milk."

"I've had my breakfast," said Mayo. "I was up
hours ago. I'll just have a coffee. Any post?"

"A letter from the National Gallery," said Hood.
"They want their picture back."

"That's not funny."

Murf looked at Hood and laughed.

"Look, sugar," said Hood, touching Brodie on the
arm, "why don't you and Murf do the dishes. I've got
a bone to pick with the klepto."

"I always have to do the dishes," said Brodie, complaining.

Murf rose and began gathering empty cups. "You
heard what he said."

"Go to it, squire."

In the parlor, Mayo said, "I'm exhausted." Hood
didn't react. "The meeting went on for hours."

"The offensive," said Hood lightly, as if repeating a
familiar joke.

"That was part of it," she said. "And we expelled
someone."

"Do I know him?"

"Her," said Mayo. "I doubt it."

"We had a visitor yesterday."

"Not the police." Mayo held her breath.

"No. A friend of Brodie's."

"I didn't think she had any friends."

"You'd be surprised," said Hood. "It was a lady—
in the technical sense."

"What's that supposed to mean?"

"I'll tell you in a minute. But first I want you to tell
me something. Where exactly did you get your picture?"

"The self-portrait? Highgate House—why?"

"Who lives there?"

"No one lives there, you fool. It's a museum."

"That's the first I've heard of it. I thought you got it from a private house. I imagined you sneaking through the window, tiptoeing down the corridors—the folks snoring in their beds. I thought it was pretty cool. She's a gutsy chick, I thought. But, for Christ's sake, it was a museum. So it wasn't such a big deal after all, was it?"

"There was a burglar alarm," she said. "There were risks. What are you trying to say?"

"Just this. You gave me the impression you knocked off a private house—and all you really did was waltz into a museum and rip off a picture. If it had been a private house you might have gotten somewhere, and if you'd chosen the right one you'd have scored in spades—you'd have had them screaming their heads off. But you're a genius. You went for a museum and came out with one picture—you could have taken a dozen!"

"What's wrong with a museum?"

"Museums don't have that kind of money. They don't pay ransoms, no one lives in them, they're empty." He sighed and said, "How'd you happen to settle on Highgate House?"

"I told you all this at Ward's—that first day."

"You were drunk. You didn't have a plan. All you talked about was a picture."

"Yes, and I knew where it was."

"You checked it out?"

"No," she said, "my parents used to take me there."

She stated it as a simple fact; but it was a revelation. It was the most she had ever told him about herself, and it was nearly all he needed to know.

My parents used to take me there. He knew her parents, he saw them on a misty Sunday in winter guiding their daughter to the museum, the mother apart, the doting father holding the girl's hand. They had planned it carefully; they knew they were paying a high compliment to the little girl's intelligence in the family outing—part of her education, while the rest of her school friends idled at the zoo. A restful, uplifting interlude, strolling among the masterpieces. Privilege. And he saw the daughter, a spoiled child, small for her age, but bright, alert, in kneesocks and necktie, noticing details her parents missed—that Bosch cripple in his leather vest, the thread of piss issuing from the bowlegged man in the Brueghel, the Turner thundercloud and tide wrack of sea-monsters' jaws, the tiger launching itself from the margin of the Indian engraving. *Look, dear, an angel.* And finally the attentive parents brought her to the Flemish self-portrait and urged her to admire the tall man in black: *What do you see through that window?* Later, they bought postcards and chatted about them over tea; but the parents never knew how that afternoon they had inspired the girl—made her see the value of art even if she could not see its beauty; how their encouragement that particular day, the origin of all her careless romance, had made that little girl into a thief.

Hood knew her parents, he saw them, because he could see his own. The same encouragement in a different museum, a different light: a Minoan snake goddess had marked his eye. They had been taught to respect art, so thievery mattered; and their parents' legacy was this taste, a hesitation. Only Brodie and Murf acted without hesitation. They could destroy easily because they had never seen what creation was—they did not know enough to be guilty; but Mayo, and he, knew too much to be innocent.

Mayo saw the strain of memory on his face. She said, "What's wrong?"

"You blew it. You're a flop."

He told her the version he had promised Murf, and what Lady Arrow had said. Mayo understood immediately, quicker than Hood himself had. She closed her eyes and he could see she was relieved—as he had been, but perhaps for a different reason: he had never wanted to lose the picture and she had worried about jail.

He said, "Maybe you'll listen to me now."

"Do you think she'll grass?"

"Not a chance," said Hood. "She's on your side—whatever side that is."

Mayo said, "You'll find out soon enough."

"Really?"

"Don't you see? That's one of the reasons I was held up last night. We expelled someone—"

"So there's a post vacant," he said.

"You can put it that way. I was trying to convince them you were clean. Well, they're convinced." Mayo lowered her voice. "There's a problem, Val. They want to talk to you. They think you can help them."

"I used to think that."

"Oh, God, don't tell me you're getting cold feet!"

"Cold feet," said Hood, sneering. "Wise up, sister."

"I knew it. As soon as things started to go your way you'd begin your consul act—the big, cool, noncommittal thing."

"I'll play it by ear."

"They're coming tonight."

"I might be out tonight."

"I told them they could count on you."

"They can count on me tomorrow. I've got other plans." He stood up and moved towards the door.

"Where are you going?"

"That shouldn't be hard for you to figure out. You've got training—you said so! You're a conspirator, aren't you? You don't have to ask questions like that. Get your raincoat and shadow me."

"Don't go now, Val. Stay awhile—it's nine o'clock in the morning! Don't make me wait, please."

"You made me wait last night, sweetheart." He looked at her imploring face. He wouldn't stay. There was Lorna, but more, he was punishing Mayo for her past, for betraying her parents' trust; the picture. *My parents used to take me there.*

"So that's it. You're going to get your own back at me. God, it's as stupid as a marriage! It's sickening. You've got other plans. All these secrets. You're hiding something from me. Why don't you just come out and say it—you're not interested in me anymore."

"But I am. Come on, smile."

"The painting," she said. "They trusted me after that. If they find out it belongs to that woman they won't like it—it's no good to them."

"I won't tell them."

"Thanks, Val," she said. "I feel such a failure."

"Bullshit," said Hood. "Think of the painting! It's yours—you've committed the perfect crime!"

"Kiss me," she said.

He hesitated, then he drew near to her.

She said, "What do you want?"

"I want to kiss you, sister."

"Don't," she said. She faced the wall and said, "Go! That's what you really want to do, isn't it?"

"No," he said. "I want to kiss you."

She turned expectantly and lifted her arms to embrace him, but Hood was on his way out of the room.

As he passed through the kitchen, he slapped Murf on the shoulder. Murf said, "Take me with you," and whispered, "I don't want to stay here with these two hairies."

"Next time, pal."

It was a lovely autumn day and Hood was so distracted by the sunshine he did not at first see the sweeper—just the father today, with his shovel and broom and the yellow barrel on wheels. The man pushed at the papers and dead leaves, then stooped to pick up a button. He looked at Hood with mistrust and said, "That your ice-cream van?"

"Not mine," said Hood.

"I can't sweep there unless it's moved."

"I don't know anything about it," said Hood, and he heard the man mutter a curse.

15

—BECAUSE WHEN IT came, he was thinking, the thunderclap and short circuit in the heavens, announcing itself there in the city like the rumble and flash of summer lightning, it would travel in every direction and be most evident here on the pitches of this bald heath: a sudden airless fissure streaking across the grass to that silent church, dividing Blackheath into two treeless slopes. Already there were no trees, so the slightest crack would heave open the unrooted ground and make a canyon of this suburb. It could be horrific: London's most mammoth sewer ran under this heath.

The morning, so beautiful, with tufts of white cloud racing in the sky, intimated a ripeness that was next to decay—the season's warning. And more than this, Blackheath, a square mile of grass, was like a roomy cemetery, all that space awaiting diggers and coffins. How lonely sat the city that was full of people! She was a widow, she who had had an imperial fortune. The princess of cities was supine with tramplings. The prospect made him sad, remembering. He had protected himself from life, which was pain, but the last pain was unavoidable. Yet if the eruption came, the fissure underfoot, the storm overhead, he might be granted the life he had denied himself, as the war had briefly proven his resourcefulness; and he came to see in the quake he imagined a humbly heroic retirement, testing him with the repeated whisper "Die!" He would say no and live.

Mr. Gawber puffed his morning pipe on the top deck of a bus. His mind, undistracted by a crossword puzzle, sped easily to thoughts of doom; he looked up from the simple puzzle and there was the unsolvable world. He lingered over his annoyance. She had rung again, as she had done a month ago, with the same weepy haste. *I must see you,* she'd said, *it's very important. You're the only one who can help me.* A dirty trick, that; singling him out to throw herself on him. *Perhaps you can stop by on your way to work. I live quite near you now—Blackheath.* But only the map made it near. In every other way it was a troublesome detour. He would not get to Rackstraw's before lunchtime. Charity blunted his anger, and he made his objection general: I'm glad we never had a daughter.

He recognized her house at once, Mortimer Lodge, the fresh coat of pale green paint and white trim subduing the Georgian plumpness. On the western edge, it faced directly onto the heath, like a fort fronting an open plain, defying intruders. It was secure, unshakable, detached, not crowded by nearby houses; and though it was not tall, its weight was apparent in the spread of its bay-windowed wings. Its hedge had body, its garden balance. The girl was luckier than she knew, but as Mr. Gawber swung open the gate he had a vision—he did not know why: perhaps it was an effect of the sunlight slanting explosively on the roof tiles—a vision of Mortimer Lodge bursting open; the front toppling forward into the fountain and bird bath and the roof caving in and a puff of smoke rising from its shattered design. He endured it, let it pass across his mind, and he was left breathless. Now the house was unmarked. He thought he had rid himself of these punishing visions, but since the day he had uttered "macaroon" to the strangers on the crossed line he had sensed a fracture in his life. It surprised him; he was strengthened by it, enlivened, like an old man who senses the onset of magic in him. He wondered if he was mad, then dismissed the thought. He was only late for work, and Araba's phone call the previous night had made his dreams anxious and disconnected (searches, a son, ruins). He thought: I hope she doesn't cry.

He pushed the bell and set a dog yapping inside. The gnome-faced woman with freckles answered the door, the puppy under her arm yelping and choking like a child in tears. He had been told this woman's name; he could not remember it. Tomorrow, seismic, was at the front of his mind. He removed his bowler hat and said, "I believe we've met."

"Araba's waiting for you," said the little woman.

"I'm in here," called Araba, and when Mr. Gawber found her in her loose blue dressing gown in the sunny room, he was ashamed for having seen the house so furiously destroyed. He had confounded himself with exaggeration—surely that was insanity, not magic? Araba said, "I'm sorry you had to come here like this, but honestly there's no one else who can help me."

"It's no trouble," said Mr. Gawber. "It gives me a chance to see your lovely house."

"You don't think it's corny? I always wanted to live in the country—I had to get out of Chelsea. It was so stifling. We're going to grow our own vegetables here."

Mr. Gawber joined her at the window as she indicated the half-dug garden, a vertical spade in a small rectangle of hacked earth, like the beginnings of a cemetery plot, her own grave. He saw frailty on the actress's face, lines of indecision he had never noticed before, deepened by shadow. It was more than the shaken guarded look that women habitually had, vulnerable in dressing gowns in their own homes; it was a threatened wincing expression, as if she had, shortly before he entered, heard a very loud noise. And dramatizing this with tragic pats on his arm she passed the unease to him, made him apprehensive, so that staring through the window to what looked to be a family graveyard he could only say, "No, I couldn't agree more."

She peered abstractedly over the hedge as if into the past, and the abstraction in her eyes entered her voice as a drawl when she said, "Wat Tyler marched over there, on that road. He was a fantastic person. He was into revolt before people knew the word. God, why aren't there people like that anymore?"

"Good question." Wat Tyler, the lunatic with the pitchfork, leading his mob of gaffers? "I wish I knew the answer."

Suddenly Araba said, "You know, I've never been honest with you."

He didn't know how to reply. He said, "I never knew Wat Tyler had been here. I'm so glad you said that. Puts it all in a new light."

"But you've always been honest with me," she said, ignoring Mr. Gawber, who was nodding studiously at the heath. "You've always told me the truth."

"I suppose I have," he said. "But there it is."

"I was really touched that you came to the play. It meant something."

"A very great pleasure," he said, and pretending

to look at his shoes he glanced at his watch. Nearly ten. What did the woman want?

"When I saw you there I knew you believed in me. You'll stand by me and help me no matter what."

He said, "It's the least I can do."

"I admire your frankness—it's something I never learned."

My frankness? What have I ever exposed? But her statement gave him courage and he said, "I think I should tell you the tax people have been onto me again." He reached for his briefcase. "I have the correspondence somewhere here."

"Don't show me!" She walked to the far end of the room, fleeing the letters he held. "I couldn't bear that. No, put them away."

He stuffed them into the briefcase. "They think we're dragging our feet."

"What have you told them?"

"The standard thing. Thank you for yours of the et cetera. We are awaiting instructions from our client et cetera. Yours faithfully." He frowned. "They think we're being a bit bolshie."

"Perhaps we are."

"I couldn't agree more."

"But that's not what I wanted to discuss," she said.

"Of course not."

"Mister Gawber, that fellow you brought to the play—"

"Mister Hood," he said. "Very interesting chap."

"Is he a friend of yours?"

"I suppose he is. I must say he was quite taken with you."

"Really," she said, and her tone softened. "I was hoping you could tell me something about him."

"There's not an awful lot I can tell you," he said. "I met him purely by accident some time ago. He's become a client." He thought of Hood. A friendly sort. He had enjoyed his company, but Miss Nightwing was causing him distress. He wondered if at a certain age one turned to other men for consolation. Women didn't turn to other women; they never lost their appetite for men—they still hungered at sixty. But he had only been at ease with men, and he was glad to be acting for Hood—that weekly check. Odd request; but it was an odd business.

"American, isn't he?"

"What's that? Oh, yes. But one of your better sort."

"The thing is," said Araba, and as she moved towards him companionably her dressing gown fell open. Mr. Gawber saw her nakedness and the shock blinded him. He went shy. She said, "The thing is, I was counting on you to tell me where he lives. McGravy and I are giving a little party and we wanted to invite him. I said to McGravy, 'I know. I'll ask Mister Gawber. He'll be glad to tell me.' "

Mr. Gawber laughed and said, "I'd love to help you out."

"Good," said Araba.

"But I'm afraid I can't," he went on. "Business. Silly rule, really. I don't divulge clients' addresses. I've been asked enough times for yours, my dear. I always say, 'My lips are sealed' and hope the person won't press me too hard."

She said, "But you've always been so frank with me."

"Exactly," he said. "I am being frank with you now. I can't tell you a thing."

"All I want to know is his address. So I can contact him for this party. Surely you understand?"

He couldn't look. The question was pardonable; but the nakedness? The dressing gown flapped. Did she know she was naked? The whiteness at the edge of his eye chilled him like snow, and he felt fear, like frost, in his own joints. He had been frozen in just that way, faced by a strange drooling dog on a footpath.

"I understand perfectly," he said almost sorrowfully to the window, which held in its glaze segments of her body. Why was she putting him through this? "But I can't help you. I must be going. I'm late for work as it is."

"Mister Gawber, I won't let you go unless you tell me." She closed in on him carelessly. He folded his arms to block the view, but saw on her face an un-reasonable wrath: his refusal had upset her—more than that, unhinged her. She took it personally. *If she touches me I'll scream.* He wanted to be out of the house, and he thought: I will never come here again for any purpose whatsoever. He said, "You're going to catch your death like that."

"I don't care." She pushed at her dressing gown, but the white fabric was her own flesh.

"It's nippy." His eyes hurt.

"Tell me—I must know!"

"This is very awkward," he said.

Araba raised one leg and put her foot on the seat of a chair. Her thigh shook. She said, "Don't you have any feelings?"

"A compromise, then." He straightened himself. He had seen under her flat belly a clinging mouse. "I'll meet you halfway. Give me a note and I'll see that he gets it. That's simple enough."

Araba said, "You've never let me down before this. Why are you protecting him? Has he something to hide?"

"I respect privacy—yours, anyone's."

"I have nothing to hide!" said Araba and opened her dressing gown, showing her body: a narrow column of ice, the coldest candle he had ever seen. Once, she had told him she was a bitch. He had denied it, but now he saw the accuracy of it. How was it possible for the actress to play a bitch and not have that malice in her? The bitch, the whore, the nag, the shrew: they lived in the actress, she gave them voice. She could not be forgiven her roles.

"Try to understand," he pleaded, memorizing the carpet's blooms.

"All right, have it your way," she said, and wrapped herself again in blue. "I'll send you a letter. But if he doesn't reply I'm bound to be a bit suspicious."

"I quite agree," said Mr. Gawber. "But I'm sure he'll be in touch with you. He seems a most depend-able sort of chap."

Araba said, "I never realized until now you hated me so much."

He tried to reassure her, but he saw how he was failing at it and he left. Outside, his confusion hardened into anger: he raged, he swore, and again in the grassy cemetery of the heath he saw the shadow of a seam preparing to part for the canyon of a mass grave, to swallow it all. The calamity—but no, it was only a cloud passing overhead. Not yet, not yet.

16

"YOU LIKE THEM?" She was wearing white thigh-length boots; the short black skirt was new as well, and standing before him she reminded him of a tropical bird with slender legs, a small-bodied heron raising her head and flicking her tail before taking flight. She walked up and down for him—the boots made her taller: not the slouching flatfooted girl anymore but a preening woman. Perhaps sensing the novelty of her height, she stood straighter and danced towards him, laughing. Then she sat down beside him and smoothed the boots. "I've always wanted ones like these. Real leather."

"Classy," said Hood. He knew they were out of fashion elsewhere, but they were still considered chic in Deptford.

"You don't think they make me look like a tart?" She narrowed her eyes and peered sideways at him.

"A little bit," he said. "Maybe that's why I like them."

"I'll go up the Broadway looking for pickups."

"You could make a fortune as a hooker," he said. "I'd take a cut."

"Funny," she said. "First time I seen you I took you for a ponce. Ron knew a lot of them. They'd come

sniffing around for him. Something about the eyes.
You've got mean eyes."

"And you've got a nice ass," he said.

"You think so?" She wriggled on the sofa. She
laughed. "Me, I'm a raver—you don't know!"

"A new skirt, too," he said. "Nice."

"Got a blouse upstairs. I'm saving that for later.
You can almost see through it."

"The hooker," he said.

She wrinkled her nose. "It don't matter."

The new clothes flattered her, and he knew they
were for him. Lately, Lorna had begun to dress up for
his afternoon visits. Suspicious at first, she had worn
old dresses and slippers in the house as if to challenge
his interest. She said, "Don't mind me—I usually pig
it around the house." But he noticed that she always
made up her face and wore a white raincoat and silk
scarf when she took Jason to the playgroup—for the
other mothers. With time she relaxed; she sat in her
dressing gown and drank coffee with him, talking with
trusting familiarity, as if they had spent the night together. Hood had not responded to her clothes; he
imagined her in other clothes, a riding outfit, a leather
suit, a great robe; he played with the idea that there
was no difference between her and a princess but
jewels. But now she dressed for him as she did for the
mothers at Jason's playgroup, and today the clothes
were new. The money had arrived.

He visited her regularly. He asked nothing of her.
If there was time they smoked the pipe. She saw nothing unusual in his visits. At one time she might have
been able to ask, "What do you want?" and demand
he be explicit. But (and like the crescent of scar over
her eye he had always meant to ask about—Weech's
work?) it was too late for that. He liked her too much
to risk embarrassing her. He believed they were as
close as friends could be, for the friendship had grown
out of a cautious study of each other's weaknesses.
Once she had said, "I thought you wanted to fuck
me," and when he laughed she added, "It's better this
way—for now." He had wanted to, but he was shamed
by his advantage—his victim's wife was also his victim

—then he decided that sex made a couple unequal with doubting tension: if sex was tried it became the only reassurance, and there was power for the one who withheld it. That part had been set aside, though for Hood it was accidental—he had only desired her the first instant he'd seen her rushing out of the house. He hadn't known who she was and then, seconds later when he remembered, the feeling died in him; afterward, he did not think of making love to her. His remoteness made her curious and inspired trust in her, and though he saw how she was uncertain of him in the early weeks when she had expected sexual sparring, that awkward hinting dance, after a month it was plain he had no further intentions and she stopped being defensive. She was perfectly naked, but he did not want another victim.

The afternoons they spent together were happy. They touched more than lovers because they were not lovers; they kissed easily, they hugged and she lay with her head in his lap. It meant friendship. No further bargain was being struck: the kisses led to nothing. With the sexual element removed they were equal, mutually protective, like brother and sister, as if they had shared a parent they both hated, now dead and unmourned. And it was partly true: Weech was in a cemetery in the blackest part of Ladywell. Hood saw her new boots and skirt as an expression of her freedom, and he admired them as a brother might, congratulating his sister's taste.

She said, "Ron never let me buy new clothes—at least not like these ones. Men are such fuckers. They like to see dolly-girls, all tarted up, false eyelashes, miniskirts and that. But not their wives."

"You think every man is like Ron."

"I didn't know any others, did I?"

"You know me."

"I used to think you were the same," she said. "Only you ain't."

"I sure ain't."

"You're the quiet type, you are. You bottle it up. I used to think, 'What's he waiting for?' "

"You don't think that anymore?"

"Now I know what you're waiting for—nothing." She pursed her lips and kissed him, holding his head, then she stamped her boots and said, "These things are killing my feet. Here, help me get the buggers off." She zipped them down to her ankles, showing the pink roulettes of the zipper on her inner thigh, and then she raised her legs playfully for Hood to get a grip. She was unembarrassed with her legs in the air, her skirt to her waist; but even holding her this way and pulling her boots off he felt no twinge of arousal.

She said, "Stop looking at me knickers, you dirty devil."

Only then he looked and saw the wrinkle fitting the parrot beak of hair where she was narrowest. "Black ones. Very sexy."

"I bought a dozen. All colors."

"You're a new woman, sweetheart," he said, tugging her boot, tipping her backward. "All these new clothes—you must have won the pools."

She looked away. "I don't know." He worked the second boot off, then she smiled and said, "Right. I won the pools. But it's a secret."

"I hope it was a bundle."

"A packet—well, enough anyway." In a resentful monotone she said, "He knew I wanted boots like these. But he always said no. Or a skirt—I used to wear skirts like these but when we got married he said I was just trying to get other men to look at me. As if he didn't look at other women! It was the same as the dog track. That's where I met the fucker—at the dogs. My father took me there a few times, and then when he died I went with my girlfriends from work. Nothing serious—just for fun, like, a little flutter on a Thursday night. Made a change from going home to the telly. It was at the track one Thursday. Ron come over and chatted me up. He's wearing this expensive suit, he tells me he's something in insurance, full of talk. How am I supposed to know he's a villain? He was a heavy punter—always showing off with his money and talking about his connections. He knows this bloke on the continent, he's got business with the Arabs. Then we got married and after that he wouldn't take me to the track. He went with his mates—Willy, Fred and them. 'That's no place for no married woman,' he says."

Hood said, "But you're not married anymore."

"No," she said, and she looked so sad he thought she was going to cry. She surprised him by saying, "He was a right bastard, he was. Sometimes I think, 'Poor bugger, he's dead,' then I remember how he used to treat me and I think, 'Good—the fucker deserved it.'"

"Maybe he had it coming to him."

"Maybe, maybe!" she mocked. "Are you trying it on? You always sound as if you're defending him."

"Do I?" She was quick; he wondered if it was so.

"Yes, you do. I tell you what an absolute fucker he was and all you do is nod your head and say, 'Oh, yeah, maybe you're right.' Jesus, whose side are you on?"

He said coldly, "It's unlucky to bad-mouth the dead. Even if they are fuckers."

"No, that's not the reason," she said. "I keep forgetting you're one of them. You're different, but you're one of them. Why aren't you like the rest of them?"

He almost objected. He so easily forgot how he had come into her life; then he remembered that he had introduced himself as one of the family. Had he said he was Weech's friend? He no longer knew. Lorna had told him all the other names, and he had given them faces and cruel teeth. He could not ask for any more, he could not reveal himself. It was too late for that: assumptions had to be taken for truth.

He said, "Maybe I am like them."

"If you was," she said fiercely, "if you really was, I wouldn't want to know you."

"Take it easy, sister," he said. "How do you know them so well?"

"I know they're filth," she said, tightening her mouth, pronouncing it, as Murf did, *filf*. "They've been over here. The other night—Monday, it was. Ernie— you know him, the little one, eyes like a rat, hair way down to here—Ernie come round. I thought it was you, so I let him in. Asking questions, but I knew he wasn't listening to me. The fucker's just going sniff, sniff."

"Why didn't you tell me this before?"

"I thought you knew," she said. "Anyway, it don't matter."

"Did he ask you about the stuff upstairs?"

"No. But I knew he was checking up. I could see the little fucker's eyes."

"I should have known." Hood was uneasy; he didn't want to be exposed, but there was a greater danger for Lorna, and he regretted that he had told her so little. At once he saw how he had toyed with her affection—his victim's wife was his victim: the thought repeated, more deliberately and so more cruelly. He said, "If they ever ask you about that loot, say you don't know where it is."

"I don't, do I?" she said lightly. She was calm, she didn't know how unsafe she was. "Like I've never been to your house, have I?"

"Right," said Hood. "So you don't know anything."

"I don't want to know anything."

Hood said nothing. For a moment he thought of telling her everything, from the murder onward, but there was a threshold in every friendship which, once crossed, made the past a deception. Then, every explanation seemed like a suppression of a greater fact, and truth looking like a lie was an unforgivable taunt.

Noticing his silence she said, "Anyway, they're your friends, not mine."

"Sure," he said to stop her. Then, "You said you were going to show me the other clothes you bought."

"What's the use? There's nowhere to go. I can't go shopping around here wearing stuff like that. The butcher's, the news agent. They'll take me for a tart."

"We'll go somewhere," said Hood, but he could not think where. They had only ever been to the park on Brookmill Road together and once to Greenwich to see the *Cutty Sark* and the Royal Observatory (he told her about Verloc; she said, "The fucker sounds like Ron"). "Where would you like to go?"

"How about the flicks?" she said. "I can sit in the dark wearing my new gear."

"Come on, think of a place."

She said, "What I'd really like to do is go to the dog track, like I used to—not with my girlfriends, but my father. He'd find me a seat where it was warm and tell me which dogs to back. He'd have a cup of tea with me and he'd put his arm around me and keep the teds away." She smiled sadly. "Sometimes we used to win. He always gave me half."

"We'll do it," said Hood. "Where is it—Catford? We'll win a bundle!"

"Not a chance," she said. "What about the kid?"

"Get a babysitter," he said. "You've got the money. Remember, sister? You won the pools."

She sat back and sighed, then she said, "I'd love to go. There are races tonight. It's Thursday."

"We're going," he said.

"Okay," she said, but she added quietly, "I didn't win no pools. It's their money. Ernie said, 'We'll take care of you, don't worry.' And then, the next day, this thing came from the bank—fifty quid deposit. I don't care, and maybe they ain't such fuckers after all. But they probably stole it off Ron."

17

THE RAILWAY ARCHES in the half-dark—the black brick spans—were shaped like the crust of a burnt-out cloister. They ran parallel to the poorly lighted road all the way from the station at Catford Bridge to the dog track. And there were dead monks underneath—or so it seemed to Hood, who preparing himself to enjoy the dog races had smoked a joint in the train—discarded cartons, peaked like the cowls of monks' habits, lay on the ground, holy casualties in the broken place, feet and hands and covered heads, and an odor of ruin. Ahead he saw the greyhound motif, a starved lunging dog picked out in lights, but between the stadium entrance and where they now stood was this shadowy rising brickwork mottled with football slogans, CRYSTAL PALACE, CHARLTON RULE, SPURS, barely legible, like the last messages of heathen raiders. The highlights were unexpected—rubbish that had the appearance of thick bushes and an impression of autumn foliage that was no more than the suggestion of darkness and the smells, verifying the dead cloister and giving it a further authority, the veiled aspect of a brittle engraving. And when the train rumbled on the spans and shook the yellow lamps on the line—but was itself hidden from this road—the sound raised the tattered smell again and corrected the engraved dimension the silence had imposed: the noise loosened it all and gave it brief life for the duration of the passing train.

Lorna said, "I always used to be afraid of this road."

"I like it," said Hood.

"Well, maybe because I saw a bloke nobbled here," she said. "I mean, killed."

It had a name, this puddly two hundred yards: Adenmore Road. London was closely mapped. No city he had ever seen had been so examined. The darkest corner had an inaccurate caption, and even the wild place, the sudden hill of hiding trees above Peckham where he'd dumped Weech's body—that, too, had a name.

Hood was surprised when Lorna chose the second-class enclosure instead of the more expensive one. At the turnstile she said it was the one she had always used with her father. The stadium was gaily lit with strings of colored bulbs, and Hood could see the smoke drifting up from the various enclosures to the floodlights on tall poles, as if the whole circus were cozily smoldering. There was no shouting, only a low roar of voices.

"There's the dogs," said Lorna. "Way over there."

The first race was about to begin. Across the track, on the far side of the stadium, six girls in hunting clothes marched in single file. Each held a sleek dog on a leash, and the sharp snouts and thin bodies were silhouetted in the lights like black metal cutouts in a row, shooting gallery targets. Then they turned under the lights and came towards the near grandstand, and up close Hood could see how young the girls were, how skinny the dogs—tottering on bony paws, panting in their tight wire muzzles.

"Aren't you going to bet on this race?" asked Hood, looking down at his program.

"Too late," said Lorna. "I always watch the dogs in the paddock before I bet. Here, they all look the same, but out back you can tell which ones are fast. That's what my father used to say."

They stood talking under the first-class enclosure which, glassed-in and high, was at the brow of the grandstand. The steamy windows were full of red-faced people who sat at tables, eating, holding pint glasses, watching the track. "Ron always went up there, so he could act big," said Lorna. She led Hood to the side of the grandstand, where people were marking programs on the terraces and hurrying up and down the stairs. Hood found Lorna a seat near the bookies, at the rail. The bookies worked rapidly at blackboards, some on stools signaled the odds with gloved hands to the far side of the stadium—pointing and clapping like deaf mutes, while the men beside them spat on their fingers and wiped numbers from the columns on the boards and added new ones. They gave a hectic motion to the race that was like the instant before panic. Each one had a satchel with his name on it, *Sam & Alec, Jimmy Gent, Pollard Turf Acc'ts,* and as the starting time grew near the activity around these men became frenzied as cash was exchanged for tickets. In this excitement Hood saw the pleasure of risk; the very sight of the men gambling aroused his desire for Lorna.

On the track, men in white smocks were heaving the metal traps into position.

"You're going to win tonight," said Hood.

"If I won a lot of money I'd take a holiday," said Lorna. "Not to Spain, but maybe Eastbourne or

Brighton. Check into one of them big white hotels on the front and look at the sea from the balcony. I always wanted to do that, live in a posh hotel and look at the sea."

"We'll do it," said Hood.

"First we have to win."

The dogs were being unleashed and helped into the traps, one by one, and Hood could hear them whimpering. They didn't bark; because of their muzzles they gave low curiously human wails, an odd lonely sound in that festive crowd of gamblers. Then the lights went out in all the enclosures and in the darkness there was silence, a hush that amplified the moans of the dogs. In the black stadium the only light was the yellow gleaming sand of the track. And over the moans a murmur that grew to a whine: the mechanical rabbit speeding towards the traps. As the rabbit shot past, the traps sprang open and the dogs leaped out, stretching themselves after it. The race itself brought a new hush to the grandstand. The only distinct sound was the rabbit singing on the wire, a humming heightened by an occasional twang.

"Five's ahead," said Lorna. Hood heard her clearly. Instead of shouts there was intense concentration. It was not like a horse race where spectators screamed at the jockeys and jumped and waved their arms. This was studied enthusiasm, a kind of breathless suspense. A man behind Hood said in what was nearly a whisper, "Come on you two dog."

The dogs sprinted past, and it was still so quiet in the grandstand that Hood could hear their toiling gasps and the scrape and skid of their paws on the track. When they rounded the last bend there was a little cheer, scattered shouts of anger or glee which ended the moment the dogs crossed the finish line: relief, jostling, and some laughter—and a flurry of losers scattering tickets at their feet.

"Let's go round to the paddock," said Lorna. "I want to pick a winner."

"Everyone's looking at you," whispered Hood. "They're saying, 'Who's that fantastic chick?' "

She laughed. "You're dreaming." But she looked

down at her new boots in prim admiration. He had
never seen her so happy, and he imagined a life
with her: a safe monotony, without incident, sur-
rendering to Deptford, the pub, the bed, the child,
the dog track, the weekend in Brighton. He wanted
more, but he was tempted by less, and he sometimes
felt this, passing the window of a south London parlor and envying the people inside having tea with
their elbows on the table. He could save her that way;
he saw in her the sad aging of every lost soul—
and it was true loss, since she had no notion of how
she had been widowed. But what kept him from
pushing the reverie further was not that it was a retreat from the life he had planned for himself but that
underlying this obvious feeling was a smaller one: pity,
the feeblest mimicry of love.

He followed her behind the grandstand to the paddock. Here it was damp, enclosed and yet open to the
sky. It was divided by a sturdy metal fence. On the
other side was a small shed; a few over-bright bulbs
inside the shed lighted patches of grass where they
stood. The rest of the lights were aimed at the closed
doors of thirty numbered stalls built against the brick
embankment of the railway line. These narrow cupboards rattled with the whimpering of the dogs locked
inside—their wails carried, as they had from the
traps, and Hood was alarmed by their frantic paw-
ings on the wooden doors. The paddock was empty,
but the cries of the dogs, and the dampness, the
spiked fence and the spotlights that showed nothing
but locked doors, gave it the appearance of a tortuous
jail compound. Hood wanted to go. Lorna said, "Wait
—here they come."

Shivering, blinking and scratching at their numbered vests, the dogs were dragged into the shed by
the kennel maids, who wore velvet riding caps and
jodhpurs. Then a bowler-hatted man in brown gaiters
—the starter—checked their collars and tried their
vests to see they were securely fastened. Men, a
dozen or more, had gathered at the fence to watch
this simple ceremony, and they conferred in whispers,
singling out particular dogs with cautious nods.

"Number Two looks like he wants a kip," said Lorna. "But that Number Three's a lively one. Got a strong back." She opened her program. "Lucky Gold—nice name."

Hood leaned to her ear. "Who are these apes hanging on the fence?"

"Villains," said Lorna, confidentially. "It's a crooked sport—attracts all the villains, like Ron and them fuckers. But my father told me what to look out for. Right here, before the race, you can spot the slow ones."

"That mutt looks like he's limping."

"The villains step on their toes—their paws, like. That one's probably been mashed. Or they give them a drink of water. Sometimes—straight—they put chewing gum up their arses. Anything to slow them up. But Number Three, Lucky Gold, he looks a fast one, he does. He's going to win."

"All this poncing about," a man clutching the fence said loudly. "That clot's just wasting time—they could have been around the track by now."

"Cheap," said another man, "filthy cheap—"

As he spoke there was a rumbling above the paddock, an approaching train. The warning was brief; the train thundered by a moment later, flashing across the arches overhead, a rapid intrusion of banging wheels drowning the voices and the dogs' whimpers. The yellow windows blurred and lengthened to a ribbon by the speed. The paddock shook and the eyes of the dogs being led out bulged in fear over the muzzles. For seconds the paddock was darkened by the loud clatter.

The men left as the kennel maids filed out with the dogs, and Hood went with Lorna to the front of the grandstand, to a window with the sign *Win and Place*.

"How much are you betting?"

She said, "A pound on Number Three to place."

"A *pound* to *place*? But you said he's going to win!"

"Who knows?"

"Put your money where your mouth is," said Hood. "Play to win—why hedge?"

"Because I might lose the lot, nitwit."

"If you're worried about losing you shouldn't be betting."

"It's just a flutter," she said. "Bit of fun. Little gamble."

"Bullshit," he said, and she seemed amazed by how serious he had become. He growled, "If it ain't risky, sweetheart, it ain't gambling."

"The big villain," she said.

He snatched her money and stepped past her to the window. "Five pounds on Number Three—to win." He took the tickets and handed them to her: "Now watch that bitch run."

He put his arm around her and kissed her. They walked arm in arm to an empty place on the grandstand steps. It was to be a long race, over five hundred meters, so the traps were across the stadium from the finishing line. But even at that distance the dogs' howls were loud, and they carried from the far side —long anxious wails from the barred traps. The lights went off and only the track shone, a sugary yellow; the rabbit started its circuit and the wire sang again. The traps banged open.

It was not clear until the dogs passed them which one was ahead, but at the turn they saw the number four dog balk and the white vest of Number Three flash to the front.

"He's in the lead!" said Lorna.

The pack darted after him, the lean dogs sprinting beautifully, low to the ground, almost horizontal in a silent chase, like gaunt racing wolves liquefying with the speed. Their names were absurd—Kelowna Gem, Tawny Perch, Aerial Miss, Star Beyond—but for half a minute their names mattered, and Lucky Gold jostled with the blue-vested number two dog, Act On, for first place. They had circled the stadium once and were now leaping around the last curve. Hood saw the second dog slowing and Lucky Gold's slender head shoot across the finish line in a burst of light as the photo was taken.

Lorna screamed delightedly. Hood said, "You're rolling in it," and helped her collect her winnings at the pay-out window.

After that win of nearly thirty pounds, they bet in the same way on the next two races, going behind to the paddock and choosing the liveliest dog before placing the bet. But both dogs lost; one was fast away but finished fourth, the other came in second. Lorna said, "I told you we should have got place tickets."

"Forget it," said Hood. "You're still in the money. Let's go up there and you can buy me a drink."

"We can't go there—you need a blue program for that enclosure. They'll chuck us out."

The first-class enclosure was just above them, a lighted ledge. They were at the margin of the track, away from the men crowding the bookies.

"There's your friend," said Lorna.

Hood was looking at the twinkling lights on the far side. It was a pleasing circus, a fine way of playing at risk. He said, "Who?"

"Willy Rutter." Seeing Hood squint she added, "Don't pretend you don't know him. He's up there." She frowned and pointed to a man leaning against the high window. "Look at him—he thinks he's big. He's looking at you."

Hood said, "I see him."

The dark-haired man, bulked at the glass, was gesturing, motioning in a friendly way. The light behind him blackened his face and showed how his hair was fluffed at his ears. But even so, in these dim features, Hood could see how mistakenly he had characterized the man. He had imagined a thug and given him a heavy jaw and fangs and an ape's shoulders. This was a smaller creature than he had pictured in his mind, a man who looked like a car salesman, waving with sham geniality. The man turned aside to face the light and Hood saw a smile on his pouchy face.

"He wants us to go up," said Lorna.

"I'm not going," said Hood, and without looking again at Rutter he steered Lorna quickly to the bar at the top of the second-class enclosure. He ordered drinks and said, "Aren't we going to bet on this race?"

Lorna shrugged. "I should have known we'd see Willy here. I'll bet he's with the rest of them. I don't want to talk to him."

"Then drink up and we'll go."

"Go? What for? I'm not leaving just because that fucker's here."

"Right." Hood looked for the man's face, the stringy head in the crowd. *There's your friend:* the man would expose him, and if he was exposed it was all over. The friendship he had contrived with Lorna would be proved a fraud; he would lose her. He did not worry about himself, but he feared for her. He said, "Let's go around back."

"What's the rush? We can give this one a miss. There's still one more race. I'll put a tenner on the last race—I've never bet a tenner before."

They watched the preparations for the race, a handicap with staggered traps in pairs along the last stretch. When the lights went out and the race began, Hood said, "Let's go to the paddock now." He did not wait for a reply. He helped her through the darkness of the enclosure, taking care not to alert her that he was running away from the man she had named.

In the paddock he instinctively looked for another exit. Seeing none he felt cornered. Lorna was at the fence, examining the dogs. The fence was a semicircle, gateless, meeting the back of the grandstand at one end and joined to the gangway, leading to the track, at the other. Beyond it, above the dogs' stalls, was the railway. He was trapped. The dogs began to moan loudly, a wolfish baying that made his own throat dry.

"I've seen all I want," said a man near Lorna, and he started away. The rest of the men left and the dogs themselves were led out. The dogs' close pelts gave them a look of nakedness, exaggerating their skinny, punished bodies, and they shook as they trotted beside the fence. From trap to trap, with the interruption of a futile chase: the agony was as familiar to Hood as waking to life.

He said, "So let's go."

"I haven't made up my mind."

"Decide at the window. It never fails." He took her arm and tried to hurry her, but as he turned, the paddock entrance, that small alley, filled with three men.

"There she is," one said, and the men started towards them. The smallest, whom Hood took to be Rutter, was in the middle; the two others marched at his elbows.

"Here comes trouble," said Lorna into her hand.

Hood faced them. The paddock was empty—the dogs, the attendants, the starter had gone for the last race, and Hood could hear the voice quacking on the loudspeaker, urging people to place their bets: *Ladies and gentlemen, the race will begin in three minutes.* In the paddock there were only the cries of the dogs locked in their stalls, and the light broken by posts and trees into blocks of shadow that half-hid the approaching men.

"Hello, Willy."

"Lorna, baby," he said. "I want to talk to you. Sorry about Ron."

Hood said, "We were just leaving."

"Who are you?" As Rutter spoke the two other men drew close to Hood, preventing him from moving on.

"He a friend of yours, Lorna?" said Rutter.

"What if he is?" she said.

"You're in the way," said Hood. "We're betting on this race."

"I got a tip for you," said Rutter. He lifted his hands and pointed at Hood. "Start talking."

"Put your cock-scratchers back in your pocket or I'll break them off."

"You didn't answer my question. You one of the family?"

"Who wants to know?" said Hood snarling and trying to keep back from the men so that they couldn't slip behind him. A dog began to yelp from his box and he started more shrill baying from the others.

Rutter said, "Because if you're one of the family, then maybe it don't matter. But I think you're crowbaring in, and the thing is, we're looking after Lorna. Aren't we, baby?"

"I can look after myself," she said.

"Ron was a mate of mine," said Rutter. "More than business. We done each other favors. When he copped it I cried like he was my own brother."

"Get out of the way, shorty," said Hood.

"Don't push your luck," said Rutter. "You can go if you want, but Lorna and me are going to have a little chat. Come on, baby, leave this geezer." He went to put his arm around Lorna, but as he did Hood chopped at his shoulder and Rutter staggered back.

Lorna screamed, and from the far side of the grandstand there was the muffled bang of the traps opening, the snare-drum mutter of the crowd, the whine of the fleeing rabbit.

Rutter clutched his bruised shoulder and yelled, "Okay, Fred! Do him! Do him!"

The taller of the two came at Hood, but the men were working to a plan he saw only when it was too late. As Hood prepared to throw Fred off, the second man jumped him from behind and began kicking him. Hood felt Fred tearing at his sleeve and he tried to swing on him, but still he felt the weight of the other on his back, choking him and booting his legs and trying to drag him down. Lorna was screaming still, and there was more noise: the thunder of the train above the dogs' howls, the deafening clatter of the tracks banging above the railway embankment. He imagined from her shrieking that Lorna had been pounced on, and he tried to reach her. But the sound smothered him and as he stumbled he sensed the paddock's lights tipping into his eyes. He was being pulled in two directions; he fought to stay upright and he felt warm blood trickling down his legs and gathering in his shoes. Then the train died on the rails. The men's grip loosened on him. He heard strangled woofs. He steadied himself to hammer the nearest man when he heard an excited stutter.

"If anyone moves, this fucker gets it in the chops."

Murf held Rutter's head in the crook of his elbow. They were almost the same size, both very short, but Murf had a demon's insect face, his earring twitched back and forth, and he stood just behind Rutter in a grotesque embrace, as if he were about to devour him. He had jabbed his hunting knife under the knot of Rutter's tie and he was moving it menacingly against his throat. Rutter had gone white, and for a moment

Hood imagined the knife halfway through his wind-pipe.

The men backed away from Hood. Lorna ran to the exit, stumbling in her new boots. Hood went over to Murf, who still hugged Rutter tightly.

Murf said, "You want to put the boot in?"

"Drop him," said Hood. He straightened his jacket and started to limp away.

Murf swung Rutter around, gagging him with the knife at his throat. Using the same childlike plea he had at the house—as if there were no knife, no thugs, as if they were alone—he said, "Now can I come wif you?"

"Come on, brother."

Part Four

18

ONCE THE BOAT was out of sight of Tower Bridge, traveling downriver on this bleak backwater lined with ghostly rotting warehouses, there were no more landmarks to distract her, and her memory was buoyed by the river's surge. Her mind began to move with the current. So much better than the bounce and stink of a taxi, though at first on the excursion boat she had felt only nausea. She had been struck by the discomfort, the choppy water under the gray sky, and up close she could see that what she had taken for turbulence were chunks of rocking flotsam, the arm of a chair, a cupboard door, a greasy eel of rope, a bar of yellow factory froth, all simulating the dance of waves. Like the boat itself: a deception. She had seen it gliding towards the quay at Westminster and had a foretaste of pleasure; but on board, the engine droned against her feet and set her teeth on edge, and then she worried that the flimsy craft might go under, slip beneath the water's garish tincture of chemicals and sink before she gained the embankment walls. She was sickened by the motion and noise and bad air, and she decided that she had been so far from the boat and water she had mistaken clumsiness for grace. She had reached for something tranquil and seized disorder; her snaring hands had put the peaceful bird to flight. The boat was frantic; it tipped and rattled; the smell of gas made her dizzy. The four other passengers huddled at the edges of the cabin like stowaways. The windows were splashed, but there was nothing to see except a zone of water distorting her landmarks and suddenly the rusty hull of a looming tug—she heard its hoot—and behind it, on a cable, its ark of sewage.

That was at the beginning of the trip. The wind had wrinkled the river's surface, she had been cold. The late-October chill had settled, an afternoon in the afternoon of the year, reminding her—as foul weather invariably did—of her age. But now the landmarks were gone and the river carried the boat and her thoughts; she remembered her errand. Her discomfort helped her to reflect: she knew she was playing a role that required moments of furtiveness, an anonymity she sometimes craved. She had asked for this accidental hour on the river to keep her appointment on Greenwich pier for the meeting later; she needed all the props of secrecy for her mood. So after the first shock of the boat, the feeling she wanted to shout, the dread she was going to vomit, the window's dampness prickling her face and that icicle jammed in her spine —after all that, she saw how right it was and she enjoyed its appropriateness to her stealth. It could not be different. The pretense warmed her. And, as always, enjoyment was a prelude to greed: she wanted to buy a boat, think of a name for it, hire an ex-convict to pilot it, moor it beside Cheyne Walk, and give a party on the deck.

Downriver, down its gray throat, seaward, the boat was borne: she could think here. *When our brother Fire was having his dog's day* . . .

Instinct, no more, had brought her this far. She had always struggled to find among the choices within her the truest expression of her will. She had groped to show herself the way through her wealth. Like the painting. That theft. It had been so embarrassing at the time she had only felt exposed and had not seen the simplest thing—that she might have managed it all herself, upstaged the thieves and been the triumphant victim of her own plot. She wished she had been involved from the very beginning. But she had discovered it soon enough—a vindication of her curiosity that made her more curious. She had once thought of selling everything and giving away the proceeds, pouring it all into the river of common hope—like this river

beneath her, murky and slow—to speed the current
and cause a flooding so great they'd be knee-deep in
it in dreary places like Cricklewood and Brixton. But
there were other stratagems (anyway, charity was the
century's most deliberate fraud—what were her do-
gooding parents but pious cheats?), and of them theft
was the greatest. The stolen painting taught her to see
her role in a different way. She thought: perhaps I
have spent my whole life encouraging people to steal
from me, because I have been too timid to give. The
most outrageous reply to money was the only one. She
had improved on Bakunin—using privilege to rid herself of privilege. She wished for others to do violence
to her wealth and yet to have her own say in their acts.
She deserved to be the victim and yet she could not be
deprived of that other role she had set for herself. She
wished to be both the terrorist and the terrorized. Her
own painting hung as hostage in the upstairs room of
the Deptford house showed her how central she was
to the drama of disorder, how her importance confounded simplicity and made all the layers of travesty
political. It was like *Twelfth Night* in Holloway
Women's Prison: the woman chosen to play the man's
part was disguised as a woman, who was revealed as
a man who was offstage a woman. And how far she'd
come! Until she had discovered the complications of
the theft her most revolutionary idea had been to sack
Mrs. Pount.

She thought: *Give the dog a bone.*

She could feel the boat's progress, the splashings at
her elbow, the window's mist on her cheek. The painting had redeemed her and, most of all, that theft was
one in the eye for Araba. She had stopped visiting Hill
Street. She said she was too busy. But Lady Arrow
knew the reason. It was not that over-praised farce
and had nothing to do with the *Peter Pan* business—
those rehearsals wouldn't start for weeks. No, a need-
less sense of rivalry had sharpened in Araba. She too
had money; she had prominence; she had her group,
the militant actors who had done little but give themselves a name—the Purple League—and disrupt
Equity meetings. Play-acting with customes and ali-

ases, their substitute for action. A mob of howling
fairies, frenzied because the best parts went to younger
stars who didn't lisp—amazing how many actors in
the League had speech impediments or were too short.
They got noisier until they landed a place with some
safe repertory company and then they fell silent: politics was a way to fame, Marxism to wealth; the furious little Trots wanted to be film stars! Araba believed
in them, or said she did; she staged their pageants, led
the attacks on the Punch and Judy shows, chaired their
meetings, loaned them money. If they disappointed
her she expelled them.

"You must come to a meeting one day," Araba had
said. It was not an invitation. Only an actress celebrated as Lady Macbeth could exclude you by seeming to invite you.

But she believed, in spite of her mockery. Of all the
people Lady Arrow had ever known only actors had
been able to combine power with glamour; and the
best were gods, moving easily from world to world.
They made you believe in that pretense. More than
their friendship Lady Arrow wanted their loyalty. It
would be like owning the priests who officiated at the
public ceremonies of a popular religion. It was, she
knew, an irrational trust that she had, but she could
not help it. Actors lived in a way she would have
chosen for herself; they could be anyone and they
could persuade others to believe in their masks. She
guessed they were weak, but she seldom saw their
weakness and for them to make weakness seem like
power filled her with approval. More than that, she
saw how in organizing plays in prisons and assigning
roles for herself she was secretly imitating them—and
what prisoner would criticize her acting ability? This
was her unspoken answer to Araba, and a way of
proving to herself that she could act well. The more
Araba avoided her, the more she tried to divine how
she might make the actress dependent, and then they
could conspire together. She wanted to be included,
but Araba kept her away, as if encouraging the rivalry. Money did not enter into it—so much the better.
But Lady Arrow had gathered that Araba did not trust

her, did not quite believe the principles Lady Arrow claimed for herself. She seemed to imply in her disbelief that Lady Arrow had a fictitious ambition. Or was she demanding proof—a tactic for ignoring her—because she was not interested in her? Araba might even be on the verge of expelling her in some casual way. Today, Lady Arrow had invited herself and Araba had allowed it with reluctance, showing interest only when Lady Arrow had said, "I'm not coming alone. There's someone I want to meet."

"Who?"

"One of my prisoners."

The river stopped, then her thoughts; the boat was turning, hooting. The spattered windows revealed nothing but the water's cold light. The engine was still. The boat bumped. Lady Arrow guessed they'd arrived at Greenwich. She walked unsteadily to the ladder and climbed to the deck.

Brodie was at the top of the ramp, waving. Seeing her, Lady Arrow felt a helpless exalted hunger for the girl, something physical tightening in her that made her strength clumsy. Desire seldom activated her mind—it pulsed at her throat and made her flesh burn as with the onset of fever. It was always like this: it broke her in two and one half hid from the other, like shame from pride. She rushed up to Brodie and kissed her, feeling huge, hoping she did not look foolish and yet not caring. She saw she had startled the young girl with her tongue and teeth, and she said, "Are you going to be warm enough in that jacket?"

"I'm all right. I liberated it from a secondhand shop." It was a school blazer, with a badge and a Latin motto on the breast pocket. Under it Brodie wore a thin jersey. The wind whipped at her lapels and pushed her long dress against her small thighs.

"We've got a stiffish walk," said Lady Arrow, feeling guilty to be so warmly dressed in a heavy coat and thick scarf. "Why don't we have a drink at the Trafalgar before we set off?"

"I don't drink," said Brodie, "but I'll keep you company."

They walked on the riverside path in front of the Naval College to the Trafalgar, where Lady Arrow ordered a double whisky. Brodie excused herself and by the time she returned Lady Arrow had finished her drink. Brodie was brighter, laughing to herself and staring with glazed hilarity at Lady Arrow.

"Have you taken a pill or something?"

"I turned on in the loo," said Brodie. "You mean you can smell it on me?"

"Rather," said Lady Arrow; then she sniffed.

"You said we were meeting this heavy actress. I always turn on before I meet people."

Outside, Lady Arrow said, "In my favorite novel there's a lovely scene here in Greenwich—an outing, like this. Do you know Henry James?"

"Never heard of him."

"That's much better than knowing his name and not reading him." She looked at the young girl's white face and thought: she knows nothing—she is free.

They cut across the park and climbed the path that led around the front of the Observatory to a road and a little hill. Although it was only midafternoon the light was failing and the ground darkening with an intimation of shadows; and the air had thickened, so that the trees that led to the far end of the hill, where some tennis courts were just visible, were dimmed by a mist so fine it was like cigarette smoke. And now the Observatory looked distant, like an old Dutch mansion on a promontory of a gray green sea.

"How is my friend Mister Hood?"

"He's not around much. I think he's got a chick."

"Has he?" Lady Arrow was momentarily jealous, then she was calm: she was with Brodie. This was what she had wanted most. "He seems quite a remarkable man."

"He's pretty heavy."

"You must bring him over to Hill Street."

Brodie laughed. "He won't come. He don't like you."

Lady Arrow stopped walking. She said, "Why not?"

Brodie went a few more paces, then turned and said, "He'd go crazy if he knew I was meeting you.

He told Murf and me not to see you. He says it's not our scene. You'll fuck us up."

"Do you think I will?"

"I'm fucked up already. Anyway, he's not my father. He can't tell me what to do."

"Good girl," said Lady Arrow, and seeing that they were alone and surrounded by trees she stopped and put her arm around the girl's small shoulders. Crushing the blazer she pulled her close—even in those thin clothes Brodie was warm. Lady Arrow said, "I'd like to adopt you—legally. Then we could be together all the time."

Brodie looked up and smiled. "You'd be my mother. Really weird."

"I'd be a nice mother," said Lady Arrow, then urgently she said, "Let me."

Brodie shrugged. "I'd feel funny."

"We could go to bed and have all our secrets there."

Brodie squinted, as if she had just then forgotten something she had always known.

"I've shocked you," said Lady Arrow.

"No," said Brodie. "A chick fancied me once. In the nick it was. I done it with her."

"So you know how beautiful it is."

Brodie screwed up her face, pretending a look of comic disgust, seeming to swallow something foul.

"Don't you?" said Lady Arrow.

Brodie was shaking her head. She said, "Yuck!"

Then she was running across the humpy top of the hill, her hair flying like a pennant as she ducked around trees, growing smaller. Lady Arrow watched: she was out of reach, running away as children always did, making no allowance for the very slow. The afternoon mist and low sky made a great brown canvas of the park on which Brodie was an elusive flag of paint among the trees, a brushstroke. Lady Arrow leaned into the steep path and trudged towards the darting figure. She stopped several times to get her breath and felt almost defeated knowing she was chasing her in the most hopeless way and could only catch her if the girl allowed it.

*

In the living room of Mortimer Lodge, Araba was saying, "But she's not one of your prisoners, is she?"

"I thought you'd like her."

"She's spoiled and she's too young." Araba sipped her mug of coffee. The mug was chipped, her jeans were stained with paint and bleach, and she sat on the arm of the sofa with a kind of awkward arrogance, like a workman in a large strange house. "I've had it up to here with these rich girls playing at politics."

"You must be joking," said Lady Arrow, and she laughed at the thought of Brodie being considered rich. But she was vindicated in her belief: Araba had taken the girl's carelessness—poverty's legacy—for freedom. She saw that Araba was annoyed and said, "She's the real thing."

"I can't stand her affectations. That blazer is a dead giveaway."

"She liberated it from a secondhand shop."

"Really, Susannah, you shouldn't waste your time with girls like that. There are so many people who need attention—why pick on one of your own?"

"So that's why you're being rude to her."

"She's not my type."

"She'd be interested in your work."

"My work would scare the daylights out of her."

Brodie entered the room holding McGravy's dog. She said, "He thought he could get away from me, but I was too fast for him."

"Poldy's got high blood pressure," said Araba. "Do be careful with him."

"How do you like Araba's new house?" said Lady Arrow.

"Far out," said Brodie. "But ours is bigger, ain't it? You can play hide-and-seek in ours."

Lady Arrow saw Araba's ears move in satisfaction. She said, "Brodie lives in a marvelous old house in Deptford with her friends."

"I imagine that must make your parents absolutely furious."

"My father run off when I was a baby," said Brodie. "And my mother, she don't have a clue."

Lady Arrow said, "I think Brodie would get on

terribly well with your friend Anna, that pretty little Trot."

"We expelled her," said Araba.

"They're always expelling people," said Lady Arrow to Brodie. "They're famous for it. It sounds such fun. I once thought of expelling Mrs. Pount, but she'd be ever so sad if I did."

"It's not funny," said Araba. "I was expelled myself not long ago."

"Who would do a thing like that?" said Lady Arrow.

"I can't go into it—not in present company."

The women were on chairs, facing each other across twenty feet of carpet, in the center of which Brodie sat cross-legged, playing with the dog. She was like a bored child forced indoors by her aunts, who made an effort from time to time to include her in the conversation and who spoke with self-conscious care, knowing they had a young listener.

"And how is *Peter Pan?*" said Lady Arrow. "They haven't expelled you from that, I hope."

"Rehearsals start in a few weeks," said Araba. "It's a headache—I've got so many other things to do. I have to take lessons on the wire. It's a complete bore, learning to fly."

"It sounds super," said Lady Arrow. "Did you hear that, my love—she's learning to fly!"

"When I was at the home," said Brodie, "they took us to see *Peter Pan* one Christmas."

"And did you like it?" asked Lady Arrow.

"The part with the pirates was pretty freaky," said Brodie. "I can't remember the rest. I think it was too long."

"Your political affairs must take up a great deal of your time, Araba," said Lady Arrow turning away from Brodie.

"The League? It's the only thing that keeps me sane."

"How many members do you have?"

"That's a reporter's question, Susannah. You know better than to ask that."

"I love secrets," said Lady Arrow. "I only wish I had some myself. Perhaps I do!"

"How did you get into it?" asked Brodie, holding the dog on her lap and letting him gnaw her wrist.

"Historical necessity," said Araba. "It had to happen. You can't ignore what's going on around you. You take it for just so long and then something snaps."

"I never thought of it that way," said Brodie.

"It can be a very humbling thing to know how much power you really have. I'm not talking about playing around with it, the political protest wank that only makes you feel good—that doesn't change anything. No, I mean, when you realize that there are thousands, just like you—"

Brodie was shaking her head, laughing softly and stroking the dog.

"I can see you're not very impressed," said Araba. "But I'll lend you a book if you like."

"I read one."

"And what did you think of it?"

"Too long," said Brodie.

"There speaks the voice of innocence—innocence is a form of laziness, isn't it? The young and their all-purpose comments. I must remember that—it was too long!"

"It's probably a fair comment," said Lady Arrow. "I don't know. I'm hopelessly out of my depth with political theory."

Araba said, "I'm so sick of the young, I'm so tired of hearing about them and seeing them courted." She turned to Brodie and said crossly, "You don't know anything, but if you listen you'll see you have a part to play."

"No," said Brodie.

"You might be surprised," said Araba.

Brodie said, "I could never play Peter Pan."

"Oh, lord," said Lady Arrow. "Didn't I tell you?"

"It's not that the book was boring," Brodie explained. "I liked the pirates. But the flying! I'd freak out on that wire. I'm afraid of heights."

"Tell her about the League," said Lady Arrow.

"I don't want to alarm her," said Araba.

"She won't be alarmed."

"Then she won't understand."

"I'm stupid," said Brodie. "Right? That's what you're saying. I'm stupid—I don't know nothing."

Araba blushed slightly and said, "We're mainly Trots, but some are outright anarchists or anarcho-syndicalists. Are you with me?"

The dog barked. Brodie giggled and patted him.

"It's a grassroots movement of workers, the only viable alternative to the existing power structure of hacks and exploiters." Araba got to her feet. "It's a party committed to action on all fronts."

"I like parties," said Brodie.

"She's really quite passionate," said Lady Arrow.

"Stuff your praise," said Araba. "We're not part-timers. And I warn you we're not joking. Any corrupt government is bound to fail—this one will, and when it does we'll be there to take over."

"Then you'll be the big shits," said Brodie.

"No," said Araba, "because then we'll hand it over to the people."

"The word 'people' is so bald," said Lady Arrow. " 'People'—that's what politicians say. Who are they, the people?"

"They're, like, mainly the straights, aren't they?" said Brodie. "It's everyone except the freaks."

"What a jolly good definition," said Lady Arrow.

"I don't think you want to hear anymore," said Araba.

"I think Brodie would like you to be specific," said Lady Arrow. "You've been awfully abstract with your people and your grassroots."

"I could scare you with specifics."

"Go on, try," said Lady Arrow, and she sat forward and took a pinch of snuff.

"Well, for one thing, we haven't ruled out the possibility of confrontation."

Brodie said, "Hey, what's this dog's name again?"

"I mean direct action," said Araba, ignoring Brodie. "In a word, Susannah—violence."

"Bombs," said Lady Arrow.

"Oh, bombs," said Brodie, chucking Poldy under the jaw, making him growl.

"It frightens you, doesn't it?" said Araba.

"Only if I think about it a little," said Brodie. "Like these clocks they use are so poky, all done up with sticking plaster and that, they can blow up when you're legging them."

"I wouldn't know about that," said Araba, but her green eyes were electric and she looked closely at Brodie.

"I'm telling you straight," said Brodie. "Sometimes they go wrong. Say the hands get muddled up and they're touching the screw and you can't see them. They're so feeble you can hardly tell when it's legged anyway. Then you twist the wires over and as soon as they, like, touch, it's the last act, ain't it?"

"What does that mean?" said Araba.

"You've had it. You're snuffed. You're wiped out."

Lady Arrow stared at her. She had been on the point of taking some more snuff, but she stopped her hand halfway to her nose and held it there, at shoulder level and a little forward, as if resting her hand on an invisible shelf. She said, "Have you some experience of these things, my darling?"

"A little bit," said Brodie, and hung her head.

"It's considered very fashionable to know a bomber," said Araba. "A few years ago it was Yorkshiremen. Then it was Africans. Now it's bombers. Your girlfriends must envy you."

"I don't have no girlfriends."

"Well, your gang."

"It's not a gang," said Brodie. "It's more a bunch of people. A family, like."

Lady Arrow said, "I've met a number of them. They're quite impressive."

"I'm sure," said Araba. "It sounds a great hoot. After that, our League would strike you as rather dull."

"If you're into bovver," said Brodie, "it might not be so bad."

"I take it you are into bother, as you say?" said Araba.

"It's the only way, ain't it? You said so yourself—everything's rotten. It's a ripoff."

"But what's your program?"

"Bovver," said Brodie. "Just bovver."

"She's a Trot way down," said Lady Arrow proudly. "A true anarchist."

"I doubt very much whether she knows the word."

"I don't," said Brodie. "It sounds like some creepy church."

"You see?" said Lady Arrow. "No theories. It's as simple as football. I love her directness. You should listen to her, Araba."

"You're welcome to stay," said Araba. "We've got plenty of room."

"She can't."

"If Hood don't find out, it's all right," said Brodie.

"No, you're coming with me," said Lady Arrow. "We can come back tomorrow. Or better still, Araba might like to visit Hill Street."

"Did you say Hood?" Araba knelt in front of Brodie, who still held the dog on her lap.

"It's this bloke," said Brodie.

"You're going to miss your lesson," said Lady Arrow standing up.

Araba looked at her watch and frowned in impatience. "Damn," she said, "I've got to go. But tell me something, Brodie—"

Lady Arrow went to the door and called Brodie: she was insistent, demanding in the tone a tired mother might use that Brodie follow her, but the fucking child wouldn't move. She said, "I'm going," but didn't go. She watched the small girl on the floor answering the actress's questions. "Don't keep her, my darling," said Lady Arrow sharply. "She's learning to fly!"

19

THEY ARRIVED LATE at Paddington Cemetery in Kilburn, and walking down the central path between the close rows of tombstones—following Mayo's instructions—Murf was apologizing to Hood for having caused the delay. At Queen's Park Station Murf had said, "Wait," and when the other passengers had gone he took a felt-tipped pen from his pocket and wrote ARSENAL RULE on the wall. He did it purposefully, clinging to the tiles with one hand and making the letters line by line like a child copying his name. He inked them in heavily. Then he walked away and turned to squint at it. He was not satisfied; he wrote it again on the wall next to the door, while Hood watched him with puzzled amusement.

"I'm really sorry about that," Murf was saying in a low voice. His feet scuffed the gravel regretfully. The long black raincoat he had bought to match Hood's flapped about him, beating like a cape in the wind. "I think I made us late."

Ah fink. He slouched ahead, his coat rising, and he kicked at the path as if blaming himself by punishing his feet. The cemetery was in darkness; the lights shining just above the wall put the whole place in shadow, whitening only the tops of the tombstones so that they were like peaks of ice chunks frozen in a still black pool. Outside the cemetery the air was soaked pale yellow, like a low cloud of poison, the effect of the sodium street lamps. The sound of their footsteps was deadened by the baffles of the tombs and they could hear their words ring once at the edge of the path and die as the echoes were stifled against the dark marble blocks. A black pool of ice; but when they had crossed it several times Hood saw the cemetery as a walled-in ruin, the sturdy cellar of an ancient toppled building, with the rows of its foundation stones exposed—these broken steeples and cracked posts, and their chains and scabs of moss, pushed up to the path. The ones that caught the light were chalky and pitted like old bones, and the wind groaned through them, making the cluttered place seem mournfully empty. This was how the whole of London might look if it was devastated by bombs: miles and miles of shallow moaning cellars.

Hood said—and he was careful not to laugh—"Do you always write that?"

The previous night, at the dog track, Murf had stopped running to mark the same slogan on the exit gate—a rash afterthought, since they had no way of knowing whether they were being chased by Rutter's men. Even fleeing, Murf had paused to use his felt-tip! On the platform at Catford Bridge he had explained, "If you do it right, it sort of jumps out at you."

"Habit," Murf said. He gathered his coat against the wind. "Couple of years ago I lived up in Penge. Arfa and me. And we had these mates. We called ourselves 'the Penge Boys'—boot-boys, like. I was a kid, about fifteen at the time, I was. Yeah, I was had up—threatenin' behavior, utterin' menaces—but I got off easy. We just hung out and we used to write stuff on the walls, 'Penge Rule,' 'Wankers Support Palace,' that kind of shit. Then you started calling the house a flipping arsenal—remember? When you saw me clocks? 'Don't let no one in this arsenal without permission,' you said. So I got this idea. Let's start advertisin'. Arsenal Rule, and that. It's like I say—it's a habit."

In the whole time Hood had known him he had never said so much about himself. Murf was silent for a minute, as if wondering about his own candor, discovering embarrassment.

Finally, Hood said, "But won't people think it's the football team?"

"Right," said Murf. "That's the funny part."

"I get it," said Hood, but he was glad it was too dark for Murf to see his face.

"Like no one knows. You write down 'Arsenal' and everyone thinks it's the team. Right? Only it ain't. Right? It's our secret family, like, and no one has a fucking clue." He chuckled. " 'Right on,' they're saying, 'Up Arsenal' and they don't even know they're supporting us. That's the best part." He showed Hood his shadowy face, his lighted ears, the glint of his earring, then he burped. "They don't know nothing, the wankers."

Hood said, "Some advertising."

They walked to the upper end of the path and paused for a moment. Nothing moved, and in that enormous tract of shadows there was no sound but the wind tearing at the half-hidden stones and grass. Startled by the silence they turned and headed down the path again, as if seeking to be calmed by the muffled crunching of their own footsteps.

Murf said, "I hate this boneyard."

He tramped against the wind, with his small head down and his black coat wrapped around him. He tottered forward, hunched like a deaf bat. And Hood could hear his murmured singing, *"Boom widdy-widdy, Boom widdy-widdy, boom-boom."*

Hood had not said anything about the night before, but he could see that Murf was glad to have been able to do him the favor. They were friends; now there was no question of it. Before, he had shown his loyalty in unlikely ways. Hood had stuck by him, defended him against Mayo's sneers, and to show his thanks Murf had redecorated the bathroom. The little deception over the painting—Lady Arrow's intrusion—had secured their friendship. Murf had tagged along behind him for that; and the fight at the dog track had lifted Murf's mood and made him candid. Yet Hood wondered how he had gone from being a boot-boy in Penge to a bomber for the Provos. He had no particular belief; he had a crude skill. Hood was amazed that Murf had been able to follow him for an entire day without once showing him-

self. He was small, but not that small. Tonight Murf
was especially grateful. Before they left the house
Mayo said that Murf was to stay behind, but Hood
insisted he come and said, "He's my secret weapon."

Now, Hood said, "You saved my life, squire."

"You mean that punk?" Murf laughed, a little bark
in his throat.

"I thought you were going to put his lights out."

"He was dead-scared." Murf laughed again. The
laughter carried to the tombstones and was flattened
into a mirthless snort that thudded at the far wall.
Murf said gruffly, "I would have cut him and all."

"Did you recognize him?"

"No. I thought you knew him." Murf looked to
Hood for a reply, but there was none and Murf went
on, "He scared your chick. I felt sorry for her."

They had gone to New Cross together in the train,
saying nothing. Lorna sat, sniffing with fright into a
hanky she held in her fist. Then Murf had gone back
to the house, and when they were alone in the street
Lorna said, "Who are you?" It sent a chill through
him, as it had that first day when she had caught
him prowling upstairs. Walking her home he tried
to explain—telling her how he had once quarreled
with Rutter, inventing reasons for the pretense of
Rutter's not knowing him. And though she half believed him she was fearful—the casual violence was
too great a reminder of her old life. She repeated that
Hood was no different from Ron: a thug, a villain,
dangerous, putting her at risk. At the door she said,
"I never want to see you again." He didn't care; he
was just playing about, using her. "I'm not even
pretty," she said. "But I know what you are—you're
a fucker, just like the rest of them."

To Murf, kicking at the cemetery path, Hood said,
"She was upset. She'll get over it."

"She seemed quite nice," said Murf. "I wouldn't
want to see her messed up."

"She'll be okay."

"Those punks," said Murf. "They're a bad lot. Hey,
you wouldn't believe it, but punks like that are always pestering the Provos."

"What do you mean?"

"They got hardware," said Murf. "They got connections. Like they know Arabs."

And Hood thought of Weech's two trunks of guns; it had been a puzzle, but now he saw that he might solve it like an acrostic, adding a dozen names to make a word with their key letters.

Murf looked at the cemetery shapes and sucked at the wind and said, "They probably come up here already and left, Sweeney and them. It's all my fault."

"Don't worry about it." Sweeney: another name. He knew nothing, but he was almost relieved to think they might not come. He wondered if he really wanted to see them and commit himself further. Once, when he had acted alone, it had all seemed very simple. His present anxiety was like a fear of crowds, the mob that would sweep him from his own motives. The origin of his doubt was the discovery weeks ago that he had made a passport for that wealthy actress he had taken a dislike to. So they were linked. But there was more: the painting stolen by the rich girl from the titled woman. They were all related! And what of Weech's arsenal? Was it also part of the family now? He resisted assigning it ownership as he had resisted anything final with Lorna, to preserve some distance and avoid the complicating sympathy of kinship. Yet it was as if by degrees he was waking to the true size of his family and seeing it as so huge and branched it included the enemy. To harm any of them was to harm a part of himself. A family quarrel: if he cut them he bled.

That was how he saw the man slipping through the gate at the far end of Paddington Cemetery, the shadow hurrying along the path. What mad cousin was this who had dragged himself from the past to plead with him?

He said, "Heads up, squire."

Murf moved behind him, whispering, *"Boom widdy-widdy—"*

The man approached and as he stepped close to them he flipped his cigarette away. It glanced against a tombstone and the tip came apart, making a shower of sparks, lighting for seconds a jar of wilted flowers and the dagger of a cross in the ground.

Murf said, "Easter—"

"Stuff your bloody password—what are you doing here, man?"

"He's with me," said Hood.

"You're supposed to be alone." The man turned. "Hop it, Murf."

"Hold the phone, squire."

"They won't like it," said the man.

"That's tough," said Hood. "He's staying."

"Then follow me," he said. "But I ain't responsible."

They walked out to Lonsdale Road, where Murf stopped briefly to chalk ARSENAL RULE on the cemetery wall. In the cemetery the man had been a threatening voice, a villainous shape. In the street Hood saw him wince; he was uncertain, with thinning hair, in a battered jacket. The light removed any suggestion of threat and showed his laborer's stoop—a careworn limping. He turned to Hood, peering up: small, close-set eyes and a wrinkled nose, a large dented chin and a crooked Irish mouth—then he looked away. He skipped slightly, getting ahead of Hood and Murf, and led them down a side street to a pub.

Before they entered he said angrily, "I ain't responsible." Then he pushed at the door.

The pub was full of hollering men, most of them red-faced and standing in wreaths of smoke, gesturing with pints of beer. A juke box played—not music, but a throb that repeated against the floor and shook the windows. Hood was used to strangers' stares, but here there was an unusual break in the chatter as they crossed the pub; he sensed attention, a sharpening of suspicion—a pause in the darts game, heads turning, low mutters—as if they had entered a private club and were intruding on a closely guarded ritual. In a corner of the bar the man said, "Wait here," then walked away.

Murf said, "I think I should split."

"Forget it. Let's hoist a few."

"There ain't time."

"They can wait."

"It don't work like that," said Murf, trying to make Hood understand. "When they say go, you go. It's like an order. And they don't want me—I can tell. So I think maybe I'll just hang out."

"I might need you," said Hood. "What if they pull a fast one on me? You're my back-up man."

"Yeah, but they won't do that. You're seeing Sweeney—he's the chief."

"Never trust the top banana, Murf," said Hood and he bought two pints of beer.

The limping man returned five minutes later and seeing them with glasses he said, "Drink up—we're going." Without waiting he pushed towards the back of the pub. Hood put down his half-full glass. Murf said, "You leaving that?" and gulped it. Arching his back he seemed to pour it straight into his stomach.

Hood thought they were headed for a back room —they were in a passageway stacked with beer crates, then squeezing through a narrow darkened hall. The man kicked a door and they were outside.

"Hey, sweetheart, you know where you're going?"

The man muttered. He glared at Murf. He said, "I told you, I ain't responsible."

Murf said, *"Boom widdy-widdy."*

The next pub was several streets away, smaller than the first and not so crowded. They entered by the back door and the man, who had grown uneasy in his movements—he had not stopped muttering and his posture had become more cramped—crooked his finger at some stairs. He said, "Up there. First on your left."

On the stairs Hood said, "Just like any other cathouse."

"I never been here before." Murf quacked the words nervously and looked around at the worn staircase.

Hood said, "Smile."

"Widdy-widdy."

Hood found the door and knocked. It opened a crack, a man showed his nose and cautious eye, then it swung open and Hood saw the table—another man seated at the far end—the dim bulb and drawn shades. The room was bare and had the musty smell of a decaying carpet. And it was cold. The men—there were only those two—wore winter coats, and the younger one at the door a flat tweed cap. Murf began to cough nervously.

"Sit down," said the man at the door, shutting it and slipping the bolt.

The man at the table smiled. He said, "Welcome."

"Where are we?" said Hood.

"The High Command," said the younger man.

Hood looked around: a dart board, a bottle of whisky, a broken lamp, a saucer full of cigarette butts. He smiled, then he sat down and said, "I hope you don't have any objection to Murf."

The man at the table did not reply to that. He sat up, and leaning across the table extended his hand. "My name's Sweeney. I know yours."

Hood shook his hand. It was a strange clasp, without weight, and glancing down Hood saw that the top of Sweeney's hand was missing and that he held a rounded stump and two small limp fingers, like a monster's claw.

"A little accident," said Sweeney. He smiled at the knob and tucked it into his sleeve. "This is Finn. How about a drop?"

Finn nodded and put the whisky bottle on the table with four cloudy glasses. He splashed some in each one and handed them out, winking at Murf. Then he touched Hood's glass with his own and said, "The offensive."

Murf said, "The offensive."

Hood said, "Any ice?"

"No," said Finn.

"My brother Jimmy's in the States," said Sweeney. "Boston. Your hometown, right? He's been there for years. Married an American girl."

Hood said, "That doesn't make us cousins, does it?"

"Mayo told me you were temperamental," said Sweeney amiably.

"She told me you had something important to say. I haven't heard it."

Sweeney quietly finished his whisky. He looked

about thirty, though he was balding. There was a toughened redness about his face, a raw lined quality in his cheeks that might have been whisky or the sun. His mouth and eyes were gentle, and he spoke slowly in the strangled accent of Ulster. Hood noticed that he held the glass of whisky with his mutilated hand, pinching it awkwardly against his chest and lifting it using his two frail fingers, as if exhibiting the damage. He said, "I thought we might have a little talk."

"Start talking."

Sweeney went at his own speed. "This organization attracts a lot of funny boyos. I mean, unstable people—mental cases." He pronounced the word in the Ulster way, *muntal*. "They belong in hospitals or with kind families, but they come to us and say they want to help." He smiled. "All they really want to do is plant a bomb somewhere—they don't care why. They're looking for victims." He nudged his empty glass. "It's made us a little suspicious of volunteers."

"What's that got to do with me?"

"You're a volunteer, aren't you?"

Hood said, "I used to think I could help. I gave Mayo a boost with her painting."

"To be sure," said Sweeney. "But an ordinary drunken layabout from some village in the Republic —or even in England—it's usually obvious why he wants to join. He's a bit lost, running away from his wife or his parents. He feels secure with us—we understand that. You're not in that category."

"How do you know?"

"We know you," said Sweeney. "We know the important things. Some of the other fellers wanted you over here months ago but I said no. We tried you out on that passport. That was a good job, but I still couldn't figure you out. What's the motive? What does a feller from a good family—Jimmy did a little detective work, you see—why does a feller earning a handsome salary in the American State Department decide to chuck it all and join a bomb factory?"

"We were all casualties in Vietnam—I wasn't the only one," said Hood softly. "Some died, but even more were born there, and I'm telling you, we'll never forget how painful it was." He thought a moment. "I found out which side I was really on, so I left to fight somewhere else."

Sweeney shrugged. "Everything's so easy for you Americans."

"You mean it's not for you?"

"It isn't. It's bloody hard." Sweeney turned to the wall to reflect. He said, "When I was twelve I had to prove myself. I broke every shop window on Feakle Street in Derry—hundreds of pounds worth of plate glass. My father was delighted. 'The Smasher' he called me. Now you," he said, pointing at Hood, "you were probably a Boy Scout."

Hood said, "I've always been suspicious of people who rap about their childhood. It's just a cheap way of avoiding blame."

"I'm a responsible feller," said Sweeney.

Hood thumped the table and cried, "You've got sitting targets!"

"That's how it looks to an outsider, I suppose. If you knew how we operated you wouldn't say that. This has been a bad summer. Our supplies dried up. I'll be frank with you—we've been burned."

"So have I," said Hood bitterly.

"Sorry to hear it. I wish there was something I could do."

"You can tell me why I wasn't contacted sooner."

"That bothered you, did it? Well, it's just as I say. I was wondering what was in it for you. Mister Hood, you were too eager."

"So you delayed."

"You could say we were waiting for a telephone call."

"But you let me do the passport."

"That's another story," said Sweeney.

"I'd like to hear it."

"It's not very interesting," said Sweeney dismissively.

Hood laughed. "I knew you'd hedge."

"Did you now?"

"But that's all right. You don't have to tell me anything." He fixed his eyes on Sweeney's. "I can always ask Miss Nightwing."

Sweeney sighed and looked at the rear of the room where Finn and Murf were sitting in silence. He said, "Murf, how would you like a beer?"

"Widdy," said Murf, blinking and bobbing forward. "Okay."

"Finn, take our friend downstairs and buy him a beer. I'll see you later."

"Heads up, squire."

When they were gone and the door was bolted again, Sweeney said, "Let's talk about Miss Nightwing." He had become genial, a mood Hood took to be a cover for his suspicion. He smiled again and said, "Jasus, so you know our Araba, do you?"

"I met her."

"I thought she had more sense than to go yapping about her sordid past," said Sweeney. "But then I never really understood the girl. It's like I was telling you. We get a hell of a lot of funny people. I don't think she's a nutcase in the usual sense, but she's certainly unstable."

"She didn't tell me anything," said Hood. "I just guessed."

"You guessed, did you? That's hard to believe."

"I was a consul. Do you think she was the first one to try and pull a fast one on me?"

"I forgot you've had training," said Sweeney. "It must have upset her. She's an emotional sort of person. Very interested in the poor and oppressed. She sees them and she cries. That is an admirable thing, but it's the extent of her political consciousness. I'll tell you, she was much better at entertaining the troops." Sweeney winked broadly. "Ah, she was wonderful at that, she was. A real morale-builder."

"That's why you gave her a passport, then."

"Not exactly. About five months back, when our American supplies dried up, we needed some contacts on the continent. Our girl Araba claimed to have a lot of helpful friends. Thanks to you we fixed her up with a passport, and off she went."

"With an ass like that she must have made a lot of contacts."

"Who knows?"

"You mean she didn't come up with the goods?"

"She wasn't supposed to take delivery," said Sweeney.

"Who was?"

Sweeney waved his mangled hand carelessly. He said, "Agents, agents."

"What are we talking about?" said Hood. "Arms? Dynamite? What?"

Sweeney smiled. "Oh, cabbages, that sort of thing."

"And you got burned."

"You're guessing again." Sweeney added wearily, "You've been talking to Araba too much."

Hood said, "I'm probably wrong, but I would have thought that if Araba made a supply deal for you and it went through, I'd have seen a little action. The big London offensive. But I haven't seen anything." He stared at Sweeney. "So I guess she burned you."

"You're probably wrong."

"I told Mayo you were delaying. She denied it, but now I understand. Araba welshed on you. That's what you get for trusting the idle rich."

"The rich only have money," said Sweeney. "But you can see why I was hesitant to take you on. Araba was just an actress, but you were a highly paid diplomat. No one had ever heard of you. All we knew was how much money you earned and where your family lived. Mother of God, I thought—he can't be serious. So we waited."

"I think you're lying," said Hood. "You talk about the offensive, Mayo talks about the offensive. But what's the offensive? It's a couple of teenagers hustling bombs into luggage lockers. Oh, and I almost forgot about Mayo's painting. That was a brilliant caper—it really had the art world up in arms, right? What an offensive."

"Have you been to Belfast?"

"No," said Hood, and he muttered, "Don't mention religion."

"You should go," said Sweeney. "You'd learn

something. Ever see a father gunned down in front of his wife and kiddies?"

"Yes, I have," said Hood solemnly.

"And what did you do about it?"

"I came here."

"Maybe you can see why we're militant."

"I don't call stealing paintings very militant."

"It's a tactic. It's better than cutting people's throats." Sweeney looked closely at Hood, then said, "If you have other ideas I'd like to hear them."

"I'll write you a letter," said Hood.

"If you're worried about Araba you can forget it. We expelled her."

"For burning you."

"It's no concern of yours. The fact is she was expelled. She's on her own now."

"Competition," said Hood.

Sweeney grinned. "Actors."

"There are a hundred more like her—aristocrats, suckers, and middle-class girls with problems. Like Mayo, who takes her bra off and thinks she's bringing down civilization. She's just a can of worms. Once, she saw a pretty picture. Then she became a revolutionary and decided to steal it. She's like a lot of them, a barbarian with taste."

"Hold it," said Sweeney. "Mayo's my wife."

Hood said, "Then you should keep an eye on her."

"I've been told that before," said Sweeney softly.

They faced each other and Hood saw an acknowledgment in Sweeney's gray eyes, a recognition bordering on the saddest affinity: they had slept with the same woman. Hood did not feel guilty; he felt ensnared by a sense of shame, and angry that he had been brought so close to this stranger. He thought: What does that make me? Another member of the family. And he could see now how it had all gone wrong, why Mayo had kept him away—or perhaps Sweeney himself, out of pride, had avoided bringing him any further into the plot. He could hardly be expected to welcome his wife's lover.

"Her name isn't Mayo. It's Sandra."

Hood said, "I don't have much to do with her these days."

"I know, but it wouldn't bother me if you did. A man sleeps with your wife. It hurts at first—that's pride. But then you realize what he's putting up with and you almost pity the poor bastard." Sweeney laughed and reached for his glass.

"I'm going," said Hood.

Sweeney faced him. He said, "You're going to help us. You've got ideas—the offensive is yours, if you want it."

"You're really in a jam, aren't you?"

"It's up to you. I think we can depend on you." Sweeney took a sip of his whisky. "I'm getting used to you."

"That's your problem," said Hood.

*

"Sweeney's a great bloke," said Murf, in the train back to Deptford. "He was like a father to me, he was. He taught me everything I know."

"Listen, Murf, most fathers don't teach their kids to make bombs."

"Then they're useless, ain't they? 'Cause that's what it's all about, ain't it?" Murf slumped in his seat. "They done my old man. Didn't give him a chance. He's Irish, so they nobble him."

Hood looked over and just before Murf turned away he saw the boy's face crease with grief: he had started to cry. Hood thought: But what have I taught him? He was going to comfort him—they were alone in the compartment—he was moved by the boy's size, his small crushed face, the ridiculous earring, and that black raincoat he wore in imitation of his own. Then he saw the handle of Murf's knife and he held back. Suddenly, as if remembering, Murf sprang from his seat, whipped out the felt-tipped pen and wrote on the compartment mirror, ARSENAL RULE.

At Deptford Station Hood said, "I'll see you later."

"The pubs are shut," said Murf.

"I'm not going to a pub."

He left Murf and walked up a side street to Lorna's where, in front of the house, he watched a crumpled sheet of newspaper dragged by the wind from the gutter to the sidewalk. It rasped against the garden wall, altering its shape, then tumbled into a tree and flapped fiercely. Hood waited a moment, studying the caught thing animated by the wind, and he was about to go when he glanced up and saw the kitchen light burning. He rang the bell and the light went off. There was no sound from the house. He knocked, then poked open the letter slot and called Lorna's name. She didn't answer. He drew out Weech's key and unlocked the door.

"Lorna?"

He switched on the light and saw her cowering halfway down the hall, preparing to run upstairs. He almost recoiled at the sight of her, and she seemed not to recognize him—she registered slow fear, the negligent despair of someone wounded or doomed. And she was wounded. Her face was bruised, her blouse torn, and there were scratches on her neck. She watched him with swollen eyes as he rushed forward and took her in his arms. He could feel her frailty, her heart pumping against his chest.

"What happened?"

"They was here—oh, God, I thought they got you too." She sobbed and then said, "I didn't tell them anything!"

"Love, love," said Hood, and heard the child cry out in an upper room.

20

THE FACE WAS a success: even the dog barked at her, and McGravy was taken in for a few bewildered seconds. She had spent the morning at the mirror working on her eyes—it was too easy to wear sunglasses, and down there sunglasses in this dreary weather would attract as much attention as a full frontal. The headscarf and plastic boots were her greatest concession, since her first thought was to go as a man. She knew she could bring it off, but how to explain it? A woman, then, but anonymous. The skin had to have a pale crêpy texture and around the eyes a wrinkled suggestion of neglect and premature aging, with dull green mascara on the lids. It took her an hour to get the right crude stripe. She labored with care for the effect and finally achieved it in exasperation, realizing afterward that what she wanted most in her make-up that day was a look of hurry. A woman went out in the morning to shop, but no matter how rushed she was she did her eyes. She aimed, with a few lurid strokes of eyeliner, at the haste and pretty fatigue of the housewife. Instead of lipstick she practiced her bite, clamping her jaw a fraction off-center to convey, in a slightly crooked grin, that her teeth didn't quite fit. Then she put on her boots and scarf and an old coat, and seeing her, Poldy had yapped in his cowardly dance of aggression, diving at her and swiveling his hind end sideways until he sniffed her and whimpered into silence.

McGravy said, "Don't tell me. Let me guess—"

"I'm in a rush," she said, rummaging in the trunk for the right handbag and selecting one in imitation leather with a broken buckle.

"Of course, you're taking the bus—Mother Courage doesn't take taxis."

"I'm not Mother Courage," she said. "I'm invisible."

"Poldy doesn't think so." But the dog had stopped barking. He was circling her cautiously, sniffing at her boots.

"And I'm not taking the bus," she said, fixing her bite and crushing the handbag under her arm. "I'm walking."

She slipped out the back door and hurried down Blackheath Hill to where it dipped at the lights. Then she was only following signs and the map she'd memorized. She had never walked here, and it was odd, for once she plunged down from Blackheath, walking west to Deptford, the light altered—filtered by a haze of smoke it became glaucous—and it was colder and noisy and the air seemed to contain flying solids.

But she had succeeded in her disguise, and the novelty of being invisible cheered her. She celebrated the feeling. There had been a time, before her political conversion, when the thought of going unrecognized would have depressed and angered her. Then she required to be seen—not for herself, a compliment to her fame, but because she believed from the moment she had become an actress that the role and the person playing it were inseparable. An actress did not become another person in studying a part: the part slumbered in her, the character—not only Alison and Cicely, but Juliet and Cleopatra—was a layer in her personality like a stripe in a cake. Once she had been asked, after a hugely successful sixties revival of the Osborne play she had taken on tour, how she had done the part so well. She replied, "But I *am* Alison." She was Paulina, Lady Macbeth, Blanche DuBois, and all of Ibsen's heroines. They were aspects of herself, but more than that their words too were hers. Acting for her was a kind of brilliant improvisation; she gave language life, she reinvented a playwright each time she performed. There was nothing she hated more than the proprietorial way a writer or director regarded the text—they wanted to reduce actors to dummies and conceived the theater as a glorified puppet show (it was this notion, and more, that made her want to ban Punch and Judy shows—her first political gesture).

Acting was liberation. The theater had shown her what possibilities people had—it was her political education. Everyone acted, but the choice of roles was always limited by social class, so the laborer never knew how he could play a union leader. True freedom, the triumph of political struggle, was this chance for people to choose any role. It was more than a romantic metaphor—she knew it was a fact. That old man, Mister Punch, leaving The Red Lion at the far end of Deptford Bridge, did not know how easily he had been cheated; in a fairer world he would have power. That took acting skill; but there were no great actors, there were only free men.

And unseen, part of the thin crowd, she was free today, stamping in her old coat and faded scarf in the High Road, biting to make her face unfamiliar. This was political proof, not simple deceit, but evidence that the woman she was this gray afternoon was unalterable in a capitalist system. Freer, the woman she mimicked would be a heroine. The mimicry was easily mastered, and though once she had needed attention, now, the very absence of it encouraged her. She could be anyone; she was no one; she could walk through walls.

Deptford—especially those angular cranes and chimneys, the low narrow brick houses, the windowless warehouses—reminded her of Rotterdam. She remembered the errand as one of her most demanding roles, though she savored it with a trace of regret: it had been robbed of completion. In the end it had failed, and yet nothing she had ever done had so satisfied her, no stage part could compare with it. It was all excitement, the smoky jangling train to Harwich, the Channel crossing that night in early summer, and then the brief electric train past the allotments on the canal to the neat station in that cheerless port. Passing through British immigration, looking the officer squarely in the eye, handing over the American passport—all of it was an achievement greater than her Stratford season. And there was that odd business with her cabin in the *Koningin Juliana*: she had been assigned a four-berth cabin but she had counted on privacy and had seen the rucksacks and stuffed bags of the other travelers and panicked. She hated the thought of being forced to sleep on this little shelf in a cupboard with three others. She had demanded a single cabin. "For your sole use," the purser had said, handing her a new coupon in grudging annoyance and suspicion, believing her to be preparing a corner for a pickup. But she had gone back and sat up the whole night in the four-berth cabin with the hitchhikers, smoking pot and haranguing them about Trotsky, and in the end she never used the expensive single cabin except to wash her face and check her disguise. She saw how the preposterous expense of the two cabins had shown her in safety how she only needed one; and she laughed at the money it was costing her to learn poverty.

Then there was Greenstain—only an Arab would misspell his own alias—with large pale eyes and a fish's lips, who had met her in the warehouse and touched her as he spoke, as if tracing out the words on her arm. His staring made him seem cross-eyed, and his lemon-shaped face, unnaturally smooth, frightened her. He had the infuriating manner that dull leering men occasionally practiced on her—repeating what she had said and giving it a salacious twang. "What have you got for me?" she said, and Greenstain wet his lips and replied, "What have you got for me?" Then she said, "Show me," and he said the same, twisting it to make it the gross appeal in a stupid courtship. He had spit in the corners of his mouth and wouldn't stop touching her arm. She was afraid, he was scaring her intentionally, and it was much worse than deceiving the immigration officers— even the friendly Dutch ones with their ropes of silver braid—because she was alone with Greenstain in that empty warehouse. He was pretending to be sly and he made her understand, using his pale eyes and greedy mouth, that he could kill her and take the money he

knew she was carrying. At last, he led her to a corner
of the warehouse and showed her the trunks. He
kicked one open and took out a gun and pointed it at
her and cackled, working his jaws like a barracuda.
She paid—the first of the proceeds from *Tea for
Three*. Greenstain counted the money, then examined each note, making her wait while he checked
the bundle for forgeries. He gave her an absurd
handwritten receipt with the name of the London
agent and took her outside. It was dark; the canal
lapped against the quayside. Greenstain belched,
then embraced her, and she looked up and in panic
memorized a word painted on the warehouse,
Maatschappij, and wondered how it was pronounced.
Greenstain ran his hands down her body and then
jumped away. For a moment she thought he might
shout. She saw him nod; he broke into gagging
laughter. "A girl!" he cried. "You are a girl!" He
pushed her lightly. Uninterested sexually, he became
almost kind, and later on the way back to The Hook
of Holland he pointed out the wartime bunkers and,
in a settlement of houses, a still solitary windmill.

Theater: Rotterdam, the deal with Greenstain, the
male disguise. Then, months later, it all went dis-
astrously wrong—no trunks, no arms, excuses from
the agent, and silence. Sweeney said, "You boobed."
Nothing was delivered and she was expelled for the
failure. She was disappointed, but she had felt safe
until that night after the play, when the American
had said, "Let me guess your passport number." She
saw how dangerously near she was to being exposed.
All the effort, all the lies and then—but she believed
it was another lie designed to scare her off—she heard
that Weech, the London agent with the trunks, had
been killed.

The November darkness enclosed Deptford; she
was anyone in the twilight, trudging home. Ahead,
halfway down the crescent, she saw the house. She
snapped open her handbag and checked her face in
the little mirror; she fixed her bite; she walked to the
gate and nudged it open with her knee.

*

Hello, more decay—the place was a shambles. Judging by the decrepit houses he had seen from the top deck of the Number One bus, it was already happening. He got off: the street stank. Perhaps it originated here, the crack that had started the slump, and was eating its way to the city, shriveling everything in its path. The sewers smelled as if they'd burst, the very bricks looked friable, and where was all that smoke coming from? It raked his eyes and made a fog of the twilight, so dense the weak light made everything small and gave the limpers on the street wraithlike, almost ghostly proportions.

He was fascinated by it. It was as if he were seeing the first evidence of the coming quake, the proof that he had been right all along. And how subtle it was! He had always thought it would be a terrible crash, thunder and lightning, screams, people holding their heads, and great steaming pits appearing all over London; buildings becoming dust and the city slipping sideways. A tremendous seizure, striking at the foundations and buckling the whole anthill from its sewers to its ramparts. Food disappearing from the shops and small children chewing their chinstraps, and ragged Londoners crowding the streets in panic, breaking his windows on Volta Road and howling at him. Confusion!

No: that was fancy's need for theater, the mind's idle picture, inaccuracy's enlargement. Catastrophe was like this, it was this—smoke, silence, emptiness and slow decay, an imperceptible leaching that was a strong smell long before it was a calamity. The knotting of the city's innards into dead hanks, not combustion, but blockage, the slowest cruelest death. And if he had not known in advance that it was going to happen he might have missed it, like an eclipse of the sun on a cloudy day. He might have thought a cup final had emptied the streets, and as for the aroma of ruin—that someone had left the lid off his overflowing dustbin or allowed his dog to foul the footpath, nothing more. But he knew the stink and smoke was calamitous, and he felt—as he made his way along the Deptford back streets—like an explorer who, having made his shocking discovery in the strange place, looks for confirmation and realizes that he is the sole witness: he will not be believed. It was an intensification of a feeling he'd had often this year, that he was the only one who knew how the country was dying, who saw its bricks crazing, its fate (as he had just read) written in blood on the station wall, ARSENAL RULE—he understood the warning. The message was everywhere, but it was ignored. He alone saw it and bore it as if it were a sorrowful secret, like the memory of his dead child. They were smiling in the High Road, in the lights from the fish-and-chip shop, beefy laborers turned to wraiths in fog that was smoke, and banging carelessly into public houses. They didn't know; ignorance was part of the disease, because the illness would kill them before they understood it was fatal.

He adjusted his bowler hat and swung his briefcase into his free hand, treading an unvarying track, as if at the edge of a precipice. He would be late for his tea, and Norah might be upset. But the fellow didn't answer his phone and didn't reply to letters—very naughty—and how else was one to put a flea in his ear? It was a curious address, and he got a further shock when he saw it in the ragged yellow lamplight, for it was how Volta Road would look when the disaster crept farther south. He looked up the road into the future.

*

She had entered by the back door with Brodie's key, and finding no one at home, had gone upstairs to look at her painting. She sat and studied it with gluttonous interest, more than she had ever summoned at home, where most of her father's collection was stacked against the wall. She had never guessed how valuable the Rogier self-portrait was until it was stolen—the newspapers had given it an extraordinary price. A lovely piece, but awfully cluttered—a very busy painting—and yet the face, the posture, the hands, the bones beneath that flesh: superb. She thought: But I would have stolen a Watteau; and then: Self-portraits always show wounded men and broken promises, not living men but dying men, the poor artist with his nose against a mirror.

She plumped the Indian cushions and lay on the floor. The theft had made a greater claim on her imagination than possession had ever done. And she liked the secrecy of this visit, prowling to the top floor and closing the curtains in the house at the margin of the city—a hide-out. It seemed to her as if she were the thief, the knowledgeable accomplice; and this was her prize. Risking her reputation, her great name, she had stolen the painting. She smiled at the wounded Fleming and felt great satisfaction, the sense of being an outlaw. And she toyed with the thought that she was resident here. This was her hidden house, her room, her loot. Here she was safe with all her secrets. The painting shimmered from the closet.

She tapped a spot of snuff onto the back of her hand. She raised it to inhale and the doorbell rang. Parting the curtains and peering down she saw a shadowy visitor, a woman, plainly dressed in an old coat and gazing up the street. She considered her snuff, then whistled it up her nose. Again, the bell. But it was her house, her painting. On the way downstairs she thought of moving in, finding a room for Mrs. Pount and having stationery printed. She opened the door, delighted to be given a chance to test her ownership.

"Yes?"

She saw the woman falter.

"What is it?"

"Jumble," said the woman. "I'm collecting for the church sale. It's on Saturday."

"Come in. I'm sure we have something for you."

Lady Arrow led her through the parlor and down the hall to the kitchen, saying, "I think it's such a splendid idea to have jumble sales. Share things out— so many people throw away perfectly lovely toast racks and napkin rings. I know my friends go all over London in search of good jumble. Here, have a seat. "I'll beaver around upstairs."

"Them tea towels would do me."

"A wedding present, I'm afraid," said Lady Arrow. She directed the woman back to the parlor and hurried upstairs to a bedroom, the one just off the landing. The bed, a mattress on the floor, was a tangle of sheets and blankets, and there were children's posters on the wall. She pulled out a drawer: rags. In the bottom drawer she found an assortment of alarm clocks and lengths of wire. She selected a clock and was on her way downstairs when the doorbell rang again.

"I say, will you see who that is?" she called, and she thought: What a farce—what a lark! She would move here, Mrs. Pount would get used to it. She heard the woman's footsteps, the door opening, the greetings. She listened on the landing.

"Yes, can I help you?" It was the woman's voice, and for a long moment there was no reply. Then a man's voice sounded, polite astonishment. But his surprised intake of air, that gasp, had traveled up the stairwell to her.

"Excuse me, is that you, Miss Nightwing?"

"Mister Gawber."

The clock in Lady Arrow's hand started to tick. She threw it hard against the wall and descended the stairs, swearing under her breath. She found Mr. Gawber and Araba in the parlor. They looked up when she entered, and masking his surprise with a smile, Mr. Gawber stood and gave a jaunty salute. Araba had removed her head scarf and changed her bite; but she said nothing. Lady Arrow thought the actress looked very gloomy and embarrassed.

Finally, Araba said, "Let's apologize and say nothing more. I hate explanations."

"Let's talk about *Peter Pan*," said Lady Arrow.

"Yes," said Mr. Gawber. "I must say, we're all looking forward to it. Norah's terribly keen."

"I'll send you tickets," said Araba.

"Tea?" said Lady Arrow.

"I was just leaving," said Araba.

"My tea will be waiting at home," said Mr. Gawber.

"I won't keep you," said Lady Arrow.

At the door Araba said, "I've got just the part for you, Susannah."

"Super," said Lady Arrow. "Now you know where to find me." She shut the door triumphantly, waited ten more minutes, and went back to Hill Street.

21

SHE HAD SAID—painfully and barely moving her swollen lips—"I don't want to talk about it now," and he kissed her again. Pity or love, it didn't matter; he saw her wounded and he was aroused, almost passionate. He touched her, felt for her breasts. She sucked air and her ribs lifted his hand. She was hysterical—she screamed; then she was the opposite, numbed and speechless. Her fright trembled away, and when he put her to bed she fell asleep at once. It was the child, Jason, whom he had difficulty in calming, but he dropped off in Hood's arms. He put him in the cot and went into the other room to lie beside her. Anger kept him awake; he blamed himself for her bruises and claw marks and he was disturbed by the fear that he could kill them for it—find the bastards and beat them to a pulp.

She had been beaten. He expected her to rebel, but she had no particular anger. She was forlorn, alone; the assault saddened her, like a reminder she was trapped—as if she'd broken her head against her own cage. She didn't cry—she wasn't even frightened. The violence that would have terrified another woman only weighted her with bruises and made her frail, brightened her eyes with fever; and lying next to her —it surprised him again—he felt her nakedness heating him, her body hot from her wounds. Now, sleeping, she was a small injured girl; but she burned against him, denying him rest.

In the black hours of the morning—around three— he knew he must roll a pill or stay awake cursing. He felt for his pouch and rolled the opium pill in the dark, then went to the bathroom for a glass of water to wash it down. Standing there in front of the sink he saw his reflection in the mirror and in his eyes those narrow crescents of yellow on the whites, the malarial stain, a mark of Hué. He swallowed the pill and closed his eyes and he was gliding from an inlet on the Perfume River, a rudder stick crooked under his arm, and in the bow of the sampan a Vietnamese girl knelt, the moon shining on her tight flank, her black mane of hair swaying as she worked with the small flame. Then she tossed her hair and smiled and passed him the pipe. It was a perfect memory: his mind had simplified the past, selected from it, and prettied it by making it whole. Twenty nights on the river had become one.

Yet he could not think of the past without embarrassment. It was primitive, mostly error or failure, and though the man in the boat had his name, it was another man, one he had grown to mistrust. So memory itself, that inaccurate glimpse of the past, he avoided or tried to suppress: he hated its futility.

He shut his eyes and saw the future. His mind plunged ahead in time, the landscape altered, his own figure dwindled. The future, always the future—why else would one fight? Memory was retreat. He rehearsed what was in store for him—not a matter of days or a month, but years and more, decades, and then he saw the same solitary man, slightly hunched, white-haired, in fading clothes, treading the dust in some tropical place, making his way in dazzling sunlight. It was what he wished to see. He closed his eyes and saw this old man who had cut himself off and chosen to end his life here, in the simplest way; a man with no country, unknown among strangers, who had rid himself of his family and who, at that distance, had fallen silent and ceased to act. A calm fugitive: he ridiculed the notion of exile—in this world there was no exile for an American.

Hood's reflections were not memory but this modest vision he hoped was prophecy—as all truth was prophetic—and though at first he felt it was the effect of his drugs (the narcotic flash, the sight of himself in the future walking up and down in Asia), the process became habit. He was older, in a palmy place as dense as Guatemala, never speaking; but the road was always the same, the foliage a deep green, and the blurred figures ignored him and passed by, water carriers, naked children, slow bulls. To live abroad was to create a mythology about yourself, more than a new personality—a liberating fantasy you could believe in, a new world. He could only live in a country where he was willing to die, and it sometimes chilled him to think that he might die here, in this strangely lighted city, on this watery island. He did not want to be known or mourned; he wished only to act and then vanish, to choose his own grave site. And it troubled him to think that the single reason he was in bed with this woman was that he had killed her husband. But who was that? Who killed him? The murderer was a man he scarcely knew.

In the morning Lorna was groggy. Rather than wake her he gave the child breakfast and took him to school.

"Are you my daddy now?" asked Jason, taking Hood's hand at the end of the road. The faithless child, he thought; he would go with anyone. But Hood couldn't blame him; the child's safety lay in this deceit—perhaps he saw it as the only way of crossing the road.

Hood said, "Do you want me to be?"

"No." And after a while he added, "My real daddy's coming back."

Hood held the child's hand, saying nothing.

"He'll duff you up when he comes back. My daddy's a good fighter."

Crossing the road, Jason tightened his grip, and he did not release it on the other side. Somehow he knew the terrifying fact without knowing any of the words.

At the school gate a group of mothers stood chatting in an oblong of sunshine. They dropped their voices when Hood approached, and he could see them avoiding meeting his eyes. They were young, several were pretty, and they looked as if they were dressed for more than a trip to the school. Jason yelled and ran to join his friends. Hood noticed how his presence had subdued the group, made the women self-conscious, awkward, with a kind of pedestrian envy and suspicion.

Hood said sharply, "Hi, sweetheart!"

They looked away. The teacher came out, an older woman in a smock, fussing with a toy, waving the mothers aside and calling the children by name. Hood was the first to leave. He had gone some distance down the road when he turned and saw them all, staring at him. He knew what they were saying: a new member of the family, her lover—or more likely, the fucker.

He got back to the house to find her up, and now he saw the disorder he had missed the night before— an ashtray tipped over, a smashed lamp, a buckled chair leg, and the carpet littered with glass shards and cigarette butts. Lorna was feebly sweeping the hallway.

"Have you seen upstairs?" she said. "I told them I didn't have the key, so they broke down the door of the spare room, where the stuff was. That's what did it—they saw it was empty. Willy starts screaming at me. The other one—I don't know his name—he done his nut. He slaps me."

"I'll kill them for this," said Hood through his teeth.

"Leave me out of it. I don't want trouble." She sighed and said bitterly, "I thought when Ron copped it I was free. No more fights, no more worrying about the police. I can live, I thought. Then this. The fuckers."

"Were they looking for guns?"

"What guns? They asked about you. They got really ugly—who are you? What do you do? Who do you work for? That kind of thing."

"And you didn't tell them anything?" He was almost incredulous, but he believed, and he was ashamed.

"Nothing," she said; she smiled at the memory of it. "Because I knew they were just trying it on, testing me like. I mean, the fuckers know you, so why are they asking all these questions? Play dumb—that's what Ron used to say—pretend like you don't even speak English." She winced and picked up the broom, and beginning to sweep she said, "Well, it didn't cut no ice. One of them grabs me—twisting me arm—and the other one starts slapping me. And Willy, he's just standing there whistling out the window."

"They'll be sorry." Hood paced the room.

"I don't know why I didn't come out with it and tell them you had all that stuff."

"Why didn't you?"

"Because I knew what they'd do. You think I'm stupid? I'm used to this. Me, they'd only slap me around—I wasn't afraid, I wasn't even mad. That's the way they are—and they don't kill women." She stared at him. "But they would have killed you."

"So you saved my life," said Hood.

"But later, after they left, I thought they might have got you. I was frantic, and I almost cried when I saw you last night." She was silent a moment, then she said abruptly, "They'll be back."

"Not if I nail them first," he said.

"They're probably looking for you now," she said. "Just leave me out of it. They're the worst fuckers—they're murderers."

"I've ruined your life," he said, and he wanted her to believe it, to take his word for it without asking him how.

She came over to him and touched his face. "No," she said. "You're good. You made me happy. I don't even know you, but I almost love you." She held him and said, "Sometimes I think everything you say is a lie. I don't care about that. If you have to lie to make me happy, go ahead—tell me lies. I don't want to know the truth if it's just going to spoil everything."

He was moved by her complete surrender; she knew nothing, and yet without belief she trusted him. They were strangers, joined by a corpse: a dead man's family. But the pity had been refined; she might not know him, but he knew her, and he feared that it would go further, to the narrowing sympathy that would deny him his future. She had been lost. He had found her, but now he saw he could only save her by sacrificing himself; that love was all loss, an early death. Yet he could not help what he had felt when he saw her so badly beaten—passion, or blunter still, a kind of lust at seeing her so wounded. Even now, holding her, feeling her frailty, he was heated, and he wanted to hurry her upstairs and make love to her.

She said, "I don't care what you do to those fuckers. But don't leave me—please."

"Don't say please."

"Last night you called me love," she said. "Say it again."

He looked down at her. "You say I lie."

"I want you to lie!"

He kissed her lightly, but as he started to speak, the doorbell rang.

"It's them," she said, and tore herself away, her eyes flashing in fear.

"Go upstairs," he said. "I'll see to them."

He got a knife from the kitchen, but on his way to the door he threw it down in disgust. It clattered on the floor and was still spinning as he dragged the door open. He sighed and dropped his arms.

"Yeah, sorry to bother you," said Murf, who was tugging at his earring with one hand and pushing at his other ear. He was nervous; the quack was in his voice. He tried to laugh. "I hope you wasn't on the job."

"Come in."

"The thing is, she's back," he said, stepping in and smoothing his ears with both hands. It occurred to Hood that this was a variation of the gesture balding men usually made with their hair, the pushing and smoothing. "The old girl—that filthy great giant,

Brodie's mate. I was having a kip, see, and I heard her come in. I gets behind the door and she sneaks around, like. I didn't know what to do, so I come over here. You want me to put the wind up?"

"Where's Mayo?"

"Out with Brodie. Either in Kilburn or maybe shopping. I don't know. They took the van."

"Maybe the offensive," said Hood, smiling.

"Not a chance," said Murf. "Like Mayo told me straight. You're going to do it now, the English offensive—you're the guv." He grinned and widened his eyes and said, "Yeah, arsenal rule!"

"So the secret's out."

"That's why I got worried. The old girl might find something and rumble us."

Hood said suddenly, "Murf, remember those guys that jumped me at the dog track?"

"The villains. Shorty and them."

"Who are they?"

"Never seen them before."

"But you can find out. They're agents—fences."

"Arfa might know."

"Go ask him," said Hood. "The guy's name is Willy Rutter. There are some others, but Rutter's the one I want. He must live around here. I want to catch him at home."

"I'll smash on Arfa's door," said Murf. "But what about the old girl?" He guffawed and showed his teeth. "Maybe she wants me to raise her."

"Forget it. Find out about Rutter."

When Murf had gone, Hood went upstairs and told Lorna who it was. Lorna lay on the bed, stiffly crouched, hugging her stomach; but hearing there was no danger, she stretched and relaxed and said, "Sit beside me."

He sat on the edge of the bed and pushed her hair out of her eyes.

"Tell me a lie."

"Okay," he said. "I love you."

"Tell the truth," she said impatiently, getting up on one elbow.

He said, "I don't love you."

She fell back. He thought she was pouting until he realized her lips were swollen that way from a slap. She said, "I don't care if you don't love me. Anyway, everyone says it, so it's just another lie. I know you like me, or else why would you stick with me?" She smiled slowly. "And I know something else."

"What is it?" He knew an instant of panic.

She said, "You're not a fucker."

"But all men are fuckers—that's what you said."

"Not you." She drew him down, hugging him and moving her face against his. And as she did he felt his cheeks grow wet, his eyes sting, but it was her tears trickling into his eyes. She was crying softly, and though she tried to control it he could hear the groan in her throat and feel the convulsion; she was sobbing. "Don't leave me," she said and held his arms tightly —so tight he felt his wrists tingle and go numb. The girl in her wept, but a woman's strength held him. "Please don't leave me—please, please, please!"

He thought: Yes, but there is something to do. He was crowded, haunted by the men who had wounded her. The punishment he planned lingered in his mind —that remained, an intrusion between their bodies as obvious as her wounds. The thought prevented him from responding to her plea, but he saw an end to it. He would get them and be finished—discard everything, abandon the house on Albacore Crescent, and begin with her. He had enough hope for her, and there was freedom in that hope. Ridding her life of those bastards would rid him of that part of his own past that now seemed a moment of uncontrolled fury, when murdering her husband he had murdered the worst in himself. He embraced her and kissed her and she sobbed, but he felt nothing except an impulse to find Rutter and hammer him. Kill that lurking rival.

She was still pleading, but her mouth was against his neck and he heard nothing.

"We can't stay here," he said at last. "Murf's coming back."

Murf arrived an hour later with Arfa Muncie. Seeing Lorna's bruises, Murf said, "Hey, who done you?" Then he changed the subject, perhaps suspecting that

Hood might have beaten her. Muncie looked alarmed; he was silent and eyed Hood carefully as if waiting for a signal to run. But Hood saw how rattled Muncie was (he was picking up Lorna's china dolls and examining their seals, and testing the firmness of chairs: the junk dealer's nervous reflex), and he deliberately put him at his ease, slapped him on the back—Muncie jumped—and said casually, "Now where does our friend live?"

"I can show you," said Muncie. "I mean, out the window."

"So he's that close?"

"No, Millwall. But you can see it from here," said Muncie, and he explained to Lorna, "See, I know these here houses. I do a lot of clearing. I never cleared this one as such, but blimey, some of the old boys around here got some great stuff for me shop. Victoriana like. Frames and that. Mirrors. Leaded windows. I flog them in the West End. That fireplace," he went on, hurrying across the room and rapping his knuckles on it in approval. "Don't look like much but you could dismantle it easy. I'd give you a good price and hump it up to the King's Road. Up there this thing's a antique. They pay a tenner for a quid's worth of grotty glassware."

Lorna shrugged and said, "You're welcome to it. Take the whole fucking lot."

"I could give you a estimate," said Muncie uneasily. He spoke to Hood. "I do valuations."

"The great Arfa. He's a thief," said Murf, pronouncing it *feef*, "but he knows his way around. Eh, Arfa?"

"Yeah. Can we go upstairs? I'll show you the place."

Hood said to Lorna, "Do you know where Rutter lives now?"

"No," she said. "All I have is the fucker's phone number."

"Stay here, honey. We'll be right down."

She said, "It's time to pick up Jason. Maybe I'll see you."

They climbed the stairs and trooped down the hall to the back room. The broken door sagged on its hinges. Murf said, "Someone give that bugger a good kick and all. Think you can flog it, Arfa? It's a antique. Heh-heh."

Muncie ignored him. He shuffled to the north window and pointed, saying, "He's over there."

Through the river haze that hung beyond the funnels of the power station and the cranes, and gave the distant buildings the look of thunderclouds in an old etching, receding into browner air and finally a gray emptiness—any London view was like a view from an island: it might have been the sea way out there, it was so flat and featureless—were more cranes, the towers of a housing estate, slate rooftops, and one squat black church steeple. The heavy layer of air pressed the low skyline and made it look as if it had just collapsed and was smoldering. Hood followed Muncie's finger, from island to island, but that was a ruined island, dead under its own stifling dust, and all the visible brickwork was dark, reddened by dampness and age. Apart from the church steeple there was nothing that held the eye, nothing to seize; and watching, Hood had the illusion of it slipping from focus, sailing away, becoming mist.

"Millwall," said Muncie, tapping the glass.

"It looks like an island," said Hood.

"It *is* an island," said Murf. "Isle of Dogs. I wouldn't live there for anything."

"That's where Rutter lives," said Muncie. "I could tell you where his boozer is, but you don't want to go there. The Swan, up Limehouse."

"Diabolical," said Murf.

"Does Rutter know you?" said Hood.

Muncie pulled his sleeve across his nose. "No," he said. He blinked. "He might have heard of me."

"The great Arfa," said Murf, grinning.

"But he knows Murf," said Hood.

"So Murf was telling me," said Muncie. "He was going to slip him a blade. That's what he said."

"I should have stuck him and all," said Murf, with a show of bravado. "I could have. A real spill. Right in the chops." He danced across the room pretending to hold a knife against an invisible throat.

"Widdy-widdy boom!" he said, thrusting with his hand. "So long, Willy-baby."

"Sure," said Hood. "Look, Muncie, I want you to be our advance man."

Muncie glanced nervously at Murf. "I don't want to get involved."

Murf made a face.

"Anyway, I'm tied up."

"The great Arfa," said Murf.

"How would you like him to lean on you?" Muncie whined.

"Widdy *boom!*" said Murf, flailing his arms, making the stabbing gesture again. He laughed in Muncie's face.

"You don't have to get involved," said Hood quietly.

"What do I do then?"

"Just find out if he's at home," said Hood. "Show us the house. That's all. We'll do the rest."

"It's simple—suss it out," said Murf. "After we take care of the geezer you can go clear out his house. Don't have to do no estimates. Get some nice stuff. Chairs and shit. Eh, Arfa?" Murf elbowed him companionably, rocking him sideways, but Muncie's expression remained solemn. He came to rest, upright again, and frowned with worry.

"He's tough is Rutter," said Arfa, pronouncing it *Ruh-uh*. "He's killed blokes and all."

"Like who?" said Murf, mocking. "Huh, Arfa?"

Hood said, "Anyone we know?"

Muncie's eyes widened and he pointed to the floor. "Yeah," he said in a whisper. "Downstairs. Her old man!"

22

SHADOW AND MIST mingled to make night in the late afternoon. Hood had said they should wait until it was dark, but darkness was not long in coming that November day. They took a bus to Greenwich, and out the side window Hood saw the haze thicken by the minute, the dense air brimming in the streets and rising up the flat-fronted houses. Walking to the tunnel entrance—a Victorian brick dome propped at the edge of the embankment—Hood looked across the river. There were not even shadows in Millwall, only a few twinkling lights and one feeble beacon. Here, some trees were fretting by the riverside, but over there—offshore—it was as if the island he had seen earlier had sunk and now, where it had been, stray boats were making distress signals. No church, no cranes, no buildings, not even mist; and though the river shimmered with snakes of light it too was empty.

"In here," said Muncie, and led them past the clanking elevator cage and down the circular stairwell to the tunnel under the Thames. It was the sort of glazed endless corridor Hood had seen when he was high, a tube of echoing tiles, without doors or windows, stretching away, and ringing with the footsteps of people he could not see. Voices chimed from the walls and his own footsteps gulped. Murf stopped once to write MILLWALL WANK—ARSENAL RULE.

On the far side of the river they emerged from the stairwell and its stink of urine and chalk to a dark muddy garden and a maze of earthworks. Muncie hurried into the road, to Rutter's; Hood and Murf sat on a bench in the little park. Greenwich, banked with lights, lay across the water, the Royal Naval College

rising from the walkway to trees and the turrets of the
Observatory, a symmetry of floodlit stone with its
lovely proportions reflected intact in the water, crusted
with a blaze of lights. To the right were the masts and
spars of the *Cutty Sark,* simulating dead trees, and
farther over the blacker precincts of Deptford—more
islands.

Hood pointed to the Naval College, which the odd
light and the falling mist gilded. He said, "That's a
beautiful building."

"Beautyful," said Murf. "Go like anything."

For a moment, Hood thought Murf was agreeing.
Then he saw how the building lighted the smile of excitement on Murf's face—an eagerness to destroy:
Murf was imagining blowing it up. Without saying
why, Hood began telling Murf about Verloc, as he had
once told Lorna—how the ponderous man in the overcoat had tried to blow up the Observatory, how he
had blown his young brother-in-law to bits. And as he
told it he reflected that the incident had no complexity:
the men had the minds of children; and the child
Stevie, who was wise, was inarticulate, ineffectual. It
was a simple tale, a shadowy outrage, a bout of madness. It started, it squawked, it was gone; a story of
self-destruction.

Murf listened, and Hood could see the Naval College exploding on his eyes. He tugged his earring and
said, "Provo?"

"Verloc?" said Hood. "No."

"No wonder he fucked it up." Murf sang, keeping
the tune in his nose. "Arfa's taking his time." He
laughed. "He's scared, he is. Thinks he's going to get
rompered." Murf sang again, stamping when he said
boom, then said, "Yeah, I should have stuck the
geezer and all."

"Look," said Hood. A low black boat was going
past, almost without a sound. It plowed the water, a
creeping shadow with lanterns on its bulkheads, and
behind it a laden barge, like a snooping whale. There
was a look of funereal stealth about it, and the small
voice that carried from the hidden deck muttered, em-
phasizing the immensity of water. It passed out of

sight and then waves began beating the river wall like an eruption of surf. The backwash made the reflections of the Greenwich lights dance in eddies, like wind through fire, feeding the blaze and making separate flames leap all over the river's surface.

Murf said, "What's that?"

A crackle, like sticks of dry kindling coming alight. Murf bowed his head to listen, but the sound was familiar to Hood. It was rain, sweeping from the Greenwich side of the river, crackling towards them, making the surface flames small and numerous. They heard it clearly before it descended on them a moment later, like the tropical rain that had surrounded Hood with this simulation of burning—a murmur from Vietnam, pattering on leaves before it drenched him, a few warning drops, then a downpour.

"We'll have to sit it out," said Hood, "or Muncie won't find us."

"We'll get soaked." Murf stood up, as if to avoid it, and walking up and down the narrow promenade next to the iron guardrail he beat his hands on his streaming coat and shouted into the storm, "Hey Arfa! Let's go, mate—stop wanking!"

Now Greenwich and all its lights were filtered through the drizzle, and as the rain grew heavier the opposite bank began to recede, losing its contours; the storm wrenched the land away by blending it with the night sky, and it diffused the lights so they matched their spangled reflections in the river.

Filfy wevva, Murf was saying, as he returned to the bench and put his collar up. The two crouched there, like wet roosting crows in their black coats, watching the river's changing dazzle, saying nothing more. For Hood, the time moved with the pace of the rain, slowly as it dripped and more quickly when the wind sprang up and blew it harder into his face. And it seemed to him as if his life was not made of action, but an absence of it, this waiting at a river's edge in rain that stopped him and moved the river.

Raising his voice against the wind, Murf said, "But I'm glad it's you."

"What do you mean?"

"This fucking offensive. You're the guv'nor now. I'm dead glad it's you." He screamed impatiently, "*Arfa!*"

Hood said, "I'm the guv'nor all right."

Murf turned his dripping face to Hood's and with hoarse enthusiasm said, "Give it to 'em, son."

"One villain at a time," said Hood. He heard a muffled cry and splashing feet and saw Muncie running clumsily from the far end of the park. "There he is."

"The wanker," said Murf. He stood up and danced in the downpour. "Hey, Arfa!"

Muncie was out of breath, his hair was plastered flat to the top of his head and hung in strings at his ears. He gasped and wiped his face on his sleeve, then said, "I seen him go in. But he's a crafty bastard. He parks his motor up the road and sneaks in by the back way. The house was dark before he come, so he must be alone."

"He doesn't travel alone," said Hood.

"Well, he ain't traveling, is he?" said Muncie, backing away slightly as if expecting Hood to hit him for contradicting him.

"Good thinking," said Murf. He laughed loudly. "The great Arfa."

"Let's go," said Hood.

They crossed the small park and entered the road, walking east, past the abandoned earthworks and a high wooden fence marked with Millwall slogans and swaying in the storm. The old church looked only blacker in its windy corner. Up another road, past more temporary fences; but nothing showed above the fences—here there were no buildings, and the streetlights illuminated only the broken cobbles of the road and the holes filling with rainwater. It looked like the newest ruin, knocked sideways and devastated, and not a soul to be seen: a glimpse of the end.

A bus lumbered past, lighted but empty, and pitching in the uneven road. It appeared from the darkness at one turning and entered the darkness beyond the last streetlamp. They walked up the street that ran along the eastern margin of Millwall, and then they saw—on a side street and set back—a terrace row of four bow-fronted houses. Somehow, these houses had been spared the destruction that was obvious around them. They stood alone on the derelict road, another island of damp eroded walls in a flat sea of rubble.

"The one with the light," said Muncie. He hunched and indicated the house, concealing his pointing finger with the flap of his jacket, as if afraid of being seen. "Right," he said. "Cheers."

"Where you going, Arfa?"

"Out of this filthy rain."

"You're already wet, you silly bastard."

But Muncie was running, stamping in the puddles. He vanished behind a fence, fleeing in the direction of Greenwich.

"The great Arfa."

"Wait here," said Hood. "I'm doing this alone."

"Let me come wif you."

"Sorry. I need you here. If anyone goes in after me, you thump him."

"Take this." Murf jerked the knife out of his sheath and handed it to Hood. "Stick the bugger. Like I should have."

Hood slipped the knife into his pocket and walked towards the house, feeling safely hidden by the driving rain. He detoured around the lighted front window and ducked down the side entrance to the rear of the house. He climbed a wobbly fence and found himself in a dark back garden, at the bottom of which was a high wall. A ladder in the weeds tripped him, and he paused and heard a boat's thudding hoot and the water's splash, and he smelled the oily air; the river lay just behind the wall, and now—his eyes growing accustomed to the dark—he saw a steel door in the bricks. The entrance was wide enough to take crates from a boat moored on the other side, Rutter's own quay.

He walked over to the house and tried the door, then raised himself for a look through the window. Locked and black; but he wouldn't kick the door down, he didn't want to give Rutter time to re-

spond. He made his way to the front of the house.
Ring the bell and wade in, he thought; give him the
chance he'd given Lorna. He waited, fingering Murf's
knife. The light burned in the front window, but the
curtains were drawn. Holding himself against the
house he sidled to the window, and easing himself
near he peered through a slit in the curtains. He
sipped air and looked again.

In a chair drawn up to an electric fire, and still in
his raincoat, was Sweeney. The man sat clutching a
drink against his chest with his mutilated hand. He
frowned and sat up, finished his drink, then stared
into the empty glass. Bastard, thought Hood. He
trembled and fought an urge to break in and kill him.
Sweeney! But another thought cautioned him, and he
slipped away.

*

"—Because it wasn't Rutter," Hood was saying on
the way back, in the echoing footway tunnel under
the river.

"Bloody Arfa," said Murf. He kicked the tunnel
floor. "But who was it?"

"Don't ask me," said Hood angrily, his voice ringing on the wall. "I don't know these creeps."

"You should have stuck him, just for the hell of it,"
said Murf. He saw Hood's rage and seemed anxious
to calm him.

"I want to get the right man," said Hood.

"Maybe it was the geezer you seen."

"Maybe," said Hood. "There's plenty of time."

"But where's Rutter?"

Hood said, "That's the funny part. He's probably
out looking for me."

"Eyes front," said Murf. "It's Bill."

A policeman in a helmet and gleaming rain cape
was coming towards them, wheeling his bicycle
through the tunnel.

"Nice old push-bike you got there," said Murf, and
grinned, showing the scowling policeman the stained
pegs of his teeth.

23

THE HOUSE ON Albacore Crescent was lighted; its plump stove-shaped front, with the windows' brightness sloping across the leafless hedge, had never looked safer or more snug, and the glow on the curtain folds gave it a stove's warm flicker. In the rising curve of the road those bright ledges attracted him; then the instant moved and he remembered he lived there. All the rest of London drifted on the shallow swell of night, hidden places that were only inaccessible-sounding names, like Elmer's End and the Isle of Dogs; but the house was secure, and the enlarging light gave it a cheerful fortified look in the darkened road.

He had just left Lorna's with Murf. After his night and day there, in the locked house where she sat like a child baffled by the pain of a nightmare; and after that glimpse of Sweeney at Rutter's in the bare room of dead air set in a reach of the river—those island prisons—he was astonished to return to his own house, which he had convinced himself was another uncertain island, and find Mayo in an apron cutting vegetables for a stew and Brodie lying in front of the television set—home! It was a cozy picture composed of safety and warmth, the stewpot bubbling on the stove, the television's blue hum, the gas fire's simmering. He had not noticed before how they were protected, and though he could see Lorna's from his upper window her house was an island as shadowy as Millwall, where she crouched, a castaway with her own wreckage. The last thing she had said to him was, "Now I'm going to give the fuckers their money back." He couldn't help her that way anymore. Upstairs, the man in the painting stared, and in another room the small arsenal was stacked; but these were props for another play. Downstairs, a more ordinary drama met his eye. He came in with Murf, and entering like laborers after a long day's work they shouted, "It's only us!" Murf looked around and said, "Now, where's me slippers and me pipe."

Murf kicked off his wet shoes and sat on the sofa with his legs outstretched. He squinted at the television and tapping his stash began making a joint.

"Where you been?" Brodie rolled sideways and screwed up her face for the reply.

"Hanging out." Murf lit the cigarette and inhaled. He passed it to her. "Anything on?"

"Nah." She puffed and winced at the smoke.

Hood was at the doorway, smiling at the little scene: Murf slumped in the chair, sucking at the joint, Brodie on the floor with her chin in her hands, her thin jersey riding up her bony back. It was a zone of complete calm, warmed by the sizzle and smell of the frying meat from the kitchen. Murf and Brodie's postures gave it a look of slatternly innocence.

"Have a seat, guv. It's lovely in here."

"I've got to talk to Mayo."

Murf swallowed smoke. He gulped as if stifling a belch, then waved the cigarette at Hood and said, "Hit?"

"Give it to her," said Hood. He peered at Brodie. "Okay, angel? How's your tattoo?"

Brodie said, "You know what you can do."

"Shut up," said Murf, digesting more smoke. "He's just trying to be matey."

Hood left them quarreling. In the kitchen, Mayo said, "I hope you haven't eaten already. I'm making something special." She worked at the counter, cutting carrots and potatoes, and as she spoke she reached over and shook the frying pan of meat cubes.

Hood saw Murf pass the kitchen door, headed for the stairs.

"Irish stew," said Mayo. "I make it with beer."

Hood said, "How did you know I'd be here?"

"This," she said. She took a letter from her apron

pocket and handed it to him. "I knew you'd be back
to collect it. It came this afternoon—express. Looks
like money."

"You should know." He glanced at it—the return
address was indecipherable (but a London postmark:
another from Mr. Gawber?)—and stuffed it into his
pocket without opening it. He continued to watch
Mayo slicing the carrots into discs. The knife was new
and there were more, all sizes, in a rack over the
counter. He said, "A new set of knives."

"Cutlery," she said, and he wondered if she was
correcting him. "The old ones were getting dull."

"What a cozy place," he said.

Mayo grunted and added the meat to the simmering broth.

The kitchen door burst open. Murf came in, laughing crossly, high and angry at the same time, and
swinging an alarm clock in his fist. He said, "Who's
been fucking with me clocks?"

"What is it, squire?" said Hood, putting a hand on
his shoulder to quiet him.

"Me clocks," said Murf. "I always leave them a
certain way, like. But someone's been messing around
—me drawer's open, like it's been fucked about.
There's one on the floor, just flung there, and look at
this one I found on the stairs. She's bust."

Hood took it. The glass was broken, the hands
twisted. He rattled it and handed it back to Murf.
"Too bad, squire."

"But who done it, that's what I want to know."
Murf was panting. He spoke to Mayo. "Was it you?"

She laughed and swiped with her vegetable knife.
"I expect it was Brodie."

"Brodie keeps her hands off me hardware."

"An intruder," said Hood, keeping a grip on Murf,
who was making furious little leaps at Mayo.

"He probably forgot where he left it," said Mayo.
"Admit it, Murf—you pig it up there."

"I ain't lying!" cried Murf. He stepped near to her
and shook the clock in her face, making the bell rattle.

"Don't you shout at me," said Mayo, sternly, her

voice dropping into a tone of command. "I've been cooking since six o'clock while the rest of you have had a little holiday. You'll want to eat it, too, but a lot of help I get! So don't come around screaming at me." She had been holding the knife at Murf. She turned and whacked at the vegetables, making the cutting board jump. "Go away—I'm busy."

Murf's face was pained. He said, "I ain't lying, but she's laughing at me."

"What's all the noise?" Brodie hung at the door, scratching the bluebird on her upper arm.

"Yeah," said Murf, "and I expect I know who it was that fucked with me clocks. Your mate, the hairy giant."

"So what?"

"So what, she says." The clock rattled in Murf's hand.

Mayo said to Brodie, "Was someone here?"

"Maybe the lady I told you about," said Brodie casually.

"Impossible. How would she get in?"

"I gave her a key."

Hood folded his arms and whistled through his teeth.

Seeing hostility in Mayo's face, and the others' attention on her, Brodie came awake. "Hey, she got a right to be here. Hey, that's her picture upstairs, ain't it? Hey—"

"I stole that picture," said Mayo, with an owner's scream of petulance, as if the picture were being claimed by a stranger.

"But it don't belong to you," said Brodie.

"It's mine," said Mayo crisply.

Hood said, "So you gave that old bull a key?"

"She bought it off me," said Brodie. "Anyway, she's okay."

"She's okay," said Murf, shaking the broken clock at Brodie. "That's why she fucked with me clocks, right?"

"I can't cook with you in my way," Mayo said.

"You're murder," said Hood in disgust, and without another word he went into the parlor. He itemized what he owned there, the Chinese objects, the carvings, the silver. Upstairs, he looked through the closets, assessing his belongings, his suit, his stack of clothes, his consular briefcase with the blank passports and the official seal, his Burmese box of drugs. There was little more to do; there was nothing else he owned. He did not look at the painting: he coveted it too much. He went into the spare room, where the televisions were, the appliances, the crates of whisky and cigarettes, and the two locked trunks with the Dutch words lettered on them. He sat on one and considered opening it, taking a pistol and keeping it. But no—they wanted them all. They'd get them.

He sat for a long time on the arsenal, smelling the stew, hearing the clank of Mayo in the kitchen and Brodie and Murf braying at the television. It was not disorder, it was the routine of any noisy family, an ordinary racket. This was a home, a family arsenal; safety was like remoteness, disturbance was elsewhere. He took the letter out and tore it open. *You Are Invited to a Peter Pan Party.* He read down the printed sheet, and at the bottom, in a large vain hand was scrawled, *Hope you can make it. A. N.* And holding the invitation and hearing the clatter downstairs he was reproached again by his safety and pitied Lorna the more. He could stay or go—it didn't matter. By accident, in this easily besieged city, he had invented his own struggle. He deserved to fail. *It's up to you,* Sweeney had said. Yes, at last; but every delay had saved him, as if inaction itself was, like the purest assault, a celebration of security. At the center of it all, in an attitude of reflection that was indistinguishable from an attitude of pain, was a mother and child. He was stirred by fear at the thought of them, for he had acted once and only now saw the truth of it—to act was to fail.

Mayo called up the stairs: dinner was ready. She conveyed it in a tone of irritation, and he heard her nagging Brodie and Murf to set the table. He went down and took his place. Brodie banged the soup bowls on the table, Murf poured beer; Mayo carried the stew in a tureen and with a housewife's disgusted pride, grumpy satisfaction mingled with resentment, ladled it into the bowls. Hood got up and turned off the television. Brodie said, "I was watching that." Murf said, "Watch your gob." She reacted obstinately, trying to float the round end of her spoon in the stew. Mayo said, "Stop playing with your food!" There was no more talk; the gas fire sputtered in the wires of the white-hot grate.

Hood said, "We're leaving," and before anyone could respond he added, "That's right—we're all clearing out."

He ate, the others watched him, and the only sound was from the shelf, where Murf's clock had begun to tick.

Finally, Mayo said, "You're crazy."

"I'm in charge," he said, and went on eating.

"You don't know what you're doing," said Mayo.

"He's the guv," said Murf.

"What about all that stuff upstairs—those televisions, that junk?"

Hood said, "We'll leave those for the next tenant."

"I feel crappy," said Brodie. She put her spoon down and made a sour face.

"So look around," said Hood. "Find anything you consider valuable, anything with writing on it—anything that can be traced to us—and put it in the van. All the rest we'll leave."

"What a dumb idea," said Brodie. "Hey, where are we supposed to go?"

"No problem," said Hood. "You can go to Lady Arrow's."

"The hairy giant," said Murf. "She'll eat you for breakfast, sister."

"What about me?" said Mayo.

"Back to your husband, Sandra." Hood was going to say more, but Mayo blushed and stared at her hands.

"I'm sticking wif you," said Murf.

"What about Muncie?" asked Hood.

"The great Arfa," he said. "I'm wif you."

"Okay," said Hood. "Then it's settled."

"And you?" Mayo faced Hood, her eyes meeting his and then faltering.

Hood said, "I'll think of something."

Brodie looked around the table, and at the walls, the floor, the ceiling. She said, "We're not going to be here anymore."

"It's a nice place," said Murf. "You don't get hassled. You can hang out here."

Brodie shook her head. "It's kind of sad."

"I don't feel hungry," said Murf.

"I made that especially for you," said Mayo, sitting up and raising her voice, "and you're going to eat it."

"Let's not have an argument on our last night," said Hood. He picked up his glass of beer and winking at Murf he said, "This is it, then. The beginning."

"Look at him," said Brodie. She scraped her chair back and ran out of the room.

Murf followed her, his arms flapping, and then Mayo said, "You're on your own now. I don't trust you."

"Then start packing," said Hood. "You're going home."

But she refused to pack. She followed him around the house, sulking, and then complaining as he collected his artifacts from the parlor. Upstairs, he filled his suitcase, lining it quickly with his clothes, and she stood next to him, accusingly, not making any move to pack. Hood said nothing. She stamped the floor angrily, as if she were being left behind; and she threatened him, but her anger was pathetic, proof of her helplessness. Because she could not do anything more she raged; she was like a wife at the moment of a divorce she had demanded as a rash threat, seeing her mistake and knowing she is lost—too late, too late. She kept her wronged face at him. He ignored her.

"Go to hell," she said, and went to bed with unnecessary noise, punching the pillow and switching off the lights and screaming when he turned them on again. He knew she wanted a scene, something final to seal it, and he had felt—with his back to her—that she wanted to hit him. Now, deprived of argument, she lay in the bed with her head under the blanket. He saw her clearly, as he once had when she had spoken of the painting: a child who was used to getting her own way, as if being a clever daughter was an incurable condition for which the only consolation was the fatherly praise of an attentive lover.

Brodie and Murf were on the stairs, in the back room, calling to each other, banging and slamming. "Don't cry," he heard Murf saying; Brodie whimpered; Murf's coaxing turned to blame—he swore and shouted, "Shut up!"

"Tell them to stop making so much noise," Mayo sobbed. She burrowed deeper into the bedclothes.

Later, when he was in bed, there were murmurs from their room, Murf insisting and from Brodie an odd pained cry. Then a muffled kicking and the small strangled howls of the two children making love. It ended with a series of brief despairing thumps, and lying there in that large house Hood believed it was the saddest thing he had ever heard.

The next thing he knew it was morning, he was being shaken. Mayo stood over him, all teeth and hair, pulling his shoulder and saying, "It's gone—the picture's gone!"

Across the room his suitcase lay open, the clothes were strewn; his briefcase was unzipped—disorder where he had left a neat pile of his belongings.

"Who did that?" he said slowly.

"I did," said Mayo. "Well, if you didn't take it, who did?"

He got out of bed cursing, righted the suitcase and rearranged the clothes. Then he went to the cupboard and saw the empty space where the painting had been, and it was as if a hollow were carved in his stomach. He had been robbed, and on his eye a dim after-image of the loss. Feeling very tired, he sat down on the edge of the bed and put his head in his hands. He said, "When did you see it last?"

"I don't know."

He loathed her for saying that. "It must have been Brodie's friend," he said. "She was here yesterday. And it's hers."

"The bitch," said Mayo. She was packing now. She pushed clothes into her suitcase.

He was glad she wouldn't have the painting, but sorry to think that he might never see the self-portrait again. He tried to picture it, but his imagination simplified it, and all he saw was a nearly expressionless face, a gesture, obscurely lit; already it was gone. He knew he would have to see it for it to speak to him. And it was odd, because in all the estrangements he had known this was the most severe. His spirit had been thieved and in its place was fatigue. He was assailed by another feeling—unexpected—an enormous sense of himself, his own smell and weakness, an absence of light; a brown reminder of mortality. The theft was like a death, and his feeling—that shabby weight of flesh, that futile sigh that did not even have anger's strength—was close to grief.

"I knew it," said Mayo, with her scream of petulance. "As soon as my back is turned—"

"Dry up," said Hood, not looking at her.

She grumbled and finished packing. She had several suitcases, a large cardboard box, and in three tea chests the dishes, the pots and pans. He had always wondered who the kitchenware belonged to—who owned the towels, the sheets, the blankets? They were in her luggage: all the furnishings were hers. The house was stripped; the furniture that was left looked useless and dirty in the empty house. But it had seemed empty from the moment he saw the painting was missing.

Brodie came downstairs carrying a shopping bag of her belongings and a guitar he had never seen her play. Murf followed with more of Brodie's things and he and Hood began to load the van. Entering the house for more of Mayo's boxes he heard her shouting in the kitchen: *I'm the one who has to answer for it, not you!* And Brodie's whine: *I couldn't help it. Anyway, it's hers, ain't it? It's not yours.* When they came out, breathless from the quarrel, Mayo still blustering and Brodie sheepishly dragging her feet, Hood said, "Off you go then, Sandra."

"I don't even know where I'm going," said Brodie. "I'm going to get anorexia again, for shit sake."

Mayo took the keys from her handbag. She started for the van, then stopped and walked back to him. He wondered what she was going to do—kiss him, slap him, shout. She was beyond caring about risk. But she said in a controlled voice, "Last night you said this is the beginning. Well, you're wrong—this is the end, but you're just too cowardly and selfish to admit it."

"Don't you believe that," said Hood. Murf had run to the bottom of the crescent. Hood saw him running back, holding a paper bag. He handed it to Brodie: toffees. Brodie started to cry.

"It's no big deal that you're handling this offensive," Mayo was saying. "There's no war here. It's happening in Ulster. If you had any guts you'd go there."

"I'm counting on you to do that."

"I'm staying in London," she said.

"Then you'll be hearing from me," said Hood. "But one last thing—don't come back here. Stay away from this house."

She said, "You'll never be happy," and started the engine.

They sat side by side, not speaking, mother and daughter, a pair of enemies. The van jerked forward, then disappeared at the turning of the crescent.

Murf said, "Now what do we do?"

"We make the house burglarproof."

"Yeah," said Murf. "Good idea. If you can find the locks."

Hood said, "You've got the lock, squire."

"Yeah." Murf smiled. "Nah. I ain't got a clue."

Hood said, "We're leaving a bomb behind."

"Yeah."

*

"A trip wire," said Murf. Now they were in the spare room, standing among the stacks of crates and televisions, the two large metal trunks. "Maybe use that

wall socket there for juice. Beautyful. Go like anything."

"You're the boss."

"Or else a battery, self-contained like. But sometimes it's hard to get a spark."

"Just one thing, Murf. Make it a fat one."

"About ten pounds should crack it. It's an old
house."

"Make it thirty," said Hood.

Murf cackled. "A thirty-pounder would get this
fucking pile to the moon. Yeah, with knobs on."

"Let's get started."

Murf opened his leather satchel and took out wire,
a small transformer, pliers, a spool of tape. Hood indicated the trunks and said he wanted the bomb wired
to the lids, so that opening the trunks would detonate
it. Murf nodded and set out sacks of powder, one bone
white, the consistency of detergent, the other a fine
gray zinclike dust.

"This here's your explosive," he said. "Safe as anything as long as you don't pack it too tight and refrain
from smoking, like." He uncoiled the wire. "This
here's your trip." He took another small object, with
a spring, a switch and a tightly wound spool of wire.
He handled it and showed Hood. He was obviously
enjoying himself and his enjoyment was tinged with
an oddly pedantic way of speaking. "Explosive? Well,
it's just a word, ain't it? You can use fertilizer, any
shit really. The world, like"—was he quoting Sweeney?
—"it's explosive right the way through. Now this,"
he said, and smacked his lips, "this here's your mousetrap. Remember that. Mousetrap. Trip. Power supply.
Explosive. Put them together and what have you got?"

"Come on, Murf. Step on it."

"You got a circuit," said Murf, taking his time.
"Okay. But there's a choice. Your trip wire. String
that bitch on the door—they fling it open—*ba-boom!*
Or your mousetrap under that floorboard there—one
step and they're fucking airborne. That's a beauty—
no wires showing—but it's bloody dangerous to leg. I
know a geezer who done himself that way. McDade.

His picture was in the paper. The Stickies give him a funeral."

"Hurry up."

"You mentioned them trunks," said Murf. "Quite honestly, I could cut some holes in them lids. For wire. They're unlocked. Fucker lifts them up. Circuit breaks. She sparks, and it's all over."

"That's the one."

"Put the powder under the floor. Get this lino up and jam a charge down there. Beautyful."

"Wouldn't it be quicker if we put the explosive in the closet?"

"Neighbors," said Murf. "Fuckers would be up in the sky—fucking astronauts. Kill innocent people. Hey, I'm telling you, the walls are thin in these here terraces. No, put the charges under the floor, then she goes straight up—*whoosh!*" He took a small drill from his satchel and made holes in the sides of the trunks, then threaded a wire and joined the lids. "No," he was saying, "can't kill the neighbors. They never done anything wrong."

"What do you want me to do?"

"Start pulling up the lino, so we can get at the floorboards. But don't tear the shit. People see lino torn a certain way and they know something's up."

Hood worked on the linoleum, peeling it from the sides of the room and rolling it across the floorboards. Murf wired the transformer, then mixed the powder in a plastic bag.

"This is the way to do it," said Murf. "Teamwork, no one bothering you. Wire it up, all the apparatus fixed, nice solid charge seated in the floor. Electric detonator. All nailed down. Them incendiaries in carrier bags are dinky little things. But this—this here's scientific."

Hood said, "Don't you want to know why we're doing it?"

Murf didn't look up. "You're the guv," he said. "I ain't asking."

They were at it for most of the morning. Murf insisted on hiding the transformer in the fireplace, which was sealed with a square of hardboard. Opening it they found it to be full of soot which had fallen from the chimney; it had to be cleaned and the soot disposed of before the transformer could be lodged inside. Murf wouldn't be hurried. When Hood said they could trail the wires along the wall and cover them with old newspapers, Murf said, "That's just sloppy workmanship," and tore up the floorboards to hide the wires. He brought to his peculiar method of destruction the laborious and precise dedication of a builder. Then they were finished, and the room was as it had been—no wires showed.

"I pity the poor fucker who messes with this baby," said Murf. "I'm knackered. How about a cup of tea?"

"Okay," said Hood.

"Hey, where are we going?"

Hood said, "Guatemala."

Murf smiled. He understood the euphemism.

They secured the windows, locked the front door, and in the back entryway Hood was saying, "That does it—"

"Half a tick," said Murf. "I almost forgot." He dug into his shopping bag and pulled out a rolled tube of old canvas. "The picture," he said, handing it to Hood. "I nicked it last night. I hope it ain't too squashed."

"Murf!" Hood held it. He felt rescued, and he wanted to throw his arms around the boy.

Murf saw Hood's gratitude and he was embarrassed. "I knew you liked it," he said. "And Mayo and that other bitch—they laughed at me."

Part Five

24

"TO BE BORN"—she lingered on the cue. Her arms were upraised in the dark thronged room. A vapor of light from outside Mortimer Lodge—the yellow streetlamps on Wat Tyler Road—was broken by the window slats and it shone in beams on her branched arms and the heads of the people watching her, sharpening the corners of the children's masks some of the actors wore. At the end of her phrase, on cue, a spotlight's dazzling velocity picked her out, and she stood charged with brilliant light, her feet apart, pausing for effect. She was mostly naked, but her skin rubbed with green powder made her seem as if she were wrapped in a tight membrane. Her breasts and hips were crisscrossed by strands of skeleton vines; her hair was cut, and her face, without make-up, was an oval of white that looked as thin as porcelain. She showed her teeth and began again: "To be born is to be wrecked on an island."

She saw fifty people in fifty postures, her actors, half-dissolved in shadow. A hush of approval from them and she continued, "The man who wrote that did not write this. But how could he know that the spirit he set into motion could be interpreted this way—"

"She looks so splendid," said Lady Arrow. Lady Arrow wore a combination of costumes. She was to play Mr. Darling and (or so Araba said) his piratical manifestation, Captain Hook. A copy of the *Financial Times* in one hand; a hook protruding from her right sleeve; a frock coat and boots. She was pleased—already the party was a success, a great improvement

253

on that other one she'd been to, when Araba lived off the King's Road, that dreary pageant they'd rehearsed for the rally at the Odeon in Hammersmith. "Come over to the Lodge," Araba had said. "We're having a cell meeting."

It was no ordinary cell meeting. For Lady Arrow this gathering of actors—a show of youth, strength, and poised optimistic anger—was a glamorous occasion. Many were beautiful. That girl over there, naked under her loose suede overalls, her breasts plumped against the straps of her leather bib, with bare arms and long hair, saying nothing—Lady Arrow could smell her from across the room and she smelled of genius. That boy dressed as a gangster pirate, with a velvet bow on his pigtail and his tight striped suit—she could eat him, clothes and all. She felt lucky, and she looked over the guests, squinting with greed and impatience, frenzied by the choice. The sight of so many perfect faces in that steamy stage-lit room was a shock that left her slightly breathless. Whatever I want. And this time she had a role to play—two roles. It made her almost mournful with excitement, and it was as if she had only acted before, performed a humdrum farce for her friends at Hill Street—her powerful friends: golden pigs and balding mice—and now in this play she was allowed a brief life without pretense.

"Tonight we improvise," Araba was saying. Lady Arrow had no lines. She had a costume—so did the others. But Araba said there was no need to rehearse the best-known English play. It was every child's first play, a fulfilled vision of his longing, and there was not a child who saw the curtain fall on the last act who did not hate his thwarting parents. By the nimblest magic it showed the fraudulent intrusion of authority and convinced the child ever after that to recapture the rule of Pan was to be free. Araba said, "Peter Pan is the saboteur of the bourgeois dream, the best English expression of the beauty of revolt. Remember, Neverland is an island—"

Lady Arrow watched with admiration. Then she

looked down and said, "Are you all right, my darling?"

Brodie, dressed as Tinker Bell, sat at Lady Arrow's feet. Her thin legs were sheathed in dancer's tights, her small breasts and tattoo showed through her blouse of pale silk, and she held a spangled wand. She shifted position and said, "I'm nervous. Hey, there's nobody here my age."

Lady Arrow was rebuked. They were all young! She offered her snuffbox and said, "Have some of this."

"Yuck." Brodie smiled and reached for her pouch. She rolled a cigarette, licked it and puffed. Then she relaxed, rocking slowly back and forth, regarding Araba with wide staring eyes. She laughed, a little drugged giggle, like chatter, causing heads to turn. "Fairy dust," she said. She made a nibbling face at them and went on smoking.

"—Or any age," Araba said. "Now, we begin."

She snapped her fingers, starting the music—the notes of a single flute, sweetly plangent, trilling as the spotlight dimmed. Araba entered the shadow at the side of the room as an armchair was dragged forward.

"I'm on," said Lady Arrow, and strode to the chair, scowling as if acknowledging applause. There were whispers, a wondering at her size. With the spotlight on her she looked enormous and slightly misshapen; she cast a crooked shadow and made the large armchair seem suddenly rather small and inefficient. She sat down heavily, raised her newspaper and began reading. She crashed the newspaper. She said, "I am responsible for it all. I, George Darling, did it . . ."

*

I know very little and I hate them, Hood thought, watching darkly from a corner near the door. If I knew more I'd probably kill every one of them. He watched the play proceed, with gaps and accidents freaking the self-conscious design. But it was the play's own heartless lines that hinted most at menace;

the actors, attempting to give it political coloring, only
drew attention to themselves.

In the fooling to upstage, improvisation's risk,
it was Brodie who got the laughs. Her popularity was
apparent from the outset, and as the play unfolded—
Peter battling with Hook for the leadership of the Lost
Boys who were trying to liberate the Neverland from
the rule of Pirates and Redskins—she realized how she
could stop everything by pulling a face or pretending
to assault another actor. During one of Wendy's
speeches she rolled a joint and had the room in
stitches. Araba called for order and began to deliver a
prepared monologue on the power of youth to destroy,
but her words were drowned in laughter, for as she
spoke, Brodie—who was alone at the side of the stage
—clawed her buttocks and then, making a business of
it, sniffed her fingers. It ended in farce: Lady Arrow
accused Araba of bullying Brodie, and gesturing with
her hook, caught Araba on the arm and scratched her.
Araba screamed and ran upstairs. So the play closed
in disorder, incomplete, a collapse; and Hood heard
one actor murmur, "Beginner's night."

He saw Brodie at the far side of the room with Lady
Arrow. But Brodie was perfectly alone and self-
contained. She pinched a roach in her fingers and
smirked at it. He was disgusted, like a man seeing his
daughter in an unguarded moment in public, among
her trivial friends: her foolishness was exposed but
mattered only to him. He was responsible; he had
taught her to roll a joint one-handed, and he was to
blame for having marked her face with this careless
mouth.

Lorna said, "They're not up to much."

"Screamers," said Hood. "They're trying to start a
revolution."

"Fuckers couldn't start a car."

"Let's score a drink," he said.

"I seen enough. Let's go home."

He admired that. She held them in total contempt.
The costumes they wore, the poses they struck, the
selfish jeering in their talk—she dismissed it as nothing. They were not even exotic to her, they had no

glamour; she seemed embarrassed to be in the same room with them.

"Mister Hood!" Lady Arrow rushed over, and ignoring Lorna, and standing eye to eye with him, said, "Araba told me you might be coming. I didn't believe her for a minute, but here you are! It's a terrible snub for me—you've never come to Hill Street. Or did you know I'd be here? Say you did!"

Hood said, "This is Lorna."

Lorna nodded hello. She wore her boots, her shortest skirt, and the jacket Hood had bought her, crushed velvet, bottle green. She looked away to avoid looking up at the much taller woman.

"Yes," said Lady Arrow, assessing her swiftly. She said nothing more.

"Isn't that Brodie over there?" said Hood.

"She's mine now," said Lady Arrow proudly. "She's made a great hit with Araba's friends, I can tell you. Quite a debut—it could lead to something, a real part. She's so natural. Darling!"

The girl raised her head and threaded her way through the room, walking flatfooted in the drooping tights, the crotch at her knees. She gave Hood a sheepish grin and said, "Hey, I didn't think this was your scene."

"Pull up your pants," he said.

"I'm stoned," she said. She made her goofy face.

Lady Arrow stooped and embraced her. Brodie resisted, but she was enfolded, and again Hood tasted a father's disgust. Brodie didn't seem to mind; perhaps she would never know, lost in that woman's arms. Hood looked at Lady Arrow's hands, one tightening on the small girl's tattooed arm, the other a knot of snails inching across the flawless skin of her belly.

"I hated that woman," said Lady Arrow. "The one who dropped Brodie off the other day. She came screaming into the house, and do you know what? She accused me of stealing the Rogier self-portrait! I understand *she* is the thief. Of course, I told her I had no idea where it is—what a shame if someone's really stolen it. I let her search the house from top to bottom. She was quite upset, said some rather unkind things about you. I imagine she's from some dreary place like Basingstoke. I need hardly add that I urged her to find my precious picture."

Hood said nothing. The painting was at Lorna's, and he had had a long look at it before coming to the party, studying it for changes as if looking at his own reflection in a mirror. The face was more familiar to him than his own, and unlike his own, a consolation. He wondered if he would ever part with it.

Lady Arrow said, "I say, did you see our little effort?"

"The last part," said Hood.

"The fracas," said Lady Arrow. "Wasn't it superb? 'And so it will continue, as long as children are gay and innocent and heartless.' "

"Putrid," said Brodie.

"You said it." Hood glanced around the room. The actors, holding glasses of wine, still wore the costumes from the play, the eye patches, the cassocks, the spectacular rags. Their voices made the room howl.

"But I won," said Lady Arrow. She smiled at Hood. "Araba's absolutely desolate—but there it is. You can't always have it your own way. I think it's a lesson to them. They're terribly nice people, but their Marxism is so moth-eaten. Things aren't like that anymore— Marx was an optimist! They stink of sincerity, and they will go on trotting out these old ideas. They sound like my father. But they're just parrots—give up your money and we'll believe you, property is theft, power to the people. Who are these people they are always talking about? They have study groups, reading lists— these ratty little pamphlets with coffee stains on the covers, Albanian handbooks of social change. Albanian! Have you ever heard such a thing? And Arabs —these filthy little desert folk—they think they're revolutionaries! No, I tell them, we are beyond Marxism now and Chairman Mao and your Arabs and that"— she spat the words—"that pinup, Trotsky. Any right-thinking anarchist would have chucked these primitives years ago. But there's hope. I must sound awfully negative to you, but there's hope in this room —you can feel it. Look around. Araba hasn't the slightest idea of what she's started, which is so often the case. Her days are numbered as an activist. Before long, they'll be looking to someone like me, and she'll be back on stage, posing for photographers, searching the papers for mentions, like Jane Fonda and Vanessa and Brando and all the rest of them."

She had spoken in a single burst and was panting from the effort of it. She smiled, as if satisfied there could be no reply, and hearing none she straightened herself with assurance. Hood shook his head. Lorna sniffed and brushed her skirt.

Then Brodie said, "But Araba's pretty."

Lady Arrow showed her teeth. It was not a smile. She said, "White trash."

She hurried Brodie away.

Hood thought: Die.

"She hates me," said Lorna. "Should be ashamed of herself, with that little girl, touching her up. Do you really know these fuckers?"

"I want to see the lady of the house."

"What's wrong with me?"

"I'll deal with you later."

"Listen to him," said Lorna, and her face clouded with sadness.

But from the moment they had entered the house he had felt close to her: it was the same desire he had known when he saw her bruised. He did want her and he cursed himself for hesitating. He feared betraying her by making her trust him too much. But the consequence of his fastidiousness was her excitement: he had not made love to her and that aroused her more than if he had. She was a hostage to an unspoken promise. He had also feared possession, dependency, complication, blame, any reduction of his freedom, any disturbance to hers. Sex, an expression of freedom, made you less free: the penalty of freedom was a reverie of loneliness.

To act, he knew, was to involve himself; no act could succeed because all involvement was failure; and love, a selfish faith, was the end of all active thought—it was a memory or it was nothing. But he had come too far, known too much to evade blame, and he sought to conclude the act he had begun on impulse that summer night. He wished to release himself with a single stroke that would free him even if it left him a cripple—like a fox gnawing his leg so he could drag himself from the trap; an amputation, true terrorism.

They got drinks from the kitchen and stood next to the stairs, watching the drunken actors (some were preening; several sang; here was one doing another's horoscope). Hood put his arm around Lorna and kissed her hair. He had overcome his horror of holding her. Once, he had not been able to touch her without feeling the pressure of her husband's corpse; now touching her reassured him and she could rouse him simply by seeming wounded or lost, which, he had come to see, was her permanent condition. Not love—it was more drastic than that, a hunger for her very flesh, and what kept him away was his fear that her hunger was greater than his and almost unappeasable.

They remained at the fringe of the party, watching what could have been another act of the improvised *Peter Pan,* a cheerier one, noisy and uncomplicated, like a spirited mob scene, all the actors talking at once. Lorna spotted several famous faces—an actor from a film she'd seen; a comedian looking oddly tense; a child star; then a girl who appeared regularly on a children's program, and she said without irony, "Jason should be here—he'd be dead pleased."

"Maybe we should go," said Hood. "I don't see the bitch."

"That one—he does the Angel Snow advert," said Lorna. "I seen him on telly."

It was the young man who had played John. His mask was off but he still wore his top hat and striped pajamas. He was not tall. He passed by as Lorna spoke and hearing her he stopped, did a humorous double take, and greeted them.

"Brother. Sister."

Hood said, "How's the family?"

"I know you," said the man. "What company are you with?"

"General Motors."

"He's funny," said the man to Lorna. "Does he make you laugh?"

She flinched. "Sometimes."

"Don't knock it," said Hood. "You're pretty funny yourself. What's your name?"

"McGravy," he said. "You probably know my sister, the so-called Irish playwright. Everyone does, mainly because her plays are banned in Ireland. Censorship made her a household word. She's not even funny, but"—he tilted his head and clicked his heels— "vee haff vays of making you laugh."

"I can do a German accent better than that," said Hood.

"Yeah, well, I guess that's cause you're Amurrikan," said McGravy in an accurate imitation of Hood's own speech.

"Try something hard. Can you do Japanese?"

"Hail!" said McGravy, sneezing the word, Japanese fashion. Then he said in a halting monotone, "I can do bettah than many lidicurous men in crabs. You know crabs? Nightcrabs?"

Lorna laughed. "He's like Benny Hill!"

"Bud Benny Hill is daking doo much of rupees and binching backsides of vooman, my goodness," said McGravy, waggling his head like an Indian. "In my country is not bermitted on estage, oh no!"

"He really sounds like a Pakki," said Lorna. She was amused; she stared at McGravy's comic face.

Hood said, "West Indian."

"What, mun? Trinnydad or Jameeka? It's a flamin' big place, mun. So many i-lands."

"Cuban."

"Hasta la vista," said McGravy, and started to go.

"Wait," said Hood. "Don't go yet. I've got a tough one for you."

"I'll bet you do," said McGravy, again in Hood's voice. "A real ball breaker, right?"

"He's putting you on," said Lorna.

"Ulster," said Hood.

"Catholic or Protestant?"

"What's the difference?"

"Fussically," said McGravy, putting his jaw out

and speaking in a heavy Northern Ireland accent, "there's no dufference. But the mumbers of the Pro'estant Uni'y Par'y tund ta talk like thus. Ya go' ta swalla some sullables."

"Catholic," said Hood.

McGravy closed his eyes. "Give me something to say."

"Say, 'Mary had a little lamb.'"

"Murry had a luttle lamb."

"Say. 'Look, I know where it is now.'"

"Luck, Ah know whirr ut uz nigh."

"'It's in an upstairs room at number twenty-two.'"

"Ut's un an opstairs rum at number twunty-tow."

Hood muttered the phrases to himself, then said, "I wish I could do that."

"If you could, I'd be out of a job," said McGravy. "Though there's not a hell of a lot of work around. I do juves—boy parts. It's my face. I'm thirty-one, but I'm cast as a teenager. If I've got this face at fifty I'll still be doing juves and foreigners with funny accents. I'm not tall enough to play a real man. Who wouldn't be a revolutionary?"

Hood smiled. "That sounds like your real voice."

McGravy bent close to Hood and said, "Kill the bastards."

"Why are you whispering? Scared someone will hear you?"

McGravy sized him up, as if trying to decide whether the taunting question deserved a serious reply. After a moment he said, "There's too much shouting."

"Are you afraid of that?"

"Yes," said the actor. "Sometimes these people scare me more than the police."

"They're safe," said Hood. "They know what they're doing."

"Sure they do."

"Then why are you afraid?"

McGravy said, "Because they aren't."

"When you said, 'Kill the bastards,' I thought you meant the police, the army, the politicians." He smiled at McGravy. "Now it turns out you want to snuff your friends."

"No," said McGravy. "I know who the enemy is."

"What happens if you fail?"

"We fail." He spoke with equivocal emphasis, doubt and certainty subtly balanced, then he added, "You see, I've played in *Macbeth*. Fleance, naturally."

"It's your funeral."

McGravy shook his head. "It's everyone's fight."

"Not mine," said Hood. "I used to think that, but it's pride that makes you think you can fight someone else's battles—in Africa, southeast Asia, here, wherever."

"Pride," said McGravy with a touch of sarcasm.

"Yes, pride, because it's their weakness that involves you. The illusion that you're strong is pride. But when they discover how weak they are the only dignified thing they can do is kill you. Notice how often it happens—the Third World is a graveyard of idealists." Hood smiled. "I'm sympathetic—sympathy is a cowardly substitute for belief. No one dies for it, but if you believe—"

"What do we have here?" It was Araba. She had changed into faded blue-jeans, tight trousers, and a jacket covered with patches. She posed next to McGravy and ruffled his hair. "I love his head—it reminds me of Lenin's."

McGravy ignored her. He turned to Hood and said, "I may see you again—maybe at the barricades."

"There aren't any," said Hood. "So don't wait for me." But he felt tender towards the man, and it was as if the actor was bearing the most fiery part of himself away: he believed; he might survive his belief.

Araba said, "I'm glad you came."

"Lorna," said Hood. "Score me another drink."

Lorna hesitated.

"Don't do it, darling," said Araba, touching her on the arm.

Lorna went for the drink.

"I knew you were the domineering type," said Araba.

"Skip it. I've got a question for you. And I know

all about you, so don't waste my time denying anything. I know you used to work for the Provos—running guns on the continent with an American passport, until you put the burn on them."

"That's a lie."

"You didn't deliver the last batch, did you?"

"I don't expect you to believe me."

"I don't care," said Hood. "I just want to know the name of your contact."

"Isn't it odd, Mister Hood? I invited you here to find out about you, and now you're asking all the questions!"

"His name," said Hood. He stepped close to her and snatched her wrist. He gripped her tightly, twisting it.

"That hurts," she said. Her eyes were bright with pain, but she made no move to resist.

Hood said, "If you don't tell me I'll slash your face so bad you'll have to give up acting."

"You're a pig," she said. "You hate women."

"I'm liberated," he said. "I treat women the same as men. And I'll kick you in the balls if you don't tell me." He realized that he was on the point of hitting her. He checked his fury and growled, "Wise up, sister."

"Let go of my arm," she said.

He threw her arm down hard.

She said, "Don't think I'm telling you because you threatened me. I don't have to protect anyone. They're bastards. They let me down. They'll do the same to you."

"Spit it out!"

"Greenstain—from Libya or somewhere. An Arab. He's in Rotterdam and he's a pouf. He might fall for you, but he won't give you anything."

"What about your contact in London?"

"He was just the delivery boy," she said. "And I don't remember his name."

"Was it Weech?"

"Yes, that's it," she said. "I thought he was the one who burned me."

"How do you know he wasn't?"

She laughed. "Because they killed him."

"Who did?"

"Some fink," she said lazily.

"What about Rutter?"

"Rutter! I don't have to tell you anything, do I? You know all the punks. That proves you're either a clever cop or the biggest crook of them all. And I've found," she went on, smiling now, "that they're usually the same thing."

"So Rutter supplies the Provos," said Hood. "But he stays put and lets guys like Weech take the rap. And you keep them all in business. You were taking a chance going to the continent. You must have liked that."

"How did you know my passport number?" she said.

"I provided it. Without me you couldn't have left the country for the Provos. Only it didn't work."

"It worked," she said. "But they hated me. They wanted to expel me all along—they were just looking for an excuse."

Hood said, "Then where's the arsenal?"

"The arsenal," she said. "Is that what you call it? Shit, if I knew the answer to that question I'd be Queen of England. Ask your friends the Provos."

"They don't know."

"Of course they don't or they would have started their offensive. And Rutter doesn't know either, or he would have flogged it long ago—he must be dying to get his hands on it. I'll tell you something, Mister Hood. I may be wrong but I don't think anyone knows what happened to the arsenal." She tasted the word again and grinned. "I saw it, I paid for it, and then it vanished. Maybe it sank in the Channel. It would serve them right if it did." She paused a moment, patted her hair, then said, "Haven't you got a theory?"

"It's just a theory," said Hood.

"Tell me."

"I have to prove it first," he said. He saw Lorna returning with the drinks.

"Shampoo," said Lorna, handing Hood a glass of champagne.

"It's a little celebration," said Araba. "I'm opening tomorrow in *Peter Pan*."

"Break a leg," said Hood, and he drained his glass in one gulp. Then he said, "That's funny—I'm not thirsty anymore. Let's go."

Araba turned to Lorna. "Don't pay any attention to him, darling. Stick with us. You're the sort of person we're trying to reach." She made a move to take Lorna's hand.

Lorna stepped aside. She glared at the actress and said, "You fucker."

*

Murf was asleep on the sofa when they entered. He lay flat, his face up, his mouth open; he was being steamrollered by a narcotic dream; he was flattened, in a posture of surrender. Hearing the door slam he sat up straight, opened his mouth to shout, then said, "What's the time?" He yawned, flopped down and turned over without waiting for a reply. There was an ashtray on the floor, and a pipe; and in the air the stale perfume of burnt opium.

Hood and Lorna went upstairs. Lorna undressed first and Hood helped her off with her boots. She got into bed. He crept in beside her. He made a tender appeal with his hands and kissed her eyes. She stiffened, as if resisting, and then she began to cry softly, her tears wetting his mouth. He felt the convulsive pressure under his hand and turned her gently.

She said, "I can't help it. I always cry." She lifted her breast to his mouth and parted her legs. He slid between, touching her; she was open, hot with liquid, straining to receive him. She reached down, took him urgently in her fingers and helped him enter, but as he did—seeming to move into fathoms of darkness—she cried out.

"What is it?" He paused.

"No," she wept, "don't stop. But don't hold me so tight."

She still ached from that beating, and the thought of it filled him with rage. But his anger was displaced. He knelt over her, and she lay back, drowning there under him, her skin as luminous as if under water; she was alone, then he embraced her, joined her, and followed her down to a brief death.

*

In the morning he awoke before she did and went downstairs, where Murf lay asleep, his mouth open, his yellow feet sticking out from the blanket.

Hood carried the telephone into the kitchen. He dialed a number and waited, watching the still dawn-green garden whitened in patches with a dew as thick as frost. Clouds were bulked above the nearby roofs.

The ringing ceased.

"Sweeney," he said. "It's Hood."

"It's seven o'clock in the morning. What do you want now?"

Nigh. "Just making sure you're home."

"That's not funny."

"And I wanted to hear your voice," said Hood. "How's your wife?"

"I don't know. Probably with her family. She lost the painting. It's the only card we have to play at the moment—I told her not to come back without it."

"I want to see you."

"You know where I am. I don't make appointments by telephone."

"Oh, and something else," said Hood. "Do you know a guy named Rutter?"

There was a pause; for a moment Hood thought he had hung up. Then Sweeney asked him to repeat the name. Hood said it carefully.

Sweeney said, "No. Why do you ask?"

"I heard he's been rumbled. The Yard's on to him."

"Never heard of him."

"I'll see you," said Hood. He hung up.

He listened, but the house was as still as the garden, and as cold. He dialed again, referring to a number in Lorna's schoolgirl handwriting, holding the wrinkled

scrap of paper to the window, the first light of day. The
phone rang and stopped.

"Rutter," he said. "Sweeney." And before the man
could reply he said, "Luck, Ah know whirr ut uz
nigh—"

25

THE LINE SPUTTERED and seemed to heat as
if it had caught fire. There was a scatter of clicks, no
ring, then the sudden honk of a human voice, "—don't
really know what to do."

Mr. Gawber moved the receiver away from his
ear and hid his face, shielding himself from the thing's
eyelike holes.

Another voice, younger, said, "But it can't get any
worse."

"I feel sure it will."

"Depend on it," said Mr. Gawber, from his stomach, woefully.

"What did you say?"

"That wasn't me."

"The market's firming up."

"No, it is not," said Mr. Gawber. "There is a great
deal of concern. The market is extremely shaky, and
I assure you"—now he was speaking over squawks
of protest—"I assure you we'll have to tighten our
belts." He put the phone down, silencing the squawks.

That was at nine-thirty, and it stirred him. It trig-
gered compassion: he wondered if he had been too
harsh. He buzzed Miss French and said, "No visitors,
no phone calls. I'm in purdah. But Monty can
bring my tea as usual."

"I'll see that you're not disturbed," said Miss
French.

"You're so kind."

He spent the rest of the morning rubbing his eyes, anxiously rehearsing his visit to Albacore Crescent. The ride to Deptford on the Number One bus; the walk up the rising street to the red brick terrace; his arrival; his explanation. His instinct was towards the making of plans, the whole of his life a simple mapping to avoid embarrassment. To be anonymous was to be independent: he had no craving to be singled out by fame or wealth. He did not want surprises to fuel his distraction.

He was anxious because he had been thwarted once before. The last time, unprepared, he had met Araba wearing that drab, unbecoming costume; and the further surprise, Lady Arrow playing hostess. How small London was in these days of distress! He had taken himself away, feeling lamed and foolish. No one had spoken of the very person who belonged there; but where was Mister Hood, and why had he canceled his standing order with the bank? The young man had left no instructions, his affairs were already in a muddle; the lump sum, which should have been on fixed deposit, was dwindling in a current account. Americans were so careless with their money, and the shrinkage alarmed Mr. Gawber, who from the first had felt almost fatherly towards him. The thought occurred to Mr. Gawber that he might meet Araba or Lady Arrow at the house once more. There again, some preparation was required. The one's income tax was still unpaid, a further demand from Inland Revenue in the pending tray; the other's insurance claim for the stolen painting wanted an underwriter's verification. Loose ends, loose ends; and the storm cone approaching as a December shadow hung over the city—a stillness, like a sacking of cloud, warning of a winter that might never end. England tossed; adrift, dismasted.

The calamity was news. The crossed lines had picked it up. And the previous week a television program he had watched with Norah foretold a new ice age. Changes in the sea currents, freak weather, desert where there had been flowers: the planet was gripped. There had been pictures of Africans—perhaps relatives of the very Mr. Wangoosa who lived in style at number thirty—starving and watching with incomprehension as the sand beat their tents to shreds; skinny livestock with sad sick eyes; children with stick-like limbs and swollen bellies. He wanted to cry. The program had shown a model globe wearing a thickness of ice like a cricketer's cap. Predictably, there were the historical snippets: snow on the dome of Saint Paul's, steel engravings of the Thames frozen over—a fairground in midstream, children skimming, a coach and four crossing the ice to Westminster. And this morning a *Times* leader about the coming ice age, matching in gloom the Financial Times Share Index which had dropped again to its lowest level ever (each day that precise phrase), plunging like a barometer. "It's like the Thirties," Monty said. And the office chorus: "Terrifying." But Thornquist and Miss French were comfortable for the moment, and they didn't know that "terrifying," a humbug word for the pickle they imagined, would not describe the unspeakable hunger and confusion, the nakedness of the event that he had already witnessed beginning.

And strange, this was his season. He had always liked—in the same degree that others hated—the days darkening into winter. Norah feared them. To her, winter was a cold tunnel she might never clear, and lately she had begun to remark on how progressively dark it was getting, how they had their tea at night. She had spent her life waiting for the sun to reach her windows; there was nothing more for her: life was a matter of temperature. She had said a thousand times, "I'd like to live in a country where the sun was always shining." Mr. Wangoosa's country? Mr. Aroma's? Churchill's Tobago? Palmerston's Jamaica? But he bore her yearning with politeness, adding only that hot countries were governed by torturers. He saw her as similar in some ways to the African savage who allowed the riddle of weather to foreshorten his existence and alter his mood until—and like those pathetic blacks in the television program—

poor Norah would simply sit in the dark and wait to die. But he could not mock Norah. He too had his fantasies, and he imagined death to be something like sitting on the top deck of a Number One bus on a December afternoon, the shop lights flaring and blazing at the windows, the black conductor grinning; a red catafalque racing him into darkness. It was death: you did not get off.

He felt it now; he was on that bus. A month ago he had traveled this way and had seen it all. But today he was reprieved. He alighted at Deptford without incident, deposited his flimsy ticket in the litter bin and started up the street. It was as he remembered it, only drearier. And gusty: the people hurried, simulating panic, as they always seemed to do on windy days. His gloom was deepened when at the brick wall with the torn circus poster—wagging tongues of paper—he saw the words that never failed to still his heart with ice: ARSENAL RULE. A necessary landmark, and yet he wished he had not seen it.

He was rising on the road. The sounds of the river reached him with greater clarity, a boat's steady poop and a distant hammering at Millwall borne across the water. He gained Ship Street and turned into Albacore Crescent, walked halfway up and stopped. Without the slightest warning, and just as he had once witnessed the demolition of Mortimer Lodge—that embarrassing misapprehension—he imagined number twenty-two bursting into flames. The roof caved in, the windows splintered, and a lighted cloud of bursting sparks and brick fragments was released. A cylinder of horrible fire heated his face. And then, as he watched, the flames died, the splinters met, and every brick fell back into place until the house regained its former solidity and was whole. But there were scorch marks above the windows; had they been there before?

The vision jarred him, and his heart was ticking rapidly as he mounted the steps and rang the bell. The echo droned on; he listened for footsteps, but he was sure on the second ring that the house was empty. No bell sounded louder or more mournful than one in an empty house.

As he turned to go he put his hand on the knob and pushed the door open. From this doorway to the back of the house there was emptiness—none of the clutter he'd seen before, and only the faintest smell of tobacco mingled with dust. Cold air, a wave of it, rolled past him from the creepy interior. He stepped inside and shut the door. A hum, like an electric purr, made him stop; but the hum was in his head, not in the house. He peeked into the parlor: two chairs, no cushions, bare walls. The dining room held a scarred table, and scabs of soot had fallen down the chimney and littered the linoleum in front of the fireplace. The kitchen was empty. He stepped into the back room, a floorboard gave under his foot and for a split second he was on his way, careening through the first inch of a black hole.

He went upstairs, disturbed by the oafishness of his own banging steps, paused on the landing, and tiptoed down the hall. Then to the top of the house, three rooms: empty.

But as he paused again his mind strayed. The front door had been unlocked: the house could not be empty. He recalled the closed room he had hurried past on the floor below. Not the bathroom, which was shut as if engaged: he could smell the soap. One looked in a bathroom at one's peril; but that other room?

He retraced his steps: down to the landing, down one flight to the closed door; and he stood in the stale cold air of the hall, taking shallow breaths.

My son is there, he thought. He had touched the doorknob. He was saddened by the chipped paint and the scars, the chill of the porcelain knob. His sadness turned to shame, and it was physical, an infirmity; his arm went dead, his fingers wouldn't work. His soul rebelled, restraining him with a tug of timid dignity. It was wrong; the place was private. The front door was unlocked: the house had to be empty. It was anyone's, but not his. For the first time in years he thought of his father and mother in a chastening way, as if when he went home they would stop him and ask him where he had been, what he had done. He had his reply. He withdrew his hand and straightened himself, and as he descended the stairs—softly, to make no noise—he thought: But my son is dead.

*

She heard his slow descent on the stairs. The front door banged shut, and she shuddered, the nervousness overtaking her now when she was out of danger. It had not been Hood; it was a cautious tread, someone checking the house, a curious neighbor, the gas man, a meter reader, a stranger. The keyhole on the bathroom door was sealed, and she had not had the courage to risk a peek. She had shot the bolt and stayed there, where she'd hidden when he entered the house. She cursed herself for not locking the front door, and starting down the stairs she reproached herself for wanting to go and lock it now. The absurdity of it. It was too late; whoever it was had come and gone, and she was safe again.

She climbed back to the landing, where she had been stopped when the front door opened, and she went up the second flight to the top floor. The front bedroom looked no emptier than it ever had. She scanned it for differences, for any change. This was the way it had always been. But the family was ended, he would never return: so emptiness was this knowledge that no particle remained, and only she could know how hollow it really was.

She looked for more, because the day before she remembered how firmly he had said, *Don't come back here.* She had half-expected to find him propped on one of those Indian cushions, studying the painting he had begun to covet. She was dispirited; she had nerved herself for a scene and was glad when the bell rang and the door opened; but that gentle step going up and down the stairs was not his.

Dust flew as she rifled the closets. She found the newspapers she had put on the shelves. She wrenched the dented mattress aside. Fur balls, a button, hairpins, a foreign coin: they aggravated her distress. And as she went through the room, searching for her painting, she could not recall anything of the lovely thing but its thick coat of yellow varnish, its coarsely woven backing, the configuration of cracks that lay over a face she could no longer see. That had always been the way: each time she saw it, it was new to her and she marveled as if it were just made before her eyes, existing only when she looked at it. Out of sight it was a blank in her mind, and as she searched she prepared herself for the fresh shock of being amazed by the face again. She was certain it was in the house. *Don't come back here:* that was proof.

But she had stopped searching. She had opened a low drawer and, on her knees, was reading the old newspaper that lined it. She was calmed, and she remained in this position for a long time, reading effortlessly a large plain story on a browning front page. Old news. It held her, fixed her, as no book ever had.

Downstairs a door opened. She registered the sound, but it vanished without meaning into her depthless mood, and she was so absorbed in the newspaper she did not start until she heard voices: "Nothing" and "Better make sure." She stood and staggered as if she had been hit, dizzy from her kneeling. She went to the door and listened. They were on the ground floor. She crept along the wall to the landing and made for the place where she had been safe before, the bathroom halfway down the stairs. But she heard them climbing.

"There's no one home."

"I'll look up here."

"Check all the rooms."

"I'll kill that bastard."

The voices were loud, careless, shouting back and forth. Not Hood. Obscure rowdy men. Their accents alarmed her; she was afraid, just hearing their brutish mispronunciations. They moved quickly through the house. She padded down the hall, her eyes aching, looking for a place to hide: not a room, a closet—or out the window?

"Smells like"—the voice ran ahead of the feet

tramping the uncarpeted steps—"like someone died here."

And noises, kickings, downstairs.

"I don't see nothing."

Nuffink: she quailed. She was at a back window. It was painted shut; she struggled to free it from the casement, and as she did—not knowing what lay below her, not caring that it was thirty feet down to a paved alleyway behind the house—she was linking the visit of the first man to this one and seeing how it fit. He had been making sure the house was empty, preparing for the others, and when he left, when she had felt safest, she was in the most danger. Her clumsy logic made her blunder. She could not open the window. She had told Murf to paint it, and he had done it like he did everything, with stupid sloppy care. She fought with it, and even as she heard the man in the hall she was blaming Murf and hating the thought of his pinched face, his ugly ears.

"Well, well, well. I don't believe it."

The man, tall, with a killer's face and strings of hair to his shoulders, stood in the doorway.

"I'm leaving," she said, and still tried to work the window open.

"Don't move." He was pale, his skin like a sausage casing. He leaned backward and yelled, "Rutter!"

"You find something?" It was the man on the ground floor calling into the stairwell.

"A bird!"

"What?"

She said, "I don't know what you're looking for. The house is empty."

"Really."

He was mocking her. She said, "I used to live here. There's no one here now."

"Except you."

"I thought I left something behind. I—"

"Who are you?" It was the second man, shorter, darker, in an overcoat and a small neat hat. He shook out a pair of glasses and used them to look at her. They softened his appearance: she almost trusted him for those glasses.

"She thinks she left something behind." -

Finks, somefink. The chewed words scared her.

"Says she used to live here."

She appealed to the smaller man, who she could see was in charge: "This is my own house. You won't find anything."

"Up against the wall, chicky."

"I have a right to know who you are. If you're policemen you have to tell me."

"That's right, chicky. Flying squad."

"I don't believe you."

"You heard what he said." The taller man stepped towards her. "Get over. Palms against the wall, legs apart."

"I don't care what you're doing here," she said, and tried to sound friendly. "Just let me go. No one will know."

"What's your name?"

She hesitated. She said, "Sandra." And it was as if, admitting it, she became that person, one she hated. She said, "Don't touch me, please."

"We're not going to hurt you."

She turned and saw that the smaller one had taken out a pistol.

"No," she said. "Please—"

"Don't worry," said the man. "This ain't for you. This is for him." He jerked the pistol at the other man. "I don't trust him with birds, see. I'll make a hole in him if he starts anything."

"I wouldn't mind and all," said the taller man. "Let's do her and get out of here. The place is empty."

"Just rooms—empty rooms. Nothing." She began to cry. "Please let me go. I'll do anything you say."

"You're giving me ideas," said the taller one.

They frightened her, and her awareness of this fear gave her the greatest sense of outrage she had ever known. She wanted them cowering, dead, chopped into pieces. Rape: she would let them; afterward, she would find them and kill them.

"Tell me what you want," she said.

"Keep her away from the window."

"Off we go," said the taller man. "Make a funny move and I'll brick you so fast you won't know what happened."

They pushed her into the hall. She thought of running downstairs. They had guns; but something else kept her from making a dash—there was nothing in the house, nothing at all, and remembering that gave her hope. Somehow, they knew about the painting. She hoped they'd find it; they could have it. But no, the house was empty.

She stayed ahead of them, walking along the landing. She said, "These are bedrooms. They're all empty."

"How many upstairs?"

"Two. No, three."

"What about this one?"

The voice was over her head. It was rough, unpleasant, deliberately threatening. She trembled; her fear was like penance, purifying her. She felt innocent, a young girl, without any blame, punished for no reason. And again she wanted the men dead, at her mercy.

"Which one?"

"Here. The door's closed."

"Empty, like the rest of them."

"The rest of them are open."

"Let's have a look."

They gathered at the door. She remembered the televisions, the junk, and Hood saying, *We'll leave them for the next tenant.* A hand moved across her shoulder. *Don't touch me.* Pure. Most of all she hated Hood: *Don't come back here.* You only said that if you had something to hide. She thought: I will do whatever they say, and be safe; the ones who fight, die.

They stepped into the room.

*

The Number One bus that had taken him to Deptford would take him the rest of the way to Catford, but he had waited twenty minutes and none had come. The queue had lengthened behind him: shoppers, laborers, schoolboys in uniforms. It was dark. He clasped his hands on his paper and relaxed, finding it restful to be so anonymous, in a bus queue in Deptford, among strangers. There were whispers of complaint about the late bus. He eavesdropped, invisible in the shadow of the bus shelter, glad that nothing was required of him but to listen.

"What's that?"

The explosion reached him as a muffled roar, too brief for recollection.

"Smashup."

"That was no smashup."

"Gas main."

"Look!"

The sky was lit, segments of low cloud touched by fire and given majestic detail, and sparks traveling up in gusts, curling above the rooftops. Now the bus queue broke, and all the people ran across the street in the direction of the flames.

Mr. Gawber stayed. He boarded the bus and went to the top deck, paid his fare and folded his paper square to complete the crossword. He clicked his pen, but he did not write. He thought: home, Norah, and tonight *Peter Pan*. It is the end of my world. He put his hand to his eyes and tried to stop his tears with his fingers.

26

"BEAUTIFUL. BEAUTIFUL." Murf was at the window, the firelight flickering on his face, catching his earring and making his ears seem to twitch. Little Jason joined him, standing on tiptoes, his chin on the sill, shrieking at the flames. "Went like anything," Murf said to the child. "It's still going beautyful. I wish Brodie was here. That cracked it and all. Look at it go!"

The explosion, a tremendous thud, a shower of bricks and glass, had come as they were having tea. It shook their plates and brought a groan from their own house. And Murf, who had just pushed a fragment of kipper into his mouth, stood up, his cheeks bulging, his eyes popping. He threw down the slice of bread he was holding; he choked, trying to swallow, trying to shout. Hood saw black fingermarks on the bread slice. Murf, still chewing, had started out the door, but Hood restrained him, and so Murf had run upstairs to watch the blaze. Then Jason and Lorna; then Hood.

Eruption: the neighborhood which had seemed to him a district of empty houses, locked and abandoned, was alive; the streets full of reddened people painted by flames, gathered in little watching groups, driven from their houses like ants roused by heat. An ambulance brayed in Ship Street. It came skidding around the crescent, its blue lights flashing in all the windows of nearby houses. Deptford itself was alight, but this fire, simulating life, reduced it to theater, and Hood could not bear to watch.

Lorna said, "That's your house!"

"Not anymore it ain't," said Murf. He laughed; he was dancing. He lifted Jason to see. "Look at the little basket—he likes it and all!"

"What's up," she said. "What the hell is this?"

Murf said, "That there's the booby prize. Hey, where you going?"

"Downstairs," said Hood.

"You won't see nothing from there."

"Who says I want to?"

Hood left them and went down to the dining room. The eaters had been put to flight. Panic showed in their leavings. The table was covered by the half-eaten meal, bones, bitten pieces still on forks, greasy glasses, the fingerprinted bread, teeth marks everywhere; and outside, the alarm, the excited shouts.

"What do you know about this?" said Lorna, entering from the hall.

"You don't want me to tell you."

"Ron." She looked at him strangely. "Ron would have said that." She pushed at the soiled plates. "No," she said, "I don't want to know."

"I have to go. A little business."

"You're running out on me. You won't come back. Like Ron."

He took her face gently in his hands. He kissed her and said, "I'll be back."

"I'm scared," she said. "You done something."

Hood said, "There's nothing to be scared of. It's all over. No one's going to bother you now."

Her expression—puzzled, fearful—had not changed. She said, "Ron," and then, "I loved him, and sometimes he loved me."

Murf was on the stairs, clattering. He looked into the room and said, "Hey, there's another ambulance. I want to see who copped it."

"Stay here."

"There must be more than one."

"If you leave this house, don't come back."

"Okay, okay," said Murf. "I was just wondering."

"People live around here. They must know us. Keep that face indoors—and stop smiling."

"They'll find you," said Lorna, moving warily, sensing danger. "They'll do you, they'll hang you, they'll take you away."

Murf said, "Well, they'll be onto Mayo, won't they? It's her house, ain't it?" He lost his certainty and said, hoarsely, "She might cough."

Hood said, "I'm going to Kilburn."

*

From the train, high on its track, making its circuit through Southwark, the city looked immense, and he realized how miles of it were unknown to him. Most of it was hidden by the obscuring glare of the sodium lamps, the buildings showing as low dark blocks, and the church steeples indistinguishable from the night sky. There was no skyline; the dark was seamless, a tide of stars on a yellow broken sea. Too large to possess, too deep to be destroyed, deaf, inert, unchangeable; the waters had closed in, the mountain had subsided long ago. So the saboteur was proved ignorant, and his every act revealed him as a stranger. He would drown.

Hood considered this. For every one who used the city as an occasion to perform, a thousand chose it as a place of concealment. In its depths bombs were stifled. His own was local, personal, a family matter; it had not been heard here. On the platform at London Bridge there were travelers still waiting in the shadows, not hiding but hidden. He had thought this world was his to move in, an extension of his own world. But he had seen it grow unfamiliar, and smaller, and he was not moving at will. He had been driven here, to a narrowing space in the vast now featureless city where if he was not careful he would be caught. You were allowed to hide if you made no sound. The city confounded like a sea; it was penetrable, but it was endless and neutral, so wide that on a train tossing between stations—those named places, those islands—you could believe you had gone under and were dead. You verified your existence by taking out the ticket once more. You were your ticket.

Replacing his ticket he touched the rolled-up painting in the inside pocket of his coat. The last business. He would surrender that and so surrender himself. He knew the face in the self-portrait now: it was the man he had killed, months ago, and he had become that man.

The train was nearly empty; there were few people at Charing Cross, and from there to Kilburn on the Underground there were only workers returning home late and tired, sitting singly, using the satchels on their knees to doze on. It was the dead hour before the pubs shut, before the theaters let out, a chain of hollow platforms all the way to Queen's Park. Five miles away there had been a bomb. Here, no one knew. The city dissolved the shock in the slow swell that hid its tiderip, and it slept on, deaf and dark.

*

He retraced the route he had taken with Murf, from pub to pub, and found Finn at the second, standing glassy-eyed in a corner of the saloon bar near the telephone, sucking at the froth on a pint of Guinness.

"Evening, sarge," said Hood. "Where's your friend?"

Finn blinked. He had a sliver of discolored foam on his upper lip. He peered into Hood's face, searching it as though studying a mirror. He said, his eyes still darting, "He's expecting you, is he?"

"Stop scratching your ass and find out."

Finn put his glass down. He nodded thoughtfully at the telephone, then chewing his lips in protest, left the bar. Hood looked around and noticed, as he had once before, that he was being eyed suspiciously by the other drinkers. He chose one and stared until the man turned away. He chose another, and he was still squinting at that man when Finn appeared, snatched up his glass and took a swig. He said confidentially, "You can go up."

"Smile," said Hood. "Business isn't that bad, is it?"

"You're keeping him waiting."

"Did you say something, sarge?" Hood went close to him and menaced him with a smile.

Finn muttered. He turned his back to Hood and faced the telephone.

"If anyone rings, tell them I'm busy."

Upstairs, the door was ajar, and before Hood could knock, Sweeney called out, "Come in!"

The room was unchanged—the dart board, a dirty ceiling, the shades drawn, the large table almost filling the rented space they called the High Command. Sweeney was seated at the far end of the table, in a pretend posture of authority. He put his mutilated hand out, but Hood ignored it and sat down at the opposite end.

Sweeney said, "Finn says you slugged him."

"Finn needs his engine tuned."

"You got me out of bed this morning. What's the big idea?"

"Like I said. I heard that guy was rumbled. Rutter. I figured if you knew him you'd better look out."

"How the hell am I supposed to know him?"

"Don't be so defensive," said Hood. "That's why I got you out of bed. To find out."

"I don't know the boyo."

"I heard you the first time. But it's odd. I see him at the dog track now and then. He's into arms dealing, and"—Hood smiled—"so are you, right?"

"London's full of arms dealers," said Sweeney. "The world is."

"But this one was dealing with your actress. I assumed he was dealing with you, too."

"Did you now? You seem to know a lot. But you did the right thing. Let me know if you hear anything else."

"I won't hear anything else."

"You might. At the dog track—Jasus, I used to go to the dog track. Haven't got the time these days. Murf knows his way around the fellas. He'll tell you what he hears. He's a good lad, is Murf."

Hood said, repeating it slowly, giving each word equal weight, "I won't hear anything else."

"No? And why is that?"

"Because I won't be listening."

"Listening's the whole game," said Sweeney. "If you don't listen you're no good to us."

"You bet."

Sweeney laughed without pleasure. He lifted his damaged hand and pointed his scarred fingers at Hood. He said, "If you've got something to say, man, say it."

"I'm quitting," said Hood. He knew what he wanted to do next. He put his hand into his inside pocket and felt for the roll of canvas. He had gripped it and was about to throw it on the table when Sweeney lurched forward.

"Take your hands out of your pockets!"

Hood showed his empty hands.

"You're quitting?" said Sweeney disgustedly. "You think you can jack it in just like that?"

"That's what I'm doing. Are you going to plead with me?"

"Listen here. No one quits the Provos. You join for life. That's what I did—that's what everyone does, including you. I said, including you. It's like a family, see. No one quits a family."

"I never joined," said Hood.

"Oh, didn't you? What about that passport you made for us?"

"A cunt's passport."

Sweeney said, "That was your membership card."

"I smartened up."

Sweeney spat. "The last time you were in here you were full of ideas. I thought we were getting somewhere. I put my trust in you."

"Your trust isn't worth a fart," said Hood. "I know. I checked."

"Where did you check then?"

"Millwall," said Hood, "the Isle of Dogs. Don't tell me you weren't there. I saw you sitting in his house, waiting for him. He's a fucker and you're his friend."

"I don't know what you're talking about."

"You're lying. You're Rutter's buddy. What did he tell you? That he was onto something big? Did he say he'd have to beat the daylights out of a woman to find out where the arsenal is?"

"I'm not saying I know Rutter, and I'm not saying I don't know him." Sweeney shook his head. "It doesn't matter."

"It matters," said Hood. "Because he's a creep and that means you trust creeps."

"I trusted you."

"So much for your offensive."

"You know Rutter, too."

"I know his victims. I know who he leaned on. You put him up to it."

"If you don't like people being leaned on, Hood, what in the name of Jasus are you doing here?"

It was unanswerable. Again he reached for the painting, to surrender.

"Hands down," said Sweeney, but it was not a threat. "You can't quit. You know too much. You're part of the family now—you know all our dirty secrets. I can't let you go."

"You won't miss me."

"I will," said Sweeney in a friendly way. "I like a fella with some fight in him. And what about our English offensive?"

"It's all yours—everything." He wondered as he looked across the room at Sweeney's grizzled face and the scar tissue shining on his damaged hand, if he had been right before in thinking that the onset of sympathy was the end of belief, and that sympathy could only curdle into pity. He said, "But the English offensive. I hope it never happens."

Sweeney said, "There was a bomb today."

"How do you know?"

"It was on the six o'clock news. Three bodies recovered. No names."

Hood said nothing.

"It sounds like the Trots," said Sweeney. "Do you know anything about it?"

"Nope."

"Southeast London—that's what they said on the news. You just came from there."

"It's a big place," said Hood. "And I wasn't listening."

"We'll be blamed for it," said Sweeney.

"You can take credit for it."

Sweeney said, "Bombing's messy. Point a machine gun at a fella and he does what you say. Show him a bomb and he'll laugh. You might be carrying a sack of flour. You have to blow him up to convince him, and that doesn't get you anywhere. Well, you know. You were in Vietnam, weren't you?" He regarded the two twisted fingers on the stump of his right hand. He said, "But Rutter's lost all the guns."

Hood stood up. "I'm going."

Sweeney sighed and said, "I'll make an exception in your case."

"Don't do me any favors."

"I'll let you quit. We'll say you had battle fatigue. You're an American, you've got no business here. It was a mistake." He smiled. "You did a lot for my wife.

She's the nervous type—she never knew anything. But she really fancied you. You should have heard her talking about you—you'd have thought you were as Irish as Paddy O'Toole, with the sun shining out of your arse."

Hood said, "I met her at Ward's. She was drunk. She told me a ridiculous story about how she was going to steal a painting."

"I hope you didn't laugh."

"She scared me," said Hood. "She was so drunk. Incapable—isn't that the word they use? I felt sorry for her."

"You're sounding like a bloody curate."

"I knew if I helped her she'd succeed."

"Don't think I'm not grateful," said Sweeney. His manner had become genial, his talk soothing. He got up and came around the table to where Hood was standing. "Maybe the mistake was mine. I listened to my wife—that's many a man's downfall. It doesn't mean we can't be friends. What are your plans?"

"I don't have any." And he thought: It's over. He was certain now that Rutter was dead: three bodies recovered. How little it had to do with politics. But perhaps Sweeney was more right than even he knew —it had always been a family affair. Weech had brought him to it, and he had had to become Weech to complete his revenge. And though he knew that tactic was a brutal amputation, it was the revenger who was left the cripple. There was nothing more. He reached into his inside pocket again.

"Keep your hands where I can see them," said Sweeney, joshing, as if Hood had misbehaved. "A parting of the ways. Let's do it the Irish way, with a jar of Liffey water."

Hood said, "Some other time."

"You can't deny me a last drink," said Sweeney, slapping him on the back. "Come on, I know a good pub."

"I thought we were in one."

"Not this piss hole. I never drink here. Bad for the discipline if your men see you drunk."

"Then why drink with me?"

Sweeney smiled. "You're not my man anymore."

Hood went first, at Sweeney's urging, downstairs and out the back door to a side street. Sweeney chatted in his friendly way, his accent broadened by his good humor; he talked about the offensive, about Ulster, about Murf and Mayo. He said, "I told her not to come back without the painting—not that I care a tinker's curse for the bloody thing. But it's all we have at the moment. And it's the principle, see. I said, it's the principle."

"How much farther?" said Hood.

They were in a dark street, lined with cars, and something Hood was unaccustomed to seeing in London—a row of trees, all the way to a lighted junction. They were tall, leafless, and looked dead, as if at any moment they might thunder down.

"Just over the road."

"I don't see any pub."

"You will in a minute," said Sweeney. "Sure, it's a beauty—" He stopped speaking, crept behind a tree and looked back. "What's that? Did you see someone down there?"

"No."

"You're not looking." Sweeney had become short of breath. He sounded asthmatic. He said, "I think we're being followed."

Bein' follered. He had been prepared for a deception, but he had not thought it would be so transparent. He obliged Sweeney by glancing down the street, going through the motions, acting at Sweeney's direction. It was, as he expected, empty. But it was familiar. He saw the wall, the white letters ARSENAL RULE in damp chalk, and he was certain.

"There's no one," he said.

"In here," said Sweeney, motioning to a door in the wall. He was making a convincing show of fear. He pushed at Hood and Hood could feel in the shove the man's trembling hand.

"That's a cemetery," said Hood.

"It is. Now hurry—I tell you we're being followed. We can duck out by the side entrance and ditch them."

Hood thought: The simplest trick of all. There was

no pub, there was no pursuer. Sweeney had taken him here to kill him. What he hated most was Sweeney's lying, his pretense of fear, the acting. Yet Hood remained calm. There was justice in this trap. Lorna was safe, and he, for his murders, deserved to die. The executioner could be ignorant of the crime. But he was appalled by the place, the empty street, the dead trees, and at the cemetery wall he resisted, hardly knowing why—because he thought it would save him, because he thought resistance was expected of him. He would not go willingly to his death. He was empty of rage, but he could play the victim and fight. He said, "I won't go."

"Move," said Sweeney. "There's someone after us."

"You're lying."

"I'm not! Now"—he pulled a pistol from his coat pocket—"get in there and be quick."

"You're going to kill me."

"Get in!" Sweeney screamed into his fist. His face shone with sweat, and still he pretended to cower behind the tree.

To be killed by this jabbering play-actor! Hood walked ten steps to the cemetery gateway and looked in. He saw the dark humps and shadows, the grim London light behind the far wall that gleamed like a tidemark of surf on the highest tombs. Appalling because it was so ordinary, so empty, so dark; it was too cold to die tonight. But he thought: If I had died yesterday, before making that phone call, it would have been worse. His life had stopped with that bomb; it had blasted away the ramparts of his heart and he had not been able to face the painting after that. He was too ashamed. He had led himself to this death, this suicide. And yet he fought against the logic. He did not want to die. Tomorrow, tomorrow. But Sweeney was armed. I will run, he thought, and if I'm saved I'll keep running.

He darted through the door and leaped towards the darkness between two monuments, his legs numb and working clumsily. Ahead of him he saw the eclipse of Sweeney's shadow in the doorway's reflection on the burying ground. He remembered Murf: *I hate this boneyard.*

Crack!

He tumbled, feeling nothing, a miraculous transparency in his mind, a winded zero in his chest. I'm dead, he thought. But he saw he was still moving quickly on all fours, a monkey motion over a clump of gravestones. He was conscious of a sensation of sudden lightness: the painting had bounced up and dropped from his pocket. He spun round and saw Sweeney on his knees, toppling, clutching his pistol.

A man in a long coat stepped inside the gate. He fired three more times into Sweeney's body, then— the long coat jumping like a skirt—ran into the street. A car door slammed, an engine roared, and it sped away until its sound became part of the city's regular swell.

But Hood had seen the man's face. A thug: he knew the face and then didn't. He saw his confusion, the brutal similarity, the shaded features, all brutes looked the same. No—he remembered where he had seen it before, silhouetted like this, in the paddock of whimpering dogs at the track—one of Rutter's men. Hood was blinded. The painting: he started back for it and saw a policeman enter, flashing a torch near where Sweeney lay. Before Hood turned again the policeman saw him and waved his feeble torch. He called out twice for Hood to stop, but Hood kept running, through the far gate, into the street; away from the shrill police whistle, away from the painting, and into the concealing city.

27

THE LAST THING he'd seen—the image he carried away from Deptford in the ride through London to the station—was the old sweeper solemnly clearing up the mess in Albacore Crescent. But it was a brief glimpse between shifting buildings, a bent figure in a winter coat, with a shovel and a yellow barrel; but it occurred to him later, long after the taxi had veered past the crescent, that it might not have been the same man. There was no boy.

At Victoria Station Murf bought a *Mirror,* and in the compartment he showed Hood the front page story: TERROR BOMB IN SOUTH LONDON KILLS THREE. Hood glanced through the item he did not want to read. . . . *thought to be a bomb factory . . . three bodies badly charred . . . no warning beforehand . . . names will not be released until the next-of-kin have been notified.*

Murf said, "You seen it?"

"What?"

Murf took the paper and put his dirty finger on the bottom line, smudging the fresh ink: . . . *the fact that the stolen painting was recovered aroused speculation that this may be the opening volley in a campaign of terror by the Provisional Wing of the I.R.A. No ransom was paid for the painting. It was found in a cemetery . . .*

Hood's face darkened. He said, "No."

Lorna said, "Don't show me."

Murf sang, *"Boom widdy-widdy, boom-boom."*

"Look, mummy. Horses!"

"Them are cows," she said.

Murf said, "It's like a holiday. Put your feet up. Get the benefit."

The early sun broke through the layers of cloud and struck the low hills, shafts of light sending the lengthened shadows of trees across the rough brown grass. And where the sun didn't hit, in the gray scooped depressions on the hillsides, there were rounded white patches, like sea foam drying on a beach, froth that had outrun the surf.

"Snow," said Lorna. Her voice vibrated with the rumble of the train.

"They get lots of snow down here this time of year," said Murf. "Not blizzards—nothing like that. But snow, *widdy-widdy boom*."

Snow, trees, cows. They were in another country, thirty miles from London. The space, the very air here, oppressed him. Hood studied the fields, sorrowing wordlessly; he had seen these fields when he had arrived in England, the yellow fields of mustard in May. Now they were brown, grief had displaced hope. I have had no life, only a sudden death. And Murf's voice, that quacking, sounded so awful.

Just before a level crossing the train's horn squawked twice. Then, at the road itself, they could see the cars backed up and winding bumper to bumper along the country lane.

"Stop, you bitches!" Murf smiled, showing the pegs of his teeth.

"It's going to be a nice day," said Lorna.

Outside, beyond the low hills the downs lay green at the horizon, and close by, in the hedges that ran along the track, the sparkle of frost just touched by the sun was becoming dew.

"How long can we stay, mummy?"

"Ask him," she said.

Hood said, "As long as you like."

"I don't want to go back to that yucky house."

Hood saw that Lorna was staring at him. He said, "He might get his wish."

She said, "I don't want to think about that. I know something's up. That's your lookout. I'm going to Brighton. It's like winning at the dogs, Brighton. The only thing is, we didn't win nothing." She sighed, then said, "They'll find you."

"No," said Hood. "No one finds you unless you co-operate."

"Yeah," said Murf. "I ain't cooperating."

"Listen to them," said Lorna.

"The little basket wants to go to the loo," said Murf. "It's okay. I'll take him. Put your feet up." He left with Jason and slid the compartment door shut.

Lorna said, "We left in such a hurry, I forgot my rollers."

"We'll buy some more."

"I don't know if I remembered to pack my heavy sweater. It's cold down there."

"I'll get you a new one."

"And Jason needs shoes."

"There are shoe stores in Brighton."

"Oh, Christ!" she said, and he thought she was going to cry.

He put his arm around her and said, "Don't worry. I'll stay with you."

"How long?"

"Until you chase me away," he said. "Until you're safe." And as he said it he wondered if she would ever be.

"You looked old just then," she said. "I don't even know you. Who are you?"

The door shot open and Murf helped Jason to his seat. He said, "Basket almost fell in!"

Lorna looked appreciatively at Murf. She said, "He likes you." She was silent a moment, then turned to Hood. "Kids need fathers."

The stations raced by. The train didn't stop. The countryside, which had appeared so suddenly at the outskirts of London, dropped from view. The square gray backs of houses, the narrow cluttered gardens, the succession of settlements became linked and continued, breaking up the view of pasture, cutting off the sun. *Favvers*.

"Excuse me." Lorna left the compartment.

"Put your feet up," said Murf. "Get the benefit. I

wish Brodie was here. She likes a good train ride." He took out his marking crayon and smiled at the wall.

Hood said, "Don't."

"I wasn't really going to." He put the crayon away.

"You didn't have to come."

"I'm sticking wif you."

"It might not be what you think."

"Yeah. Even if it ain't, I'm sticking." He fumbled in the pocket of his jacket and took out his leather stash, his cigarette papers. He began rolling a cigarette.

Hood said, "You'll be all right."

"Yeah."

Hood put his feet up, on the seat opposite.

"That's the idea," said Murf. "Get the benefit." He licked the cigarette, giving it the color of his tongue. "But I mean, where are we really going?"

"Guatemala."

"Yeah."

Jason, sniffing the strong smoke, made a face at Murf. He said nothing. He turned again to the window. Hood sorrowed for his small pathetic neck.

Murf said, "Yeah, but what'll we do when we get there?"

Hood nodded slowly and took Murf's cigarette. He puffed it, handed it back, and put his hands behind his head. The sun striped the compartment with heat; the horn blew again, long and sad, but the train sped them away from its stuttering echo.

"Smoke," he said. Then, "Smoke and tell lies."